MIDSUMMER NIGHT'S MADNESS

MIDSUMMER NIGHT'S MADNESS

JILL BARNETT
ELAINE COFFMAN
ALEXIS HARRINGTON
SONIA SIMONE

SMP

ST. MARTIN'S PAPERBACKS

MIDSUMMER NIGHT'S MADNESS

CONTENTS

A KNIGHT IN TARNISHED ARMOR
    by Jill Barnett   1
A RIBBON OF MOONLIGHT
    by Elaine Coffman   79
ENCHANTED
    by Alexis Harrington   169
THE GOLDEN MERMAID
    by Sonia Simone   253

A KNIGHT

IN

 TARNISHED ARMOR

JILL BARNETT

For Chris,
and if he ever reads this he'll know why.

O, what can ail thee, knight-at-arms,
Alone and palely loitering?

I met a lady in the meads
Full beautiful, a fairy's child,
Her hair was long, her foot was light,
And her eyes were wild.

—*La Belle Dame Sans Merci*, John Keats

CHAPTER ☾ ONE

The sight of her took his breath away.

He, a fierce and valiant knight, sat frozen atop his mount and watched the young woman from the edge of the clearing. She stood captured for a timeless moment in prisms of misty white light that spilled into the forest.

Had he not been alone, he'd have asked his men-at-arms if she were a vision—a dream borne from the weakness of a man who had fought too many battles, drunk too much, and had too little sleep. For only a vision could have hair that rippled down her back, almost touching her knees. Hair the rich fiery color of a sunset. Only a vision could look so innocent. Only a vision could sing like the angels.

To the very crowns of the trees her voice rose in song, a sound that he could only fathom was the music of heaven—clear and fresh and flawless. He dismounted and moved closer, his search for water suddenly forgotten. At that moment it mattered little that his mouth held the dusty flavor of the road, so caught was he by this young woman.

She bent down and picked up another bright yellow flower from the forest floor, weaving it into a garland of wildflowers and lush ivy that hung over her arm. She turned then, spinning on one bare foot while her hair flowed outward and her brown tunic belled slightly. She was singing a bright and merry tune—a song to the kittens that frolicked at her feet.

> *I've yearned time past to be a fairy,*
> *To fly in the pale light of the moon.*
> *With gossamer wings so light and airy,*
> *On a midsummer night in June.*

A foolish song filled with whimsy, yet somehow it charmed him as nothing had in longer than he could remember. He continued to watch her.

Soon a squirrel scurried down from a tall tree, followed by two more. They stood on their haunches and cocked their curious heads as she sang.

Three rabbits hopped from the bracken and ferns, twitching their noses and tails instead of instinctively using their speedy back legs to spring away. And the birds —hedgesparrows, robins, and hummingbirds—fluttered above her.

Odd, he thought, how the animals had no fear of her. 'Twas as if they were drawn like he was to a siren's sweet sound.

He asked himself if he had been too long at war. Had he seen so much bloodshed, been from his homeland so long that the mere sight of an English beauty made his mind play him false?

The forest was a dark place of legend, the setting for the evil side of a bard's tale, and home to trolls and witches, if one was to believe in fancy.

But fancy was not for men of war, anymore than a young woman could turn into a fairy. No, to a warrior's mind, the forest was a place for thieves and wastrels, and the best possible place for ambush.

His sixth sense told him there was no danger here. As though enchanted, this forest appeared to come alive in the joyful aura of this one small and lovely creature. And he felt it too, that full feeling of life he'd thought was long lost. Or perhaps it had never even been there.

She danced over to a small bubbling stream where she lifted her tunic and skipped from stone to stone, laughing when the birds followed her and the squirrels, rabbits, and kittens watched her from the bank.

He smiled.

God's blood . . . He asked himself how long had it been since something had touched him so. He knew the answer—too long.

She came back to the clearing, still singing and dancing. Added to her audience were bright butterflies that fluttered through the shimmering mist and a plump white duck with a trail of fluffy butter-colored ducklings that waddled like drunken soldiers from the stream.

He had never seen anything like this.

The girl picked up her flower garland and hung it around her neck, then spun again with her arms wide open and the garland flowing with her. Her song rose higher, its end sadly growing near, so he moved back where bracken was thick and the forest trees and ferns hid him and his mount from sight.

Humming now, she danced a bit closer, pausing at a rock where she picked up a pair of red leather slippers. She chattered to the animals while she dusted the leaves off a small pale foot and slid into the shoe, then propped her foot on the rock so she could tie the laces around the slimmest ankle he'd seen in months.

She finished with her other shoe and gathered the kittens into a small willow basket before she picked up her wildflower garland, this time tucking it around her small waist. She lifted the top on one side of her basket and spoke to kittens, calling them by name, silly, fanciful names that made him smile again. She moved closer to where he stood and when she was but a few feet away she set down the basket, then picked up a dark woolen mantle and swung it around her, tying it securely beneath her small firm chin.

In a gesture that almost made him groan aloud, she combed her fingers through her flaming hair and lifted it, then raised her gaze at the same time. She stood before him, completely unaware of his existence, which almost made him laugh at the irony, for he was aware of nothing but her.

She had a face that was proof of Heaven's perfection —a small nose, lips of rose, and skin the shimmering pale cream shade of dunes in the desert. But her eyes were what struck him, knocked his breath from him as surely as if he'd been struck with a Turk's lance. They weren't the familiar dark brown eyes of the Mideast, nor were they English blue, not even Celtic green.

They were the same golden yellow color of the bright wildflowers she had picked. Yellow eyes. Wild eyes, he thought, watching as she turned and moved toward the opposite end of the clearing.

He waited a few seconds, then followed slowly, using the thick grove of ash trees and heavy mist as a shield. Soon the forest ended and a meadow scented sweet with freshly mown grass spread to a ripening grainfield and on toward a craggy hillside where a castle, stark and gray and majestic, broke the blue horizon.

High above the stone walls flew the distinctive flag of the earl of Arden. Minutes later, the girl disappeared inside the gates in a stone curtain wall.

But still he stood there, his arms crossed as he leaned against the trunk of an ash tree. For the longest time— time where seconds turned into eternal minutes—he just stood there, watching . . . thinking, then making a decision with the same swiftness and gut instinct he used on the battlefield.

He moved back to the stream, knelt and took a drink while his mount quenched its thirst. He wiped his mouth and looked at his reflection for a moment, but his mind played fairy tricks on him, for he saw not his image in the silvery water, but her sweet face staring back at him.

His sense returned swiftly and he stood, calling himself a lovestruck fool. He mounted his horse, then rode toward the highway that rimmed the thick forest.

The road wound northward, a ribbon of dirt in the lush green countryside of his homeland, and at the crest of a small rise he stopped and turned in the saddle. He took one last long look at the castle known as Ardenwood. For a heartbeat he allowed himself one final golden moment of her memory.

She would be his—yes, she would, this fairy child, the woman with eyes so wild.

He vowed that she would be his, because after years of waging war and living in dry foreign lands, after years of bloodshed and waking to the clash of sword and scimitar, after years of loneliness, he wanted, needed, a little gentleness and peace in his hard life.

Then England's newest lord, Baron Warbrooke, nudged his mount around with spurs as golden as her wild eyes, and he rode away.

One month later in London

"Arden is a hardheaded old fool!" Baron Warbrooke paced the king's quarters while his liege lord watched him with royal amusement.

"Warbrooke, my friend. I bid you cease that infernal pacing. Makes me light-headed."

The baron stopped in front of the king and growled, "The man has refused my fifth—*fifth*—offer for his granddaughter!"

"What was his reason this time?"

"Same as the last four times. He adamantly refuses to force his granddaughter to wed."

"I assume you've sweetened the offer?"

The baron named a figure.

The king whistled, then muttered, "I believe *I* need to meet the Lady Linnet." He looked at his friend and laughed, then raised a hand. "Stop glowering. You've lost your sense of humor, Warbrooke."

"Any sane man who had spent three hours haggling with that stubborn old goat would no longer have a sense of humor."

"He might be a stubborn old goat now, but he has been intensely loyal to the crown for over forty years. My father owed him greatly." The king's voice lowered to a more serious tone. "As great a debt as I owe you, my friend. I will not force him."

"There must be some way . . ."

Both men were silent.

The king rubbed his chin thoughtfully and said, "I could make a royal . . ." he paused as if searching for the correct word, ". . . *suggestion* to Arden."

Warbrooke looked up. "What kind of suggestion?"

"Arden claims he will not force his granddaughter to wed."

"Aye."

"Suppose you can convince the lady to accept you? To wed you willingly. Of her own free choice."

Warbrooke was silent for a long moment, then said, "You are proposing that I pay her court."

The king nodded. "If Arden's only objection is the matter of forcing her into marriage. You need only agree to woo the girl."

Warbrooke swore viciously.

The king laughed. "Come, now. It won't be that difficult. You forget. I've seen you when you are driven to win a battle. Take this as a challenge. Your own war, the spoils of which is the Lady Linnet."

"Fine," Warbrooke snapped, beginning to pace again in agitation. "But to waylay any interference from Arden I want time alone with her." He looked at the king.

"I'll make that point when I persuade Arden to allow you opportunity to court her." The king sat silently, then laughed somewhat wickedly. "Arden's pride won't allow him to deny this. He will be forced to agree."

One month later at Ardenwood Castle

Two laundresses stood by barrel vats of steaming wash water. One of them was busy wringing out some freshly rinsed linen while the other stirred a wad of boiling soapy bedsheets with a huge wooden laundry paddle.

"They were talking about him again at supper."

"About who?"

"Him."

"Warbrooke?"

"Aye." Edith wrung out a corner of a tunic, then

added, "He might come to Ardenwood before the month is out."

Morda dropped her paddle and crossed herself, then said in a half-prayer, half-moan, "Lady Linnet . . ."

"*Tch-tch.* I know." Edith gave a huge sigh.

Morda shook her head. "Can ye imagine being wedded to such a brute? 'Tis said the king rewarded him because he'd killed a thousand men, and a few women too."

"No!" Edith said in a gasp, then leaned closer, her eyes wide. "Truly? Women?"

"Aye. He killed the women with his bare hands. Huge hands. Hairy hands. Hands the size of boar's haunches. 'Tis said he crushed the very air from their very breasts." She paused, then said in a loud whisper, "He has cloven feet."

"Like the devil himself?"

"Aye. The very same."

"'Tis a good thing Lady Linnet knows naught of this agreement. Poor wee thing, wedded to such. How can the old earl do this to his granddaughter?"

Morda shrugged. "He had no choice. My lord pleaded his case to the king, but the king favors Warbrooke. He forced the earl and baron to meet. The earl claims he couldn't refuse Warbrooke once the king was involved. 'Twas a matter of loyalty."

"I'd run away," Edith said firmly.

"To where?"

"The convent at Saint Lawrence of the Martyrs. Her great-aunt is the abbess. It's the perfect place for succor."

"Lud, that husband of yers has slapped ye in the head once too often."

"He has never hit me," Edith said indignantly. "He knows I'm stronger than he is."

"Then yer wits have gone walking to Wales. No woman can travel so far a distance alone."

"But if I were Lady Linnet, I'd hire my own protector to escort me."

"And just who would that be?" Morda raised her chin and asked in a challenge.

"William de Ros."

Morda's mouth dropped open. "The mercenary?"

"Aye," Edith said smugly. "He devours men like War-brooke for supper. Then he picks his teeth clean with their bones."

"Why, ye'd have to travel to Spain to find him. He returned from the last crusade and went off to war with the heathens there."

Edith shook her head. "He's in England." She paused for effect, then said, "At Falcon House Tavern in Waters-downe."

"And just how would she get away even if she could persuade him to be an escort? The earl would come after her."

"My lord's leaving for London again tomorrow. He'll be gone for a week. Surely that's enough time to be safely away."

A loud scraping sound echoed around the stone laundry room.

"Oh!" Morda jumped, then spun around suddenly, her sharp gaze searching. "What was that?"

Edith shrugged, then went back to her stirring paddle. "Most likely just one of Lady Linnet's cats mousing on the back stairs." After a moment she stopped stirring again and leaned on the paddle. "I wonder what will happen to all those animals after Warbrooke comes?"

Morda looked at Edith, then lifted a linen shirt from the rinse barrel. With a sharp and fierce twist, she wrung it dry. *"That's* what will happen."

Linnet slid back the peep slot and tiptoed up the small stone steps of the hidden passageway. She felt in the dark for the door handle and slowly pulled it open. She slipped into a back castle corridor and pressed against the stone walls. Her heart hammered high in her throat and she felt ill and fearful at the thought of the man— the monster among men—her grandfather would make her wed. The man must be horrid if Grandpapa had not yet even told her of him. She slowly moved toward her chambers as one of the condemned walks toward the block, head down, shoulders sagging, and her hands folded tightly in front of her.

Within a few minutes four cats trailed behind her and one still little more than a kitten nipped at her heels, then bit down on a scrap of her hem; Linnet dragging him as she walked. She stopped and turned. "Swithun! You must stop that." She bent and picked up the kitten, stroking his gray fur.

She looked down at the growing group of cats gathered so trustingly at her feet. They stared back at her with eyes full of devotion. She almost burst into tears. She hugged Swithun closer to her chest, unconsciously protecting his small neck with her hand, and she raised her chin. "No one will harm you. No one."

She spun around and ran up the stairs toward her chamber, Swithun clutched to her and the other cats trotted devotedly along behind her. She opened her chamber door, then peered up and down the corridor. When no one appeared she leaned down close to the cats and whispered, "Come, sweetlings. Crispin, Elmo, Vitus, Ambrose. Come inside. I have a plan."

CHAPTER ❧ TWO

*A*s plans went, this looked to have all the makings of a poor one.

Lady Linnet pulled the hood of her dark mantle forward and glanced around the dim tavern. It was loud, and smelly, and almost unbearably stuffy, made so by the downdraft of a blazing fire in a sooty stone hearth, and what appeared to be a veritable sea of medieval manhood raising tankards of dark yeasty ale.

For strength she took a deep breath, blanched at the stink, then stepped into the lantern light, slowly and purposefully moving toward a large table in the corner. Hearty male laughter grew louder for only a brief instant, then the crowd began to part, slowly, man by man, in front of her.

From behind she could hear the suddenness of stunned silence, until the last rowdy warrior quieted and moved out of her way. Linnet faced the one man she sought. And she had her first true taste of fear.

William de Ros sat sprawled in a chair, his long legs outstretched, his worn leather boots crossed at the ankle and propped on the table edge. It was a relaxed stance, yet instinct told her he wasn't as unaware of her as he appeared.

She glanced down, only to see his battle-scarred hand slide to the jeweled hilt of a deadly dagger that was slung almost too casually from a studded belt at his waist.

He wore a dark leather tunic spotted with spilled ale and his free hand gripped a frothy metal tankard. He had thighs as big around as her waist and they were taut, his black chausses showing the rippled power in his leg muscles, muscles that could hold in check the most deadly of war-horses.

She looked into his face again. And almost ran.

No emotion showed in his expression. Nothing but time-weathered experience and the scores of battles he was rumored to have fought, and won.

His hair was black as loam in the forest, and too long, almost barbaric in length. His gold earring was barbaric, in spite of the small cross that dangled from it. She wondered what God thought of it, and of him.

But it was his face that she would never forget. It was sharp, chiseled in raw angles, and his skin was bronzed from the harsh rays of the desert sun, where legend claimed he'd spent years as a hired warrior, a battle-scarred mercenary who sold his finely honed skills to the highest bidder.

'Twas rumored he had no crusade but avarice. No fealty to anyone, except he who held the heaviest purse. Once enough money crossed his calloused palm, the greatest fighting sword in all of England was sold, to whoever had paid the high price.

And that was why she was here. Lady Linnet of Ardenwood, youngest granddaughter of the earl of Arden, intended to buy herself a warrior.

Until she actually faced this mercenary knight whose determined jaw and keen eyes showed a ruthless intelligence she'd never before seen in any man.

Perhaps now that she saw him, she thought quickly, she would not buy *this* particular warrior. And certainly not tonight.

Suddenly gutless, she turned.

Run!

She took a quick step.

He was quicker. His arm whipped out in front of her. She caught a flash of something silver, and froze. His battle sword blocked her path.

She turned around slowly, then took a small step backward and stopped, feeling the wide steel blade of his sword pressed flatly against her lower back. The air left her lungs.

Not even a breath could be heard, though her heart's pounding grew louder in her ears. There must have been at least fifty men in the tavern, but at that very moment the room was utterly silent. Nothing . . . until the random snap of a green log in the fireplace crackled through air that was as tense as dawn on a battlefield.

Linnet watched de Ros. He paused, assurance to everyone in the room that he was in command, then he laid the sword on the table as if to say, "You may run now."

She squared her shoulders and met his gaze. His expression showed he knew exactly what she was thinking. She said the first stupid thing that came to her tongue, "I've heard you can be bought."

He said nothing, but raised his tankard of ale and drank deeply.

She swallowed thickly. "I meant your sword could be bought."

He stared at her, directly, assessing her, unnervingly so.

"Actually . . . I meant I need to buy protection," she blurted out, then winced slightly because her voice cracked.

He gave her the oddest look.

She took another breath, her mind desperate and racing. He was a man. . . . She'd give his pride a stroke. It worked with her grandfather. "I wish to buy your *powerful* sword."

He set the tankard on the table and let his gaze rove slowly from her face to her toes, where he paused, took another drink of ale as if time were his alone, then just as slowly he looked upward, stopping with interest every so often. He paused, staring at his tankard as he said almost too casually, "I see no coin."

Her knees were quivering and air felt tight in her chest. What in God's name was she doing here? She took a deep breath and pulled a sack of gold from inside her cloak, wishing it were prayer beads, and held it up.

She smiled. He didn't.

She raised her chin a notch. With a dramatic flair she tossed the gold toward the table.

The bag hit the tabletop just as she'd planned. Then she watched in horror as the bag kept going, and slid right off the edge.

It landed squarely in his lap.

Her mouth dropped open and for a horrified instant she just stared at it. With a mental groan, she closed her eyes. A heartbeat and a tight breath later she opened them.

He was staring pointedly at the bag, then he looked up, a flicker of amusement on his face.

"Ha!" someone behind her shouted. "Now we know what sword the lady wishes to buy, de Ros!"

Rowdy male laughter filled the room.

"Not merely a sword, but his *powerful* sword!" another voice shouted.

Her face flushed hot and she fervently wished the earth would just open up and swallow her. She spun around and took a step.

But again he was quicker.

His hand shot out and grasped a handful of her cloak. She couldn't move. Couldn't run.

She tried to pull free.

Slowly he drew her back toward him. She grabbed at the ties under her chin and jerked them loose. Her cloak fell away.

Run! Run!

But there was no place to run.

There was nothing before her but a wall of grinning male faces and huge bodies. She shoved at the crowd, her tears of humiliation changed into tears of fear and they fell as quickly as her heart pounded.

She could sense the mercenary standing behind her, then his shadow blocked the weak candlelight from the swinging lantern above her. His hands closed over her shoulders and he spun her around. She tried to wiggle free. But even in a blood rush of fear her strength was puny compared to his.

She took a deep quivering breath and looked up at him through a mist of frightened tears. She expected to see savagery in his expression. Cruelty, from a man so greatly feared.

But it wasn't cruelty she saw. It was something else, some odd emotion. Just as quickly that emotion disappeared and he looked away, although his hands still gripped her so tightly she couldn't move.

He turned to the crowd then pulled her flush against him with one powerful arm clamped across her collarbone.

She cried still harder, silent tears that wouldn't let her catch a full breath.

"Leave off!" His shout filled the room and the jeers and laughter died suddenly. With his free hand he tossed her bag of gold at the barkeep. "Keep the ale flowing all night, till every man has drunk his fill."

A cheer erupted as loud as a battle cry and the men shifted and charged to the tavern bar. She tried to swallow but was struck still with fear.

His mouth moved near her ear. "I won't harm you, my lady," he whispered. "Calm yourself." He turned around and released her, but didn't move away, his body providing a shield.

Linnet bit her lip and stared at the toes of her boots. He bent down and retrieved her fallen cloak. He did not give it to her, but instead laid it over one arm. She took a deep quivering breath, then another.

"Can you not look at me?"

She shook her head, knowing what she'd see if she looked up at him.

"I said I would not harm you," he added quietly.

"Perhaps you won't harm me. But neither will you help me."

He reached out and tilted her chin up with a scarred knuckle. "I've just spent your gold on a few hogsheads of ale." He shrugged, then added, "Seems, my lady, that you've already bought your protection."

She watched him uneasily.

"Come."

She looked down and saw that he held his hand out for her. It was a hard hand, calloused from the grip of a sword handle and crossed with thin and ragged white scars.

"We will speak in private."

Suspicious, she watched his expression again and saw an unexpected gentleness.

There was something more, something that told her he carried a bit of his own fear. With a sudden realization she read that fear and knew he was afraid that she wouldn't go with him.

She stared. He covered his vulnerability quickly, with the same cold and hard look he'd first given her. She stood there looking at this barbaric warrior who had only moments before frightened the very breath from her. Suddenly she was struck by something familiar about his manner. She watched him a moment longer before she knew what it was.

He was like a wounded animal that attacks in fear, strikes out and fights viciously when cornered because he is acutely aware that he can be so easily conquered. In that one instant, she understood de Ros and her fear of him waned away. Without a worry, she placed her hand in his and slowly raised her head.

His face was unreadable. He led her through the crowd toward the opposite side of the tavern. She was aware of little but the feel of his hand about hers. He held her hand with a gentle firmness. She could feel the hard callouses of his palm against hers and she could feel his warmth. Somehow that too made him seem more human.

He stopped in front of a thick oaken door near the rear of the tavern. She hesitated.

He looked at her, then gave a short bark of wry laughter as he opened the door. "I assure you, my lady, it is not the door to hell."

She looked into his face and read the challenge there. She took a deep breath and a step. "I know your words are meant to amuse, sir, but"—she raised her chin as she passed him—"there is some element of truth in every jest."

He said nothing as he followed her inside, just hung her cloak on a peg and gestured for her to sit in one of the large chairs that flanked another smaller fireplace. She sat and arranged her skirts in the silence, then looked around the room, trying to choose her words more carefully than she had earlier.

He sank into the other chair and watched her through narrowed eyes, his jaw tense, his hands stiffer than before.

"I am Lady Linnet of Ardenwood, and I need safe conduct to the convent at Saint Lawrence of the Martyrs. Tomorrow."

"Why tomorrow?" He wasn't looking at her. But instead, he sat rubbing a finger over his lips and staring at the opposite wall.

"Tomorrow my grandfather will leave for a week. 'Twill be the only chance I shall have to leave."

"The convent is near the north borders."

"Yes."

"The journey will take at least six days."

She stared at her folded hands. "I know."

He was silent for what seemed like a very long time, then he leaned back in the chair and pinned her with a hard stare. "Why?"

She looked at him then and said, "Why? Because I asked."

He started, then frowned. "Asked what?"

"How long the journey was."

He eyed her for the longest time, strangely, as if she had two heads. He looked away and cleared his throat. When he looked back he seemed to be chewing on the inside of his cheek to keep from smiling. "I'll try this again. Why, my lady, do you wish to go to the convent?"

"Because I'm being forced to wed . . ." she paused, then sighed and hung her head miserably, "the horrid Baron Warbrooke."

He said nothing.

She looked up and added, "He kills women."

Silence.

"With his bare hands. His hairy hands."

Still he said nothing, but his eyes narrowed slightly.

She gripped the arms of the chair and leaned closer. "He has cloven feet. Can you imagine?"

"Not quite," he answered through a tight jaw.

"'Twould be like being wed to the devil himself."

He stood up and slowly walked over to the fireplace, where he leaned against its stone face, rested a boot on the andiron, and looked at her without emotion.

"He's killed so very many men."

"In a war, men are killed," he said without emotion.

"Thousands of men." She looked him directly in the eye and whispered painfully, "He'll murder my animals."

He no longer stood casually, as if her words didn't matter to him. He stared into the fire. Everything about de Ros exuded anger—his tight jaw, the tick in his angled cheek, his narrowed eyes, and the fist he made with his sword hand. Even he, a mercenary knight paid to wage war, is shocked by Warbrooke's reputation, she thought.

After a moment he said, "I suppose he breathes fire and eats babies too."

"You've heard of him," she said knowingly.

He took a long, deep breath, then just watched her intensely.

She leaned forward a bit more, hoping he would agree. "I must get away and quickly. Surely you can understand why."

"Now I understand a wealth of things."

"Then you will help me?"

His expression was hard and he seemed to be trying to control some strong emotion.

"I gave you all the gold I had."

"Six days," he said so quietly she almost didn't hear him.

She stood and walked over to where he was. "'Tis not so terribly long."

He gave a wry laugh and looked at her, his expression softer. "No. 'Tis not very long at all."

"I have nothing else to give you."

He grumbled something.

She smiled then, for she saw his answer without his speaking a word. By the time he murmured "aye" she had placed her hand on his chest, where legend claimed he had no heart.

Yet there, beneath her palm, was a soft beat. The mercenary did have a heart.

William de Ros sat slumped in a chair and drank deeply from a tankard of strong beer. She had been gone from the tavern for a few minutes, long enough for him to watch her leave, then roar at the barkeep to bring four more tankards—three for himself and one for the older man who was just stepping through a door hidden in the wooden panel of the wall. William stared into his ale, then finally pinned the old man with a hard look. "It's done."

The earl of Arden didn't blink. He just calmly sat in the other chair. "So I heard."

"Is your granddaughter always so easily manipulated?"

The old earl laughed loud and long. "Hardly. It has taken me years to figure out how she thinks." He paused, then muttered something about still being a game of hit or miss.

The two men sat in awkward silence.

Arden sat up and said, "Our agreement still stands, Warbrooke. You have one week to woo her."

William de Ros, the new Baron Warbrooke, returned the man's meaningful stare. "One week to convince her I'm not the ogre she thinks? One week to court her? I suppose I will manage to find the time . . . before I go out to murder more women and roast children."

The old earl said nothing, but he didn't look chagrined either. He rested his elbows on his knees. His gaze was fixed on his hands clasped between his legs.

After a moment he admitted quietly, "I had thought to keep Linnet at Ardenwood with me. She is . . . unique. A very special part of my life. I had never thought of marriage for her. Her sisters are all wed, and wed well. I needn't barter her for another powerful man with forces to aid me. I've plenty of blood bonds."

William eyed the old man. "But then I spotted her and used my influence with the king to my advantage."

The earl looked at him with accusation in his aged eyes. "He gave you your title."

William shrugged. "As I recall your own title was bestowed in the same manner. Only by his father."

"As were those of over half the realm."

"I foiled your plans to keep her to yourself."

"I cherish my granddaughter, Warbrooke." The earl of Arden pinned him with a hard stare that matched his own. "I had thought to keep her safe, and with me."

"I will not cause her any harm. She will want for nothing. I gave you my word when we met in London."

Arden's eyes grew icier. "And I told you my terms."

"Did she know of my offers?"

"No."

"Who told her such drivel?"

The earl shrugged. "Servants talk."

"Prompted by their lords with the right tales to tell?"

The old man said nothing.

"What were you trying to do? Weight the scale in your favor? Rather like a merchant who adds chalk to the salt, Arden."

The earl returned his direct look. "If you don't care for the terms, then find yourself another woman to wed."

"I want Linnet."

"You have one week to convince her you aren't what she thinks."

"You filled her head with this nonsense."

"'Twas your idea that she not know who you are."

"I had thought to talk to her first, to ease the way before she heard of my offer of marriage. I'm not the monster you painted me."

"Your reasons for dealing with Linnet are your own, Warbrooke. I have my reasons too. I'll not force her to wed anyone. Not even a royal favorite. I gave her mother my word I would never do so. I will not break an oath to my dead daughter."

William eyed the older man, a knight who was still tall and lean but weathered by too many fights over too many years. And as angry as William was, he also couldn't blame Arden.

Until now, he had not heard of the old man's vow. It could be debated in Arden's favor that a blood oath to one's dying daughter superseded even a forced agreement. Royal or not.

William knew well that this was a time when men sold their brothers for power or for wealth. Yet here before him was a regal old knight who wouldn't betray his daughter or her memory.

And he couldn't fault the man for wanting to keep Linnet with him. Wasn't that exactly why he was wedding her himself? This strange need to have her in his life?

"At the end of that week she will wed you willingly, or not wed you at all."

William stood, his breadth almost twice that of the earl's, and he looked down at him. "She will wed me. 'Tis not a battle I intend to lose."

The earl regarded him for a time, then stood so they were almost eye to eye. "Perhaps. But my granddaughter has a special gift for getting one to agree with her ideas before one realizes they've been hoodwinked."

William handed the old earl the extra tankard, then raised his own. "I believe, Arden, that standing before me is the person from whom she inherited that trait."

CHAPTER ❨ THREE

There was only half a moon out the following night, when William stood near the eastern side of the outer walls of Ardenwood Castle. Yet there was enough moonlight for him to see once he had entered the inner bailey. He moved swiftly and silently, uncertain if the guards had been warned by Arden.

She had insisted he meet her by the chapel. He counted buildings and found the second story arched window she had described.

He whistled once.

Nothing.

He waited.

Still nothing.

Females . . .

He whistled again.

Nothing.

He counted to ten.

To fifty.

By the time—the long time—he'd reached one hundred he was not pleased.

He looked around. The bailey was quiet.

Surely Arden would not be so foolish as to attack the king's man. He drew his dagger and flattened against the rough stones of the chapel wall.

Slowly, silently, he eased along the stone wall. His instincts had never before failed him. He could always feel it when something was afoot.

He sensed that nothing was amiss. Yet . . .

He rounded the corner.

Nothing.

A second later a screech rent the air.

William froze.

Like a demon from hell, a small shadow flew out of the darkness.

Right at him.

He raised his dagger and spun around.

Sharp knife tip pricks dug into the back of his neck.

Claws of some kind of crude weapon.

He dropped to a squat, lashing out with his dagger. With his other arm he reached around and grabbed his attacker by the . . .

. . . Fur.

Fur?

He held a handful of squirming and screeching fur.

Cat fur.

"Yeooow!" The cat bit him.

"God's teeth!" he spat, holding the animal by the scruff of its neck, ready to fling the cat to Kingdom Come if the damn thing bit him again.

Lady Linnet came scurrying around the corner. She stopped abruptly. "Oh! You caught him!"

"Where the devil have you been?" he gritted.

"Poor Swithun got loose and I had to find him. But now you've found him for me." She sounded remarkably cheery.

At that moment, poor Swithun had turned his head around and wedged his sharp feline teeth into William's wrist. He held the cat out to her. "Here. Do something with it. I don't intend to stand here until dawn."

She took the cat and hugged it to her as if it were some holy relic, then she spun around. "I'll be back down in a moment," she called over a shoulder. "All I must do is fetch my things."

He grunted some response and stood there, his blood still racing from combat with a cat, something that didn't sit well with him or his warrior's pride.

But when she had turned a moment before, another image flooded his mind—Linnet spinning on one bare foot as she sang in the woods. And his pride didn't matter quite as much as it had just a moment before.

A few seconds later, around the corner of the chapel, there was a loud thud.

If she were truly trying to covertly escape, the whole castle would have known it. He shook his head and walked around the corner.

Thud!

Two large satchels lay like lumps on the ground. He looked up at the window just as another even larger cloth sack flew out the window and hit the pile below. He stared at the bundles. There was a commotion, then another sack hit the ground.

Arms crossed, he leaned against the wall and watched. Eight more sacks flew out the window.

"Pssst!"

He shoved off from the wall and looked up just as Lady Linnet poked her head through the opening. "Pssst!"

"What?"

"I'm going to lower this down. 'Tis very fragile."

Fragile? He looked at the sacks and doubted there was anything left in the castle.

He was wrong.

She lowered a small willow cage by a rope until it dangled just above the ground. "Pssst!"

"Aye?"

"Will you please lower it the rest of the way. Carefully, please."

That cat was in the cage.

He set the cage on the ground. She dropped the rope.

Moments later she came hurrying around the corner, a basket slung on one arm, tying her mantle around her neck—that same white neck in which he'd foolishly thought to sometime soon bury his lips, the same neck he was now tempted to wring.

He stood next to her "things." The pile was taller than he. She looked from him to the stack, then back. She smiled.

He crossed his arms and glowered down at her. "Are you certain, my lady, that you have everything?"

She eyed the stack again and tapped a finger against her lips, then said distractedly, "Aye. I believe so."

"And how do you propose we take your *things* on a six-day journey?"

She gazed up at him, frowning. "You sound angry. I don't understand."

He waved his hand at the pile of sacks. "Look at this."

She did. "Are you concerned that I have forgotten something?"

"God's blood, woman! You could not possibly have forgotten *anything!*"

"Shhhh. You are shouting."

"I'm whispering, dammit! How the devil can I shout when I'm whispering?"

"I too would have wagered 'twas not possible, sir, but you are."

"There isn't a knight in the realm who wouldn't shout at this. I will not strap your things to my back and play the ass."

"Oh!" she said as if suddenly enlightened. "I understand. Wait here." She spun and disappeared around the corner.

He took four very long breaths. *One . . . Two . . .*

When he reached seventy-three she came back around the corner with a rope trailing behind her. "You needn't play the ass," she whispered brightly. "I already have my own."

And she did. Rounding the corner was a tether of donkeys laden with willow cages and more bundles than a sultan's caravan.

She smiled up at him as sweet as honey and placed the rope in his hand. "Now I have everything." She patted his arm and added, "You needn't fret so. I told you I had a plan."

He stared at the rope, then dropped it and walked up and down the line of pack animals. Somewhat dazed, he turned. "You have five rabbits, two ducks, and twenty-six cats?"

"Twenty-seven." She scurried over and picked up the cage beneath the window, then held it high in the moonlight. She gave him the sweetest and brightest smile he had ever received. "You forgot Swithun."

A lone figure stood on the battlements of Ardenwood Castle, quietly watching through shrewd and narrowed eyes, as the caravan, bathed in moonlight, wended its way up the north road.

Leading the procession was the Baron Warbrooke. He had a huge bundle strapped to his horse, while Lady Linnet, perched atop a palfrey, trotted along behind him. They were followed by a line, a very long line, of loaded pack animals.

After the caravan had disappeared over the rim of the hills, the earl of Arden turned away, and smiled.

Linnet rode along behind her escort, soaking up the bright June sunshine and the lush beauty of their surroundings. And she was humming. Humming, it seemed, kept the peace.

Her cats had never traveled and they had begun to loudly meow protests that continued until well into the morning hours. De Ros was not pleased, but he had ceased flinching at the noise a few hours before, after he had muttered something about the blessed silence of rabbits.

She had begun to hum, something she did often. He stopped abruptly and turned to watch her rather intensely. She had clamped her mouth shut, only to have him turn back around and gruffly command her to continue.

Now, sometime later, they rounded a bend in the road, where, in the distance, a stone bridge spanned a winding silver river that shimmered in the long rays of the late sun. One of the cats began to screech.

De Ros reined in and turned in the saddle, his expression as black as his hair. "God's blood! And I had thought the battlefield loud. I never knew one cat could make so bloody much racket!"

"That's Dismas. He's the loudest and unfortunately he's here in front."

"Dismas?".

"Aye. After Saint Dismas."

De Ros moved his mount toward the bridge. "You named your cat after a saint?"

"All my cats," she answered brightly, trotting behind. "My aunt, she's now the abbess of Saint Lawrence convent. She taught me letters and their order by memorizing the names of the saints. Ambrose, Bartholomew, Crispin, Dismas, Elmo, Friard, Genesius, Honoratus, Ignatius, Jerome, Kentigern, Lambert, Michael, Neot, Osmund, Patrick, Quintus, Raymond, Swithun, Thomas, Ursula, Vitus, Wenceslas, Ximenes, Yves, Zeno," she recited.

"Most of those names are male."

She laughed. "'Tis why you are complaining about the noise. Male cats always whine. Being cooped up in these baskets and cages limits their territory." She paused for a moment, then added, "I've always found great similarities between cats and humans."

He stopped and turned in the saddle, giving her a long and telling look.

She blinked, then smiled. He turned back around and continued silently until they were moving across the stone bridge. The farther they traveled over the rushing river, the louder the cats became and the ducks had begun to quack too.

De Ros reined in his horse and turned in the saddle; with a pained look he glared pointedly at the cages.

She winced slightly. "'Tis the sound of the river. The ducks like it and the cats don't."

Just as she finished, four of the cats screeched so loudly even she flinched. "They're frightened. Ignatius, Jerome, Kentigern, and Lambert were tied in a sack and thrown in a stream to drown. Can you imagine anything so cruel?"

"Aye."

She opened her mouth to respond, but stopped when de Ros spun back around so swiftly he almost made her light-headed. He sat atop his still horse, staring ahead, his body straight and rigid.

In the distance, a flash of bright sunlight caught her

eye. She shielded her eyes with a hand and searched the horizon.

The sun was still high and bright enough to shine in sharp rays off the polished helm of a lone knight who blocked the road ahead of them.

With the barest of commands de Ros shifted his mount in front of Linnet.

She braced herself on the pommel of the saddle and craned her neck. "I cannot see. Who—"

"Quiet, and stay close!" he warned quietly, his hand on the hilt of his sword.

She shifted so she could see around him. The war-horse beneath the unknown knight was stomping and blowing as if the animal sensed a need to charge. Neither animal nor man wore any identifying markings. The mount's trappings were plain and the knight's shield was a field of black. His sword was sheathed, but the steel tip of his lance glinted in the bright sun.

The knight raised a gauntleted hand.

'Twas not a greeting.

He lowered his visor with a challenging snap.

De Ros, who was sans armor, cursed violently and drew his sword. He pointed to the left of the river. "Ride into those woods!" he shouted. "Quickly!" He whirled his mount around.

But she sat, frozen.

The black knight raised his shield and charged.

So did de Ros.

They pounded toward each other. De Ros's horse was small and swifter than the huge Norman breed of war-horse the knight needed to support his full armor. But the knight's lance was pointed directly at de Ros, whose speedy mount ate up the ground between them, grass and dust flying.

They were but feet apart and Linnet held her breath for a heartbeat. A silent scream rose into her throat.

An instant later, de Ros slid from his saddle, crouched down in his outside stirrup.

Linnet gasped.

The lance hit thin air.

Before the knight could rein in and turn, de Ros

launched from his mount. His arm caught around the knight's neck and pulled him off his horse.

Both men hit the ground.

There was a scuffle and they rolled into the high grasses near the river. She could not see either man. Only movement in the grass, and the sounds—the loud clank of armor and male grunts.

The knight suddenly stood.

Her heart sank.

He turned, then faced her.

Her hands flew to her mouth and her scream rose again.

Then just as quickly the black knight moved to his horse, mounted in one swift motion and, to her shock, he rode away.

CHAPTER ☾ FOUR

*H*ead throbbing, William opened his eyes. Bright sunlight blinded him for a moment. He jerked his dagger free and shot up into a squat in one swift motion.

Linnet screamed.

He cursed and flinched.

"You are not dead," she said, her eyes wide.

"Deaf perhaps, but not yet dead." He looked around. "Where is he?"

"Gone. He mounted his horse and rode off through the woods."

William groaned with disgust and sheathed his dagger.

"Are you badly wounded?" Her voice was a worried whisper.

He sat back in the grass and rested his arms on his raised knees. Pain shot through his head. He touched the knot on the back of his head and winced, then pulled his hand away. His fingertips had smudges of red blood.

"You're bleeding!"

"'Tis nothing." He started to stand.

She grabbed his arm, her eyes watchful and her brow furrowed as she tried to assist him. If it wouldn't have hurt to do so, he'd have laughed aloud. He was twice her size. She could never hold him up should he pass out again. He rose, her arm around his waist and her shoulder leaning under his arm. She laid her hand on his chest, right where his heart beat and gave him a look that was tender with concern.

His cynicism drained away as he looked down at her,

and he felt something more than just his desire to have this woman. He felt somehow bound to her by a strong sense of responsibility. And for more than just her safety. For her happiness.

He was used to taking charge of people's lives, his men-at-arms, his friend and king, those weaker and unable to fight. Such were a knight's duties—duties he accepted with pride because he had worked so long and hard to earn his golden spurs.

But he had never been responsible for something as unfamiliar to him as a woman's heart. He frowned, and a cut on his forehead sent an annoying trickle of blood into his eye. He swiped at it.

She gaped at his head, then stared in horror at his bloody hand, then slid her hand around his waist and leaned into him as she looked up. "Come. Give me your other hand and I'll help you to the river's edge and tend your wounds."

He let her help him, fighting the urge to smile. Tending him seemed to make her happy, so he went along with her, feeling strangely comfortable and staring at her hand threaded through his, then at the top of her head. Every few steps she would look up as if she expected him to faint from such puny scratches.

"Not much farther" she would say, then squeeze his hand. At the river she insisted he sit, attempting to ease him onto a tuft of bright green summer grass as she clucked and fussed.

His head no longer ached. In fact, he felt rather well. She knelt and dipped a small cloth into the river, then turned and gently cleaned his cuts.

She moved to kneel behind him, bracing one hand on his shoulder while she tended the cut on the back of his head. After a moment she said quietly, "I have never seen anyone do such."

"Have you not seen a joust?"

"Only one, but that was not what I meant. I have never seen a man swing over the side of a horse as you did."

"A trick I learned from the Turks." He watched her

come back around and kneel down next to him again, her interest captured. "They would attack on horses swifter than any war-horse, their swords swinging as they charged toward you. To survive one had to learn to ride like they did." He laughed at the way her eyes grew wide and wondered if he had looked so stunned the first time he'd seen those horsemen. "They rode like madmen. 'Twas as if they drank the wind."

She didn't respond, but seemed to be attempting to create the image in her mind. He liked that in her. She listened to him. She smiled, and he sat there, stunned by his reaction to something so simple as her smile. At that moment, had she asked, he'd have conquered the world for her.

She had busied herself by wringing out the cloth in the river. When she finished, she sat back in the grass and hugged her knees to her chest, then cocked her head. "Who was that knight?"

"I don't know." He stared at the grassy hillock where he'd first spotted the black knight. The man had taken great pains to make certain his identity was hidden. He had his suspicions that Arden had paid the unknown man, but he said nothing. Instead he turned back and watched the river flow.

"Why would he attack us like that?" Her voice was tentative.

He glanced at her. Her face was pale, emotion and fear there for anyone to see. She was truly frightened. He hadn't thought of her reaction. He was used to violence and combat. But she was a young woman who had probably led a sheltered life, especially if Arden wished to keep her from marriage as he had said. He shrugged, hoping she would drop the subject.

She was bravely trying to cover her fear and she rocked slightly, as if her thoughts were racing so that she was unaware of her body's motions. Finally she asked, "Do you think he meant to rob us?"

In a voice filled with feigned hope, he asked, "Did he take the cats?"

She stared at him blankly, then she must have caught

the amusement on his face because she began to laugh. "No," she said, shaking her head. "He took nothing."

"I must not have good fortune on my side today."

She laughed again. "I like it when you jest."

"Why is that?"

She twisted some grass, then looked up again. "Because it makes you seem more human, I suppose."

He didn't know how to respond to that. How to say he was human, as human as the next man, with the same fears and weaknesses. He just never let anyone see them. He wanted to admit that to her, but his pride stopped him and he changed the subject. "Why do you have twenty-six cats?"

"Twenty-seven," she corrected.

"Twenty-seven cats . . ." He looked at the pack animals grazing in the grass near the bridge, then added, "Five rabbits and two ducks."

She rocked back, her hands still clasping her knees and the toes of her soft leather slippers pointing daintily into the lush river grass. "Because there was no one to care for them but me. Some were starving, others, like Ignatius, Jerome, Kentigern, and Lambert were left to die. I was taught to believe that we are caretakers, put here to help care for all living things. Not to abandon them. Not to starve them, drown them, or worse. The rabbits I freed from traps. Only one has four legs. A rabbit cannot live in the forest with only one back leg." She was silent.

"And the ducks?" he asked.

She smiled. "They followed me home."

His mind flashed with the image of her running back to the castle, her arms filled with wounded animals, ducks trailing behind her, and a knight watching her with a need that was stronger than anything he had ever felt before. Some part of him wanted to have been there when she had found the animals, instead of the day he had seen her—the day she danced and sang to them.

But still he felt a lightness inside, a sense too profound to name whenever he thought of that first moment he'd seen her. He must have frowned, because a moment later he felt the trickle of blood from the cut on his forehead.

She moved toward him, kneeling just inches away, and she wiped the cut.

He spent a pleasurable few seconds judging the size and weight of her breasts, then eyed the tender white skin of her neck. She smelled of flowers and summer— exactly as he had imagined she would smell—clean and pure and intoxicating.

She slowly ran the cloth down his cheek and he was aware of more than just her scent and her shape. He was greatly aware of the gentleness of her touch. She still cleansed his face, then ran the cloth over his jaw which was becoming more tense the closer she shifted.

In a sudden motion, he grabbed her wrist and the cloth fell from her fingers. She blinked at him, startled.

He realized his grip was too hard and slackened it, then gently stroked his thumb over the thin and fragile blue veins beneath her honey-colored skin. "Enough." he said gruffly.

"Did I hurt you?"

"No." He didn't release her hand.

She returned his direct look for the longest time— time that seemed to have stopped—until she finally averted her golden eyes and stared at their joined hands.

Since the moment he had first seen her singing in the woods, he knew his life was nothing. Nothing because she had not been part of it.

And now, as he watched the top of her bent head, he wondered if he should give in to the urge that was consuming him. He wanted nothing more than to lie as one with this woman in the sweet grass.

Lie in her for all his tomorrows. But something stopped him. Some emotion that tasted of a morality he hadn't known he had.

Morality and something that had the tart flavor of a sudden lack of confidence—a weakness foreign to him. He had always known he could win any battle, so he had won. Whether his confidence had come from a foolish and youthful idea that he was invincible, or actually from bravery he knew not.

What he did know was that his confidence had left him when it came to Linnet. He felt awkward and out of place with her, afraid to speak lest he say the wrong thing. Afraid to touch her lest she recoil.

Perhaps it was because he had never had to court a woman. And he did not know how to go about it. The women he'd known had needed nothing but a look that promised long nights of hot passion or a morning's reward of silver coins.

He'd known Eastern women who were schooled in the art of bedding, women whose purpose was to satisfy a man, and who had taught him that his strongest satisfaction lay in firing a woman's passion to as hot a flame as his own.

There were the women who waited on the fringes of a battle, ready for men whose blood still ran wild, women who liked it rough and savage. And there were the skilled women of the court, who wanted to bed a new baron, the king's friend, or the man whose reputation made him some kind of sexual prize.

But he'd never known a woman like Linnet. A woman with a heart so big she cared for a herd of cats, ducks, and rabbits. A woman whose gentleness tamed a forest. And a fierce knight's wild heart.

So for the first time in his life he played coward and stood quickly, startling her.

"William?"

The sound of his Christian name on her lips almost broke his resolve. He wanted to hear her say his name again. He wanted to hear her say his name in passion.

She frowned up at him.

The look he gave her was hard and emotionless, the opposite of how he felt inside. But his stony manner covered his weakness for her, a weakness that frightened him because it came upon him so strongly and completely unbidden. He turned away.

"What is wrong?"

She sounded hurt. He had been so concerned that he would do the wrong thing. And now he'd done so. He had hurt her. He took a deep breath. "We've tarried here long enough. Half the day is gone!" he barked over a shoulder and strode toward the horses.

Away. Safely away from a battle he had no idea how to win.

CHAPTER ❪ FIVE

"*O*ne for you, Wenceslas, and one for you, Ximenes." Linnet turned and put the last of the salted fish into the cage with Yves and Zeno, then secured the latch. They had ridden with few words between them until William had finally grunted something about resting here.

A moment later he crossed the small clearing and stood behind her. "Come," he ordered. "Feed yourself." He gestured to some bread and cheese that lay upon a huge flat rock a short distance away.

She quietly followed, wondering what she had done to anger him. He hadn't looked at her again with anything remotely close to kindness. He just stared into the woods around them, like he was doing now. She followed his gaze, but saw nothing of interest.

She looked at their meager meal, then said, "I need to fetch something." She hurried over to one of the pack animals and untied a heavy sack. It plopped to the ground. She grabbed the ties and began to drag it through the dirt.

An instant later William was beside her. He hauled the sack easily over his broad shoulder and strode back toward the rock, muttering.

She followed, rushing to keep up with his long strides. "Did you say something?"

He stopped and gave her a wry look, then shook his head. He dropped the sack on the ground and sat down on the rock where he drank from a wineskin.

She knelt and untied the sack. "I brought a few things—"

He snorted.

"From the larder."

She bent and looked inside, then sat up, pulling things out. "I have pears and grapes and apples . . ." For the next five minutes she unloaded the sack.

". . . Capon with herbs, honeyed figs, and"—she held up a small crock—"pickled eel!" She frowned at the crock. "Who eats pickled eel?"

William wasn't looking at her. He was staring at the pile of food she had brought.

"What would you like?"

Now he looked at her.

"A honeyed fig?" She held up the fruit.

He did not look pleased. He was staring at her with the oddest look. Finally he shook his head and looked away.

She stared at him, her throat suddenly tight. She could not do anything to please this man. She had never had anyone treat her so coolly. Her grandfather adored her, and she could always make him laugh. Her sisters' husbands treated her like a younger sister.

But William had a wall around him that she couldn't penetrate. And it hurt her, to think he might dislike her. She stared at the food for a long time, then finally whispered, "I'm sorry."

She could feel his stare. "What?"

"I'm sorry if I did something wrong."

He sighed, then said, "You did nothing wrong."

She looked up, not understanding his mood, searching for answers. "Do your wounds pain you?"

"My wounds?" He frowned as if he had forgotten about them. "No."

She plucked at the grass and asked, "Then why are you so angry."

He looked uncomfortable and raised the wineskin and squeezed a spigot of wine into his mouth. He swallowed, then looked at her again.

She was still waiting for his answer.

"Eat," was all he said.

She didn't eat.

He took a deep breath, then shook his head. When he looked at her again there was at last a small glimmer of kindness in his expression. "I'm not angry with you," he said in that same gentle voice he'd used in the tavern. "I'm . . ." he paused as if he were trying to make a decision, then he said, "I have things on my mind."

At least she had an answer of sorts and she felt better knowing she had not angered him. They ate in a companionable silence. He even ate honeyed figs and some meat after she had offered it to him three more times.

He swallowed a fig and picked up the wineskin. He leaned down from the rock and handed it to her. "Here."

She took the wine, sensing that it was an offering of peace and knowing that he would not explain himself to her. He sat on that rock, one leg drawn up, resting his weight on one tightly muscled arm.

The small cross on his earring swung a little as a small breath of cool wind flew by them. His face was shorn of feeling, rigid as that rock and yet there was a sense of depth to this man, a vast and complex mixture of distance, hardness, and kindness all together. His thoughts were as unknown as the identity of the black knight, but she could sense his isolation. Odd how it drew her, strangely called out to that natural and fey part of her that could befriend God's wild and precious beasts.

He needed time and to be left alone. She understood that. With a small sigh, she distractedly raised the wineskin high above her face as he had done and squeezed.

Wine shot onto her forehead. She burst out laughing, knowing what a fool she must look.

Her reward was to see amusement in his expression. But no smile. For some reason she knew not why, she needed to see this man smile. He looked as if he desperately needed some laughter in his life.

She tried to drink again and came closer to her target. This time, she hit her ear. "How did you do that?"

"Experience," he said. "Years of experience."

She was determined to do this. She tried again. And

hit her chin. She laughingly swiped at the drips of wine, then licked the wine from her fingers.

His amusement drained away. He was still as stone. The look he gave her was filled with an intense hunger.

Frowning, she set the skin aside. "Do you want some grapes?" He said nothing. He stared at her mouth, so she wiped it again. She held out the wedge of cheese. "Cheese?"

He didn't move.

"Wine," she asked hopefully.

His answer was to stand up suddenly. "I need to water the horses." Then he gathered the leads and disappeared into the forest behind their camp.

Half an hour later William came back. He had stayed away until his blood had cooled. But he'd had to wade into the stream to cool it. Water dripped from his chausses onto the ground and his hair was soaked and stuck to his neck. He didn't care. He reached up to tie the leads to a nearby tree.

"Oh! You fell in the stream!" Linnet hurried toward him with a blanket. "You'll freeze to death!"

William gave her a long look and almost laughed. "I doubt it."

She stood there with the blanket in her hand, looking completely confused.

Again he was reminded of how very sheltered she had been. He still had no idea how to win her over. He felt foolish and awkward, which was as frustrating as that intense passion he felt for her but had to keep in check.

She had moved to stand close to him and tugged on his arm. He looked down. She reached up and placed her hand on his forehead, then frowned. "Your brow is cool."

"There is a God," he muttered.

"You're not fevered?"

"No," he said more sharply than he intended, then softened it with, "I am tired."

She smiled and patted his chest. "I have just the thing." She spun around and rushed over to a pile of sacks, a large pile of sacks.

"You unpacked."

"Aye," she said and dumped out one of the sacks, then grinned. "Velvet pillows. For our comfort." She dumped out another sack. "More pillows." She dumped out another. "And a feather coverlet . . ."

He leaned against the tree and watched her dump out sack after sack until the small clearing looked like the inside of a harem. Any moment he was certain she would unpack silk hangings for the tree limbs.

"I know it was here somewhere," she mumbled, and two more pillows sailed over her head to land at his feet. "Ah-ha!" She turned and held up a large yellow- and red-striped cloth. "Look!"

He stared at the cloth, frowning.

"It's a tent."

"I know." It looked to be the type of tent used in a tourney. He could see four bright yellow pennants still lying on the ground behind her.

"I brought it to sleep in. Here." She handed it to him, then stood there looking very pleased with herself. "Now we have everything we need."

"Except the poles."

"What poles?"

"The tent poles."

She began to chew on her lip.

"Poles that hold up the tent," he explained.

She snapped her fingers. "So that's what those sticks were for."

He blinked once, then began to laugh. And he laughed loud and hard.

She laughed too then said with a giggle, "'Tis a shame we cannot just use the pickled eel."

He shook his head and his laughter faded.

She touched his arm again. "I like it when you laugh," she admitted with that honesty that still jarred him. Then she foolishly smiled at him.

He stared at her for a long moment, then gave her a taste of his own honesty. "That's a sure way to get yourself kissed."

She blinked, somewhat surprised, then she said, "I always wondered how that was done."

He laughed, more at himself than at her. "So my lady has never been kissed."

She shook her head and sighed. "I always thought my first kiss would be in the garden at Ardenwood." She smiled a dreamy kind of smile. "With the moon shining and the night roses and honeysuckle blooming and by a handsome knight who had paid court to me."

"How does a lady dream of being courted?" He tried to sound casual, not giving away how important her answer was.

"How? I'm not certain. The usual way I suppose. With flowers and sweets and romance. My sisters' husbands courted each one a different way. Michael played the lute and sang love ballads to Maude. 'Twas truly touching. John wrote the most passionate poetry for Elizabeth."

William stifled a groan.

"Isabelle's husband brought her silks and scents from the East, and delicious comfits and a posy. He was very romantic."

Romantic. Something William was surely not. He couldn't spout pretty words and he'd been told his singing voice sounded like the rusted chains of a drawbridge. He said nothing, just set the tent aside and walked toward the trees.

"Where are you going?"

"We should get some sleep."

She followed, rushing to keep up with his longer strides. "But what shall we use for shelter?"

"The trees are our shelter." He shook out a blanket with a snap, dropped it, and stretched out on the ground, crossing his boots at the ankle.

She stood nearby, hugging two pillows and looking at the sky as if she expected it to fall on her at any time. "But what if it rains?"

"It is not going to rain." He locked his hands behind his head.

"Oh." She sat down next to him and began to arrange a bed. "You sound certain."

"I am certain."

She shrugged, then proceeded to lay every blanket on

her pillow pallet, then finally topped it off with the feather coverlet.

He'd sweat to death under all that, he thought.

She finally crawled underneath the covers. After a minute of peace filled silence, she said, "William?"

"Hmm?"

"Would you like some of these pillows?"

"No."

"I have plenty."

He grunted.

"Perhaps only one? On which to rest your head?"

He turned over and looked at her. She was holding out a pillow. He took it, stuffed it under his head, and closed his eyes.

She shifted around for a few more minutes, then finally lay down.

He resisted the urge to applaud.

"William?"

"Aye?"

"I have more blankets too."

"I'm fine."

"You'll freeze with only one blanket. And you did fall into the river. It must have been particularly icy. You could become ill. Especially sleeping on the ground."

"I've slept more often on the ground in the past few years than in a bed." Then he turned over and looked at her. He felt suddenly very foolish. "But you have never slept anywhere but in a bed, have you?"

"I slept in a hammock once. 'Twas quite interesting. Took me four attempts before I managed not to spill out of it. 'Twas the only time I have ever bloodied my nose." She laughed at herself, then pulled the covers over and around her and huddled under them. With only her face showing she looked like a spring cabbage.

He called himself all kinds of an idiot. Again. He should have planned a place for her to stay. Somewhere warm and with some comforts for a lady. Just as he should have planned for more elaborate food than just meager meals of bread and cheese.

He hadn't thought about what she would need. He

had been too determined to get her alone. Too ready to be with her. Too desperate to think clearly.

Now he was with her, alone, and his time was passing quickly, like water leaking from the jar of a water clock. He felt each droplet was a lost moment.

"This is rather nice," she said with a sigh. "Look at all those stars." She sounded surprised and pleased. "I don't think I've ever seen the sky like this. It's as if above us is a canopy full of stars." She paused. "Interesting . . ."

"What?"

"Somehow seeing the sky like this makes the night less dark and frightening."

He stared up at the night sky, wondering how someone could think it frightening. The lack of sunlight gave him a sense of privacy. The air was still. Cold. And it was quiet. To him there was a strange power in the darkness of the night. A peace. Battles were not fought at night.

"Do you think the tales are true?"

"What tales?"

"That all the stars are angels."

He looked at the sky and wondered at such fanciful nonsense. "Men use the stars to guide them home," he said quietly.

"Did you?"

"Aye. But I sailed home on a ship. A ship's crew uses the stars to keep on course."

"I didn't know that."

"See that bright star directly above us? That's what is called a mariner's star."

"It's very beautiful." She paused, then asked, "What is it like to sail on a ship?"

He turned, frowning.

She must have read his puzzlement because she added, "I mean, how does it feel?"

He stared at the night sky and wondered when he had stopped noticing things—the vast numbers of stars, the sweet taste of a honeyed fig, the feel of the sea. He sat up a little and rested his head on his hand while he looked down at her.

Her hands were folded prayerlike beneath the pillow

and she just lay there, calmly, looking at him with expectant eagerness.

"The sea is unpredictable. There are times when a ship can glide smoothly over the water, and other times where the sea can pound so much water into the ship that one is certain it will sink at any moment." He paused thoughtfully. "I suppose sailing is like war in a way, a battle of the elements—wind and weather and the massive seas—things, powerful things, that one cannot control."

She was quiet, then she cocked her head. "I think perhaps I'd be frightened to death. Yet you find pleasure in danger, don't you?"

He shrugged, uncomfortable at speaking so plainly of his thoughts, but he fought to keep his expression impassive. "'Tis a challenge."

She said nothing, just wiggled under her covers. He wished she would go to sleep. Then he could watch her freely, watch her sleep.

Her scent drifted to him in the midsummer air, making him aware of her in ways he'd just as soon forget. He took a deep breath, her scent as soul cleansing as fresh sea air. He stared into the night sky, then took one last look at her.

She was watching him.

He would kiss her, at any moment. He knew he would. He started to move toward her.

"William?" She spoke his name gently, as if it were natural to her.

He froze.

"Thank you," she whispered sleepily, and closed her eyes.

CHAPTER ☾ SIX

*H*umming a bright tune, Linnet wormed her way through some bushes, Quintus, Neot, and Vitus following behind while Swithun tugged on her hem. There was a small copse of gooseberry bushes here somewhere, she thought. She had spotted the bushes while trying to walk out the stiffness from being too long atop a horse.

They had traveled for most of the next day, until William had finally stopped to rest at a river bend where marsh marigolds bloomed brightly, and the trees and bushes were thick, lush, and flanked by a meadow filled with buttercups.

A little distance away she found the gooseberries, then held out her tunic and began to pick them. Within a few minutes, she had several handfuls of plump berries cupped in her skirt.

She stopped humming and glanced down at her cats. "Shall we taste them, sweetlings?" They looked up at her and she grinned. "Yes, I think we should too." She popped one into her mouth, and shuddered. They were as sour as old wine.

"Now what would you do with sour gooseberries?" They meowed. "Me too," she said, then she began to sing a silly little song she made up as she danced to the tune.

Hey fiddle diddle dee!
Hey fiddle fi.

I'd rather be a fairy,
than a gooseber-ry . . .

A handful at a time, she tossed the berries over her shoulder, and the cats scampered after them, batting them with their fluffy paws. She made a game of flinging the berries skyward and listening to them patter the ground and bushes behind her, humming and skipping to the merry tune of the falling berries. She looked at the cats and laughed. "Those berries ought to be good for something since they certainly aren't good for eating."

After a few more minutes she glanced down, just as a flash of gray fur trotted off toward the trees edging the river where a meadowlark had perched on low elm branch.

"Swithun!" she called. "Come back here!" As usual, he ignored her. She tossed away the last handful of berries and dusted off her tunic, then spun around.

William de Ros stood there, looking as tall as an ancient elm. And just as rigid.

She stared at him for a second.

He had gooseberries in his hair.

She grinned.

He didn't.

Laughter just bubbled up and she tried to stop, but couldn't. He had a plump gooseberry wedged in his earring. She covered her mouth with a hand.

He shook his head and berries flew everywhere. The cats raced anxiously around his boots, thinking he was another toy.

Now she was giggling. He glared at her, but it did no good. The gooseberry was still stuck in his earring, which didn't look barbaric now. It looked rather silly.

She dropped her hand and took a breath, smiling. "Your face is as sour as those berries." She gave him her sincerest look. "I'm sorry. Truly. I didn't know you were there." She walked toward him and stopped. He stared at her for a long moment. She reached up and plucked the berry from his earring and held it up. "You missed one."

He was silent and she cocked her head and watched

him, trying to read his thoughts. 'Twas then that she saw the flowers. Clutched in his battle scarred hand was a small posy of marigolds, maidenhair fern, and bright buttercups.

He stiffened and looked at the bouquet. She wondered what he was thinking. He looked so strange—a warrior standing before her, tall and fierce, until one noticed the flowers. 'Twas rather like watching the devil pet a kitten. Certainly not a scene one would imagine.

Very softly, she asked, "Are they for me?"

He looked as if he wanted to say something but couldn't speak. He seemed to be waging some kind of mental battle. He glanced up at the late sun and muttered, "There is no time for this foolishness."

Her heart fell a little. She didn't think the fact that he had picked flowers for her was foolish at all; she thought it was touching.

Part of her wished to put him at ease, yet she wasn't certain what she could say so she said nothing. She only gave the flowers a wistful look.

He seemed to make a decision and he turned around, then stopped and turned back. "Here," he barked and held out the flowers just a few inches from her nose.

She took the posy and in a moment of sheer whimsy she held her hand out to him. He stared at it for the longest time, then with a very intense look he raised it slowly to his lips, turned it over, and lightly and reverently kissed her palm.

She brought the bouquet to her nose, using it to hide her smile. The buttercups smelled fresh and clean— sweet as the midsummer air . . . which suddenly crackled with a vicious curse.

Stunned, she snapped her head up, then followed his angry stare.

At the edge of the meadow was another armored knight. From his helm, a blue plume nodded in the breeze and his shield was a plain field of the same color. He anchored his shield, raised his free hand. With accomplished precision he began to swing a mace.

William slowly moved toward his sword, lying forgot-

ten in the marsh marigolds where his horse was drinking
from the river's edge.

The knight charged, his mace arcing around and
around, his horse eating up the distance and sending
tufts of grass flying under the power of his wide hooves.

Linnet watched, horrified as William raced like the
wind toward his sword. She could see that the knight was
closer and faster, his horse pounding furiously toward
William—past the stream, past the bushes, under the
wide branches of the river elms.

A sudden flash of gray dropped from a tree and
landed on the mighty war-horse.

"Swithun!" Linnet called out.

The war-horse reared suddenly and shrieked, its
hooves pawing the air. Swithun screeched and clawed
the horse's hindquarters. The mace flung around and
snagged on a tree limb, jerking the mace hilt from the
knight's hand. Momentum wrapped the mace around the
tree limb with a snap, the spiked mace ball hopelessly
tangled in its own chain.

The knight struggled to control his horse, the mace
hilt forgotten and hanging uselessly from the low
branches of the tree.

William grabbed his sword and leapt onto his mount.

The knight hauled on the reins and spun the war-
horse around so swiftly that Swithun flew off. Linnet
screamed and ran. But the cat hit the water with a loud
shriek.

The knight rode off and William turned to ride after
him.

Linnet ran straight into the river. "Swithun! Swithun!"
She struggled through the current to the spot where he'd
hit the water. She slipped and grabbed at a rock.

"Swithun!"

Clinging to the rock she straightened and spotted his
tiny head bobbing away from her. She screamed,
"Swithun!" and splashed toward him, her tunic catching
on some river rocks.

William's horse thundered past her, splashing water in
all directions. He bent down and grabbed the half-

drowned cat. A second later he was in front of her, his horse blocking her from drifting downriver.

His hand shot out and gripped her arm. With a snap he hauled her up and plopped her down between his legs. He was cursing the air blue. Linnet made the mistake of looking over her shoulder at him.

He was furious.

Linnet stared up at the night sky, clear and filled with bright twinkling stars. She sighed, and looked around. There was nothing around her but dark forest and her mounds of pillows. William had said little to her since his lecture on the stupidity of leaping in the river. Especially when she admitted she'd do the same thing again.

In warring silence they had traveled until darkness made going on too risky, then they'd made camp and eaten in that same silence.

But she had felt him watching every motion she made, and it made her nervous when he watched her so intently, as if he had to do so.

She tossed and turned on the pillows she used as a pallet, then jerked her covers higher. She tried counting stars. She still couldn't sleep. But then William was not beside her.

He had waited until she was still before he crossed the small clearing. He stood above her for a moment, then he lay down and locked his hands behind his head. He was just thinking of the day he'd had, when he heard something—just a small noise. It could have been nothing but a squirrel in the trees, but he lay still, listening.

"I think I see a wolf," Linnet said.

William snapped upright, his dagger drawn. "Where?"

She stared at him with a startled expression, then pointed at the sky. "Up there. In the stars."

He sagged back down on his pallet to keep from shaking her. Star shapes in the sky, he thought with disgust.

"I'm sorry. I was counting stars and spotted it. I didn't mean to frighten you."

"I wasn't frightened."

She was quiet. William closed his eyes.

"Do you suppose the stars are different in different places. I mean do people see different stars in different places?"

Certain stars were used as guides, but the others, well, he never had thought about them.

"I see a dragon right up there. Can't you see it?"

He opened his eyes and looked at the night sky. It looked as it always did. Dark, powerful, and filled with small specks of light. Finally he said, "Where?"

She shifted closer so that their heads were right next to each other. He could have cared less about the stars at that moment. As she showed him the shape, her cheek so close to his that all he had to do was turn his head, just turn it and his mouth would touch hers.

She shifted away. "It's pleasant, sleeping under the sky. Unless it rains. That wouldn't be pleasant I imagine."

He took a deep breath. "It's not going to rain."

"How do you know that?"

"The sun didn't rise red."

"Oh." She paused, then asked, "Does that mean it will rain, when the sun rises red?"

"Aye."

"I see." She rustled underneath her mound of blankets and turned on her side toward him. He could feel her stare.

He glanced at her.

She smiled. "How do you know that a red sunrise means rain?"

He sighed. "Experience."

She was blessedly quiet. He closed his eyes and relaxed. His breath was even and he was almost asleep.

"I've been thinking . . ."

He stifled the urge to groan.

"What does it mean if the sun sets red?"

"Nothing."

"But if the sun rises red and that means it will rain, then it stands to reason that the sun setting red must mean something also." She paused, then added, "But the sun always sets red so it would not change anything or mean anything. And if the sun always sets red, then doesn't it always rise red too?"

"Good night."

"Oh. Yes, I suppose you are tired . . . riding all this way, rescuing Swithun, fighting knights, barking orders . . ."

He lifted his head and turned back to see her smiling. Exasperated, he dropped his head back on the pillow and said, "And listening to cats screech. Ducks quack—"

"And me talk?" He could hear the laughter in her voice.

"Aye, and listening to you talk."

"Good night, William."

He closed his eyes.

A few moments later she sighed. "I'll say a prayer that it doesn't rain."

"Go to sleep. It is *not* going to rain."

"Well." She sighed again. "If you're certain."

"I am more than certain. I'll lay my life on it."

"I'd say your life is fairly worthless about now," Linnet said to William with a slight smile. The comment earned her a rather pointed glare.

It had been raining for over two hours. After the first five minutes, the cats had started screeching and the ducks quacking. William and Linnet sat huddled beneath the dripping blankets he'd spread over some tree branches while he muttered something about bed hangings after all. Linnet had questioned him but he had not answered.

'Twas a soggy shelter to say the least, as soggy as her velvet pillows which were now floating a few feet away in muddy puddles. "I certainly wish I had brought those tent sticks," Linnet said, thoughtfully.

The cats screeched again and the ducks kept quacking.

William glanced at the cages. "I certainly wish you had brought just rabbits."

"It is a dreadful lot of noise, isn't it? I'm terribly sorry. I feel so sorry for them." Dismas screeched so loudly the sound rang through her teeth.

William cursed almost as loudly and stood, scowling.

She grabbed his leg. "Don't hurt him. Please. He's only frightened."

He gave her a puzzled look, then stiffened as if she besmirched his honor. "I do not kill animals," he said through a tight jaw. "Tempting though it may be in this case." With that he stalked out of the shelter into the driving rain.

Linnet watched, stunned, as William brought the cages two at a time over to the shelter of the trees. He stacked them, one atop another in neat rows, then trudged back out into the rain to get the tent and drape it over the cages.

She stood there, too stunned to move. This gruff and sometimes angry man, a hardened warrior, was doing something she was certain no other man would do. He was giving comfort and protection to her pets.

He strode back through the rain and the mud to their shelter. He must have read her thoughts because he stopped suddenly, his expression as chagrined as if she had just seen him naked. Head down, he busied himself by retying the halter leads to the tree branches and adjusting the blankets which didn't need adjusting.

She bit back a smile, then walked over to him and gently touched his arm. "William?"

He stared down at her. His black hair was plastered to his head and neck. Rainwater dripped from his brows, nose, and chin and from his clothing, even from that earring.

"Thank you."

He looked away.

She just stood there.

He jerked the corner of the blanket tightly over the limb of a tree, then stopped and said gruffly, "I couldn't take the racket any longer."

"Of course. I understand." She gave his arm a pat and turned around. She could feel his stare, but she walked back and sat down, repaying him by leaving him alone with his embarrassment.

But she felt her heart beat a little faster and a small smile of satisfaction tickled her mouth. His actions told her more about him than all the bard's tales and servants' rumors ever could. Beneath his barbaric looks, beneath the gruff and hard mercenary edges he showed the rest of the world, was a kind man.

Chapter ☾ Seven

The road had turned to mud that was thick as oat porridge and slowed their progress. The pack mules balked and brayed when the mud became deep and the cats didn't like being jostled.

William was on his own crusade, determined to rectify his past mistakes and reach the town of Wakefair by nightfall. Eventually the dirt road became rocky and drier, the mud only in ravines that dropped down from the highway.

They had been traveling for most of the day when the red knight appeared. Like the black knight he sat upon a heavy war-horse with plain trappings and both his shield and plume were red.

The visor of his helm was already down, in challenging position. He had no lance, only a sword, and he was blocking the narrow road.

William turned in his saddle. "Ride back to the center of the caravan! And woman—"

"Aye?"

"Do as I say this time!" He drew his sword and turned back.

The red knight charged.

William kicked his mount.

Seconds later they met on the narrow section of highway, met with a clash of sword blades, the power of which sent a familiar ringing up William's sword arm.

He fought hard, but the knight's war-horse was hands higher than his smaller mount. His arm was fast tiring.

The red knight sliced his sword downward. William kicked his foot out and knocked the knight from his horse. The man landed on the edge of the roadway.

William leapt from his own mount, then smacked its hindquarter and sent it charging up the road. Sword raised, he rounded the man's war-horse. The red knight had managed to stand and move from the narrow shoulder that separated road from ravine. A muffled curse came from inside the helm.

The knight raised his sword . . .

. . . And Linnet screamed.

William froze and turned. The knight knocked his sword from his hand.

William whipped around, a vile curse on his tongue.

The knight was ready. His mailed foot shot out. With the force of a catapult, he kicked William square in the belly.

William doubled over and saw stars. A second later he tumbled backward and down the ravine.

Jagged rocks jabbed his shoulders, his back, his legs. He grunted. Bracken and sharp roots scratched his face and neck. He curled into a tight ball to keep from catching a limb and breaking bones.

Down he fell, faster and farther.

Down, over more sharp granite edges and rough thorny bushes.

Down until a mud pit stopped him. He lay there, mud oozing around him, the world spinning, and more stars than Linnet could count shooting past his vision. He didn't move for the longest time. He took one breath, then another, very slowly.

"William?" She was peering down from the edge of the roadside.

He opened his mouth.

"William, please, answer me!"

He tried to speak. A moan came out.

"William? I'm coming down there."

"No!" he croaked.

Too late. Her muddy slippers crept over the edge and an instant later she was sliding down the hill on her back-

side, a fall of flaming red hair flying out behind her.
"Ouch!"

He closed his eyes and mentally cursed.

"Oh!"

He heard the sound of tearing fabric.

"Heavens!"

Gravel rained down on him.

"Uh-oh!"

He could hear Linnet crashing through the bushes and
winced. Before he could take another breath, she hit him
with a grunt.

He lay there, eyes closed, Linnet sprawled atop him.
Her chest and belly were pressed against his and her legs
lay between his own. He could feel her heart beating
faster and louder than thundering horses.

Her nose was against his chest and her hair fanned
out, twigs and leaves tangled in it. Slowly she raised her
head and shook it.

Leaves flew out and a twig slapped him in the chin.
She shoved her hair out of her face and stared down at
him. One small hand reached out to gently cup his
cheek.

"Are you terribly wounded?" she asked.

"Only my pride."

She whispered his name again. Her lips were there.
An inch away. He told himself "not yet." But her body
was soft and he wanted her. God, how he wanted her.

He relied on pure concentrated determination to control himself. He closed his eyes, which only heightened
his sense of smell, sound, and touch. Other than sight,
that left one more sensation—taste. How would she
taste?

He opened his eyes. There were tears in hers. Real
tears. Worried tears. God's teeth . . . There was only so
much a man could take.

His mouth was on hers an instant later, his hand
splayed across the back of her head, holding her to him.
She went even softer against him, as if his kiss made her
weak.

He stroked her lips with his tongue and she gave a
quiet gasp of surprise. His tongue sank into her sweet

mouth, filled it, and the kiss was just as he'd thought. She tasted of honey, of fire, and of everything he ever could need.

His other hand slid over her shoulder and slowly down her slim back to caress her bottom. She moaned against the strength of his tongue.

He held her hard against him and rolled with her, pressing her back into the soft mud, his mouth taking hers sweetly but firmly, mimicking the way he wanted to take her body—in long, slow strokes that lasted forever.

With her beneath him he pressed closer, feeling her sink into the mud but not caring, because she moaned against his mouth and gripped his shoulders.

She didn't push him away. She held him fast and kept her mouth open, her curious tongue moving in answer to his. He shifted his hips, rocking slowly against her in a steady rhythm as old as time.

It was happening too fast. Too strong. Too out of control. He fought with himself, fought his primal urge and reason. He drew his mouth away, his breath coming as fast as his passion did. He looked down into those eyes, those wild golden eyes that looked up at him with such pure wonder.

He wanted to show her what loving was, what a man and woman could be. He wanted to love her for all the days and nights left in this lonely lifetime. He wanted to die inside this woman.

But even in his heat of passion he wouldn't take her in the mud.

He moved off her and she looked up at him with a look that was half-puzzled, half-hurt.

"Here." He offered her his hand and helped her up. She looked everywhere but at him.

They were covered in mud and briars and damp grass.

He started back up the hillside, gripping onto the bushes as he tried to get a foothold. Again he gave her his hand. "Come," he told her. "I'll help you."

She placed her hand in his, but he slipped and so did his grip on her hand.

Down they went again.

He grabbed a bush and only fell to his knees. He heard a shriek and looked behind him.

She hadn't been so lucky. She was lying facedown in the thickest pool of mud in the ravine. Very slowly she pushed herself up. Two bright and surprised yellow eyes stared at him from a brown face dripping in mud.

He burst out laughing.

Her eyes narrowed and she sat back, resting her arms on her knees. He watched the mud drip from hair, nose, everywhere.

"You look like a sow," he told her honestly, not realizing that this was a stupid time for male honesty.

The mud ball hit him square in the face.

"What the hell did you do that for?" he roared and swiped at the mud.

She gave him a honeyed smile and threw another handful. Now she was laughing, laughing hard and flinging mud at him so quickly he would never have thought she could move that fast.

"Here!" she shouted. "Catch!" She hit him square in the forehead.

He sprang from the hillside and tackled her. They rolled together in the mud, Linnet shrieking while he tried to rub more mud in her face.

A few minutes later they both lay on their backs in the mud, a truce called. She was still laughing.

"You didn't play fair, William. You're stronger than I" —she slapped a muddy hand on her chest and gave him a wide-eyed stare—"a puny and weak woman."

He snorted. "Puny and weak. Ha! We could have used you at the siege of Acre, Linnet. I would have put you in charge of the catapult."

She smiled. "That is the first time you have ever called me by my name."

He hadn't realized he'd done so.

She reached over and touched him on the shoulder. "I prefer Linnet to sow."

He grinned, then stood and eyed the hillside. A second later he swept her into his arms and carried her through the ravine, heading for a place where the hillside wasn't so steep.

"William! Put me down!"

"Stop squirming and let me carry your 'puny' self."

He tossed her and grinned when she shrieked. Finally, she wrapped her arms around his neck and laid her head on his shoulder.

And he liked it so much that he carried her all the way up the hill . . . the long way.

He had never laughed with a woman, like he had with Linnet. 'Twas a strange feeling, to call a woman friend. But that was how he felt about her. Aside from her beauty, aside from her charm and the odd hold she seemed to have over him, aside from the passion she could spark in him with only a touch or a look, William actually liked her. He liked being with her.

They spent the next few nights in inns, each in their own room, a place where Linnet could have the comforts he should have thought of to begin with—baths, clean beds, warm food.

And he was loathe to admit it but he had missed her at night. He missed sleeping next to her, missed her piling enough covers atop her to thaw Hinderland, missed her punching the pillows and tossing and turning until he had to talk with her if he ever wanted to get a wink of sleep. He missed her incessant chatter about the night sky and stars and the shapes they form. He missed waking and watching her sleep.

He didn't miss the cats. That was his one peace. Some of the animals were with her, some were boarded at the inn's stables.

They were two days ride from the abbey when he heard of the fair. 'Twas midsummer's eve and the town of Noddington was having a fair—a grand event if all they had heard was true.

He had one day and one night left to win her. 'Twas all.

So he took her to the Midsummer's Fair.

CHAPTER ☾ EIGHT

$\mathcal{N}$oddington was a busy little town of stone, brick, and timber, with shops and inns that lined the small cobbled streets. Houses cuddled in close lanes with jutting roofs and bayed windows. Because of the fair the town was teeming. And Linnet could hardly take it all in.

They crossed the stone bridge to a meadow where the winding river was fringed with trees and where the fair was bustling.

Each booth, decorated gaily with batting of bright colors, sold something new and different—lengths of raye, a fabric that fairly took on the sheen of the stars, an odd-looking mechanical clock that wouldn't freeze in winter like the water clocks did and powerful crossbows, weapons of such deadly accuracy that they had been forbidden by Rome until recently.

There was hot spiced wine, fresh bread, and meat pies. Country vegetables and sweet Eastern dates. And William bought her one of everything scrumptious.

There were lively dancers and minstrels who sang songs of the magic of midsummer's eve. Puppeteers and actors became fairies and sprites, forest animals that took on human form, all to celebrate this special time of year—a time when flowers bloomed and hearts were light.

Linnet and William watched the acrobats tumble and trained dogs frolic. There was even a huge gray and wrinkled elephant that roared like a trumpet and spit water high in the air.

William bought her lengths of fine cloth, two of the raye, and a silver comb, to keep the sunset in her hair, he had told her. He filled her with comfits and sweetmeats until she thought she might burst. He showed her every sight and every new thing with patience and laughter and care.

Many was the time she caught him watching her closely, as if her happiness were the most important thing to him. But it was his smile and laughter that were the true gifts of the day.

'Twas one of the best times she had ever had, and she knew she would never think of midsummer's eve without remembering William. As she strolled through the fair she wished, somehow, to repay him. She knew his pride would accept nothing from her, nothing valuable.

She had been trying to find a gift for him when she spied a man with pilgrim badges sewn to his hat and coat. He was hawking pardons from Rome which he carried in a sack on his bent back.

"William?" She tugged on his shirtsleeve.

"Aye?"

"I think we should buy some pardons."

He frowned.

She pointed toward the pilgrim and he laughed and handed her a handful of silver coins. She shook her head. "I want to buy these," she told him.

She bought William a pardon for every curse he had spoken this past week, and a few extra for the future.

She ran back and tucked them in his arms.

He looked at them. "God's teeth! What the devil are these for?"

She gave him a wry look. "I doubt there are enough pardons in the world, William, to assuage your blasphemous tongue."

"Christ in heaven . . ." he swore with a grin. "That might just bloody damn well be."

She shook her head and followed him until he stopped to eye a collection of mail in a booth set up by the local armorer. She watched him barter and banter and bluster, and she jabbed him with her elbow when he tried to trade her cats for a mailed tunic. Finally he asked her to choose the mail and she picked one in less time than it took to blink.

"That was simple," he said, surprised. "Why that one?"

"Because it shines the most," she replied, thinking secretly that he was a knight who should have shining armor.

He bought the mail she had chosen, saying he thought he'd need it if he were challenged again.

And he was.

They had left the fair hours later, filled with drink and fresh food and fun. They were riding back to the inn to fetch her pets when the yellow knight appeared near a bend in the river.

The knight never had a chance. William took one look at him, roared an ungodly string of curses that used seven more pardons and attacked. His mail shone in the bright sunlight and his sword flashed with deadly precision, but when he sheathed his sword and drew out the crossbow he'd purchased, the knight stopped cold, turned his mount around, and rode away so fast it was almost as if he had never appeared.

William was in a better mood after that.

Soon the sun had slipped down behind the trees and the moon had risen in the dusky sky. A cart with nail studs clicked over the stones of a small bridge and haymakers were walking home with their long pitchforks resting on their shoulders.

William rode off the highway and over toward a grassy hillock.

"I thought the inn was this way," Linnet said.

"It is!"

She turned her palfrey and followed. "Then why are we traveling this way?"

"'Tis a surprise," he said with an edge of challenge, and he spurred his mount and disappeared over the hillock.

If she hadn't already been in love with William, she would have fallen the moment she saw the tent. 'Twas a tent from the Midsummer's Fair, the largest and finest

tent she had seen. Made from brightly colored fabric
with red and blue and yellow stripes, it had pennants
waving from the sharp peaks at the top and corners.

But when he pulled back the flaps and she saw all the
pillows—stacks of pillows to replace the ones she had
lost to the rain, she threw herself into his arms and cried.

"Why are you crying? I had thought to please you."

She sniffled. "You did. You do."

His look was so intent that her breath caught.

"I'll leave you to sleep," he said, then pulled back the
flap on the tent. She stopped him with a hand on his
arm. "Where are you going to sleep?"

"Outside," he said gruffly.

He still wore the mail shirt and other light armor he'd
bought.

"This is marshland. There's fog on the damp ground.
You'll tarnish your armor."

He gave her a long look, then rubbed his finger over
her jaw and across her lips. He tucked a knuckle under
her chin and said, "If I stay in here, I think I'll tarnish
more than just my armor."

She closed her eyes, knowing this decision was hers.
She opened them and looked at him. "'Tis midsummer's
eve."

"I know," was all he said.

"A time for magical things to happen."

"Aye."

The silence hung between them. Finally he started to
leave.

"William!"

He turned back.

She took a deep breath, then whispered, "I love you."

A second later she was in his arms, his mouth on hers,
and he lifted her off the ground.

"Linnet," he murmured, "my sweet bird, Linnet. God,
how I want you."

He laid her back in the pillows and joined her. Their
clothes fell away, slowly, leaving time to savor each discovery, each soft new touch, each whisper of love against
her skin, against his ear. Her name was a prayer on his
lips, his name a promise as yet unfulfilled.

For long moments he would just look at her and Linnet never felt so cherished in her life. When he touched her and kissed her, he did so as if it were the most important thing he had ever done.

He used his tongue deeply in her mouth and taught her how to respond, how to touch him. He loved her breasts, her belly and lower with his lips and mouth and sent her to the stars more times than she could imagine.

He kissed and stroked her feet and legs, and in between until she was hoarse from crying out.

She wanted William, wanted to spend every moment with him. Wanted this powerful loving between them to last forever. She told him, the moment he entered her, after the pain that made her gasp. And as soon as she spoke the words she could have sworn there were tears in his eyes.

He taught her loving, taught her caring, taught her tenderness and patience and spent eternal moments to assure her pleasure. 'Twas the most profound moment in her lifetime when she cried out and his life poured into her.

And when their breath slowed and their bodies cooled, he wrapped her hair around them and brought his lips to her ear. "You have sunset in your hair, my love. Sunset."

She smiled. "Does that mean it's going to rain?"

He laughed. "That is why I purchased the tent."

"I adore the tent. But I miss the stars. These past nights at the inns were lonely, William. I missed the sound of your breath and the stars above us."

He rose from their bed and grabbed his sword. In a flash he cut a square flap in the top of the tent. Then completely naked, he bowed, "Your stars, milady."

And it was her turn to cry.

They arrived at the abbey late the next afternoon, and a rather sorry caravan they were. The tether of pack mules, twenty-seven cats, five rabbits, and two ducks. But William and Linnet cared not, for they rode on the same horse, stopping every so often to exchange kisses and lingering looks of love.

Once a proud castle that guarded the borderlands, St. Lawrence Abbey was perched atop a lush and green English hillside. Guards with crossbows no longer stood sentinel at the battlements. The only things on those crenellated walls were doves cooing at the sunshine and a trumpeter who heralded arrivals.

Now, those who came to the abbey sought succor not from men and arms, or maurading barbarians, but from nuns skilled in healing the body, the mind and the spirit. Ducks and swans floated in the waters of the moat and sheep grazed fields. The armory, built for pounding out weapons and mail, was now just a building used for drying herbs and brewing medicinals. Lush ivy and tansy threaded with pale roses meandered up an iron trellis on the castle tower that was no longer a stronghold, but a peaceful place to find strength of mind.

William and Linnet rode through the curtain wall gates and reined in before the massive abbey doors just as matins were chiming.

He dismounted and helped Linnet down, pausing to hold her for a moment longer than necessary.

The abbey doors flew open and a bevy of black-garbed nuns trotted down the stone steps and encircled them, greeting and laughing.

"Linnet!"

She turned in William's arms and laughed, then ran to a tall and regal-looking woman. "Aunt Bess!"

Just then another person came down the steps.

"Grandpapa!"

William went as still as stone. His angry gaze met Arden's. Slowly he walked toward the steps until he faced the earl. The tension grew thick and hung like fog in the air. Slowly, the other voices tapered off.

"Arden," William snapped.

"Warbrooke."

"Warbrooke?" Linnet repeated. She spun around and looked at William. "Baron Warbrooke?"

He nodded.

There was a moment of puzzled silence as she looked from him to her grandfather, then back to him. Her face fell and he could see her reaction. "You are not William de Ros?"

"I am William de Ros, Baron Warbrooke."

"How could you? How could you do this? Am I nothing but a foolish woman to you that you would play such a cruel trick?" She looked back. "And Grandpapa? *You* knew?"

He nodded tightly.

"Why?"

"I had no choice, Linnet. 'Twas for your own good."

"Ha!" William shouted. "You didn't want me to have her, old man."

Arden cursed and charged. His fist hit William square in the chin and flattened him to the ground. "She's mine!"

"Bloody hell, she is!" William roared up and tackled Arden. They rolled in the dirt, punching and shouting, calling each other names that should have never been spoken on the grounds of an abbey.

Arden jumped to his feet and so did William. "I granted you that week alone with her!"

"You sent those knights," William gritted.

Arden wiped his mouth, panting. "They had instructions not to kill you."

Linnet gasped.

William saw red and flew at him. They tumbled again, each trying to get to the other. Arden straddled him and had his hands about William's throat while he shouted.

"Stop it!" Linnet screamed. "Stop!"

A wall of water hit them both. Arden released him and coughed. William shook the water from his head and stared at her.

She tossed a water bucket on the ground and glared down at them. "I'm not yours, Grandpapa."

William grinned.

"And you can wipe that foolish smile off your mouth, *Baron Warbrooke,* because I'm not yours either!" Tears fell from her eyes like blood from a deep wound. "I'm not some piece of land for you foolish men to wage war over! I don't belong to either of you! Do you hear me?"

Both men stared at her in dumbfounded silence.

"And you can cease your fighting because neither of you will win. I'm not going with any one of you. Do you hear me? Neither of you! I'm going to become a nun!" And with that pronouncement she burst into sobs and ran inside the abbey.

William watched the door close behind her and stared at it. And he felt more alone at that moment than he had ever felt in his hard and solitary life.

"Come, come, my dear. Stop your crying."

Linnet looked up at her aunt through a mist of tears. "I shall become a nun, Aunt. I shall."

"Tell me. Why would you want to become a nun?"

She wiped her tears. "Because there are no men in a convent."

"True. That is a high point," her aunt said wryly. "You have no idea how very many women feel exactly that way."

Linnet snorted, then said, "The more men I meet the more I understand."

Her aunt smiled, then her face grew serious. "I'm most concerned with your happiness."

"I could be happy here." She could be happy here. Someday. If she could forget.

"I think, Linnet, that you could be happy anywhere. And I'd love to have you near me, but then if I let you do this I'd be as guilty of coveting your company as my foolish brother and Warbrooke."

"But I want to be a nun."

Her aunt gave her a long and assessing look. "Could you spend the rest of your life married only to God?"

Linnet's gaze dropped to her hands.

"Devoted to Him with all your heart and soul?"

Her heart belonged to William. She had given it to him on a magical midsummer's eve. She sighed. "No. 'Tis no longer mine to give."

Her aunt reached a gentle hand and tilted her head up. "Baron Warbrooke?"

She nodded.

"Can you not find it in your heart to forgive him?"

"He lied to me and played me for a fool. I loved him."

She raised her chin. "I have my pride." She paused, then added, "And there is Grandpapa too. How could he do that to me?"

"Your grandfather has always acted before he thought. Old fool. But he loves you. More than any other member of his family. He loves you. I think perhaps he only wanted to keep you safe. Did he not tell you of the vow he made to your mother?"

She shook her head.

"He is an old fool," she muttered. "He promised her, when you were born, the day she died, that he would never force you to wed. You see, he had forced her and for all that she loved your sisters and wanted you, she was never happy. I think he always blamed himself for your mother's death. I think he tried to protect you."

Linnet thought about how her grandfather would deal with his feelings of guilt. Probably not very well.

Her aunt rose from her chair and said, "You need some time alone. Search your heart and see if you cannot understand why these men act like such fools. Pray. Ask God to help you, my dear. Ask Him to help you forgive."

CHAPTER NINE

"Do you think she truly has given up the idea of becoming a nun?"

"That's what Bess said." The earl of Arden raised his fifth tankard and leveled a stare at William. He drank deeply, then said, "I don't understand why Linnet is so angry."

William frowned into his mug. "Court a woman. God's teeth, I'm a warrior not a courtier." He was quiet, thinking of all he had done wrong. In a weak moment he began to sing *Greensleeves*.

The earl dropped his ale and slammed his hands over his ears. "Cease, Warbrooke! Bloodying my nose was enough torture for one day!"

"Can't sing," William declared.

The earl shook his head, then pounded the heel of his hand against an ear.

"I should have written her poetry," William murmured.

The earl was concentrating on pouring another round and spoke as if William hadn't. "I only wanted to keep her safe and happy. Couldn't she see that she would have to bend to a husband's will? I wanted to keep her happy and free. She's my sunlight."

"I don't kill women and eat children. She bloody well knows my feet aren't cloven."

The earl's eyes narrowed. "How does she know that?"

"Don't ask, Arden. You would just try to choke the breath from my lungs again, and I'd have to break your arm this time. God only knows how she would react to that."

"You're right." The earl gently touched his swollen eye and winced. "Never in all her eighteen years has my little Linnet been angry at me."

"Aye. She has the patience of a saint."

Arden scowled and tipped his tankard for a large drink, then said, "She must have a wealth of patience. She spent a week with you."

"I'm an ass," William admitted.

"Aye, that you are," Arden agreed. "But a damned fine and determined ass. I had to hire four different knights. They refused to take you on a second time."

"Me or Swithun?"

Arden shuddered. "Don't remind me of that cat. Bites me at least once a day."

Both men exchanged identical looks, then Arden laughed. "If it weren't for Linnet, Warbrooke, I might take occasion to call you friend."

William rubbed his bruised chin and winced. "Aye. You're quick for an old man."

"Who's old?" Arden frowned and puffed out his chest. "I'm as strong as I was when we stopped the Welsh uprising! And the third crusade was a . . ." He raised his fingers and tried to snap them. He couldn't do it. Frowning, he took another drink, then belched. He tapped his chest with a fist. "That's better. Now where was I?"

"The third crusade," William supplied gloomily.

"Aye! I can knock a man half my age from his mount! I can pleasure a lady, two in fact, and I can down a hogshead of ale and still walk a straight line!" He raised his mug high.

His eyes rolled back and he passed out facedown on the table.

William stared. The old man was snoring. He picked up his tankard, then the earl's and dumped the contents into his. "No sense wasting good ale," he muttered, then stood and stumbled out of the hall.

He walked down the dark passages of the abbey, opening door after chamber door. Ten minutes later he found the chamber he sought. It took him five minutes to light a candle, then he slumped into a small wooden chair that squeaked under his weight and rested his elbows on a desk. He searched the top, then opened a carved wooden box.

"Aha! I knew 'twould be in here." He grinned, then took out a piece of thin parchment, a quill, and a precious pot of ink.

William stared at the blank parchment, took a deep breath, then picked up the quill. He snapped the top off the ink pot, closed one eye, and tried to dip the quill tip into the jar.

Seven tries and much concentration later, he hit his target. And with his next breath he began to write.

Linnet lay in her bed beneath ten blankets, a feather coverlet, and a fur robe. Her cats, rabbits, and ducks were with her, cuddled into different parts of the room.

She stared at the dark ceiling. Her chamber was high in the abbey tower, a place for solitude. A place for thought. A place for her to cry her broken heart out.

She missed the stars. She missed the fresh night air. She missed William lying next to her. Her eyes began to fill with tears for the hundredth time.

Odd, she hadn't thought she had any tears left to cry.

A loud crash sounded from outside. She sat upright and listened sharply. There was nothing. Only quiet. The sound had awakened Swithun whose ears were still perked expectantly.

She lay back down and snuggled deeper under the covers with her gray cat curled near her pillow. A moment later a pebble bounced across the tower floor. Swithun leapt down and chased it across the room.

Very slowly, she swung out of bed and, back pressed to the stone wall, she slipped toward the window and stopped. A handful of pebbles flew through the opening.

"Psssst!" More pebbles pattered the flagstone floor.

She stuck her head out the window. "William?" she whispered.

He stood in the courtyard below with a long torch held high in one hand.

"What are you doing?"

"Shhhhh." He raised a finger to his mouth. "Can you hear me?"

"Of course I can hear you. You're shouting."

"Good." He stood a little straighter, then weaved slightly.

"Have you been drinking?"

"Aye. Just a barrel or two." He stumbled slightly, then held a piece of parchment up near the torch. Too near. A corner of the parchment suddenly flamed. With a curse he dropped the paper and stomped out the flame, then bent down and picked up the parchment. He squinted at it, then puffed out his chest. He held the torch like a conquering warrior and shouted, "Ode to a midsummer's night!"

"What?" She braced her hands on the window ledge. Swithun joined her and peered down as she leaned outside.

"Oh lady, sweet and fair"—William flung his arm out wide and the torch wavered—"with sunset in her hair."

He's spouting poetry, she realized. *Sunset in her hair . . . I love it when he says that.*

"Your eyes are golden and wild, like a forest fairy child!"

She smiled.

"Your lips are red, I'd like to bed . . ." he paused, "you. Don't bid me adieu."

She frowned.

"I dream of your face," he bellowed. "Instead of a mace."

She leaned back against the tower wall, her hand to her chest, and she giggled a little.

"Your breasts are pink as pigs . . ."

Her mouth dropped open. *Pigs?*

"And they taste like honeyed figs."

She clapped a hand over her mouth and chuckled, her face flushing bright red.

"As sure as I can fart, you will always have my heart," he finished proudly.

By then she was sitting on the floor, holding her sides and laughing so hard that tears streamed from her eyes. She wiped them, still giggling as her mind's eye still saw him standing in the abbey courtyard, where anyone could and probably had seen him, spouting the worst poetry she'd ever heard so loudly that he could have been heard in London.

But at that very moment, she knew one thing—she loved that man more than anything or anyone she had ever loved in her life.

It had grown strangely quiet outside. Linnet let go of her sides and got up. She looked out the window. The courtyard was empty.

"William?"

She heard a muffled male grunt. She gripped the stones and leaned farther out the window.

William struggled halfway up the ivy trellis. He had one long red rose clenched in his teeth.

"William, be careful! That trellis doesn't look very—"

A loud scratching crack pierced the air. The trellis wobbled for an instant, then slowly fell backward. There was a male shout of surprise, then the trellis hit the ground with a thud. The ivy rustled and Swithun crawled out of the ivy and sat atop the fallen trellis meowing.

There was a male groan. William cursed. Linnet blanched. The abbess knelt in front of her window and gave thanks. And in the hall below, the earl of Arden still snored.

The groom's stitches had healed by the day of the wedding. Such a great affair it was too, for the king himself was to stand witness to the wedding of the Baron Warbrooke and Lady Linnet of Ardenwood.

Baron Warbrooke stood in the great hall at the castle he had renamed Starwood, part of the lands granted him with his title. His wedding gift to his wife was awaiting her that night. And for years to come the folk around would talk about the huge hole Baron Warbrooke had cut in his bed chamber ceiling and filled with precious wavy glass so his wife could sleep under the stars.

'Twas a rich and warm home, with a future filled with children's laughter, love, and more animals than one could imagine. And today it was the place where many an Englishman and his lady had gathered to celebrate.

"William?" Linnet came rushing into the room, worming her way through the crowd who were stopping to wish the bride well. She found William and placed a hand on his arm. "Grandpapa still has not arrived. Has there been any word?"

"I'm certain he'll get here." William gave a bored shrug. "Eventually."

"I can't understand what could make him so very late. It only takes two days to travel here from Ardenwood."

There was a sudden racket and the earl of Arden charged into the great hall. He froze and scanned the room. His velvet surcoat was ripped and shredded at the shoulders. His chausses had holes in the knees. Briars and mud clung to his clothing and graying hair, which was plastered to his head as if he had fallen in a marsh. Dirt smudged his cheeks and hands and his lip was split and swollen.

"Warbrooke!" he roared.

Linnet stood as still as stone. Her grandfather was waving four colored plumes—one black, one blue, one red, and one yellow.

She turned to William, who was looking decidedly pleased with himself. "You didn't . . ."

"Didn't what?" he asked with feigned innocence and a distinct sparkle in his eye.

The crowd parted as her grandfather elbowed his way toward the dais. He spotted William and strode toward them with purpose. He stopped a few feet away. Linnet stood watching the two men she loved most in the world eye each other like mad dogs.

Her grandfather shook the plumes in the air and growled, "Did you send these knights?"

"Aye," William answered distractedly as he examined the nails on one scarred hand, then he added blandly. "Not to worry, Arden. They had instructions not to kill you."

Her grandfather threw down the plumes and launched toward William.

Linnet covered her eyes. But after a second of utter and curious silence, she peered through her fingers.

Her grandfather grabbed William in a giant hug, then

punched him in the shoulder like a long-lost friend. With a bellow of laughter he shouted, "Welcome to the family, Grandson! Welcome!"

After laughter and the cheers had died down, Lady Linnet of Ardenwood threaded an arm through one of Baron Warbrooke's and another through the earl of Arden's and they strolled toward the chapel. Twenty-seven saintly cats, five rabbits—four with only three legs—and two quacking ducks followed close behind.

And there before the king, before the abbess of Saint Lawrence, before all who mattered in her world, she wed William de Ros, her mercenary warrior, drunken poet, and England's newest baron.

Her knight in tarnished armor.

A RIBBON

OF

MOONLIGHT

ELAINE COFFMAN

CHAPTER ❨ ONE

Cornwall, Midsummer's Eve, 1815

The ball was a bloody bore and Quinn Westcott, the Marquess of Waverly, felt like a fool, dressed as he was, in this ridiculous highwayman's costume. He had never liked masquerade balls, and for the life of him, he could not fathom why he had let Harry Freeman talk him into coming to this one.

He should have known. Midsummer's Eve and a full moon. Lunacy at its height. What in the name of hell was he doing here?

As far as he could see, there was only one fetching piece in the entire ballroom that caught his eye—a Swiss milkmaid, her cheeks blooming with innocence, her low-cut bosom blooming with something far more interesting. But she was in the company of a rotund old walrus, who seemed to be doing a capital job of holding all the young swains at bay. For a moment, Quinn considered making a play for the chit, then decided against it. The last thing he wanted was some besotted local challenging him for the attentions of the village beauty, no matter how appealing she was.

He dismissed the milkmaid and glanced across the ballroom where his two friends Harry Freeman, Viscount Huntley, and Richard Maxwell, the Marquess of Yorkston, didn't seem to be faring much better than he was. Bored out of their minds, they looked. Catching their eye, he held up his drink and nodded in the direction of the library.

A few minutes later, three highwaymen slipped into the library. Closing the door behind them, to shut out the noise of the orchestra and all that infernal chatter, they took refuge in a sparkling decanter of fine Scottish whisky. And why not? Here they were, three grown men, peers of the realm, the picture of idiocy dressed in their highwaymen's garb—when they could have been gambling in the hells of Hanover Square, taking their pick of the wenches in Piccadilly, or carousing with the toughs in Leicester Fields.

As he leaned against the mantel and dawdled over his cigar and whisky, Quinn mellowed somewhat, but not enough to join Harry and Richard in a discussion of the late war. Having served three years in the war against Napoleon, the last year in that hell on the peninsula, Quinn found the bottle of whisky more to his liking.

Listening to his friends' discussion, Quinn's thoughts went off in another direction. It had been the war that had prevented him from paying a visit to Fairfields, the country home of Josiah Fairton, a distant cousin who had died the year before. Quinn had never met Josiah Fairton, and knew little more about him than the fact that he was a widower with no children, and upon his death, not even a nephew or close cousin could be found to receive his property.

In the end, it was decided that Quinn, being a third cousin of the late Josiah, would stand to inherit Fairfields. In truth, Quinn might not have ever visited Fairfields at all, if it had not been for one tiny stipulation in his late cousin's will.

Much to Quinn's chagrin, he learned he had inherited along with Fairfields, a ward—a child by the name of Caroline Flowers—a child he was to provide a home for until she wed.

It was the desire to rid himself of this child by packing her off to boarding school that had prompted Quinn to accept Harry's invitation to the country, Harry's country home being quite close to Fairfields.

At the time, it seemed the perfect solution. The day

after the ball, he would make his first visit to Fairfields, where he would shower the child with more toys and gifts than she had probably ever seen, then he would cart her off to Miss Porter's Academy for Young Ladies of Gentle Breeding. It was the best solution; the country home of a young, decadent bachelor was no place for a young and impressionable child.

Quinn was just pouring his third whisky—or was it his fourth?—when his thoughts were interrupted by his friends' jolly laughter. He looked up, just as Richard spoke.

"Ho, Waverly! We have hit upon a capital idea."

Quinn frowned. Whenever Richard hit upon a capital idea mischief was about. Quinn said nothing as Richard looked at Harry and they both raised their glasses in toast. "We drink to you, dear friend and hero of the peninsular war," Richard said.

"And to the best swordsman, the best shot, and by far the best rider in your regiment," Harry added, "not to mention the fastest at getting his pants unbuttoned."

Quinn scoffed at their words. "Where did you hear that?"

"It's common knowledge, old chap," Harry replied.

"Where is all of this poppycock leading?" asked Quinn. "Are you two trying to hire me out to some lonely widow?"

"We could never be so cruel," Harry said, grabbing himself in the vicinity of his heart and staggering around as if mortally wounded at the thought.

"Besides, if it was a lonely widow, we'd offer her our own services," said Richard.

"What is it, then?" Quinn asked.

"Why, we offer you a challenge, of course," said Richard with a wicked smile, bowing low, the lamplight streaking his blond head with gold.

"What kind of challenge?" asked Quinn, eyeing them with much skepticism.

"We dare you," Richard said, "to play the role you are dressed for."

"What? A fool?"

They both laughed. "Why, a highwayman, of course,

doing what a highwayman does best," Richard said, looking very much like he was enjoying all of this.

"What are you getting at?" Quinn said, his lack of amusement showing.

Harry blew a lock of chestnut hair off his forehead and grinned. "Robbing coaches."

Astonished, Quinn decided that his two friends had been idle too long. Any fool knew idle hands were the devil's workshop. "The two of you expect *me* to rob a coach, dressed in this garb?"

Richard nodded.

"All in jest, of course," Harry added.

"Of course," Quinn said, "and if I get my bloody head blown off . . . all in jest, of course?"

Richard grinned. "You won't . . . that is, *if* you are as good as they say you are."

Looking for a clever way out, and finding none, Quinn downed the last of his drink. "I accept your challenge, gentlemen," he said with a sarcastic tone. "But only because the thought of being shot for a highwayman sounds infinitely better than remaining here, at this idiot's ball, where I am sure to die of boredom."

A moment later, they were off.

The night was warm and moist. The moon was full and high in a star-struck sky. It was, after all, Midsummer's Eve. A perfect night for madness, or a merry masquerade.

As Quinn rode beside Harry and Richard, the moon danced through the trees like a ghost and lent its silver light, turning the road to a ribbon of moonlight. Black clouds moved overhead. The air hung damp and wind-tossed about them. Twice Quinn thought he heard the sound of a coach, long before he saw it.

The lamps appeared first, flickering through the mist that gathered in the low places of the road, then the great hulking shape of a coach came into view, rocking and swaying as the horses galloped through the night.

The three highwaymen pulled off the road and waited.

Night cloaked the road in purple. The wind sifted through the trees. It was Midsummer Night's Eve. A night for madness. A night when the fairy queen danced with delight and fools were about.

The coach drew closer.

Harry and Richard turned away, seeking the refuge of the shadowy darkness of the trees.

Quinn waited.

Then he rode through the mist. A phantom keeping his tryst. A knight of the road. The noblest of criminals. A gentleman bandit. The scourge of England.

The highwayman.

Mounted on a blooded black horse, high-booted with gleaming silver spurs, his clothes and cape were black as the night that surrounded him, his hat the tricorn of a gentleman. His face was hidden in shadow and masked. A rapier gleamed at his side.

Swift as a shadow he came, out of the darkness, his black horse prancing, gleaming pistol drawn.

The driver pulled back on the reins and the coach came to a rocking stop.

"Stand and deliver!"

The wind was a torrent of darkness among the gusty
 trees,
The moon was a ghostly galleon tossed upon cloudy seas,
The road was a ribbon of moonlight over the purple
 moor,
 And the highwayman came riding, riding, riding . . .

—Alfred Noyes, "The Highwayman"

CHAPTER (TWO

*S*tand and deliver?

Those were strange words indeed, considering the age
of the highwayman was long past. But the highwayman
sounded serious, his pistol was cocked, so the driver
pulled the coach of Sir Artemis Fullbright to a stop.

Inside the coach was Sir Artemis, his daughter Fanny,
and a close family friend, Caroline Flowers, on their way
home from a Midsummer's Eve masquerade ball.

To Caroline's way of thinking, the day had been too
long, the weather too hot, and the party too boring. Having the coach jerk to a stop in the middle of the night
would certainly be a dashing diversion . . . but, had she
really heard the words, *Stand and deliver?*

The night glittered like stardust as Caroline leaned her
head against the coach window and stared out, hoping to
get a glimpse of whoever had spoken those words. Seeing nothing but darkness, she felt a twinge of disappoint-
ment. She should have known better than to expect
anything dashing, diverting, or otherwise exciting in her
life. Monumental things, or at best, eventful ones, always
happened in London, not Cornwall.

Suddenly, the door was jerked open, and a highwayman, booted, spurred, and armed with a pistol, poked his head inside. He demanded the purse of Sir Artemis.

Sir Artemis, looking somewhat befuddled, sputtered his protest. "What the deuce? Is this some sort of joke?"

The highwayman flashed a brilliant smile that seemed to light up the night and said, "Hardly."

Next, the highwayman turned to Caroline, who had been so engrossed in gawking at his magnificence—which far surpassed any image of a rake she had ever invented—that until he put away his pistol and drew his rapier with a *swish,* she had not noticed that his dark, hypnotizing gaze was fastened upon her.

Her heart fluttered, then seemed to stop. Even in the moonlight, she could see the man was lean and graceful, undeniably an aristocrat. His eyes looked black against the ebony satin of his mask, cynical eyes that had seen too much. The hair that curled beneath his hat was black, and she fancied his heart would be of the same color. His nose was aquiline, his cheekbones high, his mouth mocking and yet not cruel. It was a sensuous mouth and the idea made her shiver. He disturbed her, not only by his handsomeness, but by an alarming mixture of power and sensuality that made her think he had seen and done things she could only imagine. Looking into his eyes, she felt touched by the power of darkness, drawn into something against her will.

Suddenly, his gaze left her face and traveled downward, studying her Swiss milkmaid costume. Before she could guess what he was about, the sharp, gleaming tip of the rapier came toward her. She flinched, drawing back against the cushions of the coach. Unable to retreat farther, she trembled as its cold, hard surface touched the side of her face.

Mesmerized, and unable to take her eyes from his, she held her breath as she felt the blade caress her face, then drop lower, as the tip of the rapier moved along her jawline, then followed the contour of her neck, where it paused at the hollow of her throat.

From there it skimmed the low neckline of her dress. Very, very lightly she felt it riding the swelling crest of her breasts, then come to rest in the valley between.

Embarrassment brought a rush of heat to her face, yet she shivered, wondering how she could have thought the coach overwarm and stifling only a moment ago. In truth, she had difficulty deciding if the chill was from the coldness of the rapier's metal, or the trail left by the highwayman's hot gaze.

This, she reflected bitterly, is what happens to the weaker sex, when they have neither the wit, nor the muscle to protect themselves. Here she was, the victim of a highwayman and all she could do was shiver.

Irritated with her own cowardly behavior, she dug her fingers into her knees with all her strength, and said the first thing that came into her mind. "Are you going to kill me?"

"There are many things I have considered, little milkmaid, but murder is not among them."

"Now, see here," Sir Artemis said, but his words became an insignificant sputter when the highwayman gave him a look that said the rapier's point could easily find his plump neck.

The highwayman turned back to Caroline, looking at her in that terrible, breathtaking way. "Are you afraid?"

She could not find the words to speak, so she nodded.

"Fearful when all is safe," he said in a low, lazy way that left her confused. "It isn't the point of my rapier you should fear, sweet. *Venus yields to caresses, not compulsion.*"

His words sent another cold flutter tingling along her spine. Her throat went dry, her face froze. She wanted to run and hide, but the closeness of the blade made her afraid even to turn her head away. Glancing quickly at him, she saw even that would be futile.

There was no change of expression in those hard eyes of his as he lifted the rapier.

What would he do next?

She did not have to wonder overlong.

With a sudden flick of his wrist, he began to cut the laces that crisscrossed the front of her dress and held the bodice of her milkmaid costume together. Tiny sparks of sensation played down her spine as she watched with a morbid sort of fascination as one by one, the laces came undone and the bodice of her dress gaped wide.

She did not flinch. Nor did she make a move to close her dress. And although she felt her face grow warm, she did not look away. Instead, she stared straight at him, ignoring the seduction in those eyes. Then and there she vowed, that if she got out of this scrape alive she would spend the rest of her life doing nothing more adventuresome than fussing over teacups and whipping up meringues.

She stole a quick glance at Fanny, who sat with her shawl drawn tight around her, her eyes glazed, and her mouth agape, looking for all the world like she had taken too many tots of whiskey.

No help from that quarter.

Her pleading gaze moved to Sir Artemis's great whiskered face. In response, Sir Artemis gave a Presbyterian sniff, and as if he had at last mastered the impulse to bolt, came to her defense.

With a sputter of outrage and a purpling face, Sir Artemis withdrew his purse and offered it to the highwayman. "Here, you black-hearted devil. Take the money and be gone."

Caroline quickly reached for the gaping sides of her bodice, only to find her movement hindered by the sudden reappearance of the rapier.

"Leave it," the highwayman demanded. "Hide flaws, not assets."

Feeling the blade's sharp point at her throat, Caroline's hands fell away. But it was what he said next, that made her feel as if more was bared to him than just the cleavage of her breasts.

"'Your two breasts are like two fawns, twins of a gazelle, which feed among the lilies until the cool of the day, when the shadows flee away.'"

Caroline heard Fanny's infatuated sigh. *A Bible quoting highwayman. I am doomed,* she thought

And then, the rapier was gone.

She stared at him as if he had stabbed her.

With a flashing smile and slight tip of his head, the highwayman lifted his rapier, gave a salute, then took up the purse Sir Artemis offered. As he leaned farther into the coach, Caroline could feel the warmth of his breath fan her face, feel too, the power of his arm as it slid around her, pulling her half out of the coach and into his arms.

Her eyes opened wide, seeing his were steady upon her. A scream died in her throat. She felt like a statue, unable to move, or stop the heat that spread through her, centering like a burning coal in her stomach. She could no more deny the strength and power of him than she could prevent what he was about to do.

Startled and breathless, her mouth parted in surprise. A second later, his mouth covered hers. He kissed her with a leisurely thoroughness, as if he had the rest of the night, yea, even the rest of the week, to make her first kiss one she would not forget.

The pounding in her chest was overridden by a flowing warmth that seemed to travel downward until she began to feel some part of her had always belonged to him, a part that he now laid claim to.

She moaned and heard his chuckle, then confident whisper. "If only there were time, sweet."

She would like to tell him to take his overconfidence and stick it in his ear, but she refrained from doing so, of course. It did not seem to matter that he played a game with her, or that she knew it. What he was doing felt too good, pleased her too much, and that, laced with such lush promise, was more than she could bear. She felt the burn of tears behind the lids of her eyes, the light-headed throbbing of a body at war with itself.

As quickly as he had taken her in his arms, he loosened his hold on her, widening the distance between them, yet not letting her go completely. She felt herself go limp, felt too, the rush of cool night air when his lips left hers. She looked up, into that masked face, aware only of her shaky breathing.

And then, without so much as a by-your-leave, he dropped her back in her seat. His mocking gaze traveled over her, seeing her confusion and enjoying it mightily. She had never felt the need to hit anyone before, but by all the saints in Heaven, she felt it now.

She clenched her fists, feeling a shiver of frustration and anger, not so much because he had kissed her, but because he had aroused feelings within her that she could not explain, feelings she felt only he could ease. She felt like a bride, anticipating much, then left standing at the altar.

As if sensing her thoughts, he laughed, then tossed the purse of Sir Artemis into her lap. "Keep your money," he said. "Such a kiss will see me through many a long night. It is reward enough."

His dark eyes gleaming beneath his black mask, he removed his tricorn hat and with a gallant bow in her direction, turned his prancing black stallion and rode off into the night.

Dick Turpin could not have done it better.

As soon as the highwayman disappeared into the night, Fanny came out of her stupor. "That was the most romantic thing I have ever seen," she said, her voice enraptured.

"Romantic? By God, I have reared a complete and utter idiot," Sir Artemis said. "The man is a seducer, a lecher, a libertine of the first water, an ungoverned, unrestrained, immoral ravisher of innocent women. How can you, Fanny—with all your fine Christian upbringing —possibly see what happened here as something romantic? The villain practically cut off poor Caroline's dress."

"Yes, Papa, I saw, but there was something . . . spiritual about it. After all, he did quote from the Book of Solomon." She sighed, tears shimmering in her eyes. "It was too beautiful . . . two fawns feeding among the lilies . . ." She looked at Caroline. "What I would give to have been in your place."

Caroline said nothing, merely pulling her cape over the tattered remains of her bodice. *Two fawns feeding, indeed.*

Fanny, ignoring her friend's silence, said, "Oh, how I wish I had worn the Swiss milkmaid costume tonight, instead of giving it to you."

"Enough!" Sir Artemis cried. "I refuse to have the matter discussed further. Song of Solomon . . . bah! Even the devil can quote scripture."

Seeing Fanny was sufficiently silenced, and seeing Sir
Artemis was in a peckish mood, Caroline pulled her cape
tightly about her, leaned back against the plush velvet of
the seat and closed her eyes, trying to gather her scattered wits. What was happening to her?

Part of her wanted to scream in outrage, while another
part wanted nothing more than to experience once again
that glorious feeling of being held in his arms. Heaven
help her, if that is what made a fallen woman fall, then
surely she was on her way down.

She was beginning to have an inkling—albeit a hazy
one—as to what the parson referred to when he said,
"sins of the flesh." No wonder they wanted to keep it a
secret. Why, if word ever got out, there wouldn't be a
virgin left in the whole of England.

She opened her eyes and saw Fanny gazing longingly
out the coach window, as if by willing it, she could call
the highwayman back.

Caroline closed her eyes again. Poor Fanny. Didn't she
know things like that only happened once in a lifetime?
Caroline reminded herself that it would serve her better
to forget what had just happened and to turn her
thoughts to tomorrow. Her benefactor, the Marquess of
Waverly, would be coming to meet her. There would be
no more dashing highwaymen coming to her out of the
darkness, riding down a ribbon of moonlight on a Midsummer's Eve.

Was her life destined to constantly change? First she
had endured the death of her father, only to develop a
strong love for her guardian, and her father's dearest
friend, Josiah Fairton. It had been Josiah who had given
her a home at Fairfields, and Josiah who had provided
for her future. And now, Josiah was gone, and she would
soon meet her new benefactor, the Marquess of Waverly.

Would he prove to be as kind and fair as dear Josiah?

The gentle rocking motion of the coach soon overpow-
ered her, and Caroline's thoughts began to fade. As
sleep conquered her, she had a vision of a vivid smile
and mocking black eyes. She had lost much in her life—a
mother and father to guide her, a gentle guardian who
loved her as his own, but of all the things she had lost,

she regretted the loss of the highwayman the most, for it was as if part of her destiny had been handed to her, only to be ripped from her hands.

How strange it had all been. She found herself wondering if it had really happened, or had she simply imagined it?

No doubt about it, it *was* the moonlight or the magic of midsummer. Surely it was madness, midsummer night's madness.

From somewhere beyond consciousness, in the vastness that lies between wakefulness and sleep, came the slow, lilting chant. *"Brew me a potion strong and good, a goldendrop for his wine, charm his sense and fire his blood, and bend his will to mine . . ."*

CHAPTER ☾ THREE

Quinn continued to think about her—his little Swiss milkmaid—long after he had rejoined his friends. Fascinated, he could not help recalling the way she had fired his blood, or the feel of her soft lips beneath his own.

He could not help wondering who she was.

Richard rode up beside him. "That was a jolly bit of good sport for the night, but we had best be getting away from here and fast, before the occupants of that coach have the king's own royal guards out looking for us."

Harry, riding just behind them, laughed. "Do you think anyone will believe them? It's been a good fifteen years—perhaps twenty—since there were even any *rumors* of highwaymen in these parts. If they are foolish enough to report it, I daresay they will only find themselves laughed at. In truth, if my sides were not aching from trying to hold back my laughter, I would have trouble believing it myself. You really threw yourself into the role, didn't you, old man? Kissing the chit. By Jove, that was good sport!"

"Enough!" Quinn said. "I accepted your challenge, and kept my part of the bargain. Do not speak of it again."

"Right," Harry said, but Richard only laughed and said something about living for the day when he found Quinn's vulnerable spot.

Quinn said nothing. For a moment he wondered what his friends would say, if he told them all he knew about his vulnerable spot was that she had the softest lips, the prettiest gooseberry eyes, and the most lush breasts.

Early the next morning Quinn watched with disinterest, as the last of the gifts and toys he had purchased for his ward were loaded into the carriage for the ride to Fairfields, where he would meet little Caroline Flowers.

"Where is Miss Proff?" Quinn asked, looking around for the governess he had hired to accompany the child to boarding school.

About that time, Miss Proff appeared in the doorway. "Come, come, Miss Proff," Quinn said, motioning her forward. "I would like to reach Fairfields before the child's next birthday."

"Might as well be her birthday, or Christmas," Miss Proff replied, coming down the walk and taking Lord Waverly's hand. "You've enough gifts for the next five holidays if you ask me."

"I haven't asked you," Quinn said, handing her into the carriage.

Miss Proff made a huffing sound, but climbed into the carriage without a word.

Half an hour later, the quartet arrived at Fairfields, a stately gray manor house, as the first rays of morning sun cast dazzling lights on its many windows.

Ushered into a genteel, but rather tattered drawing room, Quinn stood with his armload of toys, managing to grip a small stuffed animal by only one paw.

At last the housekeeper, Mrs. Witherspoon, appeared, moving with remarkable speed for her bulky twelve stone of solid, trustworthy flesh. "Miss Flowers will be right down," she said, coming to a sudden halt and giving Quinn and the armload of toys he bore a bewildered stare. "Would your lordship like to put those things down somewhere?" she asked, looking about her, as if trying to locate the proper place.

"No, he would not," Quinn replied.

Standing in the center of the room, flanked by Harry and Richard, with Miss Proff behind him, they stood in a state of suspension, waiting for the long-awaited appearance of the child whose life Quinn was now responsible for.

Finally the drawing room door opened and a young and very beautiful young woman stepped inside—a young and very beautiful woman Quinn had seen before. A woman he had seen the night before, to be exact, only then she hadn't been wearing a crisp dress of blue muslin trimmed in green, but the costume of a Swiss milkmaid.

"May I present Miss Flowers," Mrs. Witherspoon said. "Caroline, this is your benefactor, Lord Waverly."

Caroline dropped into a deep curtsy, but her response was muffled by the loud thud of an armload of toys hitting the floor. She frowned, looking puzzled as she glanced at the pile of toys and then at Quinn.

Richard and Harry caught on long before Quinn did, and it sent them into transports of laughter. Seeing them doubled over, Quinn had a sudden understanding.

Glancing at Mrs. Witherspoon, who looked at him with an expression that hovered somewhere between dismay and pity, he was not certain as to what he should do.

His face contorted with laughter, Harry cleared his throat with dramatic resonance, then picked up a bisque doll with yellow hair and handed it to Caroline. "You're a little old for dolls, of course, but you must forgive Lord Waverly. You see, Quinn has never been known for his understanding of the fairer sex."

Quinn clenched his jaw until he thought his teeth might shatter. His gaze went from Harry, to Richard, to Mrs. Witherspoon, and finally to Caroline Flowers, who still did not seem to grasp what was going on here. But Quinn knew with Harry and Richard present, she would not be in the dark for long.

As if right on cue, Richard stepped forward. "My dear Miss Flowers, please do let me introduce you to your governess, Miss Proff."

"Miss Flowers is not interested in your imbecile observations," Quinn said.

Caroline looked from one to the other in confusion.

Finally Harry intervened. "Dash it all, Richard, you know a child of Miss Flowers's tender years would much rather see her toys before meeting her governess. First things first, I always say."

* * *

Caroline looked first at Lord Waverly, then at the pile of toys lying scattered about the floor, and suddenly understood.

So he thought her a child, did he?

She looked at the towering man with the black hair and stormy golden eyes, unable to resist the opportunity. "Mrs. Witherspoon," she said with a straight face, "would you please see that my toys from Lord Waverly are—"

"Disposed of," Lord Waverly interjected. "It seems I have made a terrible assumption, Miss Flowers. Please forgive me. It was very foolish of me to assume you were a child." Then, turning to Richard and Harry, who were acting the picture of innocence, he said, "If you two jesters can stop laughing long enough, you can help me load these things into the carriage."

"What about her," Harry asked, nodding in Miss Proff's direction. "Want us to toss her in as well?"

"We will take Miss Proff back to the village."

"You aren't staying the night, your lordship?" Mrs. Witherspoon asked. "We have your room all readied for you."

Quinn looked at Mrs. Witherspoon and then at Caroline. "I am afraid that is out of the question now. My mistaken assumption makes my residing here, even temporarily, a bit awkward, I'm afraid."

Mrs. Witherspoon bristled, the starched front of her uniform swelling with indignation. "Miss Caro is well chaperoned, your lordship. I have acted in that capacity for some years now, and your quarters are on another wing of the house entirely. Not even the parson could find fault with such an arrangement." As if offering an added persuasion, Mrs. Witherspoon said, "It would provide your lordship with an opportunity to get acquainted with Miss Flowers."

"Tallyho!" Harry said, suddenly finding something interesting outside the window when Quinn gave him a censoring look.

Caroline noted that Lord Waverly's expression said that getting acquainted with her was precisely what he wished to avoid.

Looking as uncomfortable as a cat with its tail caught in the door, Lord Waverly said in a strained voice, "Very well."

Caroline felt a stab of anger. "Of course we would understand if you prefer to reside elsewhere," she said in a brittle voice.

"Would you now," Lord Waverly replied, with absolutely no sentiment in his cold smile. "And what is that supposed to mean?"

"It means that I am aware how we must appear to one such as yourself, who is accustomed to the finer things of life and all that London society has to bestow. I am certain that Fairfields and all its humble offerings must appear quite rustic by comparison."

The hard lines around his mouth relaxed as he looked her over. "In some areas, Fairfields far surpasses London, Miss Flowers. Besides, I look upon this as an act of benevolence."

An act of benevolence? Anger sizzled along every nerve in her body. "Pardon me, but being a simple country girl and quite provincial, I cannot help doubting we could have anything that compares with London, your lordship."

Lord Waverly approached her. "I will be happy to discuss London society with you at a later date, Miss Flowers, but for now, I have more pressing concerns."

"Such as a way to dispose of me," Caroline said, never flinching.

Much to her surprise, Lord Waverly raised his hand and carelessly drew one finger down the side of her cheek. "No one warned me that you were such a clever girl and cheeky," he said. "Don't look so distressed, sweet. I'm not going to toss you out on your lovely ear. I feel certain we can work out some . . . *arrangement.*"

Caroline heard an indrawn breath, then felt the protection of Mrs. Witherspoon's comforting arm sliding around her shoulders.

"I shall return in a few days," Lord Waverly said, in a tone of dismissal, his face emotionless and cryptic. With that, he left . . . taking his friends . . . taking the governess . . . and his toys with him.

* * *

It was becoming a habit, thinking about her. He found himself a bit fascinated, even disturbed, by the memory of her soft blue eyes, the blond hair that seemed to catch and hold all the light in a room, that amazing skin with such purity that not even a scattering of tiny freckles could mar. And then there was that mouth. Lord above, it was her mouth and the memory of kissing it that haunted him day and night.

Desire is what he felt. Disaster is where it could lead. There was no way in hell he, or any of his friends could spend a night under the same roof with her and not take her to bed. It amazed him that she had managed to hang onto her virtue as long as she had—and that wasn't much of a testimony for Kentish country lads, in his estimation. Now, in London, things would be far, far different, for there, a beauty such as Caroline Flowers wouldn't keep her maidenhead more than a fortnight.

Quinn walked to the window of the library. He had not returned to Fairfields, but remained a few miles away at Yorkston, Richard Maxwell's country estate. He frowned as he saw Harry and Richard ride up the gravel drive, Richard on a leggy bay, Harry riding his black, the same black he had loaned to Quinn the night he played the part of the highwayman. He watched them dismount, and as the grooms took the horses away, Quinn heard them laugh. He braced himself. Well he knew that they were primed to give him the devil about Miss Flowers, something they had been doing for two days.

A moment later, the library door opened.

"Well, what have we here? Brooding peerage in the height of molting season. Ye Gods, Quinn, you look like you've lost your life savings," Harry said.

Then Richard butted in with, "Cheer up, old sport. You aren't having noblesse oblige problems again, are you?"

"Of course he is," Harry said.

"Joke all you like. Things would be different, I'll wager, if the chit were either of your responsibility."

"Unlike you, I'd have no scruples. I'd take her to bed and that would be that," said Richard.

"I'll drink to that," Harry said.

Quinn scowled. "Aren't you two forgetting something?"

Richard looked blank.

Quinn did not bother to look at Harry, who he could tell, by the rattle of glasses, was helping himself to a drink, and thereby declaring himself not in the mood to argue.

"What could I possibly be forgetting?" Richard asked.

"That she is the granddaughter of a duke, and not someone to be ravished at will. I've been appointed her protector, a position of responsibility."

Harry clapped him on the back and handed him a glass of port. "Well, it's a damnable fix you find yourself in. God knows I don't envy you. I know it must be devilishly difficult to think protector with your head, while farther down, the rest of you is rearing to have a go at her."

"As her *protector*, I ought to call you out for insulting her, but as your friend, I'll give you a warning this time. Don't speak of her in that tone again."

"Well, well, well," Richard said, a cat-that-got-the-cream expression on his face.

Without giving either of them a chance to say anything more, Quinn slammed the port down on the desk and quit the room.

Half an hour later, walking his anger off in the garden, Quinn's temper had cooled somewhat—at least enough to admit that what Harry said was true. He wanted to protect her, true, but it was also true that he wanted to take her to bed—had wanted to take her to bed since he had first seen her at the Midsummer's Eve ball. And most assuredly, he had thought of little else since he kissed her. He closed his eyes against the frustration of it.

To see her eyes wide with surprise, her mouth open with desire. God, what would it be like to make love to someone so innocent?

Caroline Flowers. Her name sounded like a rich, exotic perfume, and it surrounded him like the intoxicating scent of lilacs. It was a simple name, yet the very sound of it painted a picture in his mind. Caroline Flowers. Wholesome. Fragrant. Pure.

Something she wouldn't be if he lost his control.

He stopped, thrusting his hands deep into his pockets. There was only one thing he could do, that would protect her from him and his friends. She might be too old for toys, and too old for school, but she was ripe for marriage.

Marriage?

That was just the thing. Marry her off and be free of both the responsibility *and* the temptation. Whistling a jaunty tune, he went searching for his friends.

"Cooled off?" Richard asked as he entered the library.

Quinn nodded. "Enough to ask you a favor."

Richard grinned. "Anything," he said, then with a wink, added, "short of marriage."

"Would your aunt sponsor Miss Flowers for a season in London?"

Richard looked surprised. "You know my aunt would do anything you asked, Waverly, but do you think it wise? She's a country girl and the season is only a few months off. If she isn't ready, it could prove disastrous."

Harry picked that moment to slip from the room.

Richard watched him go, then shrugged. "I'm returning to London in the morning. I'll speak to my aunt as soon as I arrive. If your ward is to have a season, you need to start grooming her right away."

Quinn gave a start. "Grooming her?"

Richard stared at him. "My God, you didn't think to send her to London as she is? Granted, she is a beauty, but beauty only goes so far. The girl is unsophisticated, green as grass. One week, and the ton would grind her down to nothing. Think about it, Quinn. Remember how it was . . . the lessons we learned? We both know it is far better to borrow experience than to buy it. To send her to London as she is, that would be ruining her. Is that what you want?"

"No," Quinn said. Polite. Candid. Dismissing. As if he had not given it much thought, and did not want to admit it. And that much was true. He wanted to be rid of the girl. It was as simple as that. He did not want to become involved in her life.

Richard had the gumption to laugh. "You don't want to ruin her. Well, that is something, at least."

Quinn walked to the window, and looking out, thoughtfully stroked his chin. Richard was right. He couldn't send her to London as she was. She would find herself flat on her back in no time.

Yet, he could not leave her here, in the same house with him, or she would find herself in a similar position.

Marriage was the only solution, and the best way to marry her off was a season in London, even if he had to "groom her" as Richard put it.

"So, what have you decided?" Richard asked.

"Sufficiently dowered and adequately groomed, she should receive an offer before the season's end."

Richard poured himself a glass of port, refilling Quinn's. "Then, let us toast to Miss Caroline Flower's betrothal. May it be quick."

Under his breath, Quinn said, "May it be painless."

CHAPTER ❨ FOUR

The first thing Lord Waverly did, prior to his return to Fairfields, was to make it known that Caroline Flowers was well dowered, and that she would be having a season in London. *That, and the fact that she was a duke's grand-daughter should get her noticed.* And noticed was all Quinn knew was needed.

A face like hers . . .

A duke for a grandfather . . .

A large dowry . . .

What mortal man could refuse?

Feeling rather good about things, Quinn said good-bye to his friends, then watched the coach drive off, taking Harry and Richard to London. He smiled to himself. Once word was out about Miss Flowers, the ton would be on the tips of their toenails, eagerly expectant.

He watched the coach disappear, then mounted his horse and headed toward Fairfields.

"Miss Caro is in the garden, your lordship," Mrs. Witherspoon announced.

"Tell her that I wish to see her in the library straight-away."

Mrs. Witherspoon looked like a woman who had something to say, but doesn't know how to say it. "But . . . that is . . . your lordship . . ."

Quinn looked at Mrs. Witherspoon, a tall, robust woman with graying black hair drawn back into a bun. But it was those black, piercing eyes of hers that made him uncomfortable, as if she could read what was in his mind. God forbid. "Get on with it, woman," he said, letting his irritation show. "Is there some problem?"

"Yes, your lordship, there is. You see, Caro . . . that is, Miss Caroline is occupied at the moment."

Quinn frowned. "What do you mean occupied?"

Mrs. Witherspoon released a long-held breath. "She is bathing the dog, your lordship."

"Bathing the dog?"

"Yes, and quite a task it is, I might add. Hector is an Old English sheepdog, you see."

"No, I don't see." *The next darling of the ton is bathing a bloody sheepdog, up to her lovely pink ears in soapsuds.* The visual image irritated him. A duke's granddaughter did not bathe dogs! Allowing his irritation to creep into his voice, he spoke much more sharply than he intended. "Sheepdog or no sheepdog, tell my wart . . . er ward, to come to the library immediately."

"Begging your lordship's pardon, but I think it would be better to give her time to change and—"

"Mrs. Witherspoon, I am paying you a salary, am I not?"

"Yes, your lordship, you are."

"Then, let me refresh your memory. I am paying you for obedience, not to think. Am I right?"

Mrs. Witherspoon nodded. "Yes, your lordship."

"Good. Now, if you would be so kind as to fetch Miss Flowers. *Now,* if you please."

"Yes, your lordship." Mrs. Witherspoon seemed to swell to twice her size, then without a word, she turned. "As you wish."

As soon as she was out the door, Quinn moved to the large mullioned window that looked out into the garden. His gaze moved across the lawn to a few lilac trees, then came to rest near the house, where a climbing rose trailed down a latticed wall. There, he spotted a large, yapping dog, soaked to the skin, looking pathetically like a stick figure. Kneeling at his side, was Caroline Flowers, looking as gay as a butterfly, and every bit as soaked as the dog, but there was nothing about her that resembled a stick figure, nor was she pathetic. *Adorable,* would have been a better choice of word. *So lovely, so golden, so breathtakingly innocent.*

Robust from country living, she wore her golden hair braided and coiled on top of her head, although a great deal of it had escaped the braid and was clustered in wet ringlets about her face and neck. Her cheeks were pink. Her mouth was laughing and he had a flash of memory of having kissed it.

He watched with interest, as she blew an errant wisp of hair out of her face, dipped the brush into the tub of water and gave the howling dog a good scrubbing. The dog tried to jump out of the tub, but she caught him. Unable to escape, the dripping mass of canine opted to shake himself, wetting everything within ten feet. Quinn, wincing, could not help admiring Caroline's laughter about being drenched. Patience, he supposed, came from living in the country.

His view was blocked suddenly, by the appearance of Mrs. Witherspoon, and he felt much as one would feel on a picnic, when a rain cloud blocks out the sun.

Quinn watched as Caroline came to her feet, tossing the brush into the water. Smiling, she said something to Mrs. Witherspoon, then looked toward the house. It was then that he noticed she had gathered her skirts and tucked them in at the waist, giving him—and anyone else who might be looking—a view of her drawers. He didn't have time to think about her behavior being scandalous, before he noticed that her undergarments were as soaked as the rest of her. Unable to look away—which any guardian worth his salt would do—he allowed his curious gaze to roam. Her skin appeared as rosy as the rest of her where the wet fabric clung. Her legs were long and well-shaped.

Suddenly Mrs. Witherspoon said something to her, and with an angry scowl, Caroline jerked her skirts loose, allowing them to fall into place, then with a furious word to Mrs. Witherspoon, she marched toward the house and out of his sight.

Seeing the globe of the world standing on his left, Quinn rested one hand upon it, thinking this made a very benevolent pose, highly appropriate, considering he was her benefactor.

The door to the library came crashing open and his ward walked in, barefoot and angry.

Hands on her hips, she said, "This had better be important. At least you could have given me time to dry off."

"I prefer obedience to perfection," he said, giving her bedraggled appearance the once-over, and regretting it instantly. The bodice of her much-pressed blue dress had a white peasant-style underblouse, and where the blue fabric fell away at the bosom, there was nothing but white fabric. Wet, white fabric with a lot of rosy-hued skin showing. The dress was too worn, too youthful, and too small for her.

Way too small.

He would have to do something about that.

Caroline crossed her arms over her bosom. "Your lordship, I am wet, as you can plainly see. I am dripping all over your floor."

"Yes, well, that can be mopped up, can't it? Have a seat, Miss Flowers. On second thought, why don't you just stand where you are," he said, looking down at the water puddling at her feet.

"What did you wish to see me about?"

"I have some news that I think you will find pleasing. I have decided to give you a season in London, and I have taken the liberty of speaking to a friend of mine, the Marquess of Yorkston, about asking his aunt, the Dowager Duchess of Carlisle, to sponsor you. With the Duchess of Carlisle's endorsement, you will be at the top of everyone's list."

"No thank you."

Quinn blinked. "I beg your pardon."

"I said no thank you. I do not wish to have a season in London, or anywhere else, for that matter."

"Why not?"

"Because I am happy here, your lordship. Why should I want to go elsewhere?"

"You are a duke's granddaughter and . . ."

Caroline laughed. "An impoverished duke, I might

add, and one whose title passed into other hands. I am the last of the line, your lordship, and my grandfather has been dead so long, I doubt anyone will even remember him. But, that is of no consequence. City life holds no appeal for me. I prefer to remain here."

"And I wish you to have a season in London."

"Please, your lordship, let me remain here, as I am."

"That is out of the question, I'm afraid."

Caroline said nothing further, but Quinn could not help noticing the muscle working in her jaw. Stubborn, she was. He wondered how long it would be before the two of them butted heads.

Obviously holding back her anger, she asked, "Will there be anything else, your godship?"

Ignoring the temptation to argue, Quinn kept his voice and his temper even. "Yes, go change your clothes, and from now on, refrain from performing such chores. That is why we have a staff."

"But I enjoy working and being involved."

"Then stick to more feminine pastimes—gardening, sewing, and such."

"May I go now?"

"Yes."

She turned away, leaving the puddle of water behind. As she walked out the door, Quinn called out, "Caroline?"

She stopped but did not turn around. "Yes, your lordship."

He sighed. "I am not trying to make an enemy of you, nor am I trying to be an ogre. I am only trying to do what is best for you."

"And for you," she said, disappearing through the doorway before he could say anything more.

Quinn looked down at the puddle on the floor, the trail of wet prints left by her bare feet, then he noticed the faint, lingering smell—not of lilacs and roses—but of wet dog. With a smile, he decided he might just enjoy being her guardian, and why not? He was already looking forward to making a lady out of Caroline Flowers.

And with that, Quinn Westcott broke into little used, and much out-of-tune whistling.

* * *

The next morning at half-past ten, Caroline was surprised when Mrs. Witherspoon announced that Charlie Morriss, the potter's son had come to call upon her.

Charlie Morriss? What would prompt Charlie Morriss to call upon her?

She went downstairs to find Charlie waiting for her, just as Mrs. Witherspoon said. More to satisfy her curiosity than anything else, she agreed to take a stroll with him through the garden.

A moment later, they strolled down the gravel path, between clumps of daisies. When they reached the stile, she glanced up at him, to see if he wished to go over, or remain in the garden.

The moment she looked at him, Charlie made a grab for her, and before she could get over the shock, he kissed her.

Caroline jerked back, giving him a puzzled look. "Charlie Morriss, what has come over you?"

Charlie, his face red, pulled the cap from his head and began twisting it in his hands. "Well, you see, Caro, me pa says to come court you, and then me brother, Will, says to kiss you while I'm a courtin'."

"I see," Caro said, knowing there was much more to this than she was hearing. "Charlie, we have been friends for a long time, haven't we?"

Charlie nodded, his head down, his gaze upon his feet, as if he were too shy, too embarrassed to look at her, and Caroline supposed that he was.

She took Charlie's arm and the two of them began walking back toward the house. "Charlie, why would your father tell you to come court me? I thought you were sweet on Clara, the miller's daughter."

"I think it was because me brother told me pa that the man what married you would get a large . . . a large . . ."

"Dowry," Caroline finished, with sudden understanding. "Well, you listen to me, Charlie Morriss. You go back and court Clara—someone you would be happy with—and tell your pa and your brother to leave you be. Tell them Miss Caroline doesn't want to be courted by anyone, you hear? And tell them too, that they are wrong, my dowry is quite small."

Charlie, looking much like a man rescued from the gibbet, slapped his hat on his head, and thanking her with a robust shaking of her hand, dashed away.

She watched him go, then walked slowly back to the house. She found Fanny sitting on a bench by the back door playing with Hector, the dog.

"Fanny, I am so glad to see you. I have the most startling news to tell you."

Fanny rose to her feet, dusting off her skirt. "And I have the most startling *gossip* to tell you."

Caro laughed. "You tell me first then, gossip is ever better for the repeating of it."

"Word is all over town, Caro. Everyone is talking."

Caro plucked a rose from the drooping rosebush. "About what?"

"The size of your dowry."

"My dowry? But it is quite small, actually. Josiah was not a wealthy man. You of all people should know that."

"I'm only repeating what I've heard," Fanny said.

"Hmmm. I wonder why anyone would deliberately start a rumor, unless . . ."

"Unless it was your new guardian," Fanny said.

"Of course it was my guardian," said Caro. Everything suddenly made sense. "I don't know why I didn't see it sooner. Of course that is the perfect way to be rid of me: marry me off to the first man who offers. And to make certain he gets an offer, he increases my dowry, and then he makes certain everyone in the whole of England hears about it. Why, I wouldn't be surprised to hear he has taken out an ad in the *Times*."

"Oh, Caro," Fanny said, patting her affectionately. "Whatever are you going to do? You cannot marry someone you don't love."

"Of course I can't, and I won't."

"But what can you do about it? Your guardian has the final say."

Caroline smiled. "I may not be able to change things, but I can certainly *delay* them a bit."

"Delay?" Fanny asked.

"I plan to put as many trees as I can in the middle of the road to matrimony. Fanny, this is war."

Caroline sat down on the bench and Fanny sat beside her. A moment later, Hector came to lay his head, wet whiskers and all, in her lap. Caro stroked his head where the tightly curled gray hair met the white around his face. "Lord Waverly wants to give me a season in London."

"A season in London?"

"Yes," Caro said, then went on to tell Fanny about the happenings in the library the day before.

"Oh, dear," said Fanny. "That explains it."

"Explains what?"

Turning to Caroline, Fanny placed her hand on top of Caro's. "I forgot to tell you *that* was the reason I came out here. Mrs. Witherspoon is beside herself. The parlor and the morning room are full of suitors."

"Suitors," Caro gasped. "For me?"

"Well, they haven't come to call on Hector," Fanny said, the chocolate-colored curls dangling beneath her bonnet bouncing with emphasis.

At the sound of his name, Hector raised his head and looking toward the door, whined.

"You stay out of this," Caro said, watching Hector as he trotted toward the house. "Traitor," she said. "Men— they are all alike."

"No matter what kind of animal they are," Fanny said, and the two of them collapsed in laughter.

They didn't see Quinn ride up, dismount, and hand the reins to the groom. For a moment he stood there, his quirt slapping the side of his leg as he watched Caroline and her friend. *They certainly seem to be enjoying themselves. Could it be that she is telling Fanny about the kiss that bumpkin gave her?*

Afraid to say anything to her for he feared he would say too much, Quinn went into the morning room by another door.

Two steps into the room, Quinn stopped abruptly. There must have been at least fifteen country bumpkins milling about. Without saying anything, he stomped through the room into the hallway and began to shout for Mrs. Witherspoon. When she did not answer, he went looking for her.

Passing the parlor, he saw it too was crammed with local buffoons, and in their midst, wringing her hands and looking as if she didn't know what to do about it all, stood Mrs. Witherspoon.

"Mrs. Witherspoon, I want to see you in the library, if you please."

Mrs. Witherspoon's mouth opened, as if she were about to voice some objection.

"Immediately," Quinn said, then headed for the library, as he added, "And if it is full of the village idiots, then I will see you in my study. For your sake, I pray it is empty."

A moment later, a huffing Mrs. Witherspoon came rushing into the library. "Oh, your lordship, am I ever glad you are home."

Quinn ignored her. "What the blazes is going on here?"

Mrs. Witherspoon looked aghast. "Why, I don't know, your lordship. I thought perhaps that you could tell me."

Quinn opened his mouth to tell Mrs. Witherspoon that he had not the foggiest idea as to why every eligible bachelor in the whole of Cornwall would suddenly show up on his doorstep. But then, he realized, that he did know.

"The dowry," he whispered.

"Beg pardon?" Mrs. Witherspoon asked, still wringing her hands on her apron and looking about the room, as if she had been advised help was on the way and she was searching for it.

"The dowry," was all Quinn said, as he stomped from the library, leaving Mrs. Witherspoon to stare, open-mouthed, after him. The success of his plan didn't send the slightest flicker of warmth into his heart.

CHAPTER ❨ FIVE

Caroline was snipping roses in the garden when Lord Waverly's shadow stretched itself across the path in front of her. She placed the tightly curled bud of a pink rose in the basket hanging from her arm and turned to face him.

Suddenly she wished she had not. Standing before her was everything she had ever hoped for: the man of all her dreams.

The perfect man. Save, of course, for the fact that he wanted to marry her . . . to someone else.

It was an odd situation: being attracted to the very man whose life she had vowed to make as miserable as possible. Well, there was no help for it. She could not let her attraction for this man sway her, for if she faltered, she would find herself married before summer's end.

Looking at him standing there, the picture of innocence, and knowing what she knew was disheartening. She felt strangely unsure of herself. This man held her future in his strong hands. This man considered her a burden. This man wanted to rid himself of her and did not care how he did it.

She closed her eyes, fearing he might be able to see what she was thinking, wanting to block his image from her mind, but like the lingering fragrance of the roses in her basket, he was still there. Even now she could see the perfection of him, the image of a man she desired with all her heart, the one man she knew she could never have.

"Well," he said, interrupting her thoughts, "are we

tired this morning, or are you simply closing your eyes, hoping I'll disappear?"

She opened her eyes and looked at him. "And would you? Disappear, I mean?"

He smiled, a charming smile and she had to remind herself that the devil was once a favored angel. Suddenly Lord Waverly reached out, brushing the bare flesh of her neck as he plucked a rose petal that had fallen inside her open collar. His voice turned soft as his gaze caressed her in a surprisingly intimate way. "And would you wish me to?"

She tried to smile, but as he stroked her cheek with the petal, all she could do was stand there gaping at him, feeling as dazed and breathless as she had the day she fell out of the hayloft when she was twelve.

Did she wish him to disappear?

"Yes," she said. All at once she had a plan, the perfect way to foil his matchmaking. He thought her a simple country lass that he could marry off at will. Well, she would give him a simple country lass, one so simple she wouldn't be ready for a season in London if she had a hundred years and just as many tutors.

She gave him a shy, simple smile. "I suppose I would want you to disappear, especially if you have any more ideas about filling the house with suitors. Why, do you know that last night, Henry Malone kept peppering my window with pebbles? And after that, some lack-talent tried to serenade me—and that was only the beginning. This morning I had fourteen love notes, three invitations to go for a buggy ride, two proposals, four bad poems—and one not-so-bad one—and a bunch of wilted daisies delivered to me, all before breakfast."

She could not have planned it better. Lord Waverly did not see any humor in her lighthearted words. He scowled and said, "How do you know it was Henry Malone?"

"Because I saw him," she said, feigning innocence, longing to burst out laughing.

"You . . . *he* came into your bedroom?"

She smiled inwardly. It was common knowledge that dear, sweet Henry couldn't find his way into the right

pew at church on Sunday morning, but she wasn't about
to tell Lord Waverly that. "No, of course he didn't come
into my room," she said with great emphasis. "I climbed
out the window."

He blinked. "You climbed out a window on the second
floor?"

She nodded, puffing herself up with pride. "Of course.
I have done it many times before, you see. Besides, how
else was I to find out who it was?"

"Charming. You climbed out a second-floor window,
not worried in the least that you might have fallen, or at
least caught one of your petticoats on the blasted tree
and hung yourself."

"Oh, I couldn't have done that, your lordship."

"I'd like to know why not."

"Because I was in my nightgown and I never wear my
petticoats with my nightgown." She looked aghast, not
because she was aghast, of course, but simply because
she thought the look appropriate.

Judging from his horrified expression, it was just the
right look.

Truly inspired now, she brought her hand up to her
bosom, and for added emphasis, she said, "Don't tell me
what the ladies in London do. Surely they don't wear
petticoats with their nightgowns!"

Lord Waverly made a strangled sound, but said nothing, so Caro, who was enjoying this immensely, went on.
"Well, anyway, as I was saying, I climbed out the window
and there stood Henry with a fistful of pebbles in one
hand and a bone in the other."

All of a sudden, Lord Waverly began to look enor-
mously interested. "A bone? He brought you a *bone?* Is
this a traditional courting custom here in Cornwall, or
am I missing something?"

This time, it was more than she could handle and the
bewildered expression on his face brought her laughter
bubbling forth. "Oh, the bone wasn't for me, your lordship. It was for Hector."

"Oh, Hector. Yes, of course. Hector—that tangled
mop with oversized feet and a dripping chin. The bone, I
suppose, was to keep him from barking."

"No, the bone was to keep him from taking the seat out of Henry's trousers, like he did the last time Henry came to shoe the carriage horses. Henry is the village smithy's son, you see."

Lord Waverly groaned. "More likely the village idiot."

Hearing his groan, Caro placed a hand on his sleeve. "Are you all right, milord?"

A helpless look upon his face, Lord Waverly said, "Nothing has been right since I inherited this bloody place." He gave her a stern, fatherly look. "Has no one ever taught you anything about proper behavior?"

She batted her eyes shamelessly. "Proper behavior? Whatever do you mean?"

"I mean, my sweet simpleton, has no one informed you that a lady does *not* climb out her bedroom window *in* her nightgown, *in* the middle of the night, to *secretly* meet some lackwit who comes courting with a pocketful of pebbles and a soup bone."

She thought back, searching her mind for the limited number of discussions she had with Mrs. Witherspoon concerning womanly things and felt like laughing. This was one time she could give him a completely honest answer. Frowning, she looked at him. "No, but I see no reason to be upset. Henry couldn't see a thing, I am certain. After all, it was dark."

"God's eyeballs! This is worse than I thought. It isn't so much that you should worry about what he could see —although that is cause for some alarm—but what he could have done."

"Done?" She played it very simple-heartedly, with wide eyes and a blank look.

"As in seduction."

Caro burst out laughing.

Lord Waverly stiffened. He began to feel that one week at Fairfields was too long. "Is something funny?"

"Milord, pardon me for laughing, but don't you see the humor in it? How could a man who comes courting with a dog bone know anything about seduction? Poor Henry. The only rake he has ever seen is the kind you find in the barn. Why, he has never been out of Cornwall, much less to London."

Lord Waverly stared at her, then the hard lines around his mouth began to dissolve. For a moment she thought he might smile. "And what, pray tell, does that have to do with anything?"

"Why, everyone knows that it is the rakes and the London dandies that know about such things. Mrs. Witherspoon said we were blessedly safe from such sinful ways here in the country."

"And of course, that paragon of misinformation, Mrs. Witherspoon, would know."

"Oh yes. She was married once, you see, but alas, poor woman, there was a terrible carriage accident on the way home from the church, and dear Mr. Witherspoon was killed."

"How fortunate for him."

She pretended not to hear. "Beg pardon?"

"And so, our sage Mrs. Witherspoon doesn't know any more than you do," he said, in a voice warm with sympathy.

"Perhaps not, but being a rake and from London, surely *you* must know."

"We are talking about your knowledge—or lack of it—not *mine.*"

"But you could teach me everything you know."

"*Someone* needs to teach you something," he said, "so it might as well be me." He took a step toward her and she quickly backed away.

This time, it was Lord Waverly who burst out laughing.

"I fail to see the humor in what has happened," she said stiffly.

"My sweet Caroline, do you have any idea what you have just asked me to teach you? You do know exactly what happens between a man and a woman, don't you?"

"Of course I do," she lied, feeling herself suddenly on uncertain ground.

"Well, then you should know that there isn't any reason for you to back away from me like a trapped fox. I couldn't possibly do those kinds of things here. Not even the worst rake would seduce a virgin in the garden in broad daylight. Not to mention it would be damnably uncomfortable."

Somehow, he had turned things around and now he was in control. To make matters worse, she wasn't certain how to turn them around again. "You make it very difficult for me to even like you," she said in a tortured tone.

"I am sure I do, but perhaps it is best that way." He gave her a curious look. "Are you cold?"

"No. How could I be cold in the summertime?"

"Then why are you trembling?"

"I always tremble when I'm upset."

"Are you upset now?"

"Yes."

"Why?"

"Because you unnerve me, milord. Because I do not understand you. Because I don't know, exactly, what it is that you expect of me. Because you make me uncomfortable."

"Pity. I could do something about that last one, but then, it isn't really my place," he whispered. She felt a tensing of her body as he reached out to dust a few rose petals from her hair. She felt the petals drift across her skin, some of them catching in the open collar of her dress. A rippling thrill rushed the entire length of her body as he opened the first two buttons of her gown, then leaned forward.

She closed her eyes, swaying on her feet, knowing he was going to kiss her there, and knowing too, that she would do nothing to stop him.

Suddenly, she felt his breath on her skin, and opening her eyes, she saw him blow the petals, then straighten, as he rebuttoned her gown.

"A lady would never allow a gentleman to do what I just did," he said. "Have you no sense of right and wrong?"

"I don't know. No one has ever done such things to me."

"And because it has never been done, you feel it is all right?"

"How would I know before it is done?"

"So, you would allow a man almost any liberties with you?"

She looked away. "I am not certain what you mean, milord." It was a shameful performance, she knew, but one did what one had to do.

He took her hand and kissed her fingertips, one by one, and when she made no move to stop him, he began to kiss the skin of her wrist, traveling up her arm to the bend in her elbow. He was looking at her now, as if she were a banquet and he was coming off a long fast. She could feel the heat rising to her cheeks. Instinct told her to slap him, but the ruse she played out said, wait to see how far he would go.

"You should never allow a man liberties such as this. Or this," he said, taking her in his arms, his mouth reaching for hers.

A sense of urgency fired her blood and she moaned, leaning against him, wanting this and more. All that he could show her, all he could teach her. She was not prepared for the softness of his lips, for the sudden rush of feeling that shot through her body. The questioning pressure of his mouth made her tingle with excitement, and she remembered having felt this way only once before—when the highwayman kissed her. Afraid she might topple over, her hands tightened around him. Everywhere she touched him, he was solid and warm. Everywhere he touched her, her skin burned. She found herself pressing closer to him, seeking the comforting hardness of his body, the dizzying warmth.

He gripped her arms and drew back. "This will never do," he said, unable to hide the shaky unsteadiness in his voice. "If a man should ever try such things with you, Caroline, you must stop his advances immediately. You cannot allow a man to take such liberties with you."

"Why not? You did."

"That was different. I was only doing it to show you, to teach you the kind of things a man might try to get away with, the things you must not give him the liberty to do."

"You still haven't answered my question. Why shouldn't I?"

"Because, it gives a man ideas, fills him with desire, and when that happens, that is, if it is allowed to continue, there can be a point of no return, a point when a man cannot stop, no matter what the woman does."

"You were able to stop," she said, noticing that he seemed to puff-up with pride as she spoke the words.

"That's different," he said. "My intentions were different, and consequently, I was unaffected by what happened between us."

She could not help it. She felt the corners of her mouth lifting with a smile. "Milford, I think you deceive yourself."

"We shall see," he said, sounding quite smug.

"Yes, I suppose we will," she said, "for having told a lie, you will have to stick to it."

She turned away so swiftly that the pink rosebud fell from her basket.

CHAPTER ☾ SIX

Quinn stared at the rosebud long after she had gone. It lay upon the ground, like an arrow of guilt pointing straight to his heart. Shame. Regret. Remorse. These were new emotions for him and he was not quite certain how to deal with them. Ignoring them seemed the simplest solution. But even that was not as easily accomplished as he would have liked.

For a moment, he simply stood there staring at the rose, then he leaned down and picked it up. The fragrance brought back the memory of her.

He looked at the pale pink bud, drawing its velvet surface across his lips. There was something about this rose that reminded him of her. The rosy paleness so mindful of her skin, and yes, even the supple softness of its petals. But there was more. Like the rosebud, Caroline was a solitary thing, a lovely creature all alone, a woman whose family was taken from her, much as the rose was snipped from the bush. And like the bud, she was lovely to look at, yet so much about her was hidden from view. He wondered then, if like this rosebud, she would open slowly, revealing the loveliness inside.

It occurred to him suddenly that he would not be the one to watch her petals gently unfold, that he would never know the secrets that were so tightly protected. With a muffled curse, Quinn crushed the rose and tossed it to the ground.

By the time he reached the house, he could hear raucous laughter and knew Richard and Harry were back from London. He cursed softly. He had not expected them back so soon. He had hoped to have things moving along more smoothly with this betrothal business before they arrived, but upon thinking about it further, he decided that having them here might be a much-needed diversion. He was fighting his attraction for his ward. Perhaps Harry and Richard were just the thing to keep him in line.

He stopped by his study to have a shot of brandy before facing the pair, knowing they would be looking for any sign of weakness. Pouring the glass half-full, he lifted the snifter to his lips.

The scent of roses filled his nostrils.

For a moment he simply stared at his hand, thinking it odd that the lovely bud had perfumed the hand that crushed it, the way Caroline Flowers had permeated his mind.

Finishing the brandy, he placed the glass on a silver tray, then went to find Harry and Richard.

"Ho, Waverly!" Harry said, looking up and seeing Quinn. "We've just had a chat with Mrs. Witherspoon. Seems word has gotten out quite well about the dowry and all that. That's jolly good news. Your matchmaking must be coming along better than you anticipated."

Before Quinn could snarl a reply, Richard spoke up. "I spoke with my aunt and I am happy to report that the Dowager Duchess of Carlisle will be happy to sponsor Miss Caroline Flowers to a season. Can you believe it? She even remembers Caro's uncle, the late duke."

Caro? "Forget it," Quinn said harshly.

Harry and Richard exchanged glances.

"Forget it, as in you aren't giving her a season?" Richard asked.

"That is exactly what I mean."

"Well, that is a jolly bit of news, and unexpected. Unable to make our mind up, are we?" asked Richard.

"May I ask why you changed your mind?" Harry asked. "She is, as you said, a duke's granddaughter."

"A duke who lost his title, his money, and his mind," Quinn replied, trying to keep any hint of emotion out of his voice. "Besides, there is, I fear, too much country in the lass. I daresay an army of tutors couldn't have her ready in time. I had hoped for a titled marriage for her, of course, but all things considered, a country squire wouldn't be a bad choice."

"So you are giving up?" asked Harry.

"No, simply changing tactics," Quinn replied.

"Is that the only reason you changed your mind?" Richard inquired.

"No, not necessarily. There were, actually, a lot of reasons," Quinn said, "but mostly it was just that I realized I could never have her ready in time."

"So what now?" asked Harry.

"I will add to her dowry, and then we'll see what happens."

What happened was that before two weeks had passed, Caroline had received fifteen offers of marriage. Of course, none of them were up-to-snuff, as Quinn put it, so he turned them all down.

"Of course," Harry and Richard agreed, giving each other a knowing look. Having a smoke in the library after dinner one evening, they were discussing the recent turn of events.

"You know, I didn't think that young parson would have been a bad choice," Harry said.

"He is as poor as a church mouse," Quinn said.

Harry smiled. "True, but with her dowry, that wouldn't have mattered much, now would it?"

"A parson has no place in his life for either money or a beautiful wife," Quinn said.

"Well then, what about Squire Peterby?" Richard asked. "He is certainly in a position to entertain both."

"Peterby is too old."

"I see," Richard said. "Hmm. How about Captain Crawley?"

"He's a lecher."

"What about Helford. His family was in tin and they are still fairly well-to-do."

"Helford is a blockhead."

Harry jumped in. "And the innkeeper, Crowder?"

"He's been married six times."

Harry tried again. "There's Sir Richard, the sheriff."

Quinn spat back. "His reputation is unsatisfactory."

"Twiler, the shipbuilder?" Richard offered.

"I don't like the look in his eyes."

"Gerran, the fisherman?" Harry supplied.

"Not even I could marry her to a man who smells like a cod."

Richard sighed. "Well, that trims the list down to Morrisson . . ."

"Too fat."

"And Carter . . ."

"Poor health."

"Grahame . . ."

"A wife-beater."

"Hastings . . ."

"An uneducated lout."

"Ramsay . . ."

"Drinks too much."

"That," Richard said, "sounds like a grand idea," and he poured himself a drink, handing one to Quinn and one to Harry, giving Harry a wink as he did.

Holding his glass aloft, Richard said, "I'd like to propose a toast. "To the impossible," he said and he and Harry downed their drinks.

Quinn did not move a muscle. "And what, may I be so rude as to inquire, is the impossible?"

Richard and Harry exchanged glances, then Richard turned to Quinn and smiled. "Finding Caro a husband, of course."

"And what is so impossible about that? She is pretty enough, and her dowry is not stingy in the least."

"My God!" Richard said. "I'll tell you what is impossible. *You* are."

"Me?" Quinn asked, doing his best to look surprised.

"Of course. You find fault with every man who comes to call. *That's* where the problem lies."

"I've done nothing out of the ordinary. They were unsatisfactory. Nothing more."

"I'm beginning to think Saint Peter himself would have been unsatisfactory," Richard said.

"If you are finding this task not to your liking, you can

return to London's decadence anytime you wish," Quinn said.

Richard laughed. "And miss the fall of the *Pride of the Peninsula.*"

"I am not the bloody Pride of the Peninsula, and I wish you would stop calling me that." Quinn paused, pinning Richard with a hard look. "What fall?"

"Yours, my friend. In case you haven't noticed, you are falling in love with the chit yourself."

"I'll drink to that," Harry said, and raised his glass.

"Here's to the Marquess of Waverly's day of reckoning," Richard said.

"Go to hell," Quinn said, and stormed from the room.

Being a man who never sulked, Quinn sulked for the rest of the afternoon.

It wasn't enough that his ward and the entire household were upset with him. Now, it appeared that even his bloody friends were against him. Not even Hector—who had never been picky about who he cozied up to—would give him a moment's time. He sighed, running his fingers through his hair. All right. He would grant that they had a point. He had been rejecting suitors for reasons that sounded ridiculous, even to him, but that was no reason to hurl accusations.

You are falling in love with the chit yourself . . .

"Not bloody likely," Quinn said, catching a glimpse of Mrs. Witherspoon out of the corner of his eye. He watched her move down the hallway. A moment later, he left his brooding and his study, and went after her.

"I say, Mrs. Witherspoon, may I have a word with you?"

Mrs. Witherspoon turned toward him, her expression telling him that she had not softened toward him one bit. "May I do something for you, your lordship?"

He glanced at her robust frame, the neat bun, the stiffly starched gray dress, the spotless apron. Something about the white apron reminded him of the blue dress Caroline had worn the day she bathed Hector. He had intended to inquire as to Caroline's whereabouts, but when the reminder of Caroline's rather shabby, ill-fitting dress came to mind, he spoke of that, instead.

"I have been meaning to speak with you about Miss Flowers's wardrobe. I find it inadequate. That is, the dresses don't seem to be suitable for courting."

"No, your lordship, they are best suited for the rag basket."

"Have you a seamstress about? One that keeps abreast of the latest fashions?"

"Yes, your lordship. We have an extraordinary seamstress and a milliner in the village."

"Excellent. Will you send for her, and please instruct her to provide Miss Flowers with a look more befitting her age. I want her to look more like the ladies in London. Her current wardrobe is far too youthful and far too countrified."

"Perhaps that is because she *was* youthful when they were made, your lordship."

Quinn could feel his face growing warm. "Yes, well, see to it, won't you?"

"Yes, your lordship. I will be happy to."

Strolling toward the stables, Quinn decided what he needed was a good ride and some fresh country air. There was nothing like a brisk run along the cliffs to clear one's head.

Rounding the corner of the vegetable garden, he suddenly came face-to-face with Caroline. She was sitting in the back of an old pony cart, a book in her hands. Bareheaded. Her bonnet tossed aside. The sunshine glorious upon her honey-colored curls. She was wearing pink and the color brought out the rose in her cheeks. Beside her was a tangle of gray-and-white fur with no beginning and no end.

"How can you tell which end is which?" he asked, thinking he liked the look of surprise upon her face.

She glanced down at Hector and laughed, and he noticed it wrinkled her nose in a most delightful way. "Well, you wait until someone speaks, then he raises his head, and you know."

As if prompted by her words, Hector lifted his head

and rose to his feet. If he had possessed anything that remotely resembled a tail, it would have been wagging, but since he was shortchanged in that area, his entire backside began to wiggle.

Distracted by the unexpected sight of her, Quinn was caught off-guard. "Would you like to go for a ride?"

"I would, except we don't have any horses for riding. We have the carriage horses, the plow horse, and the fat gray pony in the pasture."

"Well, I will have to rectify that then, won't I?" he said, noticing the way the color seemed to fade from her lovely face.

"That would be a waste of money, your lordship, seeing as how I will not be residing here much longer."

It was the first time it occurred to him that she might regret leaving Fairfields. He cursed himself for being so inconsiderate. "Well, perhaps we can bring the pony up from the pasture."

"The pony is lame and cannot be ridden."

"I see. In that case I will leave you to your book. Good afternoon, Miss Flowers."

"Good afternoon, your lordship. Have a pleasant ride."

As far as luck went, he had plenty, for Quinn decided not to ride along the cliffs, but opted instead, for a ride into town, where he hoped to find a suitable horse for Caroline. Perhaps that would lighten her mood and improve things between them.

Good fortune happened upon him when he was not more than two miles from Fairfields. Passing a small farm, he noticed a weathered sign turned on its side and hanging loosely by one nail. But even sideways, Quinn could make out what its faded letters said: HORSES BOUGHT AND SOLD

Half an hour later, Quinn rode back toward Fairfields, this time with a smart-looking white mare trotting along beside him.

Upon reaching the stables, he ignored the astonished expression on the stableboy's face and instructed him to have both horses groomed, saddled, and waiting the next morning.

After a rainy evening, morning burst forth with bright, rosy promise, and Quinn looked at that as a good omen.

Ah, there is nothing like a brief respite in the country. The two divinest things the world has got, a lovely woman in a rural spot.

Caro soon came out of the house, dressed in a worn, out-of-style riding habit the color of blueberries, but even its shabbiness did little to detract from her beauty. He was glad that he had purchased the most expensive, and by far the most beautiful horse the farmer possessed. Surely that white mare was made for a woman like Caroline.

Caro, however, upon seeing the mare led in from the paddock, stopped dead. "Is this your idea of a joke?"

Quinn was dumfounded. "A joke? What are you talking about? This is my idea of a gift. I thought you would like to go for a ride."

She dug her heels in. "I won't ride *that* horse," she said. "Nobody in their right mind would."

CHAPTER ❬ SEVEN

$\mathscr{N}$ever had Caroline seen anyone's face pass through so many shades of purple.

"Fine," he said, gaining control of himself, the deep purple of rage fading. Tossing the reins of his horse at her, he added, "You can ride my gelding, and I'll take the mare."

"Lord Waverly, I did not mean . . ."

Her words came too late. Before she could finish her sentence, Lord Waverly had sprung into the saddle, and in a whirl of dust and nickering horse, was off, thundering out of the stable yard, the mare galloping wildly, taking off like someone had set her tail afire.

"Lord love us," the groom said. Suddenly Caroline understood the expression "ride like hell," for Lord Waverly did just that.

Caroline waited for the groom to give her a leg up, then guiding the chestnut gelding into a sharp turn, she galloped off in the same direction Quinn and the mare had taken only moments before.

For two hours she searched for him, never finding him, only clues as to where he had been. At the edge of the wood, she found his hat, caught on an oak branch. At a tranquil spot beside the creek, where herons haunted the reeds, she found his quirt. And snagged on a thorny hedge, she found a good part of his sleeve, as if the hedge had reached out and yanked it from him as he passed.

Worried, she searched for another half hour. She had

just decided to return home, so she could send word to Quinn's two friends to join in the search, when out of the cover of trees burst Quinn, the mare's hooves tearing up clumps of sod as they plunged through the undergrowth.

Riding like some demon forged from the fires of hell, they came, Quinn and the mare. Quinn's face splattered with mud, his clothes in tatters, the mare well lathered, her eyes showing white.

Without the slightest slowing of pace, the mare thundered past, heading for a ditch filled with water left from last night's rain, Quinn clung to the mane with both hands, the bridle trailing out behind them. Lord Waverly, the pride of the light calvary, was hanging on for dear life.

Suddenly the mare stopped.

Quinn did not.

He sailed over the mare's head, landing on his shoulder, then rolled twice before coming to a stop in a foot of water at the bottom of the ditch. Icy fingers of fear crept down Caroline's spine.

"Bloody hell!"

She smiled, realizing by that outburst that he was all right. Probably nothing was hurt except his pride. By the time she leaped dramatically from her horse, the mare was out of sight.

When she reached him, Quinn was rising to his feet. "Hellfire and damnation! Wait until I get my hands on that bloody beast. I'll have a pair of boots from her hide by nightfall." He was panting hard, his clothes sodden and mud-spattered.

"My lord, are you all right?"

"Am I all right? *Am I all right?*" he repeated weakly, but finding the energy to go up on his toes, his voice raising several octaves. *"Am I all right?"* He glowered at her. "Considering I have been thrown against trees, over fences, into ditches, and had my face rearranged by low-hanging branches, I would say I'm in remarkable shape. At least nothing is broken, and I still have all my teeth."

She wanted to bust out laughing, but right now her task was to appear as simpleminded and gullible as possible. She sighed. "I tried to warn you," she said sweetly.

"Angel is well-known in these parts. Unfortunately, she has earned her nasty reputation."

"Angel? That beast is named . . . misnamed, Angel?"

Caroline nodded. "Officially, that is her name."

"And what is her unofficial name? Satan? Demon? The Beast from Hell?"

"She is known as The Bolter in three counties."

"Bloody hell! I've been duped. Wait until I get my hands on that farmer."

"You are new to these parts, milord, and know nothing of our ways. The farmer meant no harm. The Bolter is always passed on to the new or unsuspecting. It has become a tradition. It was his way of initiating you into Cornish life."

"Or death. Has anyone been permanently maimed by that hellion?"

She laughed. "No, milord, but most don't stay on here long enough. Once she tossed you, you would have done better to remain with both feet—or your backside—planted firmly on the ground," she said with humor dancing in her eyes.

He stared off in the direction the mare had taken. "I'll break that bloody beast if it's the last thing I do."

She laughed. "That will take both courage and craft, milord."

"With that demon it will take only one thing."

"And what is that?"

"Endurance."

"Speaking of endurance, are you up to the ride back to Fairfields?"

"As long as it isn't on that hell-horse."

"Oh, have no fear of that. I think Angel arrived at Fairfields some time ago. She probably has her nose buried in a bucket of oats by now."

"Buried . . . hmm . . . don't give me ideas."

She smiled up at him, feeling suddenly shy. She turned toward the chestnut. "Shall you mount first and I behind you?"

"No, you mount first and I'll ride behind you."

All in all, she decided she liked that idea best. It was

ever so much better to have Quinn's arms around her, than to have hers around him. Gathering the reins in her hand, she accepted the leg up from Quinn, heard him groan as he swung into the saddle behind her. Just as she was about to urge the horse forward, voices broke the stillness.

"There they are!"

They turned in unison to see Viscount Huntley and the Marquess of Yorkston coming toward them.

"Ho, Quinn, is anything amiss?" asked Harry, as he and Richard galloped closer.

When they pulled to a stop, Quinn looked at them as if nothing out of the ordinary had happened at all. "Looking for us?" he asked.

"For quite some time. Mrs. Witherspoon saw you ride off on The Bolter. She sent the stableboy to find us. We've been looking for you for a bloody hour," Richard said.

"My God!" Harry said, "what happened to your clothes. You look like you've been chewed up by something and spit out."

"Did The Bolter toss you in the ditch?" asked Richard, eyeing him with a speculative grin on his face.

"No," Quinn said, "I jumped in by myself to cool off."

"You should have tossed a little water on The Bolter while you were at it. Maybe then, she would have hung around. We saw her running like her hooves were shod with fire," Harry said. "We expected to find you tossed on your duffer, not with your arms around a beautiful woman."

"I take my blessings where I find them," Quinn said, looking down at Caroline. She looked utterly charming in her old riding habit, leaves in the tangled gold hair that framed her lovely face, so serene in its simple-minded way. How anyone could appear so intelligent one moment and so simple witted the next was beyond him.

Harry turned toward Caroline. "Mrs. Witherspoon asked me to tell you the seamstress was waiting with your new clothes. She said for us to hurry you along a bit, if we saw you."

"I forgot she was coming today," Caroline said.

"Richard, why don't you and Harry take Caroline back with you. I think I'll take a slower pace back to Fairfields, if you don't mind."

Richard raised an elegant brow. "Judging from the looks of you, it can't be slow enough. You are going to be as sore as the devil by tomorrow."

Richard dismounted and came over to the chestnut, and reaching up, helped Caroline down. "You can ride with me," he said. "Unlike Quinn, I'm not foolish enough to miss such an opportunity."

"And what is that supposed to mean?" Quinn asked, his brows knitting together.

"It's about as complex as an apple dumpling. But maybe it's too obvious, that's why you don't see it."

"You don't make any sense," Quinn said.

Richard shook his head, then helped Caroline into the saddle, climbing up behind her. Reaching around her, he took up the reins as he nudged his horse forward. "Neither do you, old man."

The last glimpse Quinn had of her was the sight of her long blond hair coming unbound and streaming out behind them, as she rode out of sight, another man's arms around her.

A moment later, they were gone, and all that was left of Caroline Flowers was the memory.

Quinn sat upon his horse thinking that was much the way things were destined to be between them. *Well, perhaps that is best, after all.* He would marry her off soon—to another man—and then, all that would be left was the memory.

He turned toward Fairfields, riding slowly, his mind not upon his aching body, but upon Caroline.

CHAPTER ❨ EIGHT

Quinn found her in the kitchen tying an apron around Richard's waist. Harry, he observed, already had his apron on. Intrigued, Quinn decided that since none of them had noticed him, he would watch them for a few minutes, primarily because his curiosity had definitely gotten the best of him, and not-so-primarily because he was not too certain she wouldn't try to put one of those bloody things on him.

He stood just inside the doorway that led to the buttery, leaning against the jamb, observing his friends and his ward.

Both Harry and Richard treated her like they were on the verge of offering for her themselves. He could not remember seeing two more lovesick fools in his life, at least not since his early years at Cambridge.

And Caroline was much more relaxed and gay around them than she ever was with him, the cunning little minx.

"I cannot believe I am in the kitchen, wearing an apron, ready to pull taffy to my heart's content," Harry said. "If the ton ever gets word of this, I'm a dead man."

"You're absolutely right," said Richard.

Quinn watched her don her smock, then set about to cover everyone's hands with butter. While Richard and Harry stood there like two idiots, staring at her with adoring stupefaction, she scraped something out of a pan and onto a marble slab.

"Are you certain it's ready?" Richard asked, giving the golden glob a questioning look.

"Yes. You poke a hole in it with your finger, like this."
She poked one dainty finger into the glossy lump. "If the
print stays, then it's ready. Haven't you ever made taffy
before?"

"Nope," Richard said, "I was too busy making . . ."
Richard paused, his face turning a bright red. "Well . . .
uh . . . never mind. Suffice it to say, I am a novice at
taffy-making."

Harry gave Richard a bemused look, then leaned over,
staring at the sticky mass. "Looks ready to me."

"So now what?" Richard asked.

"We divide it in half, then divide ourselves into two
teams, so we can pull it. Oh, dear, we need a fourth," she
said, glancing from Richard to Harry, and catching sight
of Quinn. "Lord Waverly," she shouted with much enthusiasm. "Do come and join us. We are about to have a
taffy pull."

"I don't think I'm up to that just now," Quinn said,
limping into the room. "I've been stretched and pulled
enough today, thank you very little."

But she was already coming toward him, apron in
hand, smiling at him in such a way that his body instantly
responded. Well, *that* was the only part of him that
wasn't sore, flayed, or scraped. Still, if he hadn't been so
bruised from the ride on The Bolter, he might have
bolted himself, but as it was, he was too bloody sore to
move fast enough.

A moment later, he found himself with an apron on,
standing there, as greased an idiot as his two friends,
watching her roll taffy into a ball. *God, what fools women
can make out of men.*

After dividing the taffy, she placed one section between Harry and Richard, the remaining half she shoved
in front of Quinn.

"All right, now we start pulling, but remember, you
mustn't let the taffy break," she said.

Richard and Harry, Quinn noted, leaped to the task
with much relish, and soon the two of them had strings
of taffy drooping almost to the floor.

"Now, milord, take this ball of taffy and start pulling
it, just like Harry and Richard."

Feeling like the idiot he was, Quinn accepted the ball of taffy, and as instructed, he began to pull, not paying much attention to what he was doing, since his attention was focused upon her.

Tiny beads of sweat broke out across her upper lip, and he wanted to laugh at the way her tongue kept finding its way to the corner of her mouth. He had never seen anyone so serious.

"You aren't pulling, milord. Your taffy should be getting lighter in color by now. See how much lighter mine is than yours?" She held the piece she was pulling up to him and damn his eyes if he didn't pull harder.

When the taffy was light enough in color to please her, she announced that it was ready to stretch into twisted ropes. Imagining these were ropes to fasten around the neck of that hell-horse, Quinn found he enjoyed this part best. That is, until she began to cut the twisted lengths into small pieces.

"Now what?" he heard himself asking.

"You eat it," she said, laughing and coming up on her tiptoes, bringing a piece to place against his lips. He opened his mouth, and she shoved the taffy inside. He almost choked, so surprised he was from the jolting shock of her fingers brushing against his mouth.

He looked down, drinking in the sight of her, her face damp from the steamy kitchen, her hair curling about her face, but it was the shining light of pure, unadulterated enjoyment that danced in her eyes that was his undoing. Consequently, he could only stand there and gape, seemingly paralyzed in every limb—save one.

She smiled up at him and poked another piece into his mouth.

"Keep doing that, and I might become accustomed to having you feed me," he said, feeling foolish. Only the desire to keep watching her, to see the adoring look in her eyes, prompted him to play along.

When he looked up he saw Richard and Harry giving him dark looks, and suddenly he remembered his plan. Those adoring looks of hers were not for him and in the end, they would only make it more difficult to give her up to another man.

The judgmental looks in his friends eyes prompted him to be harsher with her than he intended. "I thought the dressmaker brought your new clothes."

"Oh, she did, milord, and they are quite lovely. Please forgive me for not thanking you before now."

"It is not your thanks I want, Caroline, but to see you dressed in something besides rags. The clothes were ordered so you would wear them, not leave them hanging in your wardrobe. Have one on the next time I see you."

Without giving her the opportunity to say anything, he turned on his heels and left the room.

Caroline began gathering up the twisted ropes of taffy.

"What's wrong with him?" Harry asked.

"His mind is full of scorpions," Richard said.

Harry nodded in Caroline's direction—where she busied herself across the room—raising his brows in question, as if asking, "Her?"

"None other," Richard said. "The lad has erred and put things into motion that he is finding he regrets."

"Well, it isn't too late to change things," Harry said.

"No, but you won't be able to say that for long," Richard replied. "Mistakes have halfway marks when they can be recalled or remedied. After that, there is no turning back."

"I'm not so certain Quinn realizes that," Harry said.

"Neither am I, and that is what irritates the blazes out of me."

Out of the blue, Squire Toliver came to call upon Caroline. She was surprised, because he lived way over in Coombe Valley.

Caroline, not forgetting what Quinn had said the day before about her clothes, put on one of the new gowns, but when she looked at her reflection in the mirror, she stopped dead in her tracks.

The dress was cut low. Dangerously low. Sinfully low. Suggestively low.

She couldn't very well greet Squire Toliver with her bosom almost bare.

She looked at her reflection again. The soft-blue gauze dress was a lovely color, with small puffed sleeves and an empire waistline, *a la Josephine.* But it was too low-cut. She frowned. *One more reason to hate Napoleon . . .*

There was no way on God's green earth she would wear a gown that low-cut, and she did not give a fiddle if every woman in London, Paris, *and* Rome wore them.

She would not.

She was sitting on the bed, bemoaning her fate, for only that morning, Mrs. Witherspoon, acting on Quinn's instructions, had removed every single one of Caroline's old dresses, and now the only clothes she had were new ones. *Low-cut* new ones. Only her new blueberry-colored riding habit had a decent neckline, and she could not very well go downstairs to greet the squire in her riding habit.

A few minutes later, Mrs. Witherspoon came in. "My, my, don't you look lovely, with your hair all put up fancylike." Then Caroline turned around, and Mrs. Witherspoon's eyes nearly popped out.

"Oh, my stars and underdrawers!" Mrs. Witherspoon said.

"My thoughts exactly," Caroline said.

"You cannot go downstairs in that," Mrs. Witherspoon said. "Poor old Squire Toliver would have apoplexy."

"No," Caroline said, "I cannot go down like this, and thanks to his lordship, I have nothing else to wear, save my dressing gown and my riding habit."

"What are you going to do?" asked Mrs. Witherspoon.

"I don't know," Caro said. "Do you have any suggestions?"

Mrs. Witherspoon looked helpless. "Dear child, the only remedy I know anything about is mustard plasters" —she eyed Caro's bosom again—"and somehow I don't think a mustard plaster is what you need."

"No," said Caro, "I don't either." Without another word, Caroline headed for the door.

"Are you going downstairs?"

"No, I am going upstairs."

Mrs. Witherspoon looked puzzled. "But, you *are* upstairs," she said.

"I am going farther up," Caroline said, "to the attic."

"The attic?"

"You can go down and tell the squire that you cannot find me, that you have searched both the first floor and the second floor and I am nowhere to be found. I, of course, will be on the third floor, so you will not be telling a lie."

"The squire has ridden a long way. What if he and Quinn continue their visit through lunch? What will you do in the attic in the meantime?"

"I have been meaning to straighten things out up there for some time. This is the perfect opportunity."

"What will you tell Quinn when he asks you where you were?"

Caroline smiled sweetly. "Why, the truth, of course."

Mrs. Witherspoon smiled. "Of course."

He found her three hours later, in the dust-laden dimness of the attic, standing at one of the open dormer windows, watching a robin sitting on its eggs. She stood with her back to him, shafts of sunlight pouring around her, her silhouette a gray shadow against the summer sun's brightness.

He made his way through the years' assemblage of clutter, noticing a large trunk that stood open, filled with yellowing clothes. He came closer, stopping just behind her, close enough that he could smell her fragrance, close enough to see the scattering of fine hairs that had pulled loose from her upswept hairdo.

"I thought I might find you here. But only after I searched everywhere else."

She did not turn around. "How long have you been looking for me?"

"A good hour and a half."

"Are you angry with me?"

"I was, but that has passed."

"I'm sorry."

"I am, too," he said, "for a lot of things. Mrs. Witherspoon told me about the dress."

"I could not wear it."

"You are wearing it now, are you not?"

"Yes, but only with my mother's shawl."

He noticed then, that she had a beautiful cream-colored silk shawl around her shoulders, the long, silky strands of fringe hanging past her elbows. Suddenly, she seemed so very small, small and alone, isolated, and perhaps a little afraid. He felt responsible knowing he had made decisions that not only affected her now, but ones that would affect her for the rest of her life. He could never remember playing so callously with another person's life, and she, of all people, was not someone he wanted to hurt. Even as he stood there, he knew the folly of what he was thinking, the foolishness of what he wanted to do.

To hold her. That was all he wanted.

"Mrs. Witherspoon was concerned about you."

"She understood about the dress."

"Am I allowed to have an opinion?"

"It was your opinion that landed me in this dress, milord."

"Please. Would you show me?"

She turned toward him, slowly, obediently, her head lowered so that he could see the straight part down the middle of her head. Her hands were crossed over her chest, the silk shawl clutched tightly in her fists. With a feeling akin to pity, he reached out to her, taking her hands in his, and with a gentle tugging motion, urged them away. Beneath where her hands had been, the shawl was knotted. Using slow, precise movements, he began to untie the knot, until at last it fell away.

How lovely she was, with skin as pure and rich as cream. If he had to use one word to describe her, that word would be . . . *innocent.*

"Look at me."

She lifted her head, turning it slightly aside, too shy, or perhaps too embarrassed to look him in the eye. He lifted her chin until she was looking at him. "You are lovely," he said, "but you are also right, this dress is not for you. What looks right on the ladies of the ton becomes quite cheap on you."

She released a long-held breath, and he could see the relieved expression on her face. "I would like to have the dresses redone."

"By all means, do," he said, "but not until . . ."

Her eyes searched his. "Until what?"

"This," he said, and leaning closer, he kissed the swelling flesh of each of her breasts, where they rose above the bodice of her gown. Unable to stop, his lips searched higher, and higher, nuzzling her throat and ear with his mouth. He heard her gasp.

"Why are you doing this?"

"If I only knew," he said, then he buried his face in the curve of her shoulder, his arms coming around her, dragging her against him, against the heated hardness of his body. He felt her shudder when his hands dropped lower, to caress the softness of her buttocks, pressing her against him. "You are so lovely. Every inch of you is perfect, every part of your body seems to melt and form itself to mine. How did this happen? I only came up here to tell you it was time to come down to dress for dinner."

"I don't know. I only know it happens to me as well. My life has not been the same since you came to Fairfields. I have only felt this way once before in my life—when I fell out of the barn when I was playing hide-and-seek. I remember the sensation of falling through space; it was both exciting and terrifying, and for a moment I thought I was going to die. That is how I feel when you look at me, when your skin touches mine."

She looked into his face, searching his eyes. Guilt gnawed at him. She was being so open, so honest with him, and for the first time in his life, the Marquess of Waverly knew shame. He turned his head away, unable to bear the truth in her eyes.

"You have become so much more than my guardian," she whispered, and then she turned from him and disappeared.

Mrs. Witherspoon found him half an hour later, standing in the dusky shadows of the attic, staring out an open dormer window, a cream silk shawl in his hands.

CHAPTER ❨ NINE

The Marquess of Waverly was in a foul humor.

Everyone at Fairfields agreed he had been that way since arising that morning. No one could put a reason to it. No one dared try. The entire staff avoided him. Hector growled whenever he came near. As for Caroline, she simply left, early that morning, to visit her friend Fanny. That left Richard and Harry, who went to great lengths to stay out of his way.

Quinn's humor was so foul that not even The Bolter would have anything to do with him.

And that suited Quinn just fine.

Brooding in his study, Quinn did not bother to look up when Richard and Harry came in.

"What ill tidings do the two of you bring?" he asked, his attention riveted upon the papers in front of him.

"We've come to bring you a bit of jolly good news. There's another suitor for you to reject," Harry said. "This one is waiting in the parlor."

Quinn looked up, a scowl upon his face. "And what makes you two prophets think I'll reject this one?"

"Because you reject *all* of her suitors," Richard said, doubling over with laughter.

"And we know why," Harry said.

Quinn leaned back in his chair, the leather creaking as he lifted his feet to rest upon the top of his desk. "And why is that?"

"Because you're in love with her yourself," Richard said, "and there will never be a man who will measure up in your eyes. Why don't you call this whole absurd thing off and marry her yourself. If it's gossip you're worried about—"

Quinn sprang to his feet, the back of the chair slapping forward with a loud *thwump!* Leaning over the top of his desk, he braced himself with his hands widespread. The veins on his forehead stood out, and each word he spoke was carefully chosen. "I am not worried about gossip, and I am not in love with her. Now, why don't you tell me who is waiting in the parlor, and then get the hell out of here."

"Edgarton," Richard said. "As in the earl of."

"Edgarton?" Quinn repeated, unable to believe it himself. "Are you certain it's Edgarton?"

"Oh, it's Edgarton, all right. All six feet of him, spit-polished, combed, looking good enough to warm the coldest virgin heart." Richard looked at Harry and grinned, like he was loving this, and Quinn supposed he was.

Bastard.

As if he could read Quinn's thoughts, Richard burst out laughing, then said to Harry with mock exaggeration. "I say, don't you think it's a bloody good thing that Quinn isn't in love with her, since it's highly possible that the lovely Caroline might come to prefer the earl's attentions over his."

"By Jove, I think you're right!" Harry exclaimed, with such enthusiasm Quinn wanted to choke him. "After all, what simple-hearted lass wouldn't prefer a tall, dashing earl to a brooding, nasty-tempered marquess? Why, I hear that The Bolter ignores him now."

"No," Richard said, aghast. "She doesn't."

Doing his best to look crestfallen, Harry shook his head sadly, and said, "I'm afraid it's true."

"That's enough!" Quinn shouted, but no one heard him, his voice drowned out by the sound of hastily departing feet and clamorous laughter, as Richard and Harry made a quick and timely departure.

As Quinn walked toward the parlor, he tried to imagine what brought the Earl of Edgarton out to offer for Caroline. Whatever it was, it wasn't the dowry. Edgarton had more money than the pope had saints. What struck him as odd about all of this was the fact that since Edgarton's young wife died in childbirth four years ago, Edgarton had virtually dropped out of sight.

It was curiosity more than anything, that sent Quinn to see Edgarton. He did not waste any time before asking. Edgarton's response was immediate.

"I am offering for her for several reasons," Edgarton said. "First off, she is a country girl, and that pleases me immensely, for I prefer to live in the country. Secondly, she has not been tainted by London and the ton. Thirdly, she is quite lovely and pleasingly mannered. Aside from that, it is time I married again. I want someone to share my life with, someone to give me children. I knew the moment I saw her coming out of church several Sundays ago, that she was the one."

"I knew it was not the dowry," Quinn said, offering Edgarton a cigar.

"No, it definitely was not the dowry. In fact, I would take her if she had no dowry." Edgarton paused, giving Quinn a direct look. "So, Waverly, what is your answer? Do I have your permission to ask your lovely ward for her hand?"

Quinn looked at Edgarton. Of course, he could not fault him on his appearance, for Edgarton was a splendidly handsome man, tall, slender, with chestnut hair and gray eyes that seemed to set a woman's heart aflutter. Nor could he fault him on his lineage, which was impeccable, and being an earl, well, that meant he was second only to a duke. He was definitely wealthy, and his holdings were rivaled only by those of the king. No, Quinn could not fault him on any of those points. But none of those considerations were the reason why Quinn agreed to Edgarton's suit.

At this moment, Quinn chanced to look out the window and see Richard and Harry strolling across the yard. Still chafing from their nettling, Quinn accepted Lord Edgarton's suit, promising Caroline's hand in marriage, for one reason and one reason only: to prove to Richard and Harry that they were wrong.

There. He had done it, at last. He had given his permission. That proved he did not love her. How could a man who loved a woman promise her to another?

He did not stop to think that there might come a time when he would have to answer that question.

Caroline took the long way back from Fanny's, walking along the coastline, where the cliffs swept down to the gray-green serpentine rocks that were pounded by a wild surf, as if the churning foam's only purpose was to serve as a point of contrast between an azure sea and the pale golden sands.

She removed her bonnet, tied the strings together, and slipped it over her arm. Then she removed her shoes and stockings and placed them in the bonnet. She walked slowly along the water's edge, allowing the water to swirl around her feet, and not minding when her petticoats got a good soaking.

It was while she stood with her feet bathed in sea foam that she had a feeling she was being watched. Turning around and shielding her eyes from the sun, she saw Quinn riding down the beach toward her. For a moment, she was torn with indecision. Part of her wanted to wait here for him, to wait forever, if that was how long it took for him to realize how things could be between them. Yet, another part of her wanted to escape to the security and peace of her room, to avoid him altogether. His presence gave her no peace. Not anymore. She could not remember how long it had been since she had been able to look at him without feeling she was dying inside.

Her body grew tense, her nerves on edge as she watched him ride closer then dismount. She searched his face for some clue as to why he had come, but his emotions were too well guarded. Not one hint came to her from the depths of those dark eyes.

"I have been looking for you everywhere," he said.

She forced a smile. "I went to Fanny's, milord. Did you forget that I told you?"

The wind whipped his black hair and she wanted to reach up, to smooth it back, much as she would a child's, but she dared not. Too well she knew what it would cost her if she touched him.

"No," he said, "I remembered. I rode over there, but Fanny said you left some time ago. When I did not over-take you, and when I did not find you at Fairfields, I became concerned. It was only when I asked Mrs. Witherspoon, that I learned you sometimes liked to walk along the shore."

"Yes," she said, turning away from him to stare out over the water. "I love it here. There is something sooth-ing about the sea, don't you think? Healing, almost. Whenever I am sad or upset, I find myself drawn to the water."

"And are you . . . sad?"

"No, milord, I am not sad exactly—it is just that I would have this suitor business cleared up. It is dis-turbing to know your future is so uncertain."

"Well, perhaps I have some news that will cheer you. I have reached a decision."

She turned to look at him then, hoping, praying with all her heart that he had come to tell her that he would not force her to marry someone else, because he had come to realize he cared for her himself. He looked so handsome, so tempting standing before her with the sun-light dancing in his hair. *Tell me. Tell me that you care. Tell me you cannot bear to let me go.*

"I have just had a visit from the Earl of Edgarton."

Her whole body prickled. "The Earl of Edgarton," she repeated dully, unable to understand.

"He has offered for you, Caroline, and I cannot fault him, so I have accepted his offer and—" He stopped and looked at her. "Don't do that, Caroline. Please try to understand."

She knew what he was going to say, and she so desper-ately wanted it not to be so, that she had clamped her hands over her ears, as if by that one act, she could change the course of her life. *No . . . please tell me this is not why you have come. Tell me you have come for a hundred other reasons. Lie to me. Deceive me. Break my heart, if you must. But please do not destroy me by giving me so coldly to another. At least show some sign that you care.*

He stepped closer to her, and reaching out, took her

hands in his, drawing them away from her ears and bringing them down between them. He continued to hold them, his thumbs stroking the back of her hands as if understanding might flow from him and into her.

She pulled her hands away, then turning away herself, she began walking up the beach.

"Caroline, please . . . wait a minute. Let me talk to you. Let me explain."

Caroline broke into a run. She ran until her legs no longer felt like they were part of her body, and her lungs felt as if they would burst. When she felt as if she could run no farther, she heard the sound of his horse thundering behind her, the softly muffled sound of the hooves striking wet sand as they came closer.

Unable to outrun him, she turned, running through the water now, her movements slow and sluggish the deeper she went, her sodden skirt dragging her down. She fell once, but came quickly to her feet. It was then that she felt his arm coil around her and she was lifted, kicking and fighting, from the water.

He carried her to the beach before releasing her, where she collapsed in a heap of soggy, wet clothing, too exhausted to run, too numb to think of anything save the truth: *He gave me away.*

"Caroline . . ."

"Please don't say anything."

For a long time, he did not speak, but simply sat upon his horse, his shadow, long and dark, stretching over her. At last, when he spoke, his voice was impersonal. "Give me your hand and I'll take you home. Edgarton will be back at eight. He would like to speak with you."

"I will walk home."

"Caro . . ."

"Don't call me that, for to do so indicates closeness, a fondness, and we both know that does not exist between us."

She knew he was angry. He did not speak, but whirled his horse around, spurring the animal so hard that he leaped forward.

Caroline did not move until he was completely out of sight.

* * *

She was glad he did not force her to ride back with him, for walking gave her the opportunity to think. She was devastated, of course, for she knew she had been in love with him for some time now, always taking hope that because he had rejected suitor after suitor, he cared—hoping, praying even, that he would realize he could never give her to another simply because he wanted to marry her himself.

She sighed, feeling the pain in her lungs subsiding, and knowing that the pain in her heart would take much, much longer to go away.

It is done . . .

She barely recovered from that shock when she had another. She could never hold up under the strain of being around him day after day during an engagement. She was afraid now, terrified even, that she would weaken to the point of confessing her love for him. She realized too, that she not only wanted a short engagement, but she did not want to be married at Fairfields. She could not bear the thought of having him walk her down the aisle and callously give her away.

Upon reaching Fairfields, she quickly changed her wet clothes and arranged her hair, then went downstairs. Quinn was waiting at the bottom of the stairs for her. The moment she had been dreading had come at last.

He took her hand and drew her arm through his. Neither of them spoke as they walked down the hallway to where her future waited. If she had anything to be thankful for, it was that, upon seeing her, the Earl of Edgarton, bless him, smiled radiantly.

After making the introductions, Quinn made a hasty departure, leaving her alone with the earl.

"Why don't we take a walk in the gardens?" Edgarton said. "I have heard how much you love to work with flowers. Perhaps you will be more comfortable there."

Caroline looked into the earl's eyes. She could be thankful, at least, that they marked him to be a kind man, just as his words indicated he had the capacity for understanding. But even as she felt grateful, her mind was screaming, *It isn't Quinn . . .*

No, it wasn't Quinn, but she could have done worse.

"Thank you, milord. I would like that," she said.

Outside he took her arm and guided her to a stone bench beside a fountain. Caroline arranged her skirts about her, feeling more at ease here among her flowers, just as he had suggested.

Sitting next to her, Edgarton said, "I know this must be difficult for you, Caroline. Please believe that I will do everything in my power to make this easier for you, for it is my upmost goal to always see you happy."

"Thank you, milord."

He smiled, and for an instant she wished with all her heart that she was in love with this man, for he was truly everything she could have wished for, and more.

"Please call me William, or Will, if it suits you."

"I like William," she said, giving him a shy smile. "It was my grandfather's name, and it suits you, I think."

"Ah, yes, your grandfather, the duke. Did you know that my father was a good friend of your grandfather's? They were boyhood friends."

"No," she said, "I did not know. I know very little about my grandfather, you see."

"I'm sorry. Well, let's get on to the business at hand. I think, perhaps, that you would have many questions you would like answered. I am certain that upon finding yourself betrothed to someone you had never met, you were properly horrified."

"It is not as I would have had it."

"No, I suppose not." He paused a moment, looking down at her. "If I had it in my power to grant you anything, Caroline, what would it be?"

"An immediate wedding . . . in Scotland."

He drew back as if shocked. "Scotland?"

She nodded. "Gretna Green."

"Hmm, I see, or perhaps I don't."

She turned to look at him. It relieved her to see he was smiling. "I prefer not to have a lengthy engagement, for that would mean I would have to remain here, at Fairfields. I know I am a burden to my guardian, you see. I would like nothing better than to remove myself from—"

"I understand," he said, his hand covered hers, giving it a squeeze. "You need not explain."

"You are not upset with me?"

"How could I be? I too, would prefer such a marriage. I don't know if Quinn told you, but I was married before. My wife died in childbirth four years ago."

"I am sorry."

"I am over that now," he said. "Time, as they say, heals all wounds."

Except mine.

"Since this is my second marriage, and since I removed myself from London society a long time ago, an elopement suits me perfectly." He leaned forward and kissed her forehead. "How soon can you be ready?"

"I am ready now, William."

At that, the Earl of Edgarton threw back his leonine head and laughed. "Well, my little partridge, I am happy to report that I did secure a license before I spoke with your guardian. Perhaps it was nothing more than a spurt of masculine arrogance, or perhaps it was foolheaded optimism."

"Or perhaps it was destiny," she said quietly.

The earl smiled. "I like that reason best of all."

"I shall do everything in my power to make you happy," she said.

"You have already done that," he said. "Shall I come for you tonight?"

Her heart slammed in her chest. As if sensing her panic, he said, "If your trepidation comes from wondering if you will be forced to climb out your window, don't worry."

"I was not worried, milord. I have climbed out my window many times."

He gave her a teasing look. "Recently?" he asked.

"The last time was less than a fortnight ago."

With that, the Earl of Edgarton gave her a delighted hug. "Then by all means climb out the window. I will go now, to tell Waverly that I wish to take you to my home tonight, so that you might meet my family. Once we're in the carriage, we will make for Scotland."

And make for Scotland, they did.

CHAPTER ❈ TEN

$\mathcal{L}$ater that evening, Quinn watched the Earl of Edgarton's coach as it disappeared down the drive, taking part of his heart with it.

He had done what he set out to do. He had rid himself of his burdensome ward.

So why doesn't it feel the way I thought it would?

In his heart he knew. He could no longer deny it. He cared for her and cared deeply.

But is it love?

He couldn't answer that, but one thing he knew: He could not, would not, allow this marriage with Edgarton to take place. Strange, how it had taken the sight of her driving off with Edgarton to bring him to his senses. He could not let her go.

For now, he could only wait, until Edgarton brought her home, then he would talk with him. He would send Caroline to her room, then take Edgarton into the library, and over cigars and brandy, like the gentlemen they were, they would talk. Quinn would confess his feelings for her, and hopefully Edgarton, like the gentleman he was, would understand.

Quinn did not get to plan further, for a knock upon the door interrupted his thoughts.

"Come in."

The door opened and Mrs. Witherspoon stepped inside. "I have come to tell you, milord, that dinner is not served."

Quinn gave her a strange look. "Not served?"

"No, milord. The cook and the kitchen staff have quit."

"Quit."

"Yes, milord, and the maids, and the groom as well."

"All quit?"

"As in gone, your lordship."

"I see," Quinn said, not really seeing at all. After looking thoughtful for a moment, he inquired further. "And might I ask the reason for this hasty departure?"

"It's Miss Caroline, milord. They are sorely grieved over your callous treatment of her."

Quinn nodded. "Hmm. Well, it looks like that just leaves me and you, then, doesn't it?"

"No, milord, it does not."

"No?"

"I have quit, as well."

"Perhaps your departure is a bit hasty, Mrs. Witherspoon, for I have come to realize that I have made a grave mistake."

"Yes, milord, you have, but that will not bring the staff back into your good graces any more than it will bring Miss Caroline back."

"No, but it might if you tell them that I do not intend to allow my ward to marry the Earl of Edgarton."

Mrs. Witherspoon looked properly stupefied. "If I may be so bold, milord, may I inquire as to what you intend to do?"

"I intend to marry her myself."

Mrs. Witherspoon's face lit up. "Oh, glory be," she said, and then, "well my stars! Who would have thought it?"

"Not the staff, apparently," Quinn said.

Quinn opened his mouth to say something else, but Mrs. Witherspoon's expression became one of panic. Holding her hand up in the air, she said, "Wait, milord. I'll be right back."

He had never seen so much woman move so fast, for Mrs. Witherspoon fairly shot from the room like she had a bee in her corset.

Quinn poured himself a glass of port and stared at the door in a bemused way. Before the night was over this would all be solved. He would have his life back. He would have his staff back. And he would have his love back.

Coming back into the room a few minutes later, Mrs. Witherspoon did look a bit the worse for wear, for she was fairly rumpled, and her hair had taken on a certain wildness. "Begging your lordship's pardon, but time was of the essence. You see, the staff was on their way out, and I had not a moment's time to waste."

"And did you intercept them in time?"

Mrs. Witherspoon swelled to a self-righteous size. "That I did, your lordship."

"And have they agreed to come back?"

"They have, your lordship."

Quinn nodded. "I am relieved to hear that."

"Thank you, your lordship. And may I also say that Cook, in particular, was especially happy."

"Oh, and what did Cook say?"

"That the prodigal son had returned, and it was time to kill the fatted calf, which means she is, at the moment, lopping the head off a chicken. She also said she would have you a meal fit for a king in less than an hour's time."

"Yes," Quinn said, allowing Mrs. Witherspoon's euphoria to spread to him. "I suppose I will need my strength when it comes time to fence with the Earl of Edgarton."

Mrs. Witherspoon's face paled. "Fence? Oh, your lordship, you must not risk your life. Why, think of poor Caro, if she were to lose you about the same time she won you."

Quinn gave her a disapproving look. "And I thank you, Mrs. Witherspoon, for that vote of confidence. In spite of your lack of faith in my dueling abilities, I meant only to banter words with the earl, not to fight him."

"Oh, your lordship," she said, her hand coming up to spread over her ample bosom. "I cannot tell you what a relief that is. Now, if there is anything you need, you've only to ask. I know this must be a trying time for you, but rest assured, your lordship, that you are doing the just and right and honorable thing. It is during times like these that we learn life's biggest lessons. It isn't your fault, your lordship, that you were such a blockhead, always having to learn things the hard way. And what would we be—the staff and myself—if we did not understand that? I know you feel all alone in this, but I must tell you that it is times like these—"

"Mrs. Witherspoon?"

"Yes, your lordship?"

"Would you be so good as to shut your mouth?"

She paused. "Yes, your lordship. Will there be anything else, your lordship?"

"No, Mrs. Witherspoon, there is not. Now, will you leave me blessedly alone?"

"Yes, your lordship."

As Mrs. Witherspoon departed, Quinn added, "Please ask the staff to tell me the moment Edgarton's carriage arrives."

Mrs. Witherspoon nodded and crept quietly from the room in a mouselike way.

Quinn's optimism lasted for several hours. He did not begin to worry until half-past midnight, and the Earl of Edgarton's carriage had still not returned. As if that were not enough, Richard and Harry put in an appearance.

The two of them had been to dinner at Lady Buffington's, and by the time they arrived at Fairfields, they were looking pretty well foxed.

Quinn's news sobered them up.

"Have you sent anyone to Edgarton's? Perhaps their carriage has broken down," Richard said.

"I dispatched someone over an hour ago," Quinn replied. "If he's not back soon, I'll go to Edgarton's myself."

At half-past three, Fairfield's groom informed the three men waiting in the library that no one at the Earl of Edgarton's home had seen either the earl or his betrothed.

"They must have broken down before they got there," Harry said, "but where?"

"Are you certain they were going to his home here, and not to London to meet his family?" Richard asked.

"No," Quinn replied, "they were going to his home here unless . . ."

"Unless what?" Harry and Richard asked in unison.

"Unless they never intended to go to Edgarton's."

"Where would they have gone, then?" asked Harry.

"I don't know, but I intend to find out," Quinn replied, leaving the room.

"Where are you going?" Richard called out.

"I'm going to her room. Perhaps I'll find something there, some hint, some clue."

A minute later, Quinn lit the lamp in Caroline's room. He could see nothing out of the ordinary aside from the normal womanly clutter and was about to quit the room, when he noticed a folded piece of paper propped against the pillows on her bed.

His heart thudding painfully in his chest, Quinn put the lamp on the bedside table and reached for the note.

"Bloody hell!" he shouted.

Richard and Harry shot into the room. A second later, Mrs. Witherspoon came thundering in, her nightcap askew, her slippers flapping.

"What is it?" Richard asked.

"She's eloped," Harry said.

"How do you know?" Richard asked, looking at Harry.

"You can see it on his face," Harry said, looking at Quinn.

"Is that true, your lordship?" asked Mrs. Witherspoon. "Has she eloped, then?"

"Yes," Quinn said, "I'm afraid that's exactly what she's done." The note was addressed to Mrs. Witherspoon and Quinn handed the note to her.

She scanned the note. "Miss Caroline says here that she loves you, your lordship, and that is why she had to elope. She could not bear to have you give her away."

"I have read the bleeding note, Mrs. Witherspoon."

"Oh, yes . . . beg pardon. Of course you've read it, your lordship."

"Go back to bed," Quinn said. "There is nothing more to be done here."

"Yes, your lordship," Mrs. Witherspoon said, and turned sadly away, tucking the note deep into the pocket of her dressing gown.

Harry and Richard followed Quinn downstairs. "What are you going to do now?" Harry asked.

"I'm going after her, of course," Quinn said. "The bloody bastard has eloped with her. It's the same as kidnapping."

"Not exactly. You did give Edgarton your permission," Richard reminded him.

"I gave him permission to ask for her hand. I sure as hell didn't give him permission to abduct the rest of her."

Richard smiled and looked at Harry, who whispered something to him, then left the room. "Irregardless, you can't just abduct her out from under his nose."

Quinn turned around. "No, perhaps I can't, but the highwayman can."

CHAPTER ☾ ELEVEN

*I*ntrigued, Richard followed Quinn to his room, where he stood watching, as Quinn began to rummage through a large chest.

"Where's Harry?" Quinn asked.

"He went to tell the groom to take the saddle off his horse and to put yours on him."

Quinn paused. "Why would he do that? I've got a horse of my own."

"Yes, but yours is a chestnut, and every schoolboy knows a highwayman always rides a black," Richard said. "You did ride Harry's horse the night of the ball, when you robbed Sir Artemis, remember?"

"I did not rob him, and I will thank you to keep my activities under your hat."

Quinn was about to say he would rather take his own horse, black or not, but at that moment, Harry came in, drawing to a dramatic stop. "What? You're not dressed yet?" Harry asked.

Quinn grunted and returned to his rummaging. A moment later, he pulled out the highwayman's garb.

Richard chuckled. "Well, well, an enchanted moment."

"Go to hell, Richard."

"Do you need any help?" Harry asked.

"No, I've got everything under control."

Richard smiled at that. "Do you really think you've got a prayer, Waverly? They've been gone for some time now."

Stripped down to his underwear, Quinn was hopping around the room on one foot, trying to get his bloody foot into those damnably tight highwayman's breeches. He rammed one leg inside. "True, but they also happen to be in a carriage, and we both know how abominable the roads between here and Scotland are. Their traveling will be slow at best. Besides, if I know Edgarton, he won't expect Caroline to travel straight through. They'll stop over at some inn."

Harry raised his brows. "At an inn, you say?"

Catching Harry's drift, Quinn said, "Edgarton may be a lot of things, but he is honorable. He won't compromise her. I'm certain of that."

"For your sake, I hope you're right," Richard replied.

At that, Quinn lost his balance and had to lean against the bedpost for support. "Bloody hell!"

"I think you've got them on backward," Harry offered.

"Bloody hell!"

"Here, let me help," Harry said.

Quinn froze. "I can put my own bleedin' pants on."

"Well, in that case, I'll just *watch.*"

Once he had the pants on, Quinn grabbed the white shirt, cursing when he discovered it was wrong side out.

"Didn't your mother teach you to turn your shirts right side out *before* putting them away?" Richard asked.

"I'm warning you," Quinn said, his face turning dark.

"Yes, and I'm terrified," Richard said.

Quinn ignored him, grabbing up his boots and putting them on.

"You can wear those that way if you want to, of course, but if I were you, I'd put them on the other feet," Richard said.

Quinn looked down, seeing the toes of his boots were splayed outward like a cow's feet. If he didn't know better, he would swear someone had set out deliberately to sabotage him. He opened his mouth.

"Bloody hell!" Harry said for him.

"Where's my damn sword," asked Quinn.

"Rapier," Richard said, handing it to him.

"And here's your plumed hat, milord," Harry said,

taking a sweeping bow, the feather's of his tricorn brushing Quinn's face.

Quinn snarled and yanked the hat out of his hands. "I don't know how I was so bloody fortunate to land *two* buffoons for friends. One would have been too many."

"*Two* buffoons? And here I thought there were three of us," Richard said. "Like the Musketeers."

Quinn ignored him and began buckling his rapier around his waist. A moment later, he turned to get his coat and tripped over the long rapier hanging at his side.

He fell flat on the floor.

The way things were going, he was tempted to stay there, but duty called and he had no time to waste. "Good God! A man could get killed like this. I don't know how a bloody highwayman did it," Quinn said, trying to untangle himself.

"You've got it under control all right," Richard said.

Quinn lunged for him and Richard laughed, jumping out of the way. Looking at his friend, he smiled and said, "Are we cross?"

"As two sticks," Harry said, following Quinn and Richard from the room.

When they reached the stables, the groom was brushing Harry's black horse.

"Never mind all that brushing," Quinn said. "Just get my saddle. Time is of the essence, man."

While the groom went for the saddle, Harry said, "Maybe you should take The Bolter. I don't think there's a horse anywhere that could outrun her."

"The Bolter is white, numskull."

"Oh, and a highwayman always rides a black," Harry said in such a sincere way that Richard doubled over with laughter.

A moment later, Quinn leaped upon the back of the black and said, "Would it be too much to ask?"

Richard and Harry looked at each other and then at Quinn. "Beg pardon?" Richard said.

"Get the hell out of the doorway, so I can be on my way," Quinn shouted.

Richard and Harry made a big to-do about standing aside as Quinn rode between them.

Laughing, Richard turned to Harry and clapping him on the back, shouted loudly, as if Caroline would somehow hear, "Fear not, fair maiden, help is on the way."

"If he doesn't fall off his bloody horse first," Harry said, joining Richard's laughter.

Still grinning, they stood together, watching as Quinn thundered down the road, never suspecting that he wasn't riding Harry's horse, but The Bolter, which the groom had covered with bootblack.

Miles and miles away, a fast traveling coach sped along a lonely stretch of road, guided only by a thin show of moonlight as it made its way north. Inside the coach, Caroline stared out the window, seeing nothing, feeling nothing, numb inside. Some things hurt too much even to cry over.

She glanced at William, who slept soundly beside her. Not wanting him to see her sadness, she turned her face toward the window again.

It was on such a night, she remembered, on Midsummer's Eve, when the moon danced with the clouds in just this way, that the highwayman came. How very long ago that was, how romantic it had all seemed. It had been so very real, but now it was nothing more than a memory. Would there come a time when Quinn was nothing more than a memory as well?

Memories. What good were they? All they caused was pain. Memories did not ease her grief, or the sick feeling inside, or the frightening despair. They could not give her what she wanted, they could only remind her of what she did not have. They could not make him love her, nor lighten the burden of knowing she was soon to wed one man, while her heart would always belong to another.

She watched the moon come out from behind a cloud, a ribbon of moonlight shining down like a silver pathway, and she thought again of the highwayman, of the days before the pain. If only she could go back to that night, the night she was infatuated with a dashing highwayman. She sighed, feeling tired. How she envied William his sound sleep. For her, sleep would not come.

How could it? Regret never sleeps.

*The wind was a torrent of darkness among the gusty
  trees,
The moon was a ghostly galleon tossed upon cloudy seas,
The road was a ribbon of moonlight over the purple
  moor,
And the highwayman came riding . . . riding . . .
  riding . . .*

—Alfred Noyes, "The Highwayman"

CHAPTER ❨ TWELVE

Out of the night he came, on a mottled black horse,
riding through the mist. A phantom keeping his tryst. A
knight of the road. The noblest of criminals. A gentleman bandit. The scourge of England.

The highwayman.

Mounted on his horse, high-booted with gleaming silver spurs, his clothes and cape were black as the night
that surrounded him, his hat the tricorn of a gentleman.
His face was hidden in shadow and masked. A rapier
gleamed at his side.

Swift as a shadow he came, out of the darkness that
flanked the lonely road, a brace of gleaming pistols
drawn.

"Stand and deliver!"

The driver hit the brake and pulled back on the reins.
The coach came to a rocking stop.

Caroline felt herself thrown to the floor.

Reaching for her, the Earl of Edgarton said, "What
the blazes is going on?"

Before anyone could answer, the coach door opened.
"Get out!" the highwayman said.

Edgarton poked his head through the doorway.

"Not you," said the highwayman. "Help the lady out."

"Over my dead body," Edgarton protested.

Without hesitation the highwayman pointed the pistol at his head. "That can be arranged . . ."

Drawing his head back, Edgarton gave Caroline an odd look, then took her hand, helping her through the coach door. The moment her foot touched the first step, she felt the highwayman's arm whip around her waist and she was hoisted into midair. A split-second later, she was thrust, facedown, across his horse.

As they galloped away in the darkness, Caroline could see nothing. Soon the highwayman paused long enough to pull her upright and into his arms, then settled her comfortably in front of him. A second later, they were off again, thundering down the road, then cutting across the moors to God only knew where.

After some time, they rode into the yard of what appeared to be a modest hunting lodge. Once Caroline was out of the saddle and her feet were on solid ground, she barraged him with questions. Not bothering to answer her, he took her by the arm, ushered her inside and pushed her toward a small chair, where she gratefully collapsed. She watched him prowl about the dark room, a dark, shadowy outline.

Suddenly, the room was flooded with a warm glowing light. She watched in awe, as he turned up the lamp.

Even with his back to her, there was something awfully familiar about this particular highwayman, and she decided it had to be her gentleman bandit from Midsummer's Eve.

Transfixed, she watched as he removed his cape, his rapier, his hat. But it was when his hands came up to untie his mask that she knew.

"Quinn," she whispered, unable to believe. "It was you the night of the Masquerade Ball. I cannot . . ."

The words died in her throat. Quinn did not stop with just the removal of his rapier, hat, cape, and mask. As she watched, dry-mouthed, he began to unbutton his shirt.

"What are you doing?"

"I am going to make love to you, sweet Caroline Flowers—the loveliest flower in all of England—and soon to be the deflowered Miss Flowers."

She shot to her feet. "But, you can't."

Without another word, Quinn pulled a document out of his pocket and slapped it down on the table, face-up. "I beg to disagree with you, love. I can and I will."

She scooted to the table and read the document over. With a puzzled expression, she said, "But . . . this is a marriage license."

"Exactly."

She crossed her arms in front of her and gave him an angry look. "This gives you license to marry me, not to rape me." Even to her it sounded a bit lofty.

He smiled at her. "Come, love, you know as well as I do that it won't be rape."

She shrugged and he laughed. "Well, I had to put up some token of defense," she said, knowing that it sounded like a pretty lame excuse. "Don't you think we should wait until we are married?"

Quinn crossed the room and taking her in his arms, he said, "I will marry you, sweetheart, and soon, but God as my witness, I do not intend to take any more chances. If you had any idea what I've been through, you would understand."

"You mean you had a difficult time finding me?"

"In a roundabout-way, yes. You, of all people, should know The Bolter never takes the direct route anywhere."

Caroline's face froze with disbelief. "The Bolter? But . . . you were on a black."

"Sort of," he said, laughing. "A mottled black would be more appropriate."

She began laughing. "What happened?"

"I rode across a stream. When we came out the other side, the bottom half of my black horse had turned white."

She was laughing now. "But, surely you knew you were on The Bolter long before that."

He grinned. "Oh, I knew all right. The moment that hell-horse got the bit between her teeth, I knew."

"But how did you end up on The Bolter, and how did she come to be black?"

Quinn gave her a look, raising one questioning brow. "Bootblack, I would imagine. As for who did it . . . do you really need to ask me that? Who do you think is responsible? Who do we both know that would go to any lengths to rub horse liniment in an open wound, especially if it were mine."

"Harry and Richard," she said, laughing at the thought.

"I cannot wait until I get my hands on them."

She stopped laughing long enough to say, "It was all done as a jest, milord."

"A jest. *A jest!* Do you have any idea what it's like to be made the laughingstock of half of England? Damn embarrassing it was, passing by every farmhouse in the county, only to have a bunch of gaping rustics poke fun at my horse. I know how Don Quixote felt. I avoided towns and farms after that. Don't laugh, sweetheart, it gets worse."

She was laughing so hard she could barely talk. "How could it get *worse?*"

"It began to rain, which was bad enough, but to make matters worse, the bootblack began to run."

"Oh no."

"And that is how I ended up on a mottled horse."

Throwing her arms around his neck, she said, "I think I am ready to be ravished now, milord."

With a low growl, Quinn said, "I'm glad to hear it, because I intend to ravish until my heart's content."

"And mine," she said.

"That too," he replied.

Taking her up into his arms, Quinn carried her to a small bed in the corner, where he laid her down, then stretched his body out beside hers. She lay there in a remarkably wonderful state of enraptured delight, waiting. His mouth, heavy with desire, found hers. With a fevered response, she began to kiss him, her hands caressing the smooth muscles of his back.

"Just a minute," he whispered, then left her for a moment.

She lay back, watching him remove his clothes, until he stood before her, naked and lean, his body smooth

and golden in the lamplight. Then he began undressing
her. At last, when he was finished, he lay beside her
again, drawing her against his warm, hard body, and she
could not help thinking how this one act was both powerfully seductive and decidedly gentle. Every part of her
went limp. The blood rushed through her veins like liq-
uid fire. She felt her heart stop as his fingers wandered
along the hollow of her throat, across her breasts. When
his mouth followed the same trail his fingers had taken,
she released a long-held breath, feeling like all the liq-
uids in her body had suddenly come to a rapid boil and
were now evaporating, like water in a steaming pot.

When he drew the fullness of her breast into his
mouth, she began to feel waves of sensation rippling
downward, where she felt a strange new stirring, the
awakening of some part of her that had heretofore lain
dormant. Suddenly she knew what it must feel like to be
a rosebud, turning its face to the sun and feeling its petals open. For in truth, her body began to blossom beneath the touch of his hands, the encouragement of his
mouth.

His hands traveled lower, touching her intimately and
she drew a deep, shuddering breath and closed her eyes.
"You take me to Heaven's gate when you touch me like
that," she whispered. "I feel like you are showing me a
glimpse of Paradise."

"I haven't yet," he whispered back, "but I will."

He touched her again, and she could no longer control
her body. She began to move slowly, her movements becoming quicker, matching the rhythmic pace set by the
motion of his hand. She began to feel impatient, restless,
as if she were waiting for something . . . something
which had no memory, no name.

"Sweet, sweet, love. I think you are ready."

"I know I'm ready," she whispered.

He chuckled, the warm current of his breath fanning
out across her. She wanted, needed—what she did not
know. "Quinn . . ."

"I know, love." He shifted his weight and she felt his
thighs slip between her legs.

A perfect fit.

She could feel his hard flesh pressing against her, causing her to whimper and move against him. The taste of his mouth on hers was hot and wild, intoxicating. "How much longer?" she asked, her words faint and tense against his shoulder.

Quinn raised his head and looked down at her. "Sweetheart, you pick the most damnable times to ask questions. How much longer? Are we in a hurry, then?"

"Well, yes."

She felt him stiffen against her. "Is it that bad?"

She smiled. Men, ever getting their masculine feelings flattened. "No," she whispered, "it isn't bad, it's just that I don't think I can last much longer."

She could feel his smile as he buried his face against her shoulder. "Love . . ."

The word was soft and strangely thick, and she had a feeling he said it with great effort. Somehow, the knowledge that she affected him this much was pleasing to her. But she had no time for further thought, for his sweat-slick body arched as if driven with need.

She wrapped her arms around his neck, pressing her body closer to his. She whimpered as a burning wave of need rushed over her. When she thought she could bear it no longer, he entered her and she felt no pain, only surprise that she could feel herself dissolve, then tighten with desire around him. His body drove into her with such swift power that the world seemed to spin around them, spinning faster and faster, weaving them into a tight cocoon where nothing existed save the two of them. She breathed a sigh of relief. *I belong to him, now. Now and forever.*

The tempo of his body increased and she could think of nothing but the feel of his hips thrusting against hers. Clutching his shoulders, she could feel the moment his body was gripped by a violence that seemed to possess him. With a moan of passion, he twisted his fingers in her hair and cried out her name. The impact of it took her over the edge with him. A moment later, his body shuddered and she felt her own body quicken in response.

Several moments passed, with neither of them saying

anything. She wondered if he, like she, was afraid to speak, as if by doing so the closeness, the beauty of what they had just shared would be gone. Content to lie there in his arms, she closed her eyes, knowing her life was now complete.

Suddenly her eyes flew open and her heart began to hammer in her chest. "Quinn?"

He kissed her nose. "Yes, love."

"If it didn't hurt, does that mean I wasn't a virgin?"

"You were a virgin."

"Are you sure?"

He raised up on his elbow and looked down at her. "Are you questioning my knowledge, or disputing a fact?"

She scrunched up her face in thought. "Neither, I suppose, it's just that Mrs. Witherspoon said it always hurt . . . the first time."

"Well, how would Mrs. Witherspoon know? You did say her husband was killed on their wedding day. Now, stop worrying. You were a virgin. If you want me to put it in writing and affix my seal, I'll be happy to oblige you. Does that make you happy?"

She smiled. "Quinn, *you* have already made me happy."

"I have?"

"Immensely."

EPILOGUE

On her wedding night, Caroline stood before the mirror in her bedroom, tying the pink satin ribbon that laced the front of her gown together. Then she picked up a silver-backed brush and drew it through her hair.

Hearing the sound of someone at the door, she turned, knowing it was Quinn coming to her at last. The door opened and the brush fell to the floor with a *thump*.

There, in the doorway stood a highwayman in all his magnificence. As she stared at him, he drew his rapier with a *swish*, his dark, hypnotizing gaze never leaving her face.

Her heart fluttered, then seemed to stop. The man was lean and graceful, undeniably an aristocrat, who wore the highwayman's garb well. His eyes looked black against the ebony satin of his mask. The hair that curled beneath his hat was black, but she knew his heart was not of the same color. His nose was aquiline, his cheekbones high, his mouth mocking and yet not cruel. It was a sensuous mouth and the implication made her shiver. He disturbed her, not only by his handsomeness, but by an alarming mixture of power and sensuality that made her think this man had seen and done things she had seen and done as well. Looking into his eyes, she felt touched by the power of darkness, yet drawn to him.

Suddenly, his gaze left her face and traveled downward, as if giving her nightgown much consideration. With swift strides, he crossed the room, coming to stand before her. Before she could guess what he was about, the sharp, gleaming tip of his rapier was pointed at her. She did not flinch, but kept her eyes upon his. As the rapier's cold, hard surface touched the side of her face, she trembled. Mesmerized, unable to take her eyes from his, she held her breath as she felt the blade caress her face, then drop lower, as the tip moved along her jawline, then followed the contour of her neck, where it paused at the hollow of her throat. It skimmed the low neckline of her nightgown. She felt it riding the swelling crest of her breasts, then come to rest in the valley between.

There was no change of expression in his eyes as he lifted the rapier. She felt the metal's cool hardness leave the warmth of her breasts.

With a sudden flick of his wrist, he began to cut the satin ribbon that crisscrossed the front of her nightgown. Tiny sparks of sensation played down her spine as she watched with fascination. Holding her breath, she glanced down as one by one, the ribbons came under siege and her breasts were bared.

"Stand and deliver," he said, with a tempting gleam in his eye.

Caroline laughed, and with a seductive smile, she turned toward the bed, where she lay down. "I have a better idea," she said, opening her arms to him. "I'll lie down and *you* deliver."

With a wicked smile, the Marquess of Waverly did just that.

You may write Elaine Coffman at P.O. Box 8300-519, Dallas, TX 75205.

ENCHANTED

ALEXIS HARRINGTON

CHAPTER ❨ ONE

"*H*ow in the world did we end up with all of this lace?" Leah Whitman muttered to herself. She stood in the dark storeroom of Whitman's Dry Goods, sifting through a packing crate and pulling out reel after reel of the delicate tissue-wrapped trim. Going to the open back door where the light was better, she studied the various lists in her hands to check the items. The sun was blinding and she glanced up briefly at the silver-white sky. In the distance, withering brush peppered the yellow hills. It was high summer, and the day promised to be another scorcher. When Leah brought her gaze down to the dusty path that ran behind the buildings, she gasped. Stretched out on a long bench behind his shop next door was her tenant and neighbor, Austin Ryder.

"Good morning, Miss Whitman."

The full sun was falling on him, and she could see that he was barefoot and wore no shirt. She quickly averted her eyes from his half-naked torso. It was all she could do to make herself respond.

"Good morning, Mr. Ryder," she answered stiffly. He always seemed to exude a smart-alecky sensuality. At least that's what Leah thought, although she couldn't think of anything he'd ever said or done that could be considered rude or indecent. It was just . . . She didn't have much experience with men, but she was certain she knew Austin Ryder's type: dangerous. Too earthy, too unrefined. She chanced another peek at him. His wavy, sun-streaked hair was too long; it hung to his collarbones. Except now it fanned out around his head on the planks of the bench. He was too tall, too wide at the shoulders and broad across the chest. His eyes were too blue.

Everything about him was too much, in Leah's opinion, even if some of the women in Lost Horse thought otherwise. Indeed, she'd heard them lament the fact that he was an unfriendly loner, and could never be drawn into conversation. She might consider that to be his only attribute.

"Nice day," he remarked laconically, lifting his head and shading those blue eyes to stare at her.

She nodded curtly and returned her attention to her shipping lists, although she didn't see a single word. "Mr. Ryder, it hardly seems proper for you to be out in public like . . . like that." She gestured in his general direction.

He glanced around at the backs of the buildings, and the open prairie beyond. "This isn't exactly what I'd call public. I was back here minding my own business until you came to take a look." The tone of his voice made it sound as though she were the one in the wrong. "Besides I'd think you'd know how to break in a new pair of blue jeans."

"I beg your pardon—" she began, flipping her long braid behind her back.

"Well, you sell jeans. I'd expect that some cowboy would have told you the best way to make them fit right. You have to put them on and go for a dunk in a horse trough, then lie in the sun till they're dry."

She took another quick peek at him, just in time to see him turn over on the bench, presumably to dry the backs of the pants. The muscles in his arms and shoulders flexed with the effort.

"I should think that would be most uncomfortable," she replied with prim disapproval. Why was she continuing this indecent conversation, she wondered.

"Oh, it's not so bad without underwear."

A scorching heat crept up Leah's throat and continued on to her scalp. With not another word, she made a hasty retreat to the dim storeroom. Where was the aloofness he'd been accused of? Obviously, the man did not take life very seriously if he could loll around, wasting time on such a trivial task. To have a gunsmith, of all people, working next door another four more years . . . Why her father had leased the space to Ryder was beyond her. She could only attribute such flawed judgment to her father's failing health.

No more than two years earlier, she and Daddy had discussed expanding the dry goods store into the space next door. Only a few months were left on the apothecary's lease, and then, he'd told Daddy, he was going back to Jefferson City to retire. Whitman's certainly needed the room and Leah had made detailed mental plans for the new space. She'd even decided to give the ladies of Lost Horse a corner of their own, away from the roughness of horse harness and lamp oil. Her sister had wanted to expand their stock of vanity sets and perfumed soap. But Leah knew her customers; they worked hard and were too busy for gewgaws. They needed things to make their lives easier.

Then Austin Ryder had arrived in town. The next thing she knew, the display cases she'd pictured filled with sewing boxes and shiny scissors instead held blued pistols and long-barreled rifles. After her father died, Leah gave up her teaching job at the school to run the store. Well, at least she wouldn't have to deal with Ryder herself very much longer. It would become her sister Bethany's job. And Bethany, heaven help her, shared the sighing, moony opinion of those other women who thought he was attractive.

Leah forced her thoughts back to the papers in her hand. What had she been looking for? Oh, yes, there it was on the shipping list: one hundred yards of three-inch white French lace. She knew she hadn't ordered it. Lost Horse was surrounded by farms and ranches. The customers of Whitman's Dry Goods had no practical use for an item like that. They needed plain fabrics, serviceable housewares, seeds, nails, sturdy shoes, and clothes. Even the wedding gown she was making for herself didn't have this kind of decoration. If she hadn't ordered the lace . . .

"Bethany," she called. "Would you come here, please?"

A moment later, Bethany appeared in the doorway. Although twenty-two, Leah's little sister had never lost the bouncing, enthusiastic energy that she'd had as a girl. Her eyes fell upon the wooden reels Leah held up, excelsior trailing from them like cobwebs.

"Oh, Leah, the lace came . . . isn't it beautiful?" She sighed, delight suffusing her features. With her dark blond hair and soft brown eyes, she had a delicate, feminine beauty, like spring wildflowers. Leah's own coloring was more vivid, but she lacked her younger sister's luminous sparkle. As their father had pointed out, nature had saved the best for his last child.

"Did you order this? I was hoping it was a mistake," Leah said, putting the spools back into the crate. "You know we won't be able to sell this to anyone."

Bethany walked into the storeroom, plucked one of the reels from the crate, and unwound a length of the elegant trim. "Yes we will," she replied emphatically. "Mr. Gillespie vowed this would catch the eye of every lady who comes in. He said they'd *all* want it to make pretty dresses and ornaments for their hair—"

"Homer Gillespie? When was he here?" Homer was a smooth-talking traveling salesman who could probably, if he put his mind to it, sell a salt lick to a man dying of thirst. He'd been working this route for less than a year. It was amazing the number of peddlers and agents who found their way to Lost Horse.

"He stopped in about a month ago," she said, tracing the fine pattern with her fingers. "I think it was the day that you and Josiah went to Willowbrook to see the minister about your wedding. Somehow we got to talking about our summer full moon dances."

Every summer for as long as Leah could remember, Lost Horse had held dances at the grange hall once a month, timed with the full moon. "If it were anyone but

Homer Gillespie, I'd worry that he thought us all a bunch of pagans," Leah remarked drily.

"Well, Mr. Gillespie said the lace would make a lady's dress look as light and airy as sea foam. Isn't that a lovely thought?"

Yes, that sounded like Homer Gillespie, all right. But she supposed she couldn't blame Beth. Right after she and her sister took over Whitman's last fall, Leah herself had been duped by Homer's tactics a time or two. The six-dozen genuine Chinese back scratchers in the corner of the storeroom were testament to that. And she was much less impressionable than her sister. Beth was a bit of a flirt, but she was also a romantic dreamer, and she would have stood no chance against Homer's persuasiveness.

When Leah and Josiah married and left to oversee his new church in faraway Mountain Wells, how many other useless luxuries would the Homer Gillespies of the world sell to Bethany? Whitman's Dry Goods could be bankrupt within a year. This wasn't the first time the worry had nagged at her. She glanced at her sister.

"Oh, dear," Beth said, her smile fading. "I've done something wrong, haven't I? You've turned out to be so much smarter than I am about running the store."

Leah smiled, trying to push the worry to the back of her mind, where it had taken up permanent residence. "Don't worry, you'll catch on. I know more about this business because I spent so much time working here with Daddy before I went away to school." As a matter of fact, she'd loved it here. If her father hadn't pushed her to go to teachers college, she'd have been perfectly content to run this place. But he'd put more store in learning than shopkeeping. She knew she would miss the rich, mingled scents of coffee, leather, tobacco, and spices. But she wasn't leaving today, and there was still a lot of work to do.

She glanced at the watch pinned to her blouse front. "Goodness, it's nine o'clock already. You'd better go open the front doors and raise the shades. I'll be out in a few minutes. I just need to finish sorting out this new stock."

Her natural good temperament restored, Bethany grinned and turned to follow her instructions. She stopped suddenly, and said over her shoulder, "You just wait, Leah. I'll bet we'll sell so much of that lace, when Mr. Gillespie comes back, we'll have to order more."

Leah laughed and shook her head. A moment later she heard Bethany open the doors, and a cool breeze immediately filled the store.

She leaned into another crate and plowed through the woody-smelling excelsior, searching for the cards of buttons she'd ordered. While she wondered why the small items were always carefully packed on the bottom of the box, she heard Mrs. Foster's voice coming from the front of the store. Mrs. Foster wanted to play the organ at her wedding, and both she and Josiah were trying to think of an excuse to derail this plan. The dear woman had a generous heart, but no talent for music. Perhaps they could tell a white lie and say that they'd already—

Suddenly an ear-piercing scream that seemed to shake the very rafters propelled Leah upright as though she had springs in her back.

Dear God—

Another scream rang out, followed by female shrieking and the sound of breaking glass. Footsteps thumped across the plank flooring. Leah ran to the doorway that separated the back room from the store, just in time to see a ginger brown shape fly past her face.

Mrs. Foster was cringing at the counter, staring fixedly as though turned to stone. Her face had taken on a sickly gray cast, and she held one hand clapped to her bosom.

A creature perched on the counter next to one of the candy jars that contained peppermint sticks. Its movements were quick and jerky. With front paws that resembled little human hands, it removed the lid and plucked a piece of candy from the jar, gnashing its small teeth at everyone present.

"Leah," Bethany screeched. Her pale freckles were suddenly very apparent on her ashen face. "What *is* that thing? It just ran in from the street. Do . . . do you think it's dangerous?"

Leah couldn't say for certain. She, too, just stared at it, her mouth open. "I'm not sure. I've never seen—"

At that moment, Austin Ryder came running through the back door, carrying a gunbelt in one hand and a revolver in the other. He shouldered Leah out of the way and stood in front of her. Seeing him, the little candy thief scampered down the counter on all fours, then leaped to a high shelf and bared its teeth at him. It chattered angrily, its face a cross between that of a tiny old man and a remarkably ugly baby.

"I heard someone scream. . . . What the hell is that?" Austin stood as dumbstruck as the others.

Leah didn't move. She could hardly find her voice. "I-I think it's a monkey."

Austin lifted his Colt and trained it on the monkey who was now investigating the shelves, throwing everything to the floor like a two-year-old in a tantrum. Jars shattered, tin cans rolled under the counter, dusting powder clouded the air. Suddenly the animal let out a screech that beat any noise that Bethany had uttered so far.

"Mr. Ryder, for heaven's sake, put that gun away!" Leah demanded, her knees shaking. "You'll just shoot one of us."

Austin cocked the revolver and extended it, his hand steady, his jaw set. "Lady, I'm a better shot than that. How do you know the thing doesn't have rabies?"

Her eyes widened. "Dear God," she repeated, her voice not much more than a breath.

Hearing his words, Mrs. Foster sank to the floor in a dead faint, her dress billowing around her. Bethany rushed to her side and began slapping her wrists.

The only calm one in the confusion was Austin. He took aim with his Colt. "I've got you now, you little bast—"

"Hold your fire, sir!" A cultured voice thundered through the store.

Leah jumped; Austin lowered the weapon. All eyes turned to the tall, foreign-looking man with frost white hair and a long silver mustache. His sudden presence was as astounding as the monkey's. He seemed to have materialized out of thin air. No one moved.

"Esmeralda!" he commanded as he stepped forward, his pale eyes burning like fire. He was dressed in a long black coat and black trousers like an undertaker.

Austin turned his head. *"Esmeralda?"* he asked, lifting his brows.

The monkey, no longer defiant, skittered down from her perch. Her master held out his hand, and she scrambled to his shoulder, gripping his jacket collar. Her long tail hung down his arm like a snake.

"Esmeralda, I am very disappointed. You have been exceedingly naughty. You are a bad girl."

The monkey showed no signs of contrition. It simply chewed on one of the stolen peppermint sticks.

The stranger turned to Leah, who was getting smelling salts for Mrs. Foster, and bowed slightly. "Madame, may I introduce myself? I am Professor Xavier Sortilege, seer of truth, counsel to the royal courts of Europe, purveyor of the unusual. That is my wagon." He gestured to a vehicle parked outside. It looked like a circus wagon and his name was emblazoned on the side in bright red. "I was merely passing through your lovely town, when this *enfant terrible* escaped. You must allow me to apologize for Esmeralda. I turned my back for but a moment, and she was gone. Apparently she found your establishment too enticing to resist."

Leah introduced herself and the others. "Esmeralda . . . she's a nimble climber." There was something annoying about a man apologizing for a monkey as though it were a child. But Leah's upbringing would not allow her to say anything impolite to this mysterious vagabond.

"Professor Short Ledge," Austin, who apparently had no such reticence, said, "I assume you're planning to make good on the damages your monkey caused."

"Mr. Ryder," she admonished in a harsh whisper. She gave him a severe look before turning to help Bethany with Mrs. Foster. Leah did not appreciate being championed by a shirtless, barefoot man in wet jeans. What would Josiah say when he heard? Yet, she had to admit that a significant amount of damage had been done. It would take most of the morning to clean things up. And more than just merchandise had been lost. Who would pay to replace the glass display case the monkey had smashed with a bottle of Miracle Stomach Bitters?

The professor held up his hand. "Madame, Mr. Ryder makes a valid point. Certainly, you shall be recompensed for all damages. You have only to give me a figure." He withdrew a long slim wallet from his coat.

Leah glanced up and pushed at the strands of hair that had worked loose from her braid. His candor was unsettling, as was everything else about him. "Well . . . really, I . . ."

"Now, now, don't be shy. I insist on reimbursing you for Esmeralda's little prank." Professor Sortilege opened the wallet while he looked at her expectantly.

Leah sat back and considered the litter of broken stock. "I suppose . . . would five dollars be all right?"

"Ten dollars is more realistic," Austin put in, keeping a wary eye on Esmeralda. He still gripped the Colt, although it hung at his side.

She lowered her brows at him. Why didn't he just go back to drying his jeans and let her handle this? For a man of reportedly few words, he certainly didn't hesitate to offer his opinion. This was especially galling because she knew he was right. Well, this smart-aleck gunsmith wouldn't tell her what to do.

"*Five* dollars will be fine, Professor Sortilege." She glared at Austin Ryder, feeling as defiant as Esmeralda.

Austin gave Leah one final look, then shrugged and walked out taking his big Colt with him.

Austin Ryder padded up the stairs to his sparse second-floor living quarters to change from his damp jeans. He rummaged through the clothes hanging on hooks behind the door, looking for a clean pair of pants.

That pinched-up Leah Whitman could put any man in a sour mood, he thought. Talking to her was like trying to free the trigger on a pistol that had spent six months rusting in the weather: when you finally got the damned thing loose, you still had a rusty gun.

He supposed if she wanted to lose money just to have

her own way, he shouldn't care. After the last few years, Austin had been glad to find this quiet corner of the world. But he hadn't expected old man Whitman to die as soon as they signed the lease and leave Austin at the mercy of his school teacher daughter.

Oh, she was all right to look at, he'd give her that. With her long whiskey-blond hair that she wore in a braid, and eyes that sometimes were hazel, other times, green. She wasn't a soft, frilly woman, like her pretty sister, Bethany. Now *she* was a woman he'd consider getting to know better. But Leah was interesting. At least until she opened her mouth. He shook his head, picturing the astringent Leah and her dry fiancé, minister Josiah Campbell. The joyless pair were perfect for each other.

He stripped off the damp jeans and laid them over the chair. He would have liked to let them dry completely, but he couldn't loaf around any longer; he had work to do. He'd lost enough time dealing with the crazy professor and his pet.

Austin paused for a moment and looked at his open right hand, then closed it into a fist. When he'd pointed the revolver at that monkey, he hadn't hesitated for a second. His aim had been steady, and if the professor hadn't come in when he did, Austin knew he would have squeezed the trigger.

But shooting a mischievous monkey wasn't the same as killing a man.

Professor Xavier Sortilege agreed to Leah's price with obvious reluctance. She knew she'd been silly to insist that he pay her only five dollars, but she could hardly renege. She and Bethany spent the rest of the morning sweeping and mopping, but the air was still heavy with the odor of vinegar from the jar of pickled eggs that Esmeralda had shattered.

"Leah, do you think the monkey had anything to do with tomorrow being the summer solstice?" Beth posed. "You know funny things seem to happen around here on Midsummer's Eve. Remember when Ed Thorndike's nanny goat had a two-headed kid? And last year at the full moon dance, when Mrs. Tremaine found her wedding ring inside the blueberry pie that Elsa Robbins baked?"

Leah reached under the lower edge of a cabinet to grab an egg that had rolled to a rest there. "There's nothing magical about a two-headed kid, Beth. Those things happen on farms now and then. And Birdie Tremaine was making pies at the same table with Elsa that day. Her ring just got mixed up with the flour and berries."

"Well, that professor seems peculiar, doesn't he? Do you remember ever seeing him before or even hearing about him?" Beth asked. She maneuvered her broom to reach a sour ball hidden behind the washboards.

"No, and I wish I hadn't seen him this morning," Leah responded, unable to keep the annoyance out of her voice. The full heat of the day had settled on the store like a buffalo robe, and thanks to the professor, they were doing hot, hard work. "I'd planned to finish the stock work so I could put together some of the things I'll need in Mountain Wells."

"I hope I can come to visit when you and Josiah get settled," Bethany said, sweeping broken glass into a pile. She stopped for a moment, her hands stilled on the broom handle, her pretty face dreamy. "What a wonderful romantic adventure, going off into the wilderness together." She sighed. "You'll have such fun, building a new home, teaching the children."

Leah was on her knees on the hardwood floor, holding the dustpan. She tapped it on the planking to interrupt her sister's reverie. Bethany and her romantic fancies, she thought. "Of course you can come and visit. But as Josiah's wife, it is my duty to follow him on his mission, Beth. It's not meant to be *fun*."

Bethany swept broken glass, powder, and pickled eggs into the dustpan, making very small, deliberate strokes with her broom. "I guess you're right. Anyway, he is kind of serious."

Leah straightened. She made it sound as though being serious were some kind of disagreeable affliction. "Yes, he is, but he's an honorable man, and he's a hard worker.

He is devoted to his parishioners, and that takes up a lot of his time. I know he'll do a good job with his new church, too. The settlement has never had a minister or a teacher. They need someone like Josiah."

"I suppose. Leah, don't you think—wasn't Mr. Ryder gallant to come to our rescue this morning?"

Leah could see faint color staining Bethany's cheeks. Austin Ryder appeared in Leah's mind as she'd seen him early this morning: stretched out on that bench, bone and hard-sculpted muscle in that—that naked display.

"Bosh! He came in here waving a gun. He could have shot someone." She rubbed her nose, and then realized she'd probably left a streak of dusting powder on it.

Beth had a number of eager suitors—they were drawn to her beauty and uncomplicated mind—but she had accepted none of them. She was waiting for one man, the right one, and she hadn't met him yet, she said. Leah sincerely hoped that she didn't think Austin Ryder was the right one.

"Don't go getting any ideas about him, Beth. He's not the kind of man a nice girl should get mixed up with."

"Why? I mean, not that I was thinking of any such thing," Bethany amended hastily. "But he seems like a gentleman. Why don't you like him?"

Why, indeed, Leah thought, dumping the dustpan into a bucket. How could one resist a man who was too much of everything?

CHAPTER ☾ TWO

*L*ate that afternoon Leah looked up from her ledger to see Professor Sortilege, minus Esmeralda.

"Miss Whitman, how good to see you again," he said as he approached the counter. He looked severe and slightly mysterious in his dark clothing and brought with him the faint smell of incense. "I see that you have gotten things put to rights. However, I truly feel that you allowed us to take unfair advantage of your generous nature."

Regardless of his impeccable manners and dignity, there was something about him that Leah found odd. She glanced around, wishing that Beth were here, but she'd gone home early to get ready for the dance tonight at the grange hall. She would have left early herself because she was supposed to help with the decorations, but after this morning's disaster she had work to finish.

She closed the account book and gave him a thin smile. "That's quite all right, Professor. Sometimes things happen that are simply beyond our control."

His large, pale eyes gleamed knowingly. "Just so, Miss Whitman, just so. A chance encounter, a walk down one street rather than another, a right turn instead of a left, and *pffft*, our fates are instantly, irrevocably changed." He put his hand to his chin and considered her for a moment, then nodded as though he'd arrived at a decision. "Because you so graciously forgave the contretemps of this morning, I must offer you a small token of my appreciation, a gift. And of course, one for your sister."

"Oh, no, Professor. That really isn't necessary." Leah stepped back.

He extended a long, thin hand toward the door. "Please. I have all manner of wonders to choose from. It's the least I can do. I shall be offended if you don't accept."

"Well . . . all right," she said, feeling helpless to refuse. Heaven forbid that Xavier Sortilege be offended, after all the work he'd made for them, Leah thought wryly. She stepped out from behind the counter and followed his dark figure outside to his wagon. Large red letters on the painted canvas side proclaimed: PROFESSOR XAVIER SORTILEGE . . . SEER OF TRUTH . . . PURVEYOR OF THE UNUSUAL.

The road bustled with the usual Saturday afternoon hubbub of wagons, horses, and shoppers. From across the street, one of Mot's Regulars, the group of old men who occupied the chairs outside of Mot's Barbershop, waved to her. She waved back.

"Wait just a moment, Miss Whitman," Sortilege said, and nimbly leaped the three steps into the back of his wagon.

The canvas panel flew up like a window blind.

Inside, the wagon's walls were dark with small gold stars and planets painted on them. Gargoylelike masks, Japanese lanterns, dried herbs, a brilliant blue turban decorated with a crescent moon, all hung in the darkness.

"Step a bit closer, Miss Whitman, and I shall show you curiosities from all over the world." His voice held mystery and enticement, and despite her misgivings Leah stepped forward.

Like a magician, he snapped open a large mother-of-pearl fan. "From the Orient for the lovely Miss Bethany Whitman, with my compliments," he said, and handed it to her.

"It's beautiful," Leah admitted, taking the fan. It had a pale, iridescent gleam and was intricately carved with tiny figures of flowers and birds. She was sure its value far exceeded the amount of damage Esmeralda had caused. "Really, Professor, we can't accept something this dear." She held the fan out to him, but he pushed her hand back. His touch was cool and papery, unreal somehow.

"Of course you can. Beauty should be honored with beauty."

His statement effectively silenced any argument.

Next, the professor turned to a trunk at his feet and lifted its lid. "Let's see what the trunk holds for this kind lady, shall we, Esmeralda?"

It wasn't until that moment that Leah noticed the monkey, tethered by the ankle to one of the wagon posts. The beast let out a familiar screech and grimaced at her, showing off its teeth.

"Be quiet and mind your manners!" he ordered. "You've made enough trouble for one day." The sullen monkey turned her back on them both.

"Ah, here's an interesting item." He held out a brass lamp to her. "This comes from the exotic East and is purported to have once housed a jinn that could grant wishes to its owner."

Leah raised her eyebrows skeptically.

He withdrew the lamp. "Of course, an educated woman such as yourself wouldn't believe that nonsense."

Next the professor produced a ring with a large, dark stone. "This ring changes color to suit the wearer's humor. If she is feeling happy, the stone will be blue-green, the same color as a tranquil sea. If she is worried, the stone will become red. And should she become angry, the stone will turn as black as a storm at midnight."

When Leah said nothing, he brought out a beautiful crystal ball. It sparkled under the sun like a diamond. "Perhaps you would care to know your future, Miss Whitman? Shall we look into the crystal to see your fate?" He put on the blue turban and began waving his hands over the glass ball.

This was becoming ridiculous, Leah thought. "I already know my future, Professor. In six weeks, I will marry Reverend Josiah Campbell and travel with him to a new settlement. He'll oversee the church and I'll teach school."

Now it was the professor's turn to look skeptical, and he wagged a long finger at her. "Not much is less certain than that which we assume to be. Shall we learn the truth of it?" He held out the crystal like a king holding an orb.

Leah smiled as she closed the fan, the breeze fluffing the short strands of hair around her face. "I already know the truth," she said, deciding he wasn't as intimidating as she'd originally thought. Professor Sortilege was nothing more than a cultured charlatan, selling vaguely interesting rummage and spouting ridiculous predictions.

As she stood there, she suddenly realized that the street was empty. Where had everyone gone? Strange that it should be deserted at four o'clock on a Saturday afternoon. Even Mot's Regulars had disappeared, and not much could budge them before supper. And it was so quiet—no birds twittered. She looked over her shoulder at Ryder's shop. It, too, was closed. The note in the window said that he'd gone on an errand. She wondered why she hadn't noticed before.

A hot wind came up, sending dust devils whirling down the dry, sunbaked road, but a chill rippled through Leah. To be out here alone . . . Perhaps she should just thank Sortilege and go back inside.

"Ah, so positive of your destiny, are you?" he intoned, and his voice changed subtly.

Leah looked up at him. His eyes were riveted on her, two pale blue spheres from which she could not shift her gaze. She meant to nod, but could only stare back, transfixed.

"Then here is just the thing for you, Miss Whitman." From the trunk he produced a black velvet pouch with golden drawstrings and held it out to her.

She extended her hand as though he'd willed her to do so. The velvet was cool and soft in her fingers, its contents heavier than she would have suspected.

"Open the pouch," he instructed, and she obeyed, working loose the drawstrings. The scent of crushed lavender drifted from the folds of the fabric. She peered in and saw a necklace. Carefully, she pulled it out and found a gold chain with an odd stone suspended from it. The stone was not quite purple, not really red.

"What is it?" she asked. Her own voice sounded strange to her ears. Though she knew that it was impossible, the necklace seemed to vibrate.

Professor Sortilege sprang down from the wagon like a black cat. Taking the amulet from her hands, he opened the clasp and hung the chain around her neck. It really wasn't a proper thing for him to do, especially out on the street, but once again, she felt powerless to object. His touch on the back of her neck was ice-cold.

"This, Miss Whitman, will tell you the truth. Wear it under a full moon, and this amulet will draw your true love to you. Perhaps you are correct—your true love could very well be the good Reverend Campbell. But he might not be. Whoever he is, he will come to you. And once you have shared a kiss with him, your heart's fate will be sealed for all time."

Leah looked down at the pendant resting on her bosom. Of everything the professor had shown her, she found this irresistible. And though she disapproved of pagan charms, she could not stop herself from accepting it.

"Th-thank you, it's very nice," she mumbled, feeling a bit drowsy and light-headed.

"Wear it, my dear, most especially tonight of all nights —Midsummer's Eve, the shortest night of the year." He pointed to the stars and planets painted on the walls of the wagon. "When the sun is farthest from us, your true love will be closest. It may bring you turmoil . . . but perhaps it will bring you happiness."

When Leah looked up again, Mot's Regulars were on the barber's porch again, and horses and wagons were driving by, their bridles jingling.

The professor's wagon was only a dusty specter far down the road that led away from Lost Horse.

"What an interesting pendant, Leah," Josiah Campbell said. "I don't believe I've seen it before." The evening sun flashed on the stone, making it glow like molten red crystal against her pale blue bodice.

He, Leah, and Bethany were walking through town to the grange hall. Their shadows were long on the yellow grass that grew beside the road, and the withering heat of the afternoon had gentled. In a picnic hamper, Josiah carried Bethany's potluck supper, a robust meal of fried chicken, baked beans, and cherry pie. Bethany might not have a natural flair for running Whitman's, but Leah acknowledged that her sister did most domestic things far better than she did.

Leah had already told Josiah about their morning adventure with Xavier Sortilege and Esmeralda. Her fingers touched the amulet. "The professor felt bad about the trouble his monkey caused. I guess he gave me this to apologize."

Josiah glanced at the gold chain. "I'm sure he meant well, but do you think you should have accepted it? It looks expensive."

Leah sidestepped a rock in the road. "He insisted that I take it. He said he'd be offended if I didn't. Anyway, I thought it was . . . pretty."

She didn't bother to tell them the rest of Sortilege's tale. Leah didn't believe it herself. The frightening giddiness she'd felt when he put this amulet on her neck, well, she'd just been hungry. Her lunch had been only a biscuit and coffee. As for that bunkum about full moons, short nights, and true loves, it was just that—bunkum.

Josiah gave her a fond smile and patted her hand where it rested in the crook of his arm. "You'd better not wear it when we get to Mountain Wells. A minister's wife can't appear to be too prosperous, you know. Besides, you're pretty on the inside. You don't need adornment on the outside."

She dropped her gaze to the hard-baked road. Inner beauty. It made her think of what her mother had told her when she was young. "Let the world have its beauties, Leah. There's no crime in being plain. The sturdy and plain are the ones who get the job done."

She glanced up at Josiah. He was very highly regarded in town, and she knew that any woman would be lucky to have him for a husband. For years, he'd been kept busy with invitations from the town matrons who arranged dinners and socials to show off their eligible daughters. So no one was more astounded than Leah when, two months ago, after a short courtship, he'd asked for her hand.

He had a good face and nice eyes. His dark beard underscored his air of authority. If he decreed that she should leave Lost Horse and Whitman's Dry Goods for some remote settlement, then she knew he must be right. Just as she knew that Josiah was her true love, and no amulet or soothsaying peddler would change matters. Why, then, did she feel compelled to wear the necklace tonight?

"Maybe you should trade gifts with me, Leah," Beth said, practically skipping along in her light summer dress. "A fan might not draw so much attention."

"A mother-of-pearl fan certainly would," Leah replied.

"Did the professor give you a gift, too, Bethany?" Josiah asked.

She nodded, her expression becoming animated. "Yes, and I wish I'd been there. I'd have loved to look inside his wagon. It sounds so exciting and mysterious."

Josiah laughed. "That's our Bethany—always dreaming about what's on the other side of the horizon."

"Well . . ." Bethany made a moue that admitted this truth. "But I'd think he'd have left a trinket for poor Mrs. Foster, too. You should have seen her when that monkey jumped across the counter, Josiah. Her face got so chalky, I was just waiting for her to faint. Then when Mr. Ryder said it might have rabies, she went over like that big blue spruce Mr. Edgerton cut down at his place three summers ago. Remember that, Leah?"

"Beth!" Leah chided, but she couldn't suppress a burst of laughter. "The poor woman had the daylights scared out of her."

"I wonder if he's coming to the dance tonight. Mr. Ryder, I mean," Beth mused. "He hasn't been to one yet." She kept her eyes on the road ahead, but when

Leah looked at her, she was blushing again as she had this morning when she'd mentioned him.

She felt a spark of impatience at her sister's schoolgirl reaction. "Josiah, I've been trying to tell Beth that Austin Ryder is not a man that a modest woman should even be thinking about. And I'm sure he has no interest in our community activities."

"Who knows, maybe he *will* come tonight," Bethany said. "After all, it's Midsummer's Eve, and anything can happen. I still think a two-headed goat is peculiar. Anyway, some people think that Mr. Ryder came to Lost Horse to escape some personal tragedy, like a broken heart. Maybe that's why he keeps to himself."

Leah snorted. "Personal tragedy, my eye. Why, I wouldn't be at all surprised to learn that he was a gunslinger before he came here. H-he's much too familiar with guns." The objection sounded ludicrous even to her own ears.

"Well, the man is a gunsmith, Leah. Of course he's familiar with them," Josiah reasoned. "He's a little remote but he seems nice enough. I don't think he's anything other than what he says he is."

Men, Leah thought, lapsing into silence. They always stuck together.

When they got to the grange hall, only a few people had arrived to help set up the supper tables. While Leah and Josiah lingered outside, Bethany hurried ahead to join a group of her friends.

The whiny scrape of a fiddle being tuned came from inside the barnlike hall. Sam Weatherby's four sons had been providing the music for all the dances, weddings, wakes, barn raisings, and parties in Lost Horse ever since they were old enough to play an instrument. As it was a generally sociable town—helpful, neighborly, and tolerant of newcomers—this fondness for celebrating wasn't surprising, and the Weatherbys were kept busy year-round.

Josiah patted Leah's hand again. "I'd better help the boys set up the hay. I imagine we'll have some couples who'll want to sit awhile in the moonlight later on."

Moonlight, she thought, and touched her chain again. At every summer dance, hay bales were arranged around the grounds to provide seats for weary dancers. Of course, Josiah, Leah, and other mature townsfolk would supervise to make certain none of the young unmarried people got too cozy in the darkness.

Leah gave him a shy smile. "Maybe we—we'll be one of those couples?" Her face grew warmer still. That might not be the kind of thing to suggest to a minister. So far, except for one chaste peck he'd given her when she accepted his proposal, nothing had occurred between them. Not that it should, she decided hastily. She wasn't usually given to such romantic notions. But minister or not, shouldn't—wouldn't a fiancé want . . . a little closeness?

"I doubt I'll be able to break away from my chaperoning job. And we have to set the example for the youngsters, you know." He returned her smile and went off to join the men hoisting bales of hay.

Leah turned and went inside to help the other women arrange tablecloths over the old doors that had been set up on sawhorses to serve as tables.

She suppressed a sigh when Opal Bromfield arrived to set out dishes of her mother's strawberry preserves. Most people regarded the tough fruit spread as suitable only for tarring roofs and patching rain slickers.

"We're going to miss your help around here when you move, Leah," Opal said. "Isn't that right, Mama?" Opal was a cheerful bird of a woman whose mother had actively sought to make Josiah her son-in-law.

Her mother's mouth tightened as she regarded Leah. "Hmm, I suppose. At first I didn't think you were a suitable match for Reverend Campbell. Now I'm just glad that *my* daughter isn't the one going off to the wilderness with him. He'll need a sturdy woman like you, Leah, not someone with Opal's soft, feminine sensibilities. It won't be an easy life up there at Mountain Wells."

Leah was very aware that since she and Josiah had announced their engagement last month, some women treated her with a detectable coolness.

"I appreciate your concern, Mrs. Bromfield, but really,

there's no need to worry about me," she replied sweetly, ignoring the insult. Then she remembered what Beth had said and added, "It will be a wonderful adventure."

Corliss turned her back and began arranging the dishes with a huffy busyness. Sometimes Leah felt as though she'd committed a sin against the community in accepting Josiah's proposal. Why had he chosen her over all the eligible women in town? But it was such a good match and how could she help it if he preferred her to all the other suitable females in Lost Horse?

Soon the hall began filling with people and the Weatherby boys called them to dance. Rosewater, fresh flowers, and bay rum scented the warm summer night. The hot room, combined with the exercise, gave the dancers a powerful thirst, and Leah, in charge of one of the punch bowls, was kept busy.

At the other end of the hall, Peabody Wilson was just as busy, dispensing beer to the men. Once, Leah glanced up to see Peabody hand a mug to Austin Ryder. She was so surprised to see him, the ladle slipped from her hand and sank to the bottom of the punch bowl.

Austin had never attended any of the town's social functions before. But there was certainly no mistaking him. He looked so different from any of the other men, tall as he was, and with that long sun-glazed hair. Tonight he wore a dark gray shirt, a dark vest, and black pants that fit a little too tightly, in Leah's estimation. But there was something else about him that she couldn't define. She only knew that the women who'd worked so hard to snare Josiah for their daughters never invited Ryder to dinner. Austin Ryder wasn't a man that an unmarried girl dreamed of when she embroidered linens for her hope chest.

He stood against the wall, sipping his beer, scanning the crowd until he apparently found what he was looking for. Leah turned to see what, or who, that might be, and saw her sister dance by with a fresh-faced young man.

"Let's have two glasses of your punch, there, Leah." Mayor Hoyt's booming voice dragged her attention back to the problem of the sunken ladle. While she fished it out with a fork, the mayor continued in a jovial tone.

"Well, I guess we'll be losing you soon to the reverend. It's a mighty strong coincidence the way it worked out, him needing a teacher for Mountain Wells, and you being one and all."

Leah sloshed punch over the edge of cup she was filling. The day after Josiah proposed, he'd told Leah of this wonderful opportunity he'd just learned of. Having a wife who was a teacher would truly be divine providence, he'd said.

Leah had never considered Josiah's proposal in that light before. Why now? It had to be the heat, she decided, and the nerve-wracking events of the day.

She wiped up the spilled punch and covered her clumsiness with a laugh. "Oh, you remember my father, Mayor Hoyt. He believed that if a woman could think, there was no reason to hide it. It's a good thing I listened to him, isn't it?"

Mayor Hoyt chuckled and nodded. "It surely is, Leah. It surely is."

When the mayor finally left, Leah looked for Ryder again and noticed that he'd edged closer to the dance floor. And Bethany knew he was there. Her head kept swiveling as she moved around the floor, keeping him in sight.

Well, there wasn't a blessed thing she could do about it. When she left Lost Horse, if Beth wanted to throw herself at a gunslinger—something sinister certainly lurked in Ryder's past—she wouldn't be able to stop her. She'd said her piece about him.

Her punch bowl empty, Leah decided to step outside to escape the heat of the grange hall, and to find Josiah. She hadn't had a moment with him since the dance began. She knew if they spent a few minutes together, she could dispel the odd, niggling doubts that had crept into her mind tonight.

Outside, a breeze fanned her hot face and tugged at her hair. Purple dusk was giving way to the night. A full moon, heavy and golden, rose above the eastern horizon, lighting the countryside with a faint yellow gleam. The muted melody of a waltz floated to her from the hall. It was a beautiful evening. If Professor Sortilege's folderol

about her amulet was true, she would be saved the
bother of having to look for Josiah. The combination of
the moon and the stone should bring him right to her.

Suddenly, the odd, dizzy feeling that she'd had earlier
in the afternoon came over her again. She stopped and
put a hand to her throat, waiting for the feeling to go
away. Maybe she was coming down with something.

Behind her, a low male voice murmured, "I knew I'd
find you here." Hands came down on her shoulders and
turned her around. Before she could speak or move, she
felt a warm mouth cover hers in a slow, urgent kiss.

A confusing jumble of thoughts ran through her mind,
competing with the sensations that galloped through her
body. None of them included a desire to resist this
tender assault. *Heat . . . softness . . . sweet yearning
. . .* She smelled the faintest trace of crushed lavender,
more like the memory of a vivid dream than reality.
Then it was gone, replaced by a combination of scents
she instinctively thought of as male—soap and leather
and outdoors. Her legs were as rubbery as Corliss
Bromfield's strawberry preserves, and if not for the arms
that held her, she was sure she would have collapsed.
Comfort . . . strength . . . Josiah?

He released her, and slowly she opened her eyes to
gaze upon the man who embraced her with such posses-
sive tenderness.

Austin Ryder.

CHAPTER ☾ THREE

"Mister Ryder, how *dare* you!" Leah Whitman jumped back a good four feet.

Stunned, Austin gaped at the outraged woman and braced himself to be slapped. Leah Whitman didn't impress him as a female who would take to having her person fiddled with, and he wasn't a man who wanted to fiddle with it, anyway. And she looked furious. But the slap didn't come. She just stared at him, looking mad and shocked. No more shocked than he felt, he was certain.

"I didn't know it was you," he whispered. His face was actually hot. He glanced around to see if anyone had witnessed their encounter, but they were alone.

"Oh, so you make it a practice to sneak up on *any* woman in the dark and—and—" She spluttered in a low, angry buzz, unable to finish the sentence. But her meaning was clear.

"No! I thought you were . . . well, someone else."

"You mean you thought I was my sister."

Austin folded his arms over his chest, feeling guilty and defensive, like a kid who'd been caught stealing candy. He couldn't very well confess that she was right. Well, damn it, she never wore her hair like she wore it tonight, loose and brushed smooth, hanging down her back. But Bethany always did. God, this was awkward. Why had he ever come to this dance?

"Look, Miss Whitman, I thought you were someone else, and I'm really sorry I bothered you. Let's just leave it at that." Austin started to walk away when Josiah Campbell approached. He was a sincere but dry-spirited man, and despite her starched exterior, he didn't seem like Leah's type.

"Leah, there you are," Josiah said. "We've been looking everywhere for you." He stopped and peered at Austin through the darkness, then recognizing him, extended his hand. "And Mr. Ryder. I'm glad to see that you've joined one of our gatherings. I understand that you're the hero who came to Leah's rescue this morning."

Austin glanced at her, then shifted his weight from one foot to the other, uncomfortable with the term *hero*. She didn't look too happy about it, either. "Not really. I just heard someone scream . . ."

Campbell pressed on. "Well, come on inside. We're about to have supper, and if you haven't tried Bethany Whitman's fried chicken, you don't know what you're missing."

Austin shook his head. There was nothing he wanted more than to get away from this situation. "No thanks, Reverend Campbell. I have some work to finish." He nodded at Leah. "Miss Whitman."

Leah watched him walk away with a sense of relief. That kiss . . . besides being shaken, she felt oddly winded and dizzy, as though she'd been holding her breath ever since he first touched her.

"Let's go in, Leah," Josiah said, and pulled on her arm.

She glanced at the moon, longing more than ever to spend a few minutes alone with him. "Josiah, wait—"

He turned back to her expectantly, his beard a sharp contrast to his face in the dark. "What is it?"

"Isn't the moon beautiful?" she asked, touching her necklace. It was a lot of foolishness, she supposed, but she halfway hoped that Professor Sortilege's story was true. "Can't we stay here a moment? It's so stuffy in the hall. A minute won't matter, will it?"

"I don't think we'd better. I shooed all the other young people inside to eat. We shouldn't be the ones who come in late." He took her elbow. "Besides, it wouldn't be polite to Bethany if we missed her supper."

Leah sighed. "No, I suppose you're right." As he led the way back to the grange hall, she glanced over her shoulder at the full moon. She had her answer. If the silly amulet had any powers, Josiah wouldn't be thinking about fried chicken.

"Leah, you've hardly eaten anything of your supper," Bethany said. "Are you feeling all right?"

Around them, conversation buzzed and silverware clinked. Josiah was on the other side of the room. Next to Bethany, Chad Brewster, one of her many dancing partners, lingered in helpless infatuation, obviously hoping for a morsel of her attention.

"Yes, of course," Leah answered, a bit too quickly. "The chicken is delicious." Trying to act as if nothing had happened only made her more edgy and restless. She wished she could go home.

"How do you know? You haven't even tasted it."

Leah looked at her sister, then down at her plate. The chicken sat on her plate, untouched. "Sorry, it's so hot in here, I guess I'm getting a headache."

"I thought it was real good, Miss Whitman," Chad said, piping up.

"Chad," Bethany said sweetly. "I'm just about parched. Would you do me a big favor and get me some more lemonade?"

"I'd be happy to, Beth, uh, Miss Whitman." Nearly beside himself with eagerness, Chad grabbed her punch glass and sprang from the bench to find the lemonade.

She watched him till he was gone, then leaned closer. "Thank heavens. He's been buzzing around me all evening."

Leah poked at the chicken with her fork. "I've heard that Chad is a very nice young man with good prospects," she said. "Much more so than some of the *other* men in Lost Horse."

Bethany shrugged and frowned. "He's just a boy. I want a man who's, well, more grown up, I guess, more experienced and down to earth." She looked around the crowded hall as though searching for someone, then brought her gaze back to Leah. "I saw you outside."

Leah's heart nearly stopped. "Outside? What are you talking about?"

Beth gave her an impish, satisfied smile. "You don't have to play coy with me. I saw you and Josiah in the moonlight, and I'd guess that's what has you so unsettled. I was looking for—I was getting a breath of air myself." She primly folded her napkin. "Naturally, I came back inside before I saw anything between you, but —you're blushing, Leah, like summer geraniums! You never blush."

Well, Austin Ryder had changed that. Leah's face burned hotter, but despite her embarrassment, she was relieved. Better that her sister think she'd been sparking outside with Josiah than guess the truth.

Bethany stared across the room at Josiah. "I guess Josiah isn't a completely hopeless sobersides, after all."

Austin walked down the center of Lost Horse's main street. Except for the rustle of night creatures in the brush, it was quiet. Almost everyone had gone to the dance. He looked up at the moon. He couldn't remember the last time he'd seen one as bright and full. It was a lovers' moon. The rest of the sky was filled with stars, twinkling blue-white, and they seemed so close for a minute he thought that if he stood on the roof of his shop, he could touch them. The air carried the whispered scent of crushed lavender making him think of— He shook his head. Jesus, where did all that sappy hogwash come from?

He hadn't even planned to go to that dance. His life before he became a gunsmith had made him a deliberate, watchful man; he wasn't given to impetuous acts. What had happened tonight? How could he have gotten those two sisters confused? It had to have been more than just her hair. He only knew that he'd been watching Bethany long enough for her to notice him, too. Then she'd disappeared and something—a compelling force, he couldn't say just what—had pulled him outside. The first thing he'd seen was that moon. Then he'd seen her waiting for him, standing there looking dreamlike. Except it hadn't been her.

It must have been the beer, he decided. He'd had just the one but even now he felt a little drunk, a bit light-headed. That had to account for his error, and for the powerful arousal Leah stirred in him. A mug of beer, the sight of Bethany Whitman dancing, some moonlight, a little loneliness.

Puckery women like Leah Whitman were definitely not his type. But the longer he considered it, the more he was inclined to admit that something about her had seemed different. The way the moonlight caught in her long, whiskey-blond hair was enough to make a man look at her twice. When he'd kissed her, she'd been soft to the touch, with curves that he imagined would mold to his very well. But it was her sister he'd gone in search of, not her. All at once his attraction to Bethany had sputtered out like wet kindling.

He unlocked the door of his shop. In the gloom, the long blue barrels of rifles hanging on the wall gleamed dully. It was all too mixed up for him to figure out to-night. He'd probably have to work tomorrow, but that didn't matter. It wasn't as though he had a family to spend Sunday with. His hopes for that life had died five years ago in a saloon in Waterville.

He struck a match on the rough wall to light his ker-osene lamp and carried it up the dark narrow stairs to his room where he pulled off his clothes and flopped naked on the bed. Damn, but it was like an oven up here. The lamp flame made it seem worse. He reached out to turn it down. A soft night breeze lifted the curtains and ruf-fled the fine hair on his body.

He fell into that twilight world of half-dreams, remem-bering the look on Sarah's face when he'd gone to tell her about her little brother. She'd called him a cold-blooded killer and had flung her engagement ring at him. After that, everything in his life had gone to hell, and in the years that he'd had to think about it, he wasn't sure that Sarah had been wrong.

That thought faded when Leah Whitman's image rose in his mind's eye again. Restless and hot, he rolled over, trying to shut her out. He even tried to envision her as she'd looked this morning when she'd complained about him lying in the sun to dry his jeans: the pinched, disapproving schoolmarm. But as he began to drift off again, the picture faded.

She stood before him under an oak tree on a spring afternoon. Her cheeks were flushed with color, and her green eyes gazed up at him, half-shy, half-seductive. The sun dappled her hair with fire, highlighting its red strands. She leaned closer and put her hand on his chest, her soft lips parted in offer to his. Sweet. Her skin and hair smelled sweet, womanly. She was impossible to resist.

Austin covered her hand with his own and touched his mouth to hers, full and warm. That touch went straight to his head. He pulled her closer. The kiss grew stronger, more urgent. Under his hands, the fabric of her pale pink dress was as soft as her skin. She wore no corset and her breasts pressed into his chest. He'd never felt anything so good, or so right. Leah Whitman belonged in his arms.

"Austin," she whispered, when he released her mouth. "Make love to me . . . please . . ."

He lurched back to wakefulness, sweat-soaked and painfully aroused. Looking around the room, he was frustrated and relieved to find that he'd only been dreaming. But God, it had seemed so real. He'd felt her arms twined around his neck, heard her whisper in his ear. Even awake, he swore he could smell the faint, delicate fragrance of her. She was all wrong for him, he reminded himself, and she was engaged to the minister.

He turned over and punched his pillow. He knew he shouldn't have gone to that goddamned dance.

It was a day meant for the two of them. The spring afternoon was mild and new, and the birds twittered overhead in the branches of the oak.

Leah pressed a hand to her lover's strong chest. He smelled of leather and soap. He was the most handsome man she'd ever known, she thought proudly. His white shirt was unbuttoned to his breastbone, and she longed to put a kiss in the hollow of his throat, just there, where the shadow fell. A light breeze ruffled his sun-streaked hair, brushing it back from his shoulders. She gazed up into his eyes—when had she ever seen eyes that blue?—and beheld unmistakable, powerful desire, and love. Even though she wasn't as pretty as her sister, she knew he thought she was *beautiful,* and he had chosen her for his own.

Her lips parted as if of their own volition, and he lowered his face to hers, taking them in a moist, lush kiss. No one else had ever kissed her like this. She'd never felt *anything* like this. Hot and breathless, aware of every heartbeat. He pressed her against his long torso, enfolding her in his arms.

"Leah," he said, his voice low, intense, "let me make love to you . . . please."

Leah's eyelids flew open. Then she sat up with a jerk, her head swiveling around as she picked out the dark shapes of furniture. It wasn't spring, it was a sultry summer night. She was in her own room, in her own bed, not in a green meadow. Her heart pounded from what? Fear? Shock? Or was it something else?

Anxiously, she rubbed her forehead with her fingertips. A dream, it had been an insane, embarrassing dream, full of vivid, wanton images of herself with *Austin Ryder?* She pushed off the sheet and got up to sit in the chair by the open window. The moon had set, leaving only the stars to light the low, dry scrub beyond the yard. Perspiration stuck her thin nightgown to her body. She lifted her heavy hair off her neck and let it fall.

What had she been thinking of to cause such a dream? Truth be told, she'd been unable to think of anything or anyone else since that episode outside the grange hall. She had trouble just putting a name to it, even in the privacy of her own heart.

Carefully, reluctantly—it was like lifting the lid on a box of snakes—she went over the dream. Instead of Austin Ryder, she tried to imagine Josiah holding her, kissing her, but her mind recoiled from the image. And when she gave Josiah's voice to Austin's words she shuddered despite the heat. She slammed the lid down again and guiltily locked it.

She was a betrothed woman, due to be married in

little more than a month's time, and here she was, having unchaste, sweaty dreams about the gunsmith. A man who had only kissed her because he had mistaken her for Bethany.

If she had only stayed inside with her empty punch bowl. How would she be able to look Austin Ryder in the face when they next met? And it was inevitable that they would, with his shop next door to Whitman's. She considered and discarded two or three different scenarios, before deciding on her only possible course of action. She would be her businesslike self. After all, he was her tenant, leasing space in a building that she and Bethany owned. That gave her some advantage. She'd simply pretend that none of it had ever happened.

If she could.

On Monday morning, Leah stood on tiptoe, her back to the door, as she struggled to reach a tea tin on a high shelf. The monkey must have pushed it to the back. She heard someone come in, but she could feel the edge of the tin and didn't want to let go.

"I'll be with you . . . in a second," she said, breathless from stretching, "just . . . as soon as I . . ."

"I'll get it for you."

Leah jumped at the sound of Austin's voice right next to her. Whirling to face him, she withdrew her arm as though the tea tin had bitten her, and banged her elbow on the edge of the shelf. He winced at the cracking sound, but his eyes never left her as he easily grasped the offending can and handed it to her. She felt nailed to the floor by those eyes.

"Th-thank you," she stuttered. She knew she was blushing again, she could feel it all the way back to her ears. Her arm throbbed like blue murder, and she clamped her hand over it protectively. She felt so awkward. After the kiss, and the dream, every sensation she now experienced in his presence seemed magnified. Her grand plans to behave with aloof nonchalance evaporated in the heat of his nearness. He, on the other hand, seemed not to be bothered at all.

"I'll bet that hurt," he said, nodding at her arm. He

pulled her hand away and massaged her elbow with strong, gentle strokes. Even through the fabric his touch was warm and vital on her skin. Suddenly the pain began to fade.

The curve of his full mouth had a sculpted look. His face was broad across the cheekbones and firm jawed. Whether or not she wanted to, she couldn't deny that he was an attractive man. She managed to break their eye contact, only to let her errant gaze drift downward to see that he was wearing his new jeans. They did indeed fit him well, as though they'd been molded to his shape. For a moment she felt a troubling desire to—good heavens—put her arms around him and rest her cheek against his shoulder. Josiah never made her feel like that.

Josiah.

She eased her arm out of his grip. "What—" She cleared her throat and began again. "What did you want, Mr. Ryder?"

He dropped his hands to his sides and glanced around the store. Now *he* seemed uncertain. "I came over to get . . . coffee." He looked at her again. "Yeah, coffee."

She eyed him skeptically. His real mission was probably to see Bethany. Her sister was at home this morning, and a tart remark hovered on the tip of her tongue, but then she thought better of it.

She nodded, and went to the built-in drawers that contained coffee and spices. "How much? A pound?"

"Yeah, that'll be fine, I guess." He walked around to the other side of the counter and leaned against it, watching while she scooped the beans into a cone-shaped bag. She'd probably done this job a hundred times but she fumbled around like this was her first day. Hoping it would help, Leah turned away from him, so she couldn't see him. But she felt as if his blue eyes were burning holes in her back.

"This place was in pretty bad shape the last time I saw it. Looks like you got it back together again," he said. "What about the glass case?"

She peeked over her shoulder at him, her tension easing just a little. Whitman's was a safe subject, and she was always interested in discussing the store which was her pride and joy. "I ordered a piece of glass, but of course it'll probably take weeks to get here."

"I hope it gets to town in one piece," he said, glancing around the store. "This is a nice place you have here. I've never really had the chance to look at it before."

Leah allowed herself a private smile. "Thank you." She couldn't pretend that she didn't enjoy his compliment. Whitman's Dry Goods was like her child, a source of worry, delight, and great pride.

Her younger sister could cook, clean, and sew circles around her. Beth had always been the favorite, the more popular, and Leah never begrudged her the attention. Beth was prettier, more graceful, and something about her just, well, glowed. She excelled in all the areas where Leah lacked.

But when Leah unlocked this door every morning, and inhaled the rich, familiar scents, she truly felt at home. The colors and textures of the merchandise were a joy to her. When it came to running this store, she stood in no one's shadow. "We've been here for almost forty years. My father started out with two barrels and a couple of planks for a counter."

"It must have been hard for you to give up teaching for this," he suggested, leaning against the counter. As he moved his hair brushed his shoulders.

"Oh, no, it really wasn't. I enjoyed being a teacher, but it was really my father's idea. He thought I should be able to support myself in case I never . . ." Leah turned back to the coffee bin, leaving the sentence unfinished. She'd been about to blurt out the fact that her father hadn't expected her to find a husband. After all, she'd been twenty-nine years old when he died last year, and still unmarried.

An awkward silence fell between them.

"How come I didn't see you out on the dance floor last Saturday night?" Austin asked, softly.

"Reverend Campbell doesn't dance," she replied, suddenly feeling defensive.

"So? Lots of other men were there. You could have taken a turn with one of them." His eyes were fixed on her, expecting an answer.

Leah put the bag on one side of the scale and added a one-pound weight to the other. "I am engaged to Reverend Campbell, Mr. Ryder. It would hardly be appropriate for me to dance with anyone else." She didn't add that no one would have even thought to ask her.

He studied her hands as she added a few coffee beans to the bag to round out the pound. "I don't see a ring."

Leah folded the top of the bag. "That doesn't make a proposal any less genuine. A ring is just a-a thing, a trinket. Reverend Campbell isn't a rich man, you know."

Austin leveled a serious look on her. "When I asked— if I ever ask a woman to marry me, I'll sure as hell give her a ring to seal the bargain. Did he give you that necklace?"

Leah's hand went automatically to the amulet. Why she still wore it, she couldn't explain even to herself. "No, he didn't." His questions made her uncomfortable, but not so much that she was tempted to tell him to mind his own business. But she didn't like the direction this conversation had taken. She pushed the coffee across the counter. "Was there anything else you wanted, Mr. Ryder?"

Austin gave her a half smile, as though realizing that he'd been dismissed. He put his money on the counter and turned to leave. Then over his shoulder, he replied, "Just one more thing, I guess."

"And what would that be?"

"Do you think you could call me Austin?" He didn't wait for her answer, but continued out the door.

It wasn't until she heard his shop door open and close that Leah could finally breathe.

"Austin," she whispered.

For the next hour, Leah sat at the rolltop desk in the back of the store and tried to balance her account book, a task that usually took only thirty minutes at most. With a sigh, she pushed back her hair and dipped her pen in the ink bottle again. As she stared down at the names and amounts on the ruled page, she realized this was the third time she'd started over. Every time she touched the pen to paper, the lines and ink strokes all ran together and she'd begin daydreaming.

She rested her chin in her hand, and cast a slow, side-long glance at the wall to her right. *He* was on the other side of that wall. What was he doing? Was he working now? She could picture him sitting at his worktable like a watchmaker, his sun blond head bent, making a precision adjustment.

Willfully disregarding any sense of guilt, she allowed her thoughts to drift back to the dream she'd had the night of the dance. Feverish and sweet, it still seemed as real as the lock of hair she twisted on her finger. She imagined his mouth on hers, the barest touch of his tongue to her lips. He smelled good, so familiar. She put her hand on the back of his neck and felt his thick, soft hair beneath her fingers.

"I've brought us a treat," her sister called as she scurried in, carrying a basket.

Bethany's voice jolted Leah out of her shameful reverie, and she dropped her pen, splashing ink all over the ledger. "Oh, blast it!" She felt as guilty as if she'd been caught stealing from the collection plate in church. She turned away from her sister, certain that every lustful thought was clearly written on her face.

"Well, my, but you're jumpy," Bethany clucked, studying her. She walked to the desk and looked over Leah's shoulder. The scents of molasses and vanilla followed her. She gestured at the basket she'd left on the counter. "Leave those boring figures alone and take a break."

"You know, these 'boring figures' are going to be your responsibility pretty soon. I wish you'd spend more time getting familiar with them," Leah said, not quite able to keep the irritable edge out of her voice.

"Oh, I know, but not today. Come on, Leah," Beth cajoled. She reached back to the counter and lifted the white napkin on the basket to reveal molasses cookies. "They're your favorites."

It didn't take much to distract Leah. "All right. I'm not getting very far with this anyway." She put her pen aside and took a cookie. They were moist and fragrant with spices. "I hope you don't expect me to eat them all," she said.

Bethany shook her head between bites. "No, I thought you'd like to take the rest to Josiah later. It would do you good to get away from here for a while."

Leah smiled, gratefully latching onto the idea. Solid, unruffled Josiah. He didn't make her insides jumpy, or drag her thoughts off to private corners where they didn't belong. He might be just what she needed to get her mind off . . . off what she shouldn't be thinking of.

She glanced down at the amulet where it rested over her heart. "Bethany, do you think there really is magic?" If there was a likely believer, it would be Bethany.

Her sister regarded her with her doe brown eyes and shrugged. "You mean like spells and potions and such?"

Leah nodded.

Beth smiled dreamily, her pretty face beatific. "Wouldn't it be wonderful just to make wishes and get what you want? If I could, I'd wish for a wonderful journey to see new places, meet new people. Nothing ever changes in Lost Horse," she said. "But those things don't work, and the people who say they do, well, it's probably just because they *want* to believe."

"You mean the power of suggestion?" she asked, popping the last bite of cookie into her mouth.

Beth had to think for a moment, then she nodded. "But you're always so practical and levelheaded, why are you asking about magic?"

Leah took another cookie and picked up her pen. "I was just wondering how many people Professor Sortilege is able to hoodwink with his talk about being the 'seer of truth' and all that." She hoped she sounded casual.

Her sister laughed. "Even *I* didn't believe that nonsense." She pushed the cookie basket toward Leah. "You should deliver these to Josiah while they're still warm. Sweet spices taste best that way."

Slowly, Leah took the wicker handle in a tight grip and stared at the wall again. Heaven help her, she knew Beth was right: Professor Sortilege and his amulet were just so much nonsense.

CHAPTER ❨ FOUR

𝒜ustin sat at his workbench with the parts of a Smith and Wesson double-action revolver laid out in front of him. He carefully wiped each piece with a lightly oiled rag. The shop was like a bake oven with the doors and windows closed, and he was sweating his brains out. But the nice summer wind blowing outside was loaded with gritty dust that was no friend to firearms. As soon as he got this thing put together again, he planned to go out back and pump water over himself. For now, he only paused to drag his arm across his forehead.

He could do this job in his sleep, he knew it so well, and despite his best efforts, his thoughts began to wander. If he listened carefully, he could hear footsteps next door, and now and then female voices, although he couldn't tell whose.

It had been a damn fool thing to do, going over there like that this morning. The coffee had just been an excuse. But he couldn't stop himself. He'd felt drawn to Whitman's Dry Goods, just as he'd felt compelled to go in search of one woman last Saturday night. That one woman had turned out to be Leah.

He peered into the pistol's chambers, looking for traces of powder. What was it about Leah Whitman that fascinated him? Why couldn't he get her out of his mind? She haunted his thoughts and plagued his sleep. Maybe it was the way one corner of her smile pulled up a tiny bit higher than the other. Or it might be her eyes, the way they changed from green to hazel and back to green again. Plus she had a brain to go along with her looks. But more than anything else, he sensed that beneath her starch and simple prettiness beat the yearning heart of a passionate woman. A woman who would make one hell of a mate for the right man.

It really didn't matter what kind of woman she was, did it? She was engaged to Josiah Campbell and the sooner they married, the better. Then they'd move to Mountain Wells, she'd be gone, and that would be the end of it.

When the pistol was finally in one piece again, he put it away and exhaled a relieved sigh. Sweat ran down the column of his spine in an itchy trickle and crept over his scalp. He threw the oily rag on the worktable and headed to the back door, pulling off his shirt as he went.

Leah gripped the basket in one hand and paused in front of the closed door of Austin's shop to brush off her skirt. The hot, dry wind blowing in from the high desert in the southeast coated everything with grit.

She was not a timid woman, neither was she particularly daring. But she was about to do a daring thing.

. . . a right turn instead of a left . . . and our fates are changed . . .

Her conscience nagged like a toothache. She shouldn't be here. No, ma'am, she should have turned left and gone directly to the church to take these cookies to Josiah. But he got baked treats from Bethany all the time. He wouldn't miss these.

Austin Ryder had lived and worked here for a year, paying his rent every month, as regular as a clock. Leah was just being neighborly, nothing more. And as her sister had so sensibly noted, there was no such thing as magic. Although the amulet still hung from her neck, Leah felt that Beth's observations freed her from Sortilege's poppycock. She chose to disregard the fact that she hadn't cared one whit about anything concerning Austin before now.

She took a deep breath and turned the doorknob. She'd just say hello, drop off the cookies and leave. That's all.

But when Leah pushed open the door, she found the shop empty. It was hot as blazes, and all the windows were closed. She looked around at the glass fronted cabinets that housed rifles and shotguns, their barrels gleaming blue-gray. Pistols lay on a bed of green felt. They were arranged in order of size, from derringers up to a big navy Colt. Behind the counter, boxes of ammunition were stacked neatly on the shelves. The faint smell of metal and gun oil drifted in the air.

With no woman to clean up after him, she'd expected Austin's shop to be a disorderly hodgepodge of spare parts and unswept floors, with drawers pulled open and cabinet doors gaping.

"Hello?" she called quietly. She looked up the stairs. She knew Austin lived up there. There certainly were no cooking facilities, but she'd heard that he ate most of his meals at Pardee's Chop House down the street. "Hello?" All she heard was the sound of the walls ticking under the hot sun.

He wasn't here and after she worked up the courage to come over. Disappointed, she shifted the sweat-damp handle of the basket to her other hand, trying to decide what to do next.

Suddenly she heard the faint *bump-bump-bump* of the pump handle coming from behind the building. She walked through the shop and found the back door open.

Just a few feet away, Austin bent to wet his head under the pump spout while water cascaded over his head and straight, bare back. His jeans were wet from waist to knees.

"Hello? Mr. Ryder—"

Hearing her voice, he snapped upright. The water streamed down his naked upper torso.

"Oh, hi," he said, raking his hair off his forehead. Sparkling droplets clung to his lashes, spiking them, and making his eyes look even bluer than she remembered. He was so handsome standing in the sun with water dripping off his body and his hair slicked back.

Leah indicated the basket. She was having trouble finding her voice. "I brought you some molasses cookies."

"Really? Did you make them?" He sounded pleased.

"N-no, actually, my sister did . . ." Wickedly fascinated, she let her eyes follow the lazy course of the rivulets over his chest, through dark blond hair. They continued down his flat stomach, far below the waistband of his jeans where the top two buttons were open. A sharp line ended his tan. Beneath that border, his skin was as pale as hers. She sucked in a breath—

Seeing the path of her stare, he glanced down. "Sorry. I wasn't expecting company." He turned around and buttoned his pants, giving her a view of his well-formed shoulders and slender waist. Facing her again, he gestured at the pump. "I was working. It got hot."

"Yes," she agreed, swallowing, "it is warm, isn't it." At that moment, all Leah could remember was his comment that wet jeans weren't so uncomfortable without underwear. She felt herself being pulled to him, like a weak swimmer caught in a strong current, and knew she had to get away.

Staring at the horizon over his shoulder, she tried to make her exit. "Anyway, we had these extra cookies, and I thought you might like them." She held them out to him. "I really have to be getting back to the store."

He took the basket and set it on the bench, his eyes fixed on her.

"Leah."

She looked up into his face again. Everything she'd ever noticed about him—the bone and muscle of him, his smile, the color of his eyes, his very maleness—everything that she'd once considered to be too extreme she suddenly found powerfully, dangerously attractive. She couldn't understand why she hadn't noticed before, or why she was aware of it now. Oh, God, how had this happened to her? She didn't want to turn into one of those feckless, prattling women who sighed after Austin Ryder.

"I don't think it's proper for you to address me so informally." She could hear her own voice shaking, stealing whatever conviction her words may have held.

"I've never worried much about what's proper and

what isn't. Only about what's right." He took her wrists
in a light grip and leaned close.

"They're the same thing," she said a bit breathlessly,
trying not to give away her nervousness. She could feel
heat pouring off him in waves.

"Not always," he murmured next to her ear. Just the
sound of his voice made her eyes drift closed. "Thank
you for the cookies." Then he pressed a soft, whispery
kiss high on her cheek. She felt his wet hair drip on her
shoulder, she smelled the water on his skin, and his clean
scent. He was warm and cool at the same time. This was
wrong, she told herself, all wrong. She'd never behaved
like this in her life.

He released one wrist, and reluctantly, she opened her
eyes. His expression was serious and expectant, as
though he waited for a response from her. Or was it
some kind of permission he sought? Behind his handsome face, she thought she detected a sadness, a burden
that he carried alone. No, no, she couldn't see anything.
The temptation to linger was strong, but if she didn't go
now, she knew she might do something that would
shame Josiah's faith and trust.

She pulled her hand free and backed away. "I-I hope
you like the cookies," she babbled, and ran through the
open back door of Whitman's, hoping she wouldn't meet
Bethany in the storeroom. There she huddled in a dim
corner staring at six-dozen genuine Chinese back
scratchers until her heart stopped thundering and she
regained her breath.

For the next couple of days, Leah avoided Austin. She
made certain she didn't walk past his windows, but went
around the building instead. She stayed away from the
open storeroom door whenever she thought he might be
out in the back. And she made a deliberate effort to
concentrate on Whitman's and her own upcoming wedding.

But she couldn't stop thinking about him. She never
should have gone over there, she scolded herself again
and again. Sometimes, when things were especially quiet
in Whitman's, she might hear him bounding up or down

the stairs next door. She remembered the tender feel of his mouth on her cheek when he'd kissed her, and his gentle grip on her wrists. Of course, that led her to thinking about the way he'd looked, staring at her with sky blue eyes, his wet hair creating streams that ran down his chest and past the open buttons on his jeans.

What she also couldn't get off her mind was Bethany's lack of aptitude for merchandising. It kept Leah awake nights. At least it did when she wasn't thinking about Austin Ryder. All of this went a long way toward making Leah short-tempered and irritable, a decided change in a woman who generally kept her feelings to herself.

Desperate to make up for her wanton, disloyal dreams and thoughts, Leah sought to spend more time with Josiah. But he was usually busy, writing sermons or volumes of instructions to Mr. Parkerson, the minister who would take over Lost Horse's church. The rest of his time was occupied with seeing to the preparations for their trip and helping his congregation.

He stopped by late one quiet afternoon when she was going over the books with Bethany, explaining to her for the third time Whitman's policy of extending credit.

"But if people can't pay, why do you let them buy things?" Bethany asked, her smooth forehead creased with effort. She sat on a stool next to Leah, the ledger book open between them on the desk.

With the patience acquired from her years at Lost Horse school, Leah pointed to a name in the book. "Here's Tom Wickwire. He's a good example of what I mean. You know that Tom is a farmer, and usually, farmers see cash only when they sell their crops. The rest of the year, they get by on credit at the blacksmith, the feed store, Whitman's, and so on. They couldn't survive otherwise. In the fall when their crops come in, they get paid and then they pay us. I know that Tom and the other farmers are good for the money, and they'll come to pay us—or rather, you—sometime in September. Does that make it a little clearer?"

Beth bit her lower lip, then nodded slowly. "Yes, I suppose. Except—"

Just then Josiah walked in, rubbing his hands together

with glee. His white collar and dark clothes were as dusty as a cowboy's, but that didn't detract from his ecclesiastical dignity. "How are my two favorite ladies this afternoon?" He seemed positively delighted, as though he harbored some wonderful secret. Leah had never seen him so animated. His good spirits were contagious.

"Oh, Josiah, I'm so glad you stopped by." Maybe he'd be able to distract her from thoughts of Austin. "It seems like ages since you've been over for supper. Won't you come by tonight?" she asked, urgently hoping that he'd accept.

Beth perked up immediately, closing the ledger book with a thud. "If Josiah is going to have supper with us, I won't be able to spend any more time helping you with this, Leah. You know I haven't had time to go to the butcher store today, what with going over these accounts and all."

Leah had taught school long enough to recognize a bored, inattentive student.

"Never mind about any of that," Josiah said, nearly bursting with excitement. "We'll have lots of time to eat together, years and years. But right now, I want to show you—both of you—the wagon I bought. Come out and see it."

"How thrilling, Leah," Beth exclaimed, jumping up from her seat in a swish of skirts and petticoats.

"Well . . . all right," Leah replied, her buoyancy deflated. She put aside her pen and rose from her chair.

They followed him out to look at the object of his enthusiasm and found a broken-down covered wagon. Its grayed canvas hung in ribbons that fluttered in the languid breeze. The pair of mules that were hitched to it looked only slightly better than the burden they pulled.

On the other side of the street, Mot's Regulars watched with great interest.

Leah sent a dubious look to Beth, but her sister was busy examining the wagon with a fascination that illuminated her pretty features.

"Oh, Leah, this really will be an adventure," she rhapsodized. "Think of all the wonderful new things you'll see."

Obviously, they both saw some merit in the vehicle that Leah did not. When she looked at Josiah, she noticed that the door to Austin's shop was open. He sat at his worktable, assembling a rifle. As if knowing precisely the right moment, he looked up just long enough for their eyes to connect before he went back to his task.

"It's a prairie schooner," Josiah announced proudly, running a hand over one of the wide wheels. "It made the trip all the way out here from Missouri back in 'fifty-three. You can't find quality like this anymore."

Leah tried not to laugh, but one chuckle got away from her before she choked it back.

"I know it isn't new," he admitted a bit defensively, "but it's sturdy and I'm sure it can be repaired. I'm still looking for an ox team to pull it. Of course, it needs a canvas. And it's not as big as I'd hoped, so I'm afraid we'll have to leave that old desk of yours here. But I know you won't mind, Leah." It was an assumption, not a question. "With all the schoolbooks and Bibles and tools we need to pack—the really important things—there just won't be room for it."

Leah looked in the small wagon box again. "Oh, dear, I suppose that's true," she said, trying to keep the dismay out of her voice. She'd counted on taking her father's desk; it would be a way she could carry part of Whitman's with her to her new home. Of course, Josiah knew best. The books were more important. It was just that the desk had meant so much to her.

Pausing long enough to detect her distress, Josiah made a passing attempt to cheer her. He patted her arm and said soothingly, "Now, now, Leah. It will be all right. Once we get to Mountain Wells, you'll have so much work to do, there won't be time to miss that desk. And maybe in three or four years, we can come back to Lost Horse and get it."

"Josiah's right," Beth put in. "You don't need that old desk. You have a wonderful new life. And I'll take care of it for you in the meantime. It will be sitting right here waiting for you."

Three or four years. She glanced back at the storefront and a funny little shiver whipped through her. If Whitman's was still here in three or four years.

"I see you're still wearing that necklace," he said with a smile, but a slightly disapproving tone.

Leah automatically reached for the pendant and covered it with her hand. "I didn't think you'd really mind."

Josiah shrugged, then gave Leah a quick, dry peck on the cheek. "Just so you take it off before the wedding." He bid them good-bye and climbed up to the wagon seat. "Thanks for the supper invitation," he said, taking up the lines, "but I still have a lot to do before we leave. Maybe next week—" With that, the two sorry-looking mules lurched forward and the wagon took off, leaving Beth and Leah in a haze of dust.

As soon as he was gone, Bethany turned and said brightly, "I'm going to run along now, since you don't need me anymore today."

"But—" Leah began to protest, then thought better of it. There was no point in trying to make her stay any longer this afternoon. "That's fine, Beth. I'll probably be late. I need to finish some things."

"All right. I'll keep your supper warm for you." She turned to leave. "Oh, Mr. *Ryder.* How nice to see you again."

Leah glanced over her shoulder and saw Austin leaning against his doorjamb. He stood with his arms folded over his chest, and his ankles crossed. The sleeves of his wheat-colored shirt were rolled up, revealing his long-muscled forearms.

"Ladies," he acknowledged.

"We weren't able to persuade Reverend Campbell to join us for supper this evening. Perhaps you might favor us?" Bethany asked.

Leah shot a quick, horrified look at Beth, who was giving him her most becoming smile.

"That's very kind of you, Miss Whitman, but I have something I need to attend to," he said, and Leah recognized the tone an adult would use with a child.

Obviously disappointed, Bethany bid them good-bye, letting her gaze linger on Austin.

Feeling suddenly lonely, Leah shaded her eyes with

her hand and watched her sister cross the street. Bethany waved at the old pensioners on Mot's porch as she passed, and one of them said something to her. Leah couldn't hear what, but Beth's clear, carefree laughter floated back to her.

With a tired sigh, Leah turned to go back into the store and pulled up short when she saw Austin still standing in his doorway. He was watching Bethany, too, with a speculative expression. Then he focused on her.

He nodded in the direction that Josiah had taken. "That was quite a wagon the reverend bought for you."

She laughed nervously. "He didn't buy it for me. Josiah would never do that." Austin raised his brows at her, making her think about what she'd said. "I mean, he was thinking of everything we need to haul to Mountain Wells."

"Everything except your desk." He considered her with those clear blue eyes. The breeze lifted one blond streak of his hair and blew it behind his shoulder.

Leah's ears grew warm, realizing he'd heard the entire conversation. "He was right, of course. Josiah is always right. The desk isn't important."

"I think it's important to *you.*" He remained where he stood, leaning against the doorframe, and once again Leah had the feeling of being drawn to him. How seldom anyone thought of what might be important to her. This man did, and he was little more than a stranger. She studied the few feet of planking that separated them, and imagined crossing it to feel his hands on hers again.

When she glanced up, he wore the same expression she'd seen the last time they talked, the day she took the cookies to him. Like he was waiting for her to say something, do something. What, she couldn't imagine, but she didn't dare think about it. Her thoughts were already scandalous enough.

"Good afternoon, Mr. Ryder," she said, edging toward her door.

"Austin," he corrected softly.

She inhaled deeply and forced her eyes away from his. "Austin."

Then she hurried inside.

CHAPTER ☾ FIVE

For the rest of the afternoon, Leah moved around in a distracted fog, going through the motions of her work, but with her mind on Austin Ryder. Emmaline Stevens asked for sugar. Leah measured out salt. Hector Bosson stopped in for horse liniment, and she gave him a bottle of vanilla extract. She thought the day would never end.

When six o'clock finally came, it was with a sense of relief that Leah locked the doors and drew the shades. The shade pull was still in her hand when she heard a voice behind her.

"Hello."

She whirled to find Austin standing in the doorway between the storeroom and the counter. He carried a big napkin-covered tray.

He smiled and nodded at the tray. "I had Pardee's Chop House put supper together for us. I thought you might be hungry."

"Us?" she said. "Surely you didn't mention my name."

He gave her a steady look. "No, I told Mrs. Pardee I was having supper with a friend. Is that true?"

She glanced around the store—for what? Someone to rescue her from the temptation to share a meal with this man? Or for a reason to say yes? Leah was finding it more and more difficult to maintain a sensible perspective about him, and he wasn't making the job any easier.

"I appreciate the thought, really I do, but I have a lot of work—"

"Come on, Leah, I brought dishes and everything," he

coaxed. He put the tray on the counter and pulled off the blue-checked cloth. "Hmm, let's see. Mrs. Pardee gave me a pot of stew, and fresh bread and butter." He looked up at her again. "It smells good."

Leah dropped the shade pull and came closer, wary but curious. Yes, it did smell good, and she hadn't eaten much since breakfast.

"Oh, all right," she relented, her heart uplifted. "There's a stool behind you next to the desk. We can eat there."

They spread the dishes between them on her desk. Austin ladled the stew while she sliced the bread. The scents of the stew and warm bread brought back her appetite.

"I have something that will go with this," she said, reaching for a jar of blueberry jam on the shelf. She spread the jam on the buttered bread and took a large bite. It was the most delicious thing she'd ever tasted; suddenly her taste buds were awakened. In fact, all of her senses seemed particularly keen. She could hear the wall clock ticking softly near the front door. The color of the jam was beautifully vivid. The glass jar in her hand felt cool and smooth.

Austin looked up from his stew and chuckled. "See? You *are* hungry." Reaching for his napkin, he wiped her upper lip. "You've got blueberry on your face."

Leah laughed sheepishly and picked up her own napkin. It was nice to have someone fuss over her. Austin had a light, caring side that she hadn't expected.

"It's good to hear you laugh," he remarked, using her knife to spread butter and blueberries on his own bread. "I've gotten the feeling that it's not something you do very often."

The observation surprised her. "I'm not a giggler, if that's what you mean. Now, Bethany—she's a giggler. Her laugh is like music. At least that's what my father used to say. I guess I've always tended to be more serious."

Austin hooked one boot heel on the rung of the stool and munched his bread. "Even when you were growing up?"

Leah nodded. "I'm eight years older than Bethany, so I was expected to behave correctly and set a good example for her. She was so delicate and pretty, everyone naturally felt protective of her."

"I guess that must have been hard for you sometimes." He speared a cube of beef with his fork. "She's not prettier than you."

No one had ever told her that before! Her gaze fell from his crystal blue eyes to her lap and she smoothed her napkin. "No, Bethany is much lovelier than I am. And I'm her sister—I only did what was proper."

Austin groaned impatiently. "Damn, there's that word again. You mean it was proper to sacrifice your happiness for her?"

"I haven't done that! Why, look at my engagement, for example. I'd expected Beth to be settled with children of her own long ago. I didn't think that anyone would ever ask—well, I didn't know if I'd decide to get married. But Josiah chose me to be his wife, and I'm going to Mountain Wells, even though—" She caught herself, but not in time.

He watched her, apparently waiting for her to finish the sentence. When she didn't, he gently prompted her. "Even though?"

"Even though I'll miss this old place," she admitted. "I practically grew up working here. And Beth, she's not suited to this life. I suppose I'm worried."

"Things could change. You never know what's around the next corner. Maybe Josiah will decide that he doesn't want to go to Mountain Wells." He popped a piece of bread crust into his mouth and looked her straight in the eyes. "Or maybe you'll change your mind."

"No, I won't. What about you—"

"Me? I wouldn't want to go to Mountain Wells, either. I like Lost Horse."

"No, I mean haven't you ever had to do something you didn't really want to because it was the proper thing?"

Austin let his eyes drop from Leah's to her pendant. He could have sworn the damned thing was glowing slightly, as though a flame burned within it. He stared at it, transfixed, and without warning his memory carried him back five years to a rainy night when his life changed. When he glanced up again at Leah's open, waiting expression, he felt a compelling urge to tell her about that night. He couldn't imagine why; he'd never talked about it with anyone. He only knew that he *had* to tell her, that she'd understand.

He laid his napkin down next to his plate and leaned closer to her. "I know all about doing the proper thing. It was a lesson I learned when I was the sheriff in Waterville, Kansas."

"You were a *sheriff?*"

He almost laughed at the surprise in her wide eyes. "For three years. The pay wasn't great, but it was enough for a man to get married on. I was going to settle down with Sarah, make a nice little life with her. She didn't like my job much—for a while, Waterville was one hell of a cow town, with the shootings and barroom scrapes that go along with cow towns." He shrugged. "Although I think what happened to me could have happened anywhere. But for all the fights I jumped into, and drunken cowboys I arrested, I killed only one man." He expected a reaction from her, but she sat, just listening, hardly breathing. Austin went on. "Sarah had a brother, and Tom Allen was a mean, rotten kid on any day. Full of whiskey, he was no better than the devil himself. One night, a barboy came running to my office to say his boss wanted me to come and get Tom. He was drunk and waving his gun around, threatening the customers. Bad for business, he said." He put his fork and the knife across his plate. "Well, I got to the saloon, and yeah, there was Tom, acting like a jackass, spoiling for a fight. One thing led to another, and he drew on me. Drunk as he was, he was still fast. Tom was either going to kill me, or I was going to kill him and save myself. I saved myself. I tried to explain it to Sarah, but she didn't see it that way. She said I didn't do the 'proper' thing, and called me a murderer."

"But surely she didn't expect you to let her brother kill you."

He leaned his back against the wall and considered
her eyes. They were hazel tonight. When he spoke, his
words were quiet. "I've had five years to think about it
and to this day, I'm not certain she didn't. So that's why I
think that what's proper and what's right don't often
cross paths."

Leah nodded. "And you became a gunsmith?"

"Eventually. I sure couldn't be a lawman anymore. A
lawman ends up drawing his revolver now and then. It's
part of the job. But after I shot Tom, I'd freeze every
time I had to pull that gun. I was lucky I didn't get killed,
too. So I quit. But I tried my hand at a lot of different
lines of work before I came here."

She studied him, her head tilted as though measuring
him as a man. "I don't think you're a killer," she pronounced finally.

Leah's words were unaccountably comforting. He
didn't know why; they hardly knew each other. But he
guessed he knew as much as he needed to.

Smiling at her, he replied, "Well, I'll tell you one
thing. I could have shot at that damned monkey of the
professor's without a twinge."

"Austin," Leah whispered. Her voice was so fluttery next
to his ear that it gave him goose bumps.

In this green meadow they were alone, the only man
and woman in the world. Her hazel-green eyes, fringed
with dark lashes, pierced his soul with their innocent passion. He tightened his arm around her waist and kissed
her again. The inside of her mouth was slick and warm
where his tongue grazed it. The feel of her breasts
against his chest started a fire in his blood that burned
hotter with every passing second, fanned by the scent of
lavender and the softness of her hair.

He pulled away from her lips and pressed kisses to her
throat, while his hand moved to her breast. As he
touched her, she gasped, and he knew she was surprised
and aroused.

The buttons on the front of her pink dress opened
easily, almost magically, under his fingers. Beneath, the
thin fabric of her camisole he could see the dusky rose

shadows of her nipples. Her eyes drifted closed, and she leaned into his hand.

"Leah," he groaned.

"Yes, Austin . . . yes."

The ripe promise in her low-throated words was all he needed to hear. He lay her on the soft bed of new grass, the oak branches overhead rustled in the light breeze.

He lay beside her, propped on his elbow, and lifted her hand to his mouth to kiss her fingers. Then he opened her hand and pressed another kiss into her palm. She drew his head to her open bodice.

A full-grown woman and yet sweetly naive. He knew no other man had touched her. She was his alone. And he needed her now.

"I love you, Austin."

Austin Ryder rolled over in his hot, tangled bedding, but he didn't find sleep again till an hour before dawn.

"I love you, Leah."

She sat in the chair by her window, looking at the dark yard below. The words kept playing in her mind, again and again. Behind her, her bed was an uncomfortable jumble of twisted sheets. A soft wind lifted her white curtains, and a half moon slipped down the western side of the night sky.

This was torture. At night she couldn't put her head on her pillow without seeing Austin Ryder walk across the landscape of her sleep. And every dream was more brazen than the last. Tonight, she'd allowed him to un-button her dress, and to put his hand on her bare skin. Allowed him? No, she'd encouraged him. And it had felt wonderful.

In that meadow she'd never seen anywhere but in these dreams, he'd called her name. He spoke it next to her ear, so softly that his breath had ruffled her hair and given her goose bumps. The desire in his eyes was unmistakable. She gripped the arm of her chair. And worse, oh, God, worst of all, when he'd lifted her left hand to kiss it, she'd seen a flash of gold on her ring finger. She actually dreamed of being married to Josiah, and making love with Austin.

Damn that Xavier Sortilege, Leah thought harshly. And damn Esmeralda, too. She'd been content and happy before they walked into the store. She knew what her future would be. Now everything had changed.

Early the following day, while a trace of dew still misted the dry scrubland surrounding Lost Horse, Leah walked to Whitman's. The days of summer were wearing on, and dawn came a bit later each morning. A faint pink glow tinted the treetops and Ned Gorling's white geese as they wandered along the road in search of breakfast.

Today she'd almost left the amulet on her dressing table. What if it really was the cause of all her problems? But as soon as that idea crossed her mind, she'd stubbornly put on the necklace. It was absolutely ridiculous to think that a gold chain and a chunk of stone could create havoc in her life and give her shameful thoughts about a man she had regarded with disdain just a few short weeks ago.

She thought again of what Austin had told her about being a sheriff. She'd felt certain he'd been involved with the law somehow. Except she'd thought he was on the other side of it. Apparently the ladies in town were right, little did they know: Austin had come to Lost Horse to escape a personal tragedy. And that made things even harder for Leah. Rather than making him seem weak, in her view he was all the more attractive.

When she arrived at Whitman's, her eyes strayed to his upstairs windows. She hadn't seen that side of the second floor since he'd leased the space. But she knew what the scanty furniture looked like, and it wasn't at all difficult for her to imagine him asleep on the bed. It would be warm in that room. She could picture him lying nearly naked on the mattress, boneless and relaxed, with just a sheet thrown over his hips. His one-day beard cast a shadow on his jaw, and her imagination drifted down his throat to his chest to watch it rise and fall with the nearly imperceptible breathing of deep sleep. A combination of tenderness and ardor stirred within her, followed immediately by scorching embarrassment. She looked up and down the quiet main street, as though her every thought was visible to anyone who might be look-ing at her.

Weren't her dreams about Austin bad enough? she wondered as she dragged her gaze from his bedroom window. Now her mind was straying to forbidden images during her waking hours.

She walked quickly to her own door and unlocked it. Immediately the wonderful scents of three decades filled her head. As honored as she was that Josiah had chosen her to be his wife, she'd told Austin the truth: a wave of homesickness swept over her whenever she thought of leaving the store and worse, leaving it in Bethany's charge. If only they could stay on in Lost Horse for a while after they married, to begin their new lives here, and to give her a little more time with the store. But nothing in life remained the same, she thought as she walked to the back door, no matter how much we might wish for it. She wished she had Bethany's adventuresome spirit.

In the dim storeroom, she found the chamber sets that she planned to wash and move to the front window. She picked up a bucket to go out to the pump for water.

As soon as she put her hand on the knob, she was again struck with a vague feeling of light-headedness, as though she'd stood up too fast. But she hadn't been sit-ting. The bucket slipped from her hand and hit the floor with a thud. Fresh air would make her feel better, she decided, opening the door. The sun was bright and she shaded her eyes as she breathed deeply. If these spells didn't go away, she'd have to go see Doc Baxter. His diagnosis would probably be lack of sleep.

Finally, the feeling passed, and she was about to step out of the door when she saw something bright on the stoop.

Her heart flip-flopped in her chest, in a battle of joy and fear. At her feet was the basket that she'd taken to Austin filled with cookies. He had returned it to her filled with flowers. Black-eyed Susans, bachelor's but-tons, daisies, Queen Anne's lace, and graceful stalks of lavender, all damp with dew, tumbled out of the basket. They were beautiful.

As Leah reached down to pick up the basket she heard the sound of water splashing. She leaned out the door and saw Austin shaving in front of a mirror hung on the wall. A towel was slung over his bare shoulder and his razor flashed in the morning sun. His jeans were buttoned this time, but they hung so low, they seemed suspended on his hipbones.

He was achingly handsome, she thought. She looked at his shoulders, at the light and shadow created by the movement of muscles under his skin, at the tight, narrow tapering of his waist. She knew she shouldn't look at him this way, but he was impossible to ignore.

"Austin?" Her voice sounded small and high to her own ears.

Austin looked up at the sound of Leah's voice. She stood in the doorway, clutching the basket of flowers he'd left for her, looking hesitant and vulnerable. Her high-necked white blouse and dark green skirt made her look much younger than he'd guessed her to be.

With one quick glance in the mirror, he scraped the last of the lather off his face and wiped it with the towel. Then he threw both the towel and the blade on the bench, and walked slowly toward her.

She gestured at the basket. "Thank you for the flowers. I . . . well . . ." Her cheeks turned a becoming shade of pink, and her eyes were wide and full of emotion she couldn't hide.

"I know that you've felt it, too," he said simply.

She nodded then lifted the pendant from its resting place on her bosom and held it out to him. "It has to be because of what the professor told me about this amulet he gave me. He said if I wore it under a full moon, it would draw my true love to me, and if I kissed that man, we'd be bound for life. Then you kissed me at the grange hall dance. You weren't supposed to. Josiah was supposed to kiss me. And now this is happening to us. But I know it's only the power of suggestion. It *must* be. There is no such thing as magic."

"Maybe not, Leah," he said, smiling at her, "but the

professor didn't tell me that story. I didn't even know about the necklace. And I can't stop thinking about you. Or dreaming about you."

Her pink cheeks reddened. "But—but I'm engaged."

He didn't want to be reminded of that. Instead, he stepped closer and ran his hands up and down her arms, rucking the fabric of her sleeves. He'd never noticed before the spray of pale freckles across her nose. Or the graceful arch of her silky brows. "You might change your mind."

"I'm to be married," she said again, looking around as if someone might be watching.

"*I* might change your mind."

"No, no, I shouldn't be out here with you. It isn't proper."

"I told you I don't give a damn about what's proper," he said, passion lowering his words to a rumble. "I only care about what's right. It's right with you and me." Austin could hardly believe he was saying this. He'd never expected to tell that to any woman again, much less Leah Whitman. But he meant it.

He gripped her hand and stared down into her pretty, upturned face. Her faint, sweet fragrance went right to his heart, compelling him to kiss the corner of her mouth, the smooth soft spot below her ear, the tip of her nose.

"Leah," he whispered, and with a small, anguished cry, she dropped the basket and flung her arms around him.

Inexorably, the plans went forward for the marriage of Leah and Josiah, as if they had a life and momentum of their own. And even though she stopped wearing the amulet, she and Austin took every opportunity to meet. Theirs was a difficult secret to keep. She wanted to chatter about him to anyone who would listen. Of course, she couldn't, but if it was noticed that she'd stopped complaining about her tenant, it wasn't remarked upon.

She found him easy to talk to, and she learned things about him she was certain he'd shared with very few others. He talked about his years as a sheriff. She touched on the edges of her history as the responsible older sister. He had good ideas for Whitman's, and she suggested ways that his gunsmith shop might expand.

And whether they were talking or not, they couldn't keep their hands off each other.

Sometimes she'd go to his shop early in the morning and they'd spend a half hour together, sharing fevered, urgent kisses, made all the more intense by the secrecy forced upon them. Other times Austin would come to her if she was working late, bringing supper from Pardee's. Inevitably, the brief evenings would end with the two of them in each other's arms, frantically trying to get enough of what was never enough.

During a fitting for her wedding gown, she'd stood before her mirror while Bethany pinned up the hem. Looking at the white fabric, she felt like the biggest hypocrite in the world. It wasn't that she was no longer a virgin, in the technical sense. The fires between her and Austin burned hot (though not as hot as hellfire, she was miserably positive), but their relationship remained unconsummated. Just barely.

To justify the time she spent at the store, Leah used the very real excuse that she was tying up all of the loose ends before turning over the business to Bethany. Her sister was showing infinitesimal improvement in her business skills, easing Leah's mind to the same degree.

Elation and guilt wracked her whenever she thought about Austin, which was most of her waking hours. Her sense of duty ran strong and deep. Austin had said that right and proper were not always the same. But doing the proper thing had never produced so much guilt—or rapture—as her relationship with Austin. What was she going to do? she asked herself again and again.

"You can't marry him, Leah," Austin said early one morning as they sat on the bench behind the building eating breakfast. The low sun glinted off the gold streaks in his hair, and made him squint. The wedding was two and a half weeks away. "We're meant for each other. I can feel it and I know you can, too. Do what's right, not what's proper." A muscle in his jaw tightened.

"But if you give your word to someone, it *is* the right thing to honor on your pledge. Isn't it, Austin?"

"Not if both of you will be miserable," he said. He put down his coffee cup and took her hands in his tight grip. "Do you love him?"

"Josiah is a good man, he's fair and decent. I have a lot of respect for him. Everyone in Lost Horse respects him."

"That's not what I asked you, Leah. Do you *love him?*"

She dropped her gaze to her lap. How could she say yes? Love had never been mentioned, not when Josiah proposed to her, or at any time since. And although she'd known him for years, they'd spent very little time together since they became engaged. He'd been so busy getting ready for their trip, and she'd been occupied with Whitman's. When she didn't answer, Austin raised her chin with his finger, forcing her to look at him.

"I'll tell you what I think," he said, a trace of anger in his voice. "I don't think Josiah Campbell was planning to marry. Then he got the offer to go to Mountain Wells, and they told him if he could bring a school teacher along, it would be that much better. And which woman in Lost Horse fit that bill?"

Leah's insides clenched, but she said nothing. The seed of this troubling suspicion had already been planted by Mayor Hoyt at the last grange dance.

Austin continued, his voice tight. "And somewhere along the way, you got the idea that you aren't pretty enough, or desirable enough to attract a husband, so when Josiah asked to marry you, you accepted."

After a lifetime of living in her sister's shadow, Leah knew in her heart she hadn't merely accepted the proposal. She'd been grateful to get it. Pathetically grateful.

"Do you mean that he doesn't care for me at all?" She tried to keep the hurt out of her voice, but it trembled with choked back tears.

He pulled her into his arms and drew her head to his shoulder. His voice lost its anger and became suffused with tenderness. "No, honey, I don't mean that at all. I know Campbell is a good man. He cares about people, and I know he respects you." He rested his chin on the top of her head and let out a deep sigh. "I just wish you weren't marrying him."

Leah rested her cheek against his shirt, and wondered why heartache was the reward for doing what was right.

Chapter ❨ Six

"Do come on, Leah," Bethany called from the hall. "We were supposed to be at the grange hall at seven o'clock. It's already seven-fifteen and Josiah went on without us."

"I'll be there in a minute," Leah answered. She looked under the dresser scarf and pulled open drawers. She patted the pockets of her dresses where they hung in the wardrobe. She scanned the floor and peered beneath her dressing table.

It just wasn't here. The amulet was nowhere to be found. Even though she no longer wore it, she'd look at it from time to time, trying to decide if it had truly brought her and Austin together. Taking it off hadn't dimmed their attraction to each other.

She'd been so distracted lately, she'd probably put it in some safe place. Except now she couldn't remember where that might be. Not that she'd planned to wear it tonight. Not after what had happened when she'd worn it to the last dance. Everything in her life had been turned upside down and become hopelessly complicated.

Even though the necklace didn't have any mystical powers, there was no point in tempting providence by wearing it again. But she didn't like not knowing where it was.

"Lee-ah!" Bethany called again, her impatience obvious in her singsongy tone.

Leah smoothed her hair and took a deep breath, hoping that this dance tonight would be uneventful.

* * *

The festivities were well underway and her punch bowl empty as Leah looked for Bethany to take her place with the ladle so she could get some air. But when she finally spotted her sister, headed toward the door, she saw a sparkling red-purple stone resting on the bodice of Beth's dress.

Her amulet! Now she knew why she couldn't find it. Bethany had taken it without bothering to ask. And she must have put the necklace in her pocket while they walked over here so Leah wouldn't see it. They'd certainly discuss it when they got home.

Leah glanced around for someone else to spell her when Monroe Eggins found his way to her table.

"Here's Lost Horse's next bride. They've got you in charge of the refreshments again, eh, Leah?" Monroe was one of Mot's Regulars. He was a jolly, red-faced man with whom she usually enjoyed talking when he came to Whitman's to buy his tobacco. Tonight, though, her mind was elsewhere. The best she could manage were polite, distracted responses.

"Me and the boys was just sayin' the other day what a lucky man your Reverend Campbell is," he continued. He nodded toward Josiah where he stood talking with the crowd of young people in the doorway. "Not only did he get a good woman, he got a school teacher just when he needed one. Yessiree, a lucky man."

Leah, who'd also been looking at Josiah, turned her eyes back sharply to the old man's florid face. Was that what *everyone* thought? But she smiled at him politely. "Thank you, Mr. Eggins."

"We're sure lookin' forward to your weddin'. We ain't had one here since last October when the widder Sherman finally landed old Tater Ramsey. She was right pleased she got him afore the winter snows commenced. Those cold nights get mighty long up to her place, y'know." He let out a cackle that reminded Leah of a hen that had just laid an egg.

"I'm afraid I'm out of punch just now, Mr. Eggins," Leah interjected over his high-pitched chortle, hoping to distract him and send him on his way.

Pulling out a big white handkerchief, he mopped his sweating forehead, then stuffed the square of linen into his back pocket. "What? Oh, don't you fret about me none, Leah." He opened his jacket to reveal a silver flask. "I got all the punch I need right here."

He waved as he shuffled off, and Leah watched him go with a feeling of relief. It was hot and stuffy and she wanted a break. She made her way to the door, looking for Josiah.

Outdoors, the heat and noise of the dance faded, and Leah heard the faint call of crickets. She wandered a bit farther over the dry grass and found a hay bale to sit on. It was a lovely evening, not too warm, and lighted by a full moon. It seemed bigger and more golden than last month's moon, the one under which Austin had kissed her that first time.

Austin. He wasn't here tonight, and she should be grateful for that, she supposed. It would be difficult to have both Josiah and him in the same room—even a room as big as the grange hall—and pretend indifference. If Josiah even noticed.

Several people had mentioned they were looking forward to her wedding. One week from tonight, she would be Mrs. Josiah Campbell. In one week she'd be gone from Bethany and Whitman's, gone from Lost Horse. Gone from Austin.

She put her elbows on her knees and rested her chin in her hands. It couldn't go on like this. It wasn't fair to any of them. She'd have to decide. She looked across the moonfrosted landscape to where couples were seated on hay bales. While none of them were engaged in what she would have once referred to as immodest behavior, she noticed heads together and arms linked. She felt, rather than saw, the affection and yearning that emanated from them like an invisible energy. Was she only aware of that energy now that she had experienced it?

One couple was more demonstrative than the others. They stood in the deepest shadows of the oak tree and clung to each other with a palpable, desperate passion. Their behavior was indeed immodest. Sighing, Leah supposed she'd better go and see if she could find Josiah to speak to them. She certainly didn't feel equal to the task.

She rose and walked toward the hall, glancing back at the two. For a fraction of a second, she saw what she thought was the small red spark of a match flare between them. That grass was too dry to be carelessly lighting matches. The whole field could go up.

As she neared the hall, she paused to brush the hay off her skirt in the yellow light pouring through the open doors. Around the lanterns by the door, moths fluttered in circles, bumping the glass chimneys.

"Leah, there you are. I've been looking for you." Bethany hurried up to her from the darkness beyond. Her usually creamy skin was flushed as if with a fever and her doe brown eyes were wide. Her breath came in short gasps as though she'd been running.

Leah clutched her arm. "Beth! What happened? You don't look well."

"I'll be all right, but really, Leah, I think I'd like to go home now." Suspended from its gold chain around Bethany's slim neck, the amulet glowed like an ember in the lantern light.

"Yes, of course, we'll leave right now. I'll just tell Josiah."

"No. No, you stay. I can get home by myself. I'll be fine." Leah had never known Bethany to act like this.

"But you can't walk unescorted. It wouldn't be proper." The word slipped out before she had a chance to think. Proper—it was what Austin talked about.

"I'm not worried," Beth said. "I just want to get away from here. I need some time to myself. Please." She gave Leah a searching, almost anguished look that scared Leah.

Leah released her arm with some reluctance. "All right, Beth," she said quietly. "You go on. I'll be home soon."

Bethany whirled and sped across the grass. When she reached the road, she picked up her skirts and ran. Leah watched her until she was out of sight. What could have happened to her? Had someone said something, done something to hurt her?

Suddenly Josiah came around the corner of the building.

"Oh, Josiah," she said. "I'm so glad I found you."

"Leah, what's wrong? You look upset," he said.

"It's Bethany. I don't know if she's ill or hurt—she wouldn't tell me. But she ran away, saying she wanted to go home. It worries me that she's out there by herself. Will you go find her, please, Josiah, and make sure she gets home safely?"

He turned to look at the direction Bethany had taken, his face full of concern. "Yes, of course I'll go. She shouldn't be wandering around at night by herself."

Just then she felt a light pinch on her elbow. With a start, she turned to see Austin.

"Hello, Miss Whitman," he said with the right amount of formality. "Reverend."

"Mr. Ryder, wait. If I could have just a moment of your time," Josiah said, his tone commanding, challenging.

Leah froze, her heart bumping around in her chest like a bee in a jar. She watched Austin turn slowly toward them, a chill, blank smile fixed on his face. Suddenly, she knew what an outlaw might have felt facing Austin over the point of a gun. God, no, she thought, please don't let this be happening. Josiah didn't know—couldn't know . . .

"What can I do for you, Reverend?" Austin asked evenly.

"Mr. Ryder, you could do me a tremendous favor, as a matter of fact." Josiah looked as tense and tightly drawn as she'd ever seen him.

Austin straightened, squaring his shoulders. The wind blew his hair back behind his shoulders. "And what might that be?"

"If you could see Leah home, I'd appreciate it very much. I need to attend to a small emergency, and I don't know if I'll be back in time to escort her myself."

Leah quietly released her breath.

Austin relaxed ever so slightly, too. "Sure, I'd be happy to."

Josiah nodded once and rushed off.

Austin pulled her aside. "I hope you're ready to leave now because I want to talk to you," he said, his voice stern.

"Wh-why?" She'd never realized how intimidating he could be.

"I think you know why." He took her arm and led her away from the din of music and laughter. Leah felt the tension in his hand where it gripped her elbow. He maintained his silence as they walked through the darkness, and she was afraid to break it.

Austin didn't speak because he was so angry, he was afraid he'd say something he'd regret. He knew what he had to do, but he also knew that when he'd said the words, there would be no retracting them. It tied his stomach in knots.

He felt Leah's apprehension as she walked beside him. He wished he could reassure her, but deeper than his anger was jealousy. He was jealous of Josiah Campbell, and it made him feel small.

As they neared her house he stopped and turned to her. The moon highlighted her eyes and hair. She looked like an angel, beautiful and ethereal. If only someone had told her how pretty she was while she was growing up she might not have felt compelled to marry a man she didn't love, and who didn't love her, just because he'd asked.

"I didn't like the feeling I had back there, Leah—that a minister was going to accuse me of fiddling around with his fiancée. I don't like sneaking around, or having to pretend that you're nothing more than a neighbor to me. And I hate like hell that next Saturday night, he's going to take you into his bed and claim what's mine."

"Austin!" Leah gasped, but he continued. He had to get the words out before his courage failed him.

"That's the plain truth. I don't like any of it. But I can't change it. You're the only one who can. It's time, Leah. You have to decide. Me or Josiah Campbell."

"Austin, not tonight."

He held up his hand to stop her protests. "When, then? The wedding is only a week away."

"Just a couple of days. Please?"

He threw up his hands. "Why not wait till the morning of the wedding? There's no hurry," he snapped. He felt his anger slipping away from him.

"Austin, tomorrow or Friday—it is all the same. If I decide not to marry Josiah, it will be just as humiliating to him."

He nodded. "All right, a day or two. And I'm going to stay away so that you can make up your mind. When you've decided, you know where to find me."

She looked small and defenseless. The idea of not seeing her was hell. But he knew he'd better get used to it if she decided . . . He pulled her into his arms, savoring her softness. Breathing in the fragrance of her, he ran his hands down the silky length of her hair. "I want you to be happy, Leah. But I want to be happy, too."

"I know. I want that for all of us."

He tipped her face up to his and covered her mouth with a long, desperate kiss that came from the bottom of his heart. Then he released her. "Go on in, now. I'll wait to hear from you."

"Good night, Austin." She walked toward the house, her skirts brushing over the grass and scattering seeds in the moonlight. Just before she reached the front door, she turned and gave him a little wave.

Austin waved back and waited until she was inside. Then he headed toward the shop, feeling more alone than he did the day he left Waterville.

Leah dragged through the next few days. She barely slept, and when she did, her dreams of Austin were filled with the pain of separation. She'd see him standing in front of his shop, begging her not to leave, while Josiah put her on that rickety wagon and took her away. The dreams were so vivid, sometimes she woke up crying.

Once, she'd glanced up at his window and saw him standing there, tall and so very handsome, watching her. He sent her a questioning look, but all she could do was shake her head and hurry into the store. After that, she began worrying about him. Sometimes he'd close the shop in the middle of the afternoon, and she wondered if he was sick or losing interest in his business. She owed him an answer, but all she'd done was wrestle with the consequences of either decision.

Bethany was strangely subdued, but she refused to admit that anything was bothering her. The necklace reappeared on her dressing table, and Leah chose to let the matter die. Sometimes her sister would disappear for hours, and Leah had no idea where she went. If she asked, Beth would become evasive and her face would redden. She came to the store almost grudgingly, with the bored belligerence of the worst student she'd ever had.

On Friday afternoon, Mrs. Pardee came to Whitman's. She would be baking Leah's wedding cake because she owned the largest oven in Lost Horse. "Tomorrow is your big day," she said, and gave Leah an arch smile. "Have you decided how many layers you'll need?"

Bethany, who was sitting at the desk struggling with the ledger book, heard this and sent Leah a teary-eyed look before she jumped up and ran to the storeroom. Alarmed, Leah hustled Mrs. Pardee out of the store, promising she'd come down later to discuss the cake.

"Beth?" Leah called. What in the world had gotten into her sister? She found Bethany sitting on a stool in the corner, dabbing at her eyes with her handkerchief. She didn't look up, and idly fingered the spools of lace she'd ordered from Homer Gillespie. "Bethany, honey, won't you tell me what's bothering you?"

When she finally spoke, her quiet voice trembled so with tears that Leah's heart ached for her. "Please, Leah, can I leave? I just don't want to be here today."

Leah walked over and crouched before her, taking one of her cold hands between her own. Beth refused to look at her. "Bethany, what is it? What's troubling you?"

Her gaze flicked to Leah's for just an instant, and she saw raw, naked guilt in her sister's eyes. Then she looked down again. "I don't want to talk about it, that's all, Leah. Please don't ask me anymore."

Leah released her hand. "All right, but if you change your mind, will you let me know? We're sisters, *family.*

We should be able to go to each other when we're in trouble."

Beth remained silent.

Leah sighed. "Go ahead and take the day off. I can manage."

Immediately, Beth brightened and jumped off the stool so fast it teetered. Her skirts whipped around the doorframe and Leah heard her footsteps pound over the plank flooring and out the front door. She sank down on the stool.

She was at a loss as to what to think. She looked at the closed back door. There was only one person she could talk to and she couldn't go to him. She missed Austin keenly.

The days had slipped by quickly. Her time was almost up. She hadn't seen Josiah all week, either, and she had to admit that seemed strange, even if it was true that this was a marriage of convenience.

Leah knew she had to talk to Josiah, before she made any decision, if only to reassure herself that he'd chosen her for something other than her teaching certificate. If she went down to the church now, it would mean closing the store, but surely she had the right to do that if tomorrow would be her wedding day.

It was a sultry afternoon, one that held the promise of a thunderstorm toward evening. As she passed Mot's Regulars, and the apothecary's, and the feed store, people waved to her, and offered best wishes. She was so much a part of this community; how could she bear to leave it for that remote wilderness? Yet how could she cheat these people and Josiah out of the wedding they'd so looked forward to?

The church was a modest little structure with a bell out in front. It was embraced on both sides by ponderosa pines that kept it cool even in the hottest summer. Behind it ran a shallow, sparkling brook. It was a very romantic site for a wedding.

As she climbed the two front steps, the door swung open suddenly, and Josiah stood there.

"Well—Leah, uh, what a surprise!" He looked harried, as though he were late for an appointment.

"I haven't seen you all week, Josiah. Not since you took Bethany home. I-I was wondering how you are." She almost felt embarrassed to be bothering him.

"I didn't think I was supposed to see the bride before the wedding." He laughed in a forced, preoccupied way, and continued down the path. "Don't worry, I'll be here tomorrow. Ten o'clock, right?"

"Are you on your way somewhere? Maybe I could walk with you." She found herself running to keep up with him.

"I'm on my way to offer spiritual counseling to a troubled parishioner. I don't think you should be there." He turned and walked backward to face her but didn't stop.

"But I could walk part of the way with you. Josiah, there's something I'd like to talk to you about." She heard the note of anxiety in her voice, despite her efforts to sound calm.

He paused and put his hand to his bearded chin. "I'll tell you what. If I can, I'll stop by the store later this afternoon. Otherwise, we can talk about it tomorrow. All right?"

She stared at him. He had a kind face. She knew that he was a good man. But it bothered her that he never seemed to have time to spend with her. Was this how her life with him would be? "All right, Josiah," she said softly. "All right."

He patted her hand. "That's a good girl. Whatever it is, we'll get it sorted out after the wedding. You'll see. It will be just fine."

She watched him hurry away, left behind once more. At that moment the realization came to her with amazing clarity, like a summer's night lit by lightning. She couldn't marry Josiah Campbell. When she thought of him, no emotion stirred any longer. Not even gratitude.

She still liked Josiah. But she loved Austin.

And that made all the difference.

Chapter ☾ Seven

*N*ow that Leah had reached her decision, she felt amazingly free and light. She would not marry Josiah tomorrow morning. She wasn't the first woman to change her mind. Far better to disappoint a few people than to live a life of regrets. It would not be easy to tell Josiah, but she looked forward to the joy of telling Austin. She practically flew down the street. Outside, she stopped and smiled at Whitman's sign with sheer happiness. She would never have to leave her store.

Leah bounded up to Austin's door, only to find it locked. She knocked, thinking he might be upstairs, but she heard only silence. The way both he and Bethany kept disappearing and acting mysteriously, she'd just about worried herself gray-haired. He was bound to come back with his dinner; he always did. She'd leave him a note.

"Please meet me next door as soon as you—" No, wait. She sat with the pen suspended over the paper. How much more fitting to meet him under the big oak next to the grange hall. After all, that's where it had all begun for them, under a full Midsummer's Eve moon, with the most wonderful kiss she'd ever experienced.

She wrote the note and put it in an envelope, then took it out to his back door and wedged it in the frame where she knew he'd see it.

For the next two hours, she puttered around in the store, rearranging stock and filling the candy jars. She was too excited to concentrate on anything else.

At last she heard the muffled sound of footsteps in the shop next door. He was back. She listened as he walked from front to back, envisioning his hand on the knob as he opened the back door. When she heard it, she went to the mirror in the storeroom to smooth her hair. In the glass, she saw that her cheeks were nearly crimson with elation. She certainly wouldn't need to pinch any color into them. She cocked her head at the sound of the front door slamming, followed by boot heels running over the planks. His footsteps were like music to her yearning heart.

She came out of the storeroom and headed toward her own door.

I'm coming to you, Austin . . . I'm coming.

The sun was just setting into a flame red horizon when Leah turned down the road toward the grange hall. Her pulse thundered in her head. Joy and anticipation filled her with such happy exhilaration, she couldn't remember the last time she'd felt so good.

There it was, up ahead on the left side of the road, that wonderful old tree. And in the gathering dusk, she saw his sun streaked head and felt such an outpouring of love for him, she lifted her skirts and ran the last few yards.

"Austin!" she called.

But he wasn't alone.

Bethany was with him.

A sense of impending calamity descended upon Leah, but she wasn't sure why. She only knew that something was very wrong.

"Oh, Leah," her sister said, with a hard brightness. "I didn't expect to see you here."

From the other side of the road, Josiah approached. "Well, this is a surprise." He laughed awkwardly. "What are we all doing here?"

Yes, what were they all doing here, Leah wondered.

"I guess our secret is out," Beth said. Her face was white as paper as her eyes skittered to Josiah, then Leah. She moved a step closer to Austin and regarded him shyly. "You know I told you I was waiting for the right man . . . well, I've found him."

"Now, just a—" Austin began, but Bethany leaned against his arm and interrupted him.

Beth gave her a shaky smile. "I know that Austin will be able to help me figure things out at the store when you and Josiah go off to Mountain Wells. I've been kind of worried about that."

Leah gaped at her sister, feeling as though a horse had kicked her in the stomach. Or a man had stabbed her in the back.

She glanced at Josiah, who looked the way she felt. Of course—the news was stunning, even to the uninformed. Only Austin wore that cool, blank expression she'd seen before. Certainly, he did. He probably didn't expect Leah to find out that he'd been philandering with both of the Whitman sisters.

"Leah—" Austin said.

Finding her voice, Leah jumped in. She didn't want to hear anything he had to say. She jammed her clammy hands into the pockets of her dress. "I'm sure Mr. Ryder will be a tremendous help after we've gone, don't you think so, Josiah?" As she said this, she stared at Austin, whose only response was the tightening of his jaw.

"Uh, yes, certainly, a big help," Josiah bumbled.

Suddenly all the pieces fell together and made sense. Austin had originally been interested in Bethany. They both knew it; after all, he'd thought it was Beth he kissed at that first dance. He'd as much as told her so. Then at the last dance, Beth had worn the amulet and, oh, God, Leah, realized. They were probably the passionate couple she'd seen under this very tree. No wonder Beth had been upset. Leah had been rattled, too, when he'd kissed her. His kisses were so—consuming. Apparently, the only thing that the professor's amulet had revealed was that Austin was attracted to Beth. And if he convinced Leah to let Josiah go to Mountain Wells alone, then he'd have *both* sisters. Outrage and desperate hurt collided in her heart. Did he really think she wouldn't find out? He was ten times worse than she'd originally believed.

Leah linked her arm in Josiah's. "Well, Bethany, if a

woman is going to marry, that's the secret to happiness— finding the man who's proper for her. And Josiah is the proper man for me."

"Naturally we hope you'll be at our wedding tomorrow morning, Mr. Ryder," Josiah added.

Austin gazed steadily at Leah. "Sorry, I'm going to be busy tomorrow. As a matter of fact, I really should be getting back to the shop. But I hope you'll be very happy."

Leah's throat felt like it had a rock in it as she watched him walk away on long, straight legs, with his head up. With her voice barely under control, she turned to Beth.

"We have a big day tomorrow, Bethany. We'd better go home ourselves. Josiah, are you coming with us?"

His expression was pensive and he glanced up at the green canopy of the oak. "No, I believe I'll sit here for a while. You two go on."

"All right, then. Come on, Bethany."

Her sister let her eyes linger on Josiah a moment longer. "Good-bye, Josiah."

"Good-bye, Bethany."

In the darkness, Leah sat at her desk in Whitman's Dry Goods, staring blankly at the pigeonholes. She could hear the soft ticking of the wall clock, but there were no telltale footsteps on the floor or stairs next door. Austin wasn't there, and right now she wouldn't care if he walked out into rangeland beyond Lost Horse and disappeared forever.

Her handkerchief was a damp wad in her hand. At least she'd managed to stop crying. For thirty minutes she'd huddled here, sobbing out her anguish behind the drawn window shades.

She'd intended to go home with Bethany, but didn't think she could bear to talk to her about Austin. And what would she say, anyway? Would she tell her, *Don't trust Austin Ryder, Beth. I've been trysting with him myself for the last six weeks, even though I'm engaged to Josiah.* A little moan crept up her throat at the thought. Instead, she'd made an excuse to Beth and come here.

It might strike people as odd, if they knew, that in her

mourning she'd chosen the store as her refuge. But it wasn't odd to her. This store had always felt more like home to her than the place where she slept. The house had been their mother's domain, and Beth's after she died.

Plain Leah had Whitman's Dry Goods.

Plain Leah, who'd felt beautiful for a little while, when that beguiling, defiling fraud Austin Ryder had showered her with flattery.

Again and again she pictured that dreadful scene at the grange hall. She could still see him standing under that oak with Beth, obviously stunned to be found out. That smooth expression didn't fool her. But everything else had. The long, searching looks, the things he'd said to her, the way he'd touched her, the dreams . . .

Leah pressed her fist to her mouth to keep the humiliation and grinding heartache from turning into tears. She'd known from the beginning that what she was doing wasn't proper *or* right, that she was abusing Josiah's trust by letting Austin coax her into lustful thoughts and behavior. And worst of all, this behavior had come to her so easily with Austin, it had felt so natural.

It had felt like love.

And now? She leaned back in her chair and drew a trembling breath that began in her soul. There was nothing left to do but marry Josiah tomorrow morning, just as they'd planned. She couldn't bear to remain in Lost Horse and run the daily risk of seeing Austin.

Over the past few weeks, she'd gained enough perspective to realize that she and Josiah weren't an ideal match, but they'd probably fare well enough. In time, her respect for such a good, kind man would grow into quiet, contented devotion. Perhaps tonight's shame would fade, and so would the love for the sun-blond gunsmith that, despite everything, lingered in her heart. The wound was yet too raw, too new for anger to settle in. Right now, all she felt was pain.

Just then, she heard the front door open. Leah spun around in her chair, terrified that Austin's bad grace had led him here to try and somehow justify or explain his actions.

Instead, in the unlighted gloom, she recognized the silhouette of her sister.

"Leah?" Her voice sounded broken and childlike.

"Beth!" Relieved, she fumbled in the drawer for a match, then lit a candle. "I'm back here."

Bethany approached slowly. When she stepped into the narrow circle of candlelight, Leah saw that she looked just as wan and miserable as she had for the past two weeks. The brittle joy she'd shown earlier at the grange hall was gone. Even her hair looked limp. Had she learned the truth about herself and Austin?

"I waited for you to come home . . . I wanted to talk to you."

Leah stuffed her hankie into her pocket and busily pushed at some papers on the desk. "Oh, I just wanted to check on a couple of things. It's my last chance, you know." She smiled up at Bethany. "What is it, dear?"

Beth clenched her hands together so tightly, her fingers were white. "I know you've wondered if something is bothering me. Well, I-I need to tell you about it before tomorrow, before you go away," she said, sounding grief-stricken. "Especially since I don't know when I'll see Josiah and you again."

After days of trying to pry Beth's troubles out of her, Leah tiredly wished she'd decided to reveal them sooner. But she had to pretend that nothing was wrong, so she pasted an encouraging expression on her face and motioned her to the stool next to the desk. "You know I'll help if I can."

Beth sat cautiously, as though she might decide to bolt at any second.

"Remember the dance a couple of weeks ago? The night I left early?"

Leah nodded.

"I ran away because something so very strange happened, I just didn't know what else to do." She glanced up at Leah, her eyes edged with tears, then lowered her face to her tightly folded hands in her lap. Leah heard her take a deep breath. "You know how hot it gets in the grange hall, and I'd been a bit light-headed ever since we got there. So I decided to go outside for a while. But it was even more than that. When I walked to the doorway and looked up at that big full moon . . . I felt, I don't know, *pulled* out into the yard, like I couldn't help myself."

Involuntarily, Leah gripped the arms of her chair. She remembered very well that feeling. Beth had been wearing her amulet that night. Could she bear to hear how her sister fell under the spell of Austin Ryder and a full moon? Struggling to keep her emotions curbed beneath a carefully bland expression, she gathered her courage to listen to the rest of Bethany's story.

"Well, I wandered out to that big oak and sat on the hay bale. It was such a beautiful night." She looked across the dark store, deep in the memory of it, and for a moment her troubled face smoothed out. "The stars looked like a million bright crystals up there, and the moon turned everything silver-gold. The grass smelled sweet. I think I heard a coyote howling in the hills far away—it was like I could see and hear and smell *everything.*" She glanced at Leah. "I guess that sounds funny, doesn't it."

Leah shook her head. "No, Beth," she replied softly. "I know what you mean."

"Then," and she began wringing her hands, "then I heard a voice behind me, a man's voice—"

Leah's grip on the chair arms tightened. Oh, God, why did Bethany feel she had to tell her this? Wasn't it enough that she'd always been the prettiest, the most popular, the best loved? Couldn't she be content with those things?

Beth's voice began to quiver, and her breath came in hitches. "And he said, 'Leah, I heard you were out here.' I-I didn't mean for it to happen! I knew he was looking for you, but the next thing I knew, I was kissing him, and he was kissing me back. I never—no man *ever* kissed me like that before. But as soon as he did, I fell in love with him. And then he said he loved me! It all happened so fast."

Surely hell couldn't be worse than this, Leah thought, biting her lip to keep it from trembling. It couldn't be worse than listening to a story that made her feel like a knife was twisting in her heart. Austin had never told Leah that he loved her. Why Beth was so upset, she couldn't begin to guess. It seemed that once again, she'd gotten what she wanted.

Tears ran down her sister's cheeks. Her face was contorted. "After that, we started sneaking around to be together. I f-felt t-terrible about it, and so did Josiah, but we couldn't stay away from each other. H-he wanted to tell you, and to cancel the wedding. But I told him we couldn't do that to you, that it would break your heart. You deserve some h-happiness in your life, Leah."

Leah released her lip from her teeth when her jaw dropped; her breath left her lungs as though she'd been punched. "What? You mean that you and Josiah—for the last two weeks, Josiah and you—?" She couldn't get enough air to finish her sentence. Here she'd believed that it was Austin who'd swept Beth off her feet, Austin who loved her. But Josiah Campbell?

Bethany wiped at her red eyes with her handkerchief, but it was a pointless exercise. The tears kept coming. "I know I'm a wicked, horrible person! I tried to stay away from him, but the harder I tried, the more I wanted to be with him. He was different when we were together. He listened to me, and wanted to know what I thought of things. He's very smart, not a boy like Chad Brewster. But he's *your* fiancé. So tonight I sent him a note, asking him to meet me at the grange hall so I could tell him good-bye and see him one last time before your wedding. Then Austin came by, and I saw Josiah coming. When you showed up, I was afraid you'd guess the truth, so I made up that story about Austin."

Stunned, Leah slumped in her chair and stared at Beth.

"I'm so sorry, Leah," Beth grieved, gearing up for a fresh round of sobs. "I know I've made a mess of everything. Whatever are we going to do?"

"Do?" she asked blankly. "There's nothing else we can do. It's too late to call off the wedding now. All the guests have been invited; Mrs. Pardee has baked the cake." She sat up straight, her decision made. "We're going to do the proper thing."

* * *

Austin sat at his worktable, trying to put the hammer back into an army revolver. This was a simple job, but the damned thing kept slipping. His frustration was such that he had to stop himself from hurling the entire business through the front window. Instead he dropped it on the tabletop and rubbed his gritty eyes with the heels of his hands.

He hadn't slept or eaten since Leah lured him out to the grange hall yesterday to tell him of her decision. He still wasn't sure what part Bethany had to play in all of this. He couldn't imagine why she'd pretended that they were lovers, but Leah had sure been quick to believe it. He'd seen it in her eyes, in her accusing, condemning expression. Then to invite him to the wedding. A grim chuckle rumbled up from his chest. Nothing like pouring salt in the wound.

After he'd left that happy scene, he walked aimlessly around town, trying to understand how the woman who'd rested so easily and comfortably in his arms just as easily believed that he'd played her for a fool.

He'd even gone to the Whitman house last night, like a goddamned idiot, to try and talk to Leah, to tell her that Bethany made up the whole strange story. But he'd stood outside and knocked on the door for ten minutes, and no one answered. Not even when he called to the darkened windows. It was hard to believe that neither sister was home. Finally, he wondered what the use was, and walked out to the foothills beyond Lost Horse. From there, the little town looked peaceful as it slept under the blanket of night. No one would guess the trials and troubles that lay under those roofs.

He put his elbows on the tabletop and rested his forehead in his hands. Maybe if he'd told her he loved her, he thought with an edge of desperation. He'd never told her that. Maybe she didn't know.

It didn't matter now. Lease or no, once he finished the work he'd promised, he'd be moving on. He was looking for a home when he found Lost Horse, he could find another one.

From outside he heard the muffled sound of celebration, and he wearily pushed himself to his feet to go see what was happening. It was good to get out of that chair; he'd been sitting in it since he got back at three this morning and his legs felt dead.

He wandered out to the sidewalk and glanced down the street. Jesus, the entire town must be down there, he thought, as he watched the crowd move away from the churchyard. Josiah Campbell and his bride, her white gown dazzling in the summer sun, were surrounded by the throng of well-wishers. They were coming this way, he realized, probably on their way to the wedding breakfast he'd seen tables set up for.

Sighing, he went back inside, unable to endure the sight of the woman he loved, a woman he'd come to think of as his own, lost forever to another man.

He returned to his worktable, trying for the fifth time to put the damned hammer back in the army Colt. The party was passing the store, and Austin kept his eyes on his work, trying to ignore the pain in his tight throat.

Suddenly, the door to his shop swung open, and he looked up to see Leah standing before him. She looked so beautiful, so radiant, it took him a moment to realize that she wasn't wearing white, but pink. He rose from his chair again. Beyond the window, Bethany, in her sister's wedding gown, led the happy crowd on the arm of— Josiah Campbell?

"Wh-what . . ." It was all he could manage.

Leah laughed, weak with relief at seeing him again. "Oh, Austin! Thank God you're here. When we couldn't find you last night, I was so worried that you'd left town. Will you come and have breakfast with the newlyweds?"

"What the hell is going on?" he demanded.

She came forward and took his hands. He looked so haggard and worn-out, her heart ached for him. This had been hard on all of them. "First you have to tell me that you forgive me for not believing in you, and for jumping to the very worst conclusion."

He still looked baffled. "Well, I guess—"

"It must be true about the amulet the professor gave me, Austin. It worked for us and it worked for Beth and Josiah."

"Leah, what are you talking about?"

"You already know our part of it. Xavier Sortilege told me the necklace would draw my true love."

Austin nodded impatiently.

"The night of the last dance at the grange, Bethany borrowed the amulet and when she went outside under the full moon it drew Josiah to her. Heavens, I even saw them in the shadows of the big oak and didn't realize who they were. I wish I had known," she said. "It could have saved us a lot of trouble. So they've been sneaking around for the last two weeks just like we were. That's why poor Bethany has been so miserable. She felt guilty and angry that she was in love with a man who was engaged to her sister."

Austin shook his head. "That doesn't really explain why she claimed that the two of us were involved."

Leah squeezed his hands. "She'd sent a note to Josiah, just like I sent a note to you, telling him to meet her there because she was going to tell him good-bye. But when we all got there, she thought she was protecting Josiah by telling us that she's interested in you. She came here to tell me about it last night. When I learned the truth, I looked everywhere for you. I-I was so afraid you'd left."

"God, what a complicated mess," he muttered. "It makes my head hurt to think about it. So now what?"

"Well," Leah said shyly, "now Beth and Josiah are going to Mountain Wells, and I'm staying in Lost Horse to do what I know best."

Austin leveled his blue gaze on her. The tone of his voice changed subtly. "And what's that?"

"Love you, and run Whitman's Dry Goods."

He smiled at her, a sweet, poignant smile. "You know, I thought that maybe the reason you'd decided to go with Josiah was because I'd never told you how much I love you. And for that, I'm sorry."

He pulled her into his arms and kissed her with the same tenderness, the same urgency, that he had that first night. Oh, how she'd missed the feel of his strong embrace, and the place on his shoulder where her cheek rested so well.

He backed up slightly and looked at her gown. "I see you're wearing my favorite dress."

She raised her brows. "I haven't worn this for a long time. You've never seen it before."

"Yes, I have. I've unbuttoned it in my dreams lots of times."

Leah gasped. "I had that dream, too."

"Did you let me make love to you?" he murmured, kissing her throat.

Her voice was no more than a whisper. "I asked you to. But in my dream I wore a ring, and I was worried sick that I was married to Josiah and committing adultery."

"You were wearing a ring because you were married to *me.*" He lifted the amulet to look at the stone. "And you've put this on again?" he asked.

She couldn't help but laugh. "Who am I to argue with Midsummer's Eve magic?"

Alexis Harrington loves to hear from her readers: P.O. Box 30176, Portland, OR 97230.

THE
GOLDEN
≽ MERMAID ≼

SONIA SIMONE

My sincere thanks to Earl and John Crabb for their generous assistance in all matters nautical. Any errors that remain are entirely my own.

—Sonia Simone

CHAPTER ☾ ONE

*I*f there was one thing practically guaranteed to raise a proper ghost, it was a bonfire at Midsummer's Night. Nell Jolley brushed her damp hair back from her forehead, frowning at the tropical night sky. A storm was building off the reef, and she could smell the electric lightning in the air. She blew gently on the pile of glowing twigs and driftwood, cursing herself for not listening to Auntie Mab's instructions more carefully.

Auntie had told Nell how to cast the spell that would call forth the restless spirit of Despicable Jack, scourge of the seven seas. The pirate had been dead, buried in unconsecrated ground, for a hundred years, but the legends had it that he still had a thing or two to say—to the person who knew how to call him.

And the old fisher woman known throughout the Florida Keys as "Auntie Mab" certainly knew how to call up a pirate's ghost. Everyone knew Auntie held an impressive collection of arcane knowledge, which she normally kept to herself. But Nell had helped repair Auntie's nets and haul in her lines so many times, for so many years, that the old woman had gradually relinquished to Nell the secrets of the strong, ancient magic she claimed had first come over from Africa with the slaves—magic that had little to do with the brisk modern efficiency of the 1880s world they lived in.

Nell frowned down at the smoldering pile. She'd been so certain she knew how to make a good bonfire—she'd seen Auntie do it on the beach a thousand times. Dry

moss in a little pile at the center, long sticks of dry driftwood arranged in a spiderweb around. Simplicity itself.
But nothing was ever truly *dry* on Forgotten Key; the
ocean was too fully a part of their lives, washing over
everything.

The wind slapped the bonfire with torrents of rain.
The untidy jumble before her did not at all resemble the
blazing conflagrations that Auntie lit.

Still, Midsummer's Night was Midsummer's Night—
there was no second best. If she wanted to talk to Despicable Jack, she'd have to get the spell right by midnight
or wait another year.

She finally managed to get a small but sturdy orange
flame out of her little fire, and she carefully set some
larger bits of wood on the pile, building it to a modest
blaze.

Nell looked at it skeptically. It wasn't much, but it
would have to do. She only hoped the ghost wouldn't be
too particular. It seemed to her that a marauding pirate
who'd been dead for a century could hardly make a fuss
over minor details.

Nell fished in her skirts for the collection of magical
charms Auntie had told her to assemble: the claws of a
blue crab, the husk of a spider's shed skin, a picture
painted by no man's hand, the tail feathers of a black
chicken, and a scrap of a net that caught no fish.

Of the lot, the spider's skin had been the hardest to
find, and Nell had finally caught a spider and kept it in a
glass jar, feeding it bugs until it grew so fat it split its old
skin to reveal a glossy new one beneath. The picture
painted by no man's hand had been easy once Nell had
given it a moment's thought—a waterlogged daguerreo-
type salvaged from a local wreck. And the net that
caught no fish was a bit of dark netting from a rather
extravagant lady's hat, another bit of salvage.

Nell looked down at her treasures now. They were,
she realized ruefully, a little worn for wear. But Auntie
had told her, "Ain't no relation between pretty and
magic," so Nell supposed they would do well enough.

One by one, Nell threw the magical objects into the
fire. She saved the chicken feathers last, wrinkling her

nose at their burnt stink. "Despicable Jack, you damn spawn of evil, I call you forth from your unholy resting place!" Nell recited, from words she had carefully memorized. "Come up from that place of wickedness and show yourself, for you be tied tight to me, Nell Jolley, and I no let you go until you reveal your secret!" Nell privately had thought it a trifle odd that Despicable Jack, who was by all accounts a Frenchman, would respond to Auntie Mab's eccentric dialect, but Auntie was insistent; the words had to be repeated exactly.

A groaning came from down the beach, and Nell peered into the blackness. The wind, perhaps. "Show yourself, Despicable Jack. You be bind to me!" Nell dug through her pockets for the last magic item—a black string knotted tightly to a white one, symbolizing the wicked Jack's subjugation to Nell, who certainly didn't want him to do anything nefarious. She waved it three times over the bonfire, just as Auntie had taught her. If Nell were going to take responsibility for calling him back from the dead, she'd have to make sure he behaved himself.

Nell peered again into the night, but she could make out nothing. The bonfire smoke made her eyes tear, and she rubbed them, blinking quickly. "Oh, come on, Mr. Jack! I promise, I won't keep you long. I just want to ask you a question." Nell scowled. Maybe the bonfire wasn't big enough after all. Or maybe she should have taken *all* of General Jackson's black tail feathers, and not just the four she'd managed to pluck before the rooster scuttled to a safe spot under the chicken house.

"Goddamn and double goddamn," came a masculine voice from the beach.

Nell's blood froze. Good heavens, it had actually worked. She had summoned the ghost of Despicable Jack. She bit her lower lip hard, to keep herself from dispatching him back where he'd come from. "Mr. Jack? Is that you, Mr. Jack? I hope I haven't disturbed you."

"Who's there? Is that a woman's voice?" the ghost called from the beach, sounding more irritated than ethereal. "Who in hell—er, in their right mind would be out on a night like this? What are you, some kind of madwoman?"

"If I hadn't come out tonight, I would never have found you," Nell pointed out, very sensibly, she thought.

The voice cursed again, then apologized. It wasn't a French-sounding voice, as she'd imagined it would be, but a thoroughly American one. "Was it being buried in American soil that makes you sound like one of us?" she asked, wondering if ghosts appreciated small talk. But she truly wanted to know. "Or are you speaking in some strange, spirit-language? Would a Spaniard hear you speak Spanish?"

The voice moved closer to the fire, and Nell could see it was attached to a long, lean form, looking bedraggled as a wrecked schooner. She swallowed hard. Somehow she hadn't thought the ghost would be so . . . corporeal.

"What the hell are you talking about?" The ghost moved closer to the fire, and Nell instinctively moved behind it. Auntie had said the fire would protect her. And Despicable Jack would only appear before her as long as the fire was lit. Nell eyed the bucket of rainwater behind her with some small measure of comfort. She could snuff him out as easily as she would a match.

"Your accent. I would have thought you'd sound French," she explained. Pity he wasn't a smarter ghost. Still, all she needed from him was a single, simple piece of information that he couldn't possibly have forgotten. "You do remember things, don't you?" she asked, suddenly nervous. "From before, I mean?"

"You mean from my ship? Yes, of course I do. I've just had a bit of a forced landing—not a wreck, more of a rough knock. And I'm hardly a mental invalid. But—you're nothing but a girl!" The voice sounded shocked.

"You don't scare me, Mr. Jack!" Nell said nervously. "I brought you here and I can send you right back, so don't get any funny ideas."

"What the devil are you talking about?" the voice asked, so clearly puzzled that Nell almost felt sorry for him.

"From the place of torment," Nell explained patiently. Auntie had warned her that ghosts could be a little dim.

"The night's not as rough as all that," the voice said wryly. "I've been through worse." The ghost moved closer to the fire, and Nell's breath caught in her throat.

He was nothing like the legends said. Despicable Jack was supposed to be a massive hulk of a man, six feet across at the shoulders, with legs like tree trunks and a beard that hung down to his belly. This man was clean-shaven, lean and sinewy, tall, but hardly a giant. His calves were wet, as if he'd been wading in the surf, and his hair and shoulders were soaked.

And his eyes were not the eyes she would have expected. They were a light, warm brown. Laughing eyes.

"They're supposed to be black," she mused.

"Black?" Despicable Jack looked utterly dumbfounded as he sat on the sandy rocks and began to remove his boots. "What are?"

"Your eyes. *Black as the pit of hell itself,* that's what all the stories say. That's very distressing. I shall have to tell Auntie, of course, but I'm not sure she'll believe me."

Despicable Jack looked at her as if she were the most puzzling chimera a man had ever set eyes on. "Poor thing, you're quite cracked, aren't you?" he said finally, turning his attention back to his boots.

Nell swiped her hair back from her eyes and regarded him with righteous outrage. "I most certainly am not *cracked,* as you put it. Anyway, I hardly think a man who's been dead for a hundred years, much less one with your unsavory reputation, has a right to call people names."

"Absolutely around the bend," he said, his voice soft. He peeled off his socks, which were dripping wet, and began to wring them out. "No offense, mind. I happen to rather like crazy people. But I can't believe they let you run around loose this way. Don't you have any family?"

"Of course I have, not that it's any business of yours. Honestly, I don't think that a man who once murdered a hundred men in a single day has any right to cast aspersions on another person's faculties!"

Despicable Jack grinned, a surprising flash of white

that echoed those laughing eyes, and Nell remembered with a scalding flush the second part of that story—that Despicable Jack had ravished a hundred ladies that same evening.

"You're right. I wouldn't dream of it," he said.

Nell tried to manage a severe expression. "Now then, Mr. Jack, I have only one question for you, and you can get on about—about whatever it is you normally do. Where did you hide the Bathing Maenad?"

"What?" The grin disappeared from the ghost's face and looked as if it would never come back again. He pushed himself to his feet, lithe as a cat rising from a nap. "What the hell do you know about that, girl?"

"My name is Nell, Nell Jolley, and you can't frighten me," she said, hoping that ghosts couldn't tell when a person was lying through her teeth. "Auntie warned me you'd be full of bluff and bluster, but you just remember, I can send you back where you came from with a single pail of water."

"A pail of water. I see." Despicable Jack gave her a look that suggested he clearly didn't believe her.

Nell wasn't worried. Not much, anyway. He was very much as Auntie had warned—large, irritable, and inclined to be bossy. "No you forget your power over him," Auntie had warned. "And no you let him forget it neither."

"Don't worry, I won't send you back too soon," she said, trying for a reassuring tone. "All I want to know is where you hid the Maenad. She can't be any use to you anymore, you know. Not . . . down there."

"Down there? You mean New Zealand?" Despicable Jack asked, sounding incredulous as he sat down to pull his still-soggy socks over his feet. "How on earth did you know I'd been to New Zealand?" He shook his head, as if something had confused him. "Listen, young . . . lady . . ." He peered at her, as if trying to determine that she truly *was* a young lady. "If you think I'm going to tell you what I know about the Bathing Maenad, you're even battier—How do you know about her, anyway? She's valuable, of course, but hardly of much interest to—" He squinted at her again. "To young ladies."

"My father told me," she said warily. "He's a scientist, he studies old bones and antiquities."

"Old bones?" Despicable Jack asked, frowning. He pulled on his boots, stood, and brushed the sand from his pants. "Good God. What did you say your surname was?"

"Jolley. Nell Jolley. And my father is Theophilus Jolley. He's just a little bit famous—oh, but I expect you don't know about such things. Down there, I mean." She flushed a little—it was hard to know if it were proper to refer to a ghost's eternal damnation.

"New Zealand gets the papers from London, even if it does take a month or two," the ghost mused, his forehead wrinkling. "But I know your father from other sources."

"You keep your hands off my father!" Nell said sharply. "You bind to me, remember? The spell was very clear on that point." She waved the black-and-white string to illustrate her point. "And I expressly forbid you to haunt my father."

Despicable Jack peered at her, blinking at the smoke from the fire. "Interesting way you have with words, girl. He told me about you, of course, but he never mentioned . . . well . . ." The ghost's nod took in Nell's entirety, from her damp unbound hair to her bare feet.

"You've spoken with my father?" Nell could scarcely believe her ears. "I don't believe you. My father would have no truck with spirits, particularly not bloodthirsty ones. He's a scientist, he doesn't even believe in you."

Despicable Jack ran one large, tanned hand through his hair, letting it come to rest on the back of his neck. If he weren't the scourge of the seven seas, his eyes would have seemed almost amused, Nell decided.

"The longer this conversation goes, the less I'm sure I believe in *you,*" he said.

"Don't be impertinent," Nell snapped.

"God forbid," the ghost muttered, the faintest hint of a smile returning to his lips.

Nell realized with a start that she hadn't checked the time for some minutes. "Blast!" She pulled her father's watch out of her skirt pocket. Eleven fifty-eight. Two minutes left to work good magic. Auntie Mab had been very explicit on this point: the half hour before midnight was for benevolent magic, the half hour after midnight was for evil. Nell still hadn't gotten what she needed from the ghost, but if she kept him much longer, he was free to work evil magic instead of good.

"Come on, you've got to tell me, quickly now, where is the Maenad? And remember, you bind to me, so no tricks."

The ghost bent his head so that she could not see his face, but his cheek creased as if he were smiling. "Ah, it's a bit complicated to go into right now. Why don't we talk about it tomorrow?"

"Tomorrow?" Nell blinked. She'd had no idea he would be so accommodating. "Is that all right? I mean, you don't have to go back . . . back where you came from?"

The ghost looked over his shoulder out to sea. "For tonight. I'll see you tomorrow, then. Run along home, crazy Nell. Your father will be worried about you."

"But the fire . . . can I just leave it like this?" She looked down at the small glowing pile of coals at her feet, the crab claws blackened from the fire.

"I'm sure you can. I think the mangroves are too wet to catch fire, don't you?"

"And you won't . . . you know, disappear?"

"Not for good," Despicable Jack answered, the grin back on his face.

Nell realized to her dismay that he was actually rather handsome. "How will I find you again?"

"Oh, don't worry, Nell Jolley," the ghost said. "I'll find you. You have my word."

Nell gave him an appraising look. She wondered just how good the word of a pirate's ghost could be, but decided she had no choice but to trust him. "Very good. I'll see you later, Mr. Jack."

The ghost again cast an eye to the beach, where the waves were driving against the rocks with building force. There was a loud crack, but Nell could see no lightning. He began to look rather agitated, and Nell supposed he was being summoned back to the spirit world.

"Look here, I have to go, Nell," he said, "but I'll see you tomorrow."

And with that, the ghost of the bloodthirstiest pirate ever to maraud the Spanish Main stepped out of the circle of light of her dying bonfire and melted into the blackness of the night.

CHAPTER ☾ TWO

*A*t six o'clock the next evening, Sebastian Kane knocked firmly on the door to Theophilus Jolley's sea-side house. Glancing around, Sebastian thought he could see the seeds of Jolley's daughter's madness.

The cottage's windows were ringed in decorative rows of starfish and seashells, radiating like the petals of a sunflower. The red painted door was large, out of pro-portion with the rest of the little house, and Sebastian suspected it had been salvaged from a wrecked ship. Red geraniums hung in profusion from planters set above the door, but came to an abrupt halt at about four feet off the ground, as if chopped by a pair of scissors.

The door opened and a thin man with a perfectly round head squinted up at him through thick spectacles. "Dr. Kane, is it?" the man asked.

"Professor Jolley, this is a great honor," Sebastian re-plied holding out his hand. "I hope I haven't kept you waiting, I had a bit of trouble with the *Minerva.*"

"Nothing serious, I hope," Jolley said, concerned.

Sebastian smiled. "Not at all, she just took a little bump on the nose."

The professor seized Sebastian's hand, his round face creasing with good humor. "Oh, this is very good, very good indeed. I've been looking forward to this evening for some time."

The cottage's interior was even more outlandish than the outside. In one corner, a heavy gilt mirror, half ruined by seawater, had been inlaid with chips of some pearly shell. The east window was framed by a delicate tracework of sea horses, and a pair of slightly dented silver candlesticks were ringed by crab claws no bigger than Sebastian's thumbnail. In the middle of the table was a heavy silver bowl of mangoes, which perfumed the whole of the cottage with their ripeness.

"Your house is . . . astonishing, Professor," Sebastian finally managed. "I've never seen anything like it."

Jolley's round face creased into another smile. "Yes, it's lovely, isn't it? It's all Nell's doing, of course. I've never had what one might call an aesthetic bent. My brother, you see, he's a wrecker over on Indian Key, and he can't resist little Nell. Always doted on her, from the time she was a tiny thing. He brings bits and pieces from the wrecks, and Nell makes what she calls her improvements."

"Improvements," Sebastian repeated, with another disbelieving gaze round the place. It was preposterous, completely beyond the pale, and yet . . . Sebastian had to admit, there was a kind of insane charm to it all.

"Nell, dear, come down and say hello to our guest!" Professor Jolley shouted up the narrow stairs.

Sebastian suppressed the urge to tug at his cravat. "It's very . . . enlightened of you, Professor, about your daughter. Not to keep her shut up, I mean."

Jolley looked at him, blinking his round eyes in surprise. "Is that what men are doing with their daughters these days? Well, well. There's no need out here on Forgotten Key, I assure you, Dr. Kane. It's just the two of us, you know, and the fishermen. They all keep an eye out for her."

"And you aren't concerned she might . . . harm herself?"

"Nell?" Jolley wrinkled his high forehead, seeming for a moment to stare off into some unknown distance. "Never much occurred to me. Suppose it's possible, mind, but not, statistically speaking, very likely."

Sebastian heard a faint scurrying overhead, and a pair of familiar bare feet appeared at the top of the stairs. He gave in and tugged at his cravat, giving himself another inch of breathing room.

Nell Jolley was not the child she had seemed to be last night. She was, in fact, a startlingly pretty young woman. Her shabby smock of the night before had been replaced by a sea green morning dress. Entirely inappropriate for dinner, of course, and Sebastian noted that a long curving water stain along the bodice had actually been accented with rows of embroidery and seed pearls. Still, the girl had put up her ginger curls, and apart from the bare feet she looked merely a trifle eccentric.

Professor Jolley took her lightly by the elbow. "My dear, this is Dr. Kane. He's going to work with me on the project I mentioned to you, the Pompeiian statuette."

Nell was watching Sebastian with thinly disguised dismay. "But you're—you're—"

"Sebastian Kane," Sebastian said, extending a hand in greeting.

Nell ignored it as she peered up at his face. "You tricked me."

Sebastian raised his eyebrow. "I beg your pardon?"

Her chin raised an inch, and she fixed him with surprisingly determined eyes the color of creamy jade. "You pretended you were Despicable Jack."

"I can promise you I didn't," Sebastian said smoothly. "In fact, I have never made the acquaintance of anyone bearing that name."

Professor Jolley rested a hand on Sebastian's arm. "Oh, that's the local name for Jacques D'Epiques."

Sebastian was startled for a moment. "The pirate? But he's been dead a hundred years. Surely they're not still telling fairy stories about his ghost."

"May I remind you," Nell said, with creditable iciness, "That your precious statuette is also said to be nothing but a fairy story."

Sebastian blinked, taking another look at the girl he'd been thinking of as Crazy Nell. He realized she wasn't mad at all—at least not in the normal understanding of the term. "You thought he was me. You thought I was the pirate, Despicable Jack. That's what you called me last night."

"Last night?" Professor Jolley looked faintly disturbed. "I say, I would very much appreciate it if someone could fill me in. It appears I haven't been paying close attention."

"Don't trouble yourself, Father," Nell said, patting the old man on the arm and leading him to a comfortable chair. "I'll fetch you a glass of sherry." She looked over at Sebastian, and bit out, "Will you have some as well, Dr. Kane?"

"Thank you," he said pleasantly, taking a chair. He nearly leapt out of it again when he felt a faint nibbling at his ankles. He looked down to meet a pair of shrewd yellow eyes. "What the devil ?"

Professor Jolley leaned over, peering hard into the corner. "Oh, that's Sophia. Don't mind her. She's very interested in new people, always has been, since she was a kid."

Sophia, who was a plump black-and-white goat, looked steadily up at him. She appeared to be chewing something.

"Are those goats in the house again?" Nell asked from the kitchen. "Don't let them get into the flowers."

Professor Jolley rescued a handful of black-eyed Susans from Sophia's jaws, restoring them to the high-buttoned ladies' boot they'd been arranged in. "It's a stormy night, dear, let them stay. You know how the lightning frightens Sophia. She was just investigating Dr. Kane."

"And Heinrich will be right behind her," Nell said, emerging from the kitchen with three mismatched glasses on a chipped lacquer tray. "Heinrich isn't nearly so agreeable as Sophia is."

"I see," said Sebastian, who didn't at all. He was still wondering how Nell kept the boot full of flowers from leaking water all over the mahogany table. "Heinrich is also a . . . ?"

"A goat. Yes. He's wretchedly bad-tempered, and I'm afraid despite his daily bath he smells a bit. But for some reason Sophia appears to dote on him." Nell looked appraisingly down. "Silly girl. You were such a clever goat before you began mooning over that overbearing male."

"Marriage changes a woman," Sebastian said wryly, taking a glass of sherry from the tray.

"Turns her from a freethinking person to a slave," Nell said pleasantly, sprawling in a large upholstered chair. "How do you know my father, Dr. Kane? He was very pleased to get your letter."

Sebastian was taken aback. First the little whirlwind mistook him for a ghost, and now she spouted reformist nonsense when she wasn't talking to her goats. "I-I've been reading his articles for years. Since he was at Oxford. I've come to accept his theory that some of the most interesting artifacts at Pompeii slipped into the hands of thieves."

"Illicit hordes," Jolley said, drinking deeply from his sherry as he eased back into his chair. "Exquisite treasures, fragments that could tell us so much of how the Pompeiians lived, what they thought, how they dreamed."

Nell laughed. A single ginger curl had escaped her hairpins, but what should have looked unkempt struck Sebastian as being oddly alluring. "From the sketches and the catalogs, I'd say they only dreamed of one thing —each other."

Sebastian looked at her sharply. "What do you mean by that?"

"Well, it's quite erotic, isn't it? Their art, I mean." Her eyes held his, strangely sultry, though the rest of her face was as fresh and innocent as a child's.

Sebastian could feel his face heating, and it made him angry. Who did this spoiled hoyden think she was, to shame herself this way in front of her father? Not to mention the fact that she was making Sebastian feel like a prize idiot. "I don't think the subject is appropriate for mixed company."

"They were the original Owenites, don't you see?" Nell said, leaning forward in her chair, her silver earrings tinkling like bells. "Apart from their economic system, of course, that was barbarous. But the women! Marriage wasn't slavery to them, it was true companionship. If love soured, a couple went their separate ways. Think of it, Dr. Kane! No unhappy marriages. Men and women chose each other openly, with perfect honesty and freedom."

Sebastian was no prude. He'd spent too many hours in dockside taverns for that. But this was a respectable girl, sitting in a chair in her father's house, talking about gross immorality as if it were utopia. "What you describe is no better than free love, Miss Jolley."

"Exactly!" she said, settling back triumphantly in her chair. "The only true way for men and women to live together in harmony is through the frank, open sharing of free love. Marriage as it's now constituted is nothing better than chattel slavery."

"Good God, this is outrageous," Sebastian said.

"Now, Nell," Jolley said mildly. "Dr. Kane isn't accustomed to unconventional ideas in young ladies, and it's very bad manners to shock him."

Sebastian knocked back the rest of his sherry, shaking off the goat Sophia, who was nibbling tentatively at the cuffs of his trousers. This had to be the most bizarre night of his life. It wasn't just the girl who was crazy, the old man was cracked as well. "I'm not shocked. I just happen to think your daughter could use a good spanking."

"There, you see?" Nell said, pointing at him. "These are the 1880s, and the man still advocates violence to keep women subservient. Positively medieval." She leaned over and patted him. "You shouldn't feel badly about it, though, Dr. Kane. Practically all men are as unenlightened as you are."

Sebastian shut his eyes briefly. "Thank you, I feel much better now."

Nell brightened. "Oh, good, I'm so glad. Would you like some more sherry?"

Professor Jolley looked at a loss, blinking thoughtfully as if trying to remember how he lost control of the conversation. "Ah, Dr. Kane, how exactly do you come by your interest in antiquities? You are no longer at Cambridge, is that right?"

Sebastian accepted Nell's offer of another drink, grateful for the change in subject. "I lost my taste for shutting myself in cold stone libraries. Universities take the classics and turn them into something dead, moldered half to dust. I wanted a way to live the old stories, to remember how I felt when I was a boy and dreamed I was Jason, or Ulysses. I guess I'm just looking for my golden fleece." Sebastian broke off, feeling foolish as he stared into the boot full of yellow flowers. This mad place was rubbing off on him.

Jolley nodded. "You became an adventurer."

"A scholar as much as an adventurer, I hope," Sebastian said. "I promise you, Professor Jolley, my methods are strictly scientific. But my classroom is the world."

Nell had tucked her knees beneath her. She looked eleven years old again, the way she had last night, dreamy and endearingly awkward. "That sounds perfectly wonderful. Have you been to millions of places?"

"I've been to quite a few. Most of them in search of the Bathing Maenad."

"She'll bring you your heart's desire, or drive you mad with longing's fire," Jolley said, chuckling.

Sebastian swatted away a larger goat, whom he supposed was Heinrich. Nell was right—the animal had a distinct odor, mixed with the unmistakable scent of Pear's soap. "Excuse me?"

"That's what the sailors say about the Mermaid," Nell said. "That's what the locals here call her, you know, the Golden Mermaid. The glory of Despicable Jack's treasure, an ancient marble mermaid swimming in pure gold."

"She's not a mermaid, she's a maenad," Sebastian said, still annoyed with Nell.

"I know perfectly well what she is," Nell sniffed, "*and* I know what the maenads did, so there's no sense in avoiding the subject on my account. I think they sounded rather sensible."

"I thought you might," Sebastian said dryly. Of course Nell would approve of wild women who fornicated at will and tore the occasional young man to pieces. How could she not? "Anyway, I doubt she's swimming in pure gold. Gilt, more likely. If she exists at all."

"But you agree with me, that she does exist," Jolley said, looking suddenly more serious than Sebastian had seen him all evening.

Sebastian let out a sigh. "I can't ignore the evidence.

Certainly the criminals who conducted the first digs at Pompeii couldn't have been trusted not to pocket the occasional treasure. And rumors of the Bathing Maenad were rampant for another forty years, popping up all over the globe."

"Turkey, Cuba, New Zealand, Brazil—that last is quite a dead end, by the way."

"Yes, I read your paper on the subject. It sounds like it must have been quite a journey." Sebastian grinned.

Jolley poured himself another sherry. "No sign of the Maenad, but the natives there are fascinating. They brew a drink that would give you visions to frighten Dante. And they last for three days."

"I'll keep that in mind," Sebastian said.

"I don't much recommend the experience," Jolley said ruefully. "Now then, what were we saying?"

"The statue," Nell reminded him. "We think she's here, somewhere in these islands."

Jolley fished around behind him, giving Heinrich a light thump on the nose for having nibbled the professor's notes. "Remind me again why we keep these wretched creatures, Nell."

"Don't be unkind, Father, Heinrich and Sophia are like family. Anyway, it was your idea to let them in the house. I'll put them out if you like."

Jolley shook his head no. "I can feel a storm brewing, and I won't have Sophia frightened again." He fished around in the sheaf of papers, finally retrieving an ink-blotted map. "Here you are, y'see? It's a bit out of the way, but four different men who'd sailed with D'Epiques say this is where he hid his treasure, including the Maenad. D'Epiques sank Merriwether's ship for it. Merriwether was the New Zealander who stole it from the Brazilian Indians, who raided it from the private collection of some colonial governor or other."

"Who presumably bought it from the men who stole it from the original dig."

"More or less," Jolley agreed. "Gets a bit fuzzy the longer back you go. But I'm sure D'Epiques was the last to have it. The stories stop altogether after he dies."

"So why hasn't some enterprising local already found it?" Sebastian asked.

Jolley shrugged. "Maybe they have. But I think it would have turned up if they had. I have men keeping an eye on all the usual channels. There aren't many who've done the work I have, who have all the pieces of the puzzle and have taken the time to put them together." Jolley smoothed the map on the table. "I think the Maenad is somewhere on one of these islands." He circled them with his finger. "Probably this one. I was there four months ago, to see what I could find, but it's a fair-sized island. D'Epiques's treasure could be buried, hidden in the stump of a tree, set under a pile of rocks, heaven knows. I spent a week there and didn't find a whisker."

"So that's where we're going anyway."

"Every single one of D'Epiques's men mentioned some distinctive limestone formations. The treasure is there," Jolley said with certainty. "D'Epiques was a clever fellow, he would have kept his treasure somewhere secure. I need your sharp young eyes to see what I missed the last time."

Sebastian nodded. And, no doubt, Jolley needed Sebastian's young back to roll a few boulders back and see what they hid. "Fair enough. When do we leave?"

Jolley pushed himself to his feet. "That's just it," he said, waving his map to punctuate as he paced the wooden floor. "I'd like to start right away. Hurricane season's almost on us, and I want to get in all the sailing I can before it begins."

"Sophia, no, don't!" Nell cried. The little goat had propped her cloven feet up on Professor Jolley's thighs and was attempting to eat the waving map. Suddenly Sebastian realized what had so uniformly cropped the geraniums.

"I say, Sophia, terribly bad manners, you know," Jolley said, trying to gently wave her off.

Heinrich trotted over to defend his lady love, butting Jolley in the back of the thighs. Jolley lost his footing for an instant, and Sophia took advantage of the moment to push firmly against his hip with her small feet, knocking him clear to the ground.

"Father, are you all right?" Nell jumped up to help the professor, who was sitting on the floor with a distinctly rueful expression.

"Yes, I think so," he said mildly, giving Sophia a frown. "Ungrateful creature."

Nell started to help her father to his feet. "I'll go make you a nice cup of tea."

"That would be—oh! Ah! Yes, ahem, I don't think I want to stand on that ankle. I've twisted it again."

"Oh, Father, no!" Nell cried, helping him to the sofa. "It took a month to heal last time!"

"Is it swollen?" Sebastian asked, kneeling by the professor and rolling up the older man's pant leg. "I don't think you've broken anything, but there might be a sprain. Does it hurt?"

"I'm rather afraid it does," Jolley said ruefully. He pushed himself up, trying to stand.

"Father, you mustn't overtax it so soon!" Nell chided.

"Your daughter's right, Professor," Sebastian said.

"Stuff and nonsense." Jolley tried to push them aside. "Just let me walk on it for a few minutes and I'll be right as rain."

"You weren't right as rain last summer," Nell said. "You must be more careful with it this time. No clambering around for a month at least."

"Professor Jolley, I'm sorry about this, but you see what it means," Sebastian said.

Jolley peered up at him, blinking. "There's nothing wrong with my ankle, young man, that a little healthy exercise won't cure."

"A little rest would suit it better. Professor, you don't need to come with me. I have all the maps, and your notes are very thorough."

"It'll take you too long without me," Professor Jolley grumbled. "I'm coming, and that's the end of it."

"We'll lose a great deal of time if you twist your ankle again while we're looking," Sebastian pointed out reasonably. "I can cover a great deal of ground quickly, and with your notes, I'm sure I can find the statue."

"You're going alone?" Nell asked sharply. "To find the Golden Mermaid?"

Sebastian looked at her, annoyed. "Do you see any alternative? How long did you say it took his ankle to heal properly the last time he twisted it?"

"A month," Nell said reluctantly.

"If I don't find the statuette in a month's time, I'll come back here and we can continue the search next year, after hurricane season." Sebastian worked to keep his voice calm and eminently rational.

"You must think we're awfully gullible," Nell said, frowning fiercely. "First you come here and sweet-talk my father into handing over his notes, and now you think you'll just traipse off and retrieve the Bathing Maenad for yourself."

Sebastian found himself fighting his anger. "I think you ought to be leaving these decisions to your father, who seems entirely satisfied of my—"

"I think we can reach a sensible compromise," Jolley broke in. "Dr. Kane will take my maps and notes and go off in search of the Maenad, and Nell, you will accompany him." He turned to face Sebastian. "She knows a great deal about these islands, and she has always helped me with my work. She'll be as helpful to you as she is to me, I'm quite sure."

Nell was still looking at Sebastian as if she expected him to run off with the silverware. She shook her head. "That won't do, Father, you need someone here to look after you."

Sebastian spoke at the same moment. "I don't allow women to accompany me on expeditions."

Nell glowered at him. "I should have guessed. You're among the worst of your lot, aren't you? Intent on keeping women as nothing but mindless chattel."

Sebastian scowled. "As a matter of fact, the last thing on earth I want is to keep you as chattel. You're right, your place is here, looking after your father. You'll only be in the way on an expedition."

"I've twisted my ankle, not broken my neck," the professor said, sounding for the first time a little cross. "I don't need a nursemaid. And you needn't worry about Nell getting in the way, Dr. Kane. She'd make you a good assistant."

"No, she won't," said Sebastian flatly. "Your daughter is very charming, Professor, and I'm sure she would be a great help," he said, hoping his lie didn't sound too obvious. "But the keys are still lawless, full of dangerous men. I'm not going to allow Nell to put herself in danger."

"Piffle," Nell said contemptuously. "We've lived here for ten years, and I've never seen anyone dangerous."

Sebastian ignored her. "You must understand, sir, that even a sparsely populated island like Forgotten Key cannot compare with the wholly desolate places indicated on your maps."

Professor Jolley's blue eyes softened, as he glanced at his daughter. "Ah, yes, I hadn't thought of that. Thank you for reminding me, Kane, you're quite right. We couldn't risk it, certainly not."

"Father!" Nell said hotly. "You aren't going to *listen* to him, are you? He's just trying to take the Golden Mermaid away from you! I *knew* he was sneaky, and here's the proof!" Nell shot Sebastian an angry glower.

"I will return here in three weeks time," Sebastian said, "to check on your health and inform you of my progress. If your maps are correct, and I suspect very much that they are, this will be quite a coup for both of us, Professor."

Jolley smiled and nodded. "It's been a long time. I quite lost my scientific reputation, you know, chasing after her. She always seemed a little beyond my grasp. But since we've come here, the last pieces have fallen into place. With my knowledge and your sharp eyes, we'll find her yet."

Sebastian smiled. "I have a good feeling about this. I'll bring the Maenad back to you, see if I don't." He stood and took his hat and coat from the hat stand. "You just spend your energies looking after that ankle."

"I have no intention of letting you fleece my father this way," Nell said, looking back and forth between the two men. The cool green of her eyes burned with outrage.

Sebastian placed his hat firmly on his head. "You don't have any choice. I admire your loyalty, but your suspi-

cions are misplaced, something I think your father un-
derstands very well. I'll see you in three weeks. Good
night."

And with that, he turned on his heel and left, carrying
the professor's maps and notes tucked beneath his arm.

He should have been pleased by the way he'd handled
the girl, he thought, shutting the door behind him. He'd
been firm, rational, and unyielding—always the best tack
with women who were inclined to be emotional. But
something nagged at the back of his mind, suggesting he
hadn't seen the last of the barefoot girl called Nell
Jolley.

CHAPTER ☾ THREE

*S*ebastian awoke late the next morning, cursing himself for being a lazy bastard. It must have been well past seven, and he'd planned to wake at first light and set sail. But his dreams had been strangely compelling ones, and for the first time in years, he'd been tempted to curl up and doze a little longer when the morning sun first hit his face.

The sun was warm now, painting his gleaming little sloop with soft yellow light. Sebastian rolled neatly out of his berth, stretched mightily, and set to work.

Within a half hour the sails were hoisted and trimmed, and he was on the move. Another voyage, another search for the Bathing Maenad, who seemed to laugh and slip coyly from his grip every time he caught a glimpse of her. "This time's different, you troublesome wench," he said aloud, grinning as he tacked to starboard. "I've got you well and truly this time, and you won't wriggle away from me again."

The sails snapped as they caught the breeze, and Sebastian took a deep breath of the fresh salt air, letting it wash over him, cleanse him. He was close, now, he was sure of it. Somewhere in the maze of the keys the Maenad slept, waiting for him to find her. And this time, Sebastian wouldn't be disappointed.

Nell had a cramp in her leg that felt like it might be fatal. Surely the human body was never meant to crouch like this, folded awkwardly in a fetid, airless box.

Nell hated boats, and she always had. She was content enough to help Auntie Mab polish her decks and repair her nets, but to actually sit in one of these vile things while it bobbed around in the sea—ugh. Nell forced herself to stop thinking about it. If experience were any guide, she'd start to get vilely ill within the hour, and there was no sense hurrying the onset.

A nasty twist in her stomach told her it was too late. She found it very difficult *not* to think of a thing, once she'd started. If only there were a breath of fresh air in the chain locker. But the place was like a coffin. A hot, smelly coffin. Nell tried to stretch out her leg for a moment, and her bare feet dipped into a pool of stale still water. She jerked her foot out again. God only knew what might be swimming around in *that*.

She wouldn't be down here forever, she reminded herself. Just long enough that it would be too late to turn back. She thought of her father with a guilty twinge, but he'd been right—in the morning his ankle would hardly be sore at all, and Uncle Bartholomew would be coming by tomorrow with his usual delivery. The pantry was well-stocked, and a sore ankle wouldn't keep her father from milking Sophia. Nell's father would do very well without her, and it was more important to protect his lifelong dream than it was to fix his lunch and dinner while his ankle healed.

The boat heaved sharply to one side, and Nell's stomach heaved with it. She wrapped her arms around her torso, sank back into her hiding place, and reminded herself to breathe through her nose. "Well, Sebastian Kane, whatever else you are," she muttered, closing her eyes, "I hope you're a fast sailor."

Sebastian checked his charts again, and squinted to make out the rocky shapes around him. The keys were clustered thickly together, and it was crucial that Sebastian not lose track of where he was. He held the sheet firmly, the wind whipping his hair as he looked from the glare of the sun off the pale charts to the cool dark clusters of green islands. He'd never seen colors quite as lush as they were here, though those of the Mediterranean came close. But this place was more changeable, more unearthly. A fitting sleeping place for the Maenad, after all.

He sailed that way for hours, lost in the unceasing rituals of the sea. Ring-necked gulls coasted apace with the *Minerva*, cocking their curious eyes at him before flying off to attend to their business. Ospreys dove in his wake, carrying wriggling silversides as they came up again, and once he saw a massive frigate bird come down for a strike, close enough that he could hear the sharp hiss of wings.

The day was so idyllic Sebastian nearly forgot how changeable these subtropic waters were. Almost before his eyes, the sky gathered close around him, dark green and petulant. The waves, which had been playful and even, began to chop, and seawater slapped over the sides and onto the deck.

Sebastian moved quickly but without haste. He was not concerned. Sailing in these waters, one often encountered brief storms. He'd catch the wind while it was strong and usable, and fold the *Minerva* quiet as a sleeping sea gull when the storm built, waiting it out.

The air smelled sharp, electric. Sebastian squinted up at the enclosing darkness. The sky opened with an ominous crack, and a jagged spear of lightning split the grayness.

Sebastian cursed. So much for taking advantage of the early storm winds. He grunted as he pulled at the sails, cursing again as he loosened the lines. The heavy, wet sails flapped in the gusting wind as if to protest.

The sky was like a living thing, becoming thick and menacing, folding its wings around him as he tied down the sails. He swore he could almost hear it groan, like a woman's voice, mournful and low.

He secured the boom and heard it again, that sorrowful groan. He'd never heard anything like it—a bird, perhaps?

He cocked his head and listened more carefully. The sound was coming not from the sky, but from beneath him, in the chain locker. He peered down at the hatch. "What the hell—"

The hatch thumped, as if shoved from inside, and Sebastian stepped back, startled. It thumped again, and the groan rose up. More like a human voice than a bird's. "Excuse me?" came the voice. "Excuse me, are you up there, Dr. Kane?" The hatch thumped again, vigorously this time. "I'd like to be let out, please."

He released the hatch. A pair of slender hands braced themselves around the square opening, then pushed hard against the deck, and a tangled head of ginger hair appeared.

"What the hell—" Sebastian cried out again, more shocked than angry.

"Please," came the small, unhappy voice, "which way to the . . . ?"

Sebastian forced his jaw shut and motioned his thumb aft.

The slim hands braced themselves again, and Nell Jolley pushed herself up onto the deck, staggered to the rail, and was neatly and thoroughly sick.

"What the *hell* are you doing on my boat?" Sebastian thundered, his dark eyes as black now as the encroaching sky.

Nell sank down gracelessly to sit on the deck. She didn't feel any better for having been sick at last. In fact, she sincerely hoped the boat would be splintered into a thousand pieces, so she could sink quietly and be devoured by some merciful shark. "Throwing up," she said simply.

Sebastian's face grew, if anything, even darker. "Besides that," he growled.

He didn't feel sorry for her, of course, and Nell supposed she shouldn't expect him to. She felt more than sorry enough for herself. "I stowed away."

"You did what?" He sounded like he'd never heard of such a thing in his life.

"In the chain locker."

"You've been down there all this time?"

Nell nodded, trying not to jar her head too much. If she could just keep from moving at all, she might be all right. Maybe. "Scrunched up on top of the chain," she said, her voice a hoarse whisper.

Sebastian swiped one hand through his hair, visibly containing his temper. "Suppose you tell me just why you would do something that stupid."

"Because I'm an idiot," she said.

"Besides that."

Nell sighed. "To keep an eye on you."

The sky cracked open again, and a fork of lightning lit the sky. The sky darkened behind Sebastian's shoulders, the great gray-green clouds like wings of some vengeful angel.

"To keep an eye on me!" he shouted above the rising wind. "That's wonderful, just wonderful. Who's going to keep an eye on *you?*"

Nell could only blink rather stupidly, and wonder if the storm would take mercy on her and sink them. Oh, only then Sebastian would lose this pretty little boat, and that would probably make him even angrier. So perhaps that wouldn't be a good thing after all.

"Don't worry about me, I won't bother you anymore," she said bravely, holding the rail tightly. "I'll just stay here out of your way."

Sebastian looked up at the sky. A howling sound was building, coming at them like the scream of a banshee. "Get down below, to my cabin. I'll join you if I can."

Nell shook her head violently, which only made her stomach clutch in warning. "No, thank you. I prefer to stay up here."

"I don't give a rat's—er, backside what you prefer to do," Sebastian said abruptly. "It's not safe for you on deck, and I have enough to do without fishing skinny redheaded brats out of the water. Go."

Nell tried a wan smile. "I'm afraid I can't, because I think I shall have to be sick again." She felt as if her face were as green as the churning water.

He shot her a sudden look. "You didn't—you weren't, er, unwell all over the chain, were you?"

"Of course not. I do have some manners," she said, thrusting her shoulders back with as much dignity as the situation permitted.

For a moment, Sebastian almost allowed a glimmer of a smile to crack through the cloud of anger in his face. Almost. "There's a basin in the cabin. Go." He pointed to a neatly painted white wooden door at the front of the cockpit.

"But surely you don't—" Nell began.

"Go," Sebastian said. His tone would admit no argument.

Nell scuttled across the deck, hanging onto the odd collection of rails and ropes that boats always seemed to have. By the time she reached the cabin door, she thought that she might need to make use of that basin even sooner than she'd expected.

Sebastian's cabin was spare and spotless, and Nell felt like she was defiling it with her mere presence. She gingerly made her way to the narrow bed and sat back on it, relieved not to be standing anymore. She shut her eyes and breathed deeply through her nose, trying to think about lovely solid, dry land beneath her feet.

After a few moments she actually felt less terrible, and she opened her eyes to look around the cabin. Not the tiniest detail was out of place—another thing Nell hated about boats. People who lived in them were, without exception, unnaturally tidy. Sebastian's cabin was filled with heavy volumes of books, kept from sliding from their shelves by wooden slats, but other than that there was no sign of a scholarly mind. No crumpled scraps of paper, no round inkwell stains, nothing.

The boat gave another mighty lurch to one side, until Nell felt like the horrid thing might turn upside-down completely. Something had come loose on the deck outside and began to bang rhythmically. Nell could hear Sebastian curse. She groaned and curled up into a small, fragile ball, holding weakly to the side of the bed. She wished there were wooden slats to keep her from being hurled about the cabin, as well as to protect the books. But there was no remedy for it; she would have to hang on until the storm subsided, or be dashed to the wall like a butterfly in a hurricane.

She lay her head gingerly on the pillow. It was just possible that she had not done the right thing by stowing away on Sebastian's boat. Maybe he was just as her father said he was—eminently trustworthy and respectable. But Nell was very sure of one thing, she was paying more than a fair price for her sins.

Somehow, the monotony of the boat's violent rocking combined with her own exhaustion finally sent Nell into a dreamless sleep. She awoke again after what seemed like hours, and wondered for an instant if the wretched boat was sinking after all. But she was safe and sound, and the churning in her stomach had even eased for the moment. The boat's movement had changed, from a savage bobbing to a mere soothing rock. She took a deep breath, rubbed the sleep from her eyes, and sat up.

Up on deck Sebastian was letting out a long stream of highly inventive curses. Nell raised an eyebrow and smiled. Perhaps he was not so hopelessly respectable after all. She hopped out of bed, pausing to see if the nausea returned. But she felt perfectly well—in fact, she was starving. She smoothed her skirts, finger-combed her curls, and opened the cabin door.

The storm had settled down to a warm, thick rain. Sebastian had dropped anchor, and now he stood on the deck, putting his broad back into hauling up a rope and looking like some Hellenic demigod. His dark eyes squinted against the water running down his face, and he looked brown and vibrant and warm against the cold gray-green of the sky, like a lion against a ground of green marble. There was nothing of the cool scholar about him now. Nell was surprised at how unutterably pleasurable it was simply to watch him there, working and cursing, his hair a dark slick against the creamy wool of his fisherman's jersey.

He caught a glimpse of her and grimaced as he pulled in the last few feet of his rope. "What the hell are you doing on deck? I told you to stay below."

"I'm hungry," she said simply.

He turned away from her to his ropes. "Too bad. You should have thought of that before you stowed away. From now on, you do as you're told. Mutiny's a hanging offense."

Nell settled herself fairly comfortably on the steps to

the cabin. "You wouldn't hang me, it would upset my father terribly," she pointed out.

"Don't tempt me." Sebastian looked down into the water and let out another curse.

"Is the boat broken?" Nell stood again, climbed the two steps to the deck, and peered over the railing.

"Get back in the cabin, you're getting soaking wet," Sebastian said, looking decidedly ill-humored at the rivulets of water running down the neck of his jersey.

Nell shrugged. "I've been wet before. It'll wash the salt out of my hair."

Sebastian looked down. "For God's sake, you don't even have any shoes on! Get below deck, woman, before you catch your death out here."

"You don't either," Nell said, pointing to his bare feet.

"That's different, I'm a—" Sebastian began.

"A man?"

"And a sailor. That's different."

"Well, I hate shoes, they're silly and they pinch," Nell said. "I never wear them, and I'm not about to start for you. Besides, I didn't bring any."

Sebastian shut his eyes for a moment, letting the rain run down his face. Nell watched him, strangely fascinated. "You mean to tell me," he said finally, "that you've followed me on an expedition, after your father and I both told you not to, and you didn't even bring any shoes? You really *are* crazy, aren't you?"

"No, of course I'm not crazy—" Nell began, a little offended.

"You're out of your mind!" Sebastian shouted.

"I don't see why you're making all this fuss over something as insignificant as a pair of shoes."

Sebastian turned his back on her and began tying down a sail with an impressive-looking knot. "You're right, I've got much more important things to worry about."

"Like what?" Nell asked.

"Our bowsprint's broken."

"Oh." Nell was quiet a moment, watching his face. He looked angry, but not cold-angry. His anger was warm and vibrant, and his brown eyes shone like embers.

"Well?" he snarled finally. "What are you looking at?"

"You. You're interesting. Are we shipwrecked?" Nell's hair was beginning to get heavily wet, and she lifted it back off her nape and gave it a squeeze, releasing a thick drench of water.

"You don't seem very concerned," Sebastian said. He really did look quite cross. "God knows where the nearest inhabited land is. It'll take me hours to repair this, which means the rest of today is a complete waste."

Nell shrugged. "Have you got some matches?"

"Matches?" Sebastian looked nonplussed. "Well, yes, of course I have matches, but there isn't any—"

Nell waved her hand dismissively. "Matches are all we need. We could build a fire without them, but it's very tiresome. And I'm not so good at building fires as I am at some things." She frowned, thinking of the bonfire on the beach that she'd used to summon Despicable Jack.

"You're not building a fire on the *Minerva*," Sebastian said, looking extremely firm.

"I wasn't thinking of staying on your precious boat," she sniffed. "If you think I'm going to make my dinner on hardtack and that nasty water you keep in barrels, you'd better think again."

"And just what," Sebastian asked, his voice thick with sarcasm, "are you going to do instead?"

Nell stepped to the edge of the boat, rolled up her thin sleeves and squinted at the key beyond the reef. It looked large enough and was thick with scrub and short trees. "I'm staying over there," she said, pointing at the little island. She brushed her hair out of her face, held her breath, and jumped into the water.

CHAPTER ☾ FOUR

*I*t took Sebastian a long, stunned moment to react. Then he peeled off his jersey, peering down into the water to see where she'd gone down. Blast that infernal little female! She must be delirious—seasickness could do that sometimes, as dehydration drove one slowly out of one's wits. He felt a pang of guilt twist at his stomach.

He was ready to jump in after her when her ginger head, dark now with water, bobbed up, and she grinned up at him. "I almost forgot—bring the matches, will you? I hope you have something waterproof to carry them in!"

Sebastian only stared at her, unsure what response he could possibly make. He fell back on one he'd been making with distressing frequency lately. "Are you out of your mind?"

Nell whipped her hand through her hair to get it out of her face, treading water easily. "What's wrong now?"

"What's wrong is that you're supposed to be resting in that cabin, not swimming around like some kind of lunatic mermaid!"

Nell ducked her head and bobbed up again, swinging her hair out of her eyes and grinning up at him. "Can't you swim?"

"Of course I can swim—that isn't the point," Sebastian said. Now that he was certain she was all right, he was ready to kill her himself. "Get back up here and stop fooling around."

Nell shook her head no. "Get back on that *thing*"— she gestured to the *Minerva* with her chin—"when I could be on dry land? No thanks." She ducked under the water again, came up, and began to swim toward land with slow, capable strokes.

"Your dress will pull you down and you'll drown!" Sebastian called after her.

Nell laughed. "Don't forget to bring the matches!" And with that she swam away from him, all but flipping her tail.

Sebastian cursed bitterly and glanced around to be sure the *Minerva* was secured. Her anchor was dropped and she was a safe distance from the reef. The storm had subsided to little more than a gentle shower.

Suppressing the desire to land a swift kick on the sloop's sleek cockpit, Sebastian went to his cabin to rummage for matches, his machete, Professor Jolley's notes, and a few changes of clean clothes. He dropped them all into his leather satchel, slapped his old dark hat on his head, then stepped back up onto the deck. Nell was still swimming off in the distance, though she must have long since reached the shallows where she could wade. He lowered the dinghy into the water, dropped his parcel of goods after it, and clambered down the rope ladder. Taking one last worried look at the *Minerva,* he sighed and set his back to the impossible task of catching up with Nell Jolley, human whirlwind and mermaid extraordinaire.

Though the sandbar was littered with shells and seaweed tossed up by the storm, Nell could have kissed the beach when she reached it, dead jellyfish and all. Some time while she'd been swimming, the rain had stopped entirely, and even now the warm sun was beginning to dry the arches of red mangrove roots. Her dress was heavy on her shoulders, drenched in seawater, and she knew if she didn't get it off she'd start to itch. She cast a glance behind her, toward the *Minerva,* which bobbed patiently just beyond the reef. Sebastian was rowing toward her, looking rather less patient.

Nell sighed. Well, Sebastian Kane would just have to wait a few hours to vent his temper, because she had no intention of waiting for him on this beach, soaking wet

and clammy with saltwater. It wasn't a very *big* island—
he'd find her if he needed her. She squeezed the water
out of her hem as best she could and headed south, looking for a protected inlet. Now that she was back on land
again, this wasn't looking like such a bad idea after all.

A short while later, Nell was lying in the sun, feeling it
sink into her very bones. She'd settled on a protected
cove ringed by joewood trees and red spikes of key pine-
apple. The chorus of frogs and the slow drip of rainwater
from the trees had all but lulled her to sleep when she
heard an irritable male voice calling out to her, sounding
very disgruntled indeed. "Damn it, brat! Where in blazes
are you? I don't have time to spend all afternoon looking
for a stowaway!"

Nell sighed and shifted her weight, opening her eyelids
a slit against the sun. She'd found a nice rocky pool of
fresh rainwater, as she'd known she would, and rinsed
herself and her dress in it. The dress was hanging over a
palmetto, steaming in the ever-warming sun, and Nell
herself was basking as nude and happy as a seal. She
practically *never* got to do this at home—father had begun muttering about impropriety some time around her
thirteenth birthday, and her uncle had nearly had a fatal
apoplexy over the habit quite some time before that.
Given Sebastian's general grumpiness and his thoroughly
unenlightened view of females, Nell suspected he would
fall more into her uncle's camp than her father's.

"I'm over here, but, um—maybe you should stay
away!" she called, pushing herself to sit upright.

"Is something wrong? Are you in danger? Where are
you?" Sebastian's voice was harsh and urgent, and she
could hear him thrashing around in the brush, surprisingly near.

"No, it's not that, it's just—"

She was interrupted by Sebastian himself, slashing
through the thicket of ferns and vines with a wickedly
curved machete, his face a hard mask of determination.

He stopped short when he saw her, and made a sudden, choked gurgle. His face instantly flamed to the color

of a ripe guava, and he quickly turned his back. "Jesus! I beg your pardon, Miss Jolley."

Nell grinned. "You called me Nell before."

"That was when you . . . when I . . . what the hell do you think you're doing? What if some pirate or smuggler saw you—that way? Anyway, you'll ruin your complexion." His shoulders were very square and his spine was straight and tall as a mast.

Nell fought the strong urge to giggle. "What would a pirate be doing this far inside the reef? He wouldn't have any more luck getting past it than you did."

Sebastian made a low, angry growl. "He might be burying his ill-gotten gains."

"Really, Sebastian, you're being very fanciful. Have you been reading two-penny novels? Buried treasure indeed." Nell stood and lightly brushed the sand from her legs and backside.

His fists clenched at his sides. "*I'm* being fanciful? You're the one who's lolling about out here like some kind of siren."

"It wasn't me who lured you onto that reef," she teased. "I thought you were a better sailor than that."

He was silent a moment, but the mounting tension in his back and shoulders spoke eloquently enough. His hands flexed as if he were thinking about strangling her with them. Nell thought that it might not be such a good idea to tease him, after all.

"You brought a machete, that was very intelligent of you," she said, as a kind of peace offering. "I hadn't thought of that."

"There are a lot of things you haven't thought of," he said stiffly. "How long until your dress is dry?"

Nell looked over at it. "Oh, I don't know, it depends on how warm it gets. A few hours, I suppose."

Sebastian reached into the satchel he carried and pulled out a few garments. "Put these on while you wait. You'll look like a boiled lobster otherwise."

He threw them awkwardly back to her, and they landed in a clump of marlberry. Nell stepped forward and picked them up, a clean white linen shirt and trousers made of some coarse but soft weave. "Thanks very much," she said, slipping the shirt over her head. It felt delightfully cool on her sun-warmed shoulders. She stepped into the trousers and yanked at the drawstring, cinching them around her waist. "It's all right, I'm dressed now."

Sebastian turned warily around. He seemed angry at first, then his expression dissolved into something strange, something she didn't quite understand. He stepped toward her and gently buttoned the shirt placket, until the collar was fastened right up to her throat. "That's better," he said softly.

She didn't think it was better at all, she thought it was confining and overwarm and silly. But for some inexplicable reason, she didn't want to say that. "Thank you," she said instead, her voice as quiet as his own.

They tramped around the island for an hour before finding a camp Sebastian considered suitable. Nell kept trying to point out some pretty but useless feature of the landscape. Sebastian ignored her, plodding across ropy mangrove or slicing through choking tangles of vines with equal determination. She had caused more than enough trouble for one day, and Sebastian didn't intend to let her talk him into camping in some unprotected stretch of beach just because it had pretty flowers nearby.

Finally they came onto an inlet beneath a group of odd, massive chunks of pitted limestone. The rocks would provide good cover if they ran into trouble. The deep pits in the limestone would catch fresh water, too, if it rained. *When* it rained, Sebastian corrected himself.

He set down his pack and flexed his shoulders. He should have been exhausted—fighting the storm, dealing with the *Minerva*'s broken bowsprit, and then chasing after Nell like a hungry raccoon after a fiddler crab. But he didn't feel tired at all, he felt strangely invigorated. Probably the effect of the salt air, and the knowledge that, though he had been delayed, the Maenad was close. He had everything he needed—maps, notes, Jolley's collected observations. Some of those would be useful and some would not, but he intended to track down every single lead. The Maenad was here, and he would find her.

"We're here," he said.

"Finally," Nell said, sitting on a rock to rub her feet. "I thought you were going to walk our legs off."

"We needed to find a safe camp," Sebastian said gruffly.

"I don't know what you're worried about." Nell reached up to pick some purple flower, tucking it behind her ear. "This is paradise, remember?"

"I don't intend to end up with a smuggler's knife at my throat." He cast her a stern look. "Which is not, in case you need reminding, the worst thing that could happen."

Nell shrugged infuriatingly. "I suppose."

Sebastian itched to get a look at Professor Jolley's notes. There was something naggingly familiar about that limestone formation. "Since you were so keen on coming out here, see if you can go find us some dinner."

Nell sighed. "Yet another case of your treating women like chattel, I see."

"How does this sound?" Sebastian said, keeping his voice low and even. "You go fetch us some dinner, and I won't take you over my knee and give you the hiding you've been asking for all day?"

Nell's eyes widened, and she scuttled to her feet. "I see. Threats of violence, now, is it? Well, if that's the way it's going to be, I'd better get to work."

"Good idea," Sebastian said, trying hard not to actually snarl.

"Wouldn't want to bring down the wrath of my lord and master," Nell sniffed.

"Go!" Sebastian roared.

Nell jumped a little. "All right, all right!" She tucked her dress, nearly dry now, under one arm and scooted off toward the other side of the limestone boulders.

Thank God, a man finally had a little privacy. Sebastian rummaged through his satchel and found Professor Jolley's notes, folded safely in their oilcloth wrapper. He flipped past the pages of maps and charts, and the sketch of Jacques D'Epiques's personal mark—a lusty-looking mermaid tipping a bottle of rum to her lips. Finally he found Jolley's drawings, careful duplicates of those made by a disreputable but sharp-eyed blockade runner in the last war. The man was old now, but he had kept his drawings and had allowed Jolley to make copies of them.

Sebastian flipped through the stack of pages. Yes, this was the one he had in mind. He squinted over at the largest rock in front of him, and then back down at the page. The shape on the bottom wasn't quite right, but that shadow on the far left was very similar.

He stood and walked closer to the rock, trying to get the angle right. He could see Nell, crouching among the mangroves in the marly surf, getting her pants legs wet and playing with what looked like a piece of string. Her dress lay forgotten by her side, once again soaked in seawater.

He sighed. Maybe they'd be able to find some coconuts or something for dinner—Nell Jolley certainly wouldn't be much of a provider.

It was clearer now from this angle; this was definitely the formation Professor Jolley had sketched in his notes. Sebastian's breath caught in his throat as the golden afternoon light spilled over the white limestone. It glowed almost as if it knew what it hid.

Sebastian breathed deeply to clear his head, and slowly closed the folder of notes. This pleasant little island, with its lush vines and scent of ripening fruit teasing the air, turned out to be the very place Professor Jolley thought it most likely they would discover the Bathing Maenad.

CHAPTER ❨ FIVE

*S*ebastian heard an angry squeak and turned his head to see Nell frowning and muttering to the sea. She still held that ragged bit of string, one end tied to something Sebastian couldn't make out. The surf was playing lazily with it, curling the string first one way and then another, while Nell squatted quite still. A foam of marl and tannin lapped over her feet and soaked the rolled cuffs of her pants.

Instinctively, Sebastian curled his hand protectively over the sheaf of maps and notes. God help him if Nell realized this was the island where the Maenad was hidden. The girl was a veritable walking disaster. He couldn't quite blame the storm on her; that would be irrational. But the damnable creature kept up a constant stream of nonsensical chatter—she was as fanciful as a butterfly, and about as useful to him. A butterfly at least wouldn't require being fed and clothed and looked after.

Of course, if she hadn't gotten it into her fool head to jump ship and swim to the island, Sebastian might have taken days to sail around and find himself right here again. But that was sheer lucky coincidence, and nothing more.

He edged back from the white gleam of the limestone, tucking the papers in his satchel without making a sound. She was still playing at her odd game with the sea, looking for all the world like the pretty bedlamite he'd taken her for the other evening on the beach.

No, Nell Jolley most certainly did not need to know

how close he was to finding the Bathing Maenad. And she was so easily distracted by her own fancies that it would be no trouble at all to keep it from her.

By her own estimate, it took Nell over three-quarters of an hour, but finally she had five fat crabs tied up neatly in the folds of her discarded dress. She could see their hard, rounded backs and the menacing forms of their claws beneath the wet cloth, but she had them securely. "Rough luck, chums," she said with a smile. There was nothing on earth as lovely as the taste of a crab plucked from the ocean and steamed up for supper within the hour.

Sebastian seemed odd when she returned, distant and distracted. He seemed to cast his eyes everywhere but on her, and he'd almost forgotten to be grumpy.

"Back already, are you?" he asked, his voice strangely hearty. "Well, don't worry, I think we can find some roots and grubs to dig up in the woods. This isn't the first time I've been stranded in the tropics, and you can find a good deal to eat if you keep your wits about you."

Nell stared at him a moment. "What on earth are you talking about? I have five crabs wrapped up and ready to cook. All we need are some palm fronds, and there are plenty of those right along the beach."

Sebastian looked up, startled, and then back down again at the wriggling bundle at Nell's feet. "Oh! I see. I didn't realize. Crabs, eh? That was very clever of you."

"I found a dead fish among the roots," she said, pointing to the stand of mangrove. The trunks blazed with the mellow evening light. "Once you've found the right bait, the rest is easy. Tide's going out, or they would have been even bigger."

Nell thought she could just see him testing the air with his nose, but she'd washed her hands thoroughly in the sea, until they smelled only of salt and the fresh, tangy smell of ocean. She didn't care for the smell of dead fish any more than he did.

"Do you want me to cut the palm fronds for you? They may be too rough for your hands."

Nell looked at him, squinting. This didn't seem like

the same Sebastian at all. She preferred the old one. Better a grumpy man who could pass for a bloodthirsty ghost than one who wouldn't meet her eyes with his own. "Of course not," she said gruffly. "I'm not some helpless drawing-room female. Lend me your knife and I'll go do it myself."

"Be my guest," he said mildly, handing the machete to her.

She walked off toward the palm trees, swinging the machete loosely in one hand, wondering just what in blazes Sebastian Kane was up to.

As the sun fell, casting purple shadows across the grouping of boulders, Sebastian slowly allowed his guard down. For a girl whose intent in coming was to keep an eye on him, Nell wasn't much of a snoop.

She was, he had to admit, a better provider than he'd given her credit for. She'd rinsed the crabs in a rock pool, trussed them neatly with a piece of vine, and put them between two layers of palm fronds to steam. The only thing she couldn't manage was the fire, but he'd made rough camps often enough to be a fair hand at that. Just before the sun went down she slipped away and came back a few minutes later, her arms laden with clusters of sea grapes.

Sebastian cracked another crab claw and sucked out the sweet white meat. He had to smile when he thought of his offer to go dig her some roots and grubs. He might have been able to find something that would keep their stomachs from cramping with hunger; Nell had provided them with a feast.

"You really do look like a nefarious pirate when you smile like that," Nell said, leaning back against a flat rock, warming her bare feet by the fire.

"You mean D'Epiques?" Sebastian said, his smile widening.

"Exactly." She answered his smile with one of her own. "Despicable Jack was supposed to be taller, though, and much bigger around. And he had a great black beard that hung past his belly."

Sebastian shrugged in mock humility. "Sorry if I don't measure up."

"You've got a temper to match his, even if you don't have arms like tree trunks," she said, her eyes dancing in the firelight.

"I'm not as bad as all that, am I?" Sebastian said wryly. "I didn't force you to walk the plank, after all. You did that yourself."

Nell laughed aloud, and Sebastian was startled by how pleasing he found the sound. Her voice was low and sweet, like the sound of church bells.

"I just couldn't stand another moment on that . . . *thing.*" She gestured widely out to the ocean, in the rough direction of the *Minerva.* The water glittered with stripes of phosphorescence on the tides.

"How can you swim like an otter and not care for boats?" Sebastian asked.

Nell shrugged. "I love the sea, I feel at home here. Boats have nothing to do with it. I've made just enough peace with the things to sit on Auntie Mab's deck and mend her nets with her, but that's as far as I'll go. As soon as the anchor's pulled up, I begin to go green."

"It's all in your mind, you know," he said. "A nervous condition. After a few days at sea, you'd forget all about it."

"I think a few days at sea would kill me," she said with a shudder. "And I can assure you, my mind is not the affected area. It's my poor stomach that can't take it." She threw back her head and laughed again, exposing her throat to the warm light of the fire. She'd taken too much sun today, and she was lightly pink all over, like the horizon at twilight.

Sebastian flushed as he realized she truly would be pink all over. He slammed his self-control down as if he were clamping the lid on Pandora's box, but it was no use —the vision of her lying there, lazily brushing sand from herself while she looked at him through those half-shut, strangely sultry green eyes, sent his pulse pounding with the force of a tidal wave.

"It's what you deserve for stowing away," he said gruffly, moving one arm to shield the uncomfortable swelling beneath the soft, loose canvas of his sailor's trousers. "What on earth could have put such an idiotic notion into your head?"

She looked at him levelly, her eyes still warm, but strong and steady as well. "I care very much for my father, Sebastian. You don't know him like I do. All you can see is his intelligence, but I know how trusting he is of any fellow with a sharp mind and a quick tongue. He'd still be teaching at Oxford if he weren't so inclined to put his faith in charlatans claiming to be scholars."

Sebastian shut his eyes for a moment and nodded, understanding. Professor Jolley had become a laughing-stock in his quest for the Maenad. He had finally left Oxford in disgrace after convincing a benefactor to sink thousands of pounds into an expedition to find her, only to lose it all as the rogue they'd hired quite literally sailed off with the cash, leaving the professor and his benefactor equally empty-handed.

"Do you believe it exists, then?" Sebastian asked quietly, after a long silence.

"My father does, with all his heart, so I have to," Nell said thoughtfully. "But I almost wish it didn't. If you do find it for him, it will be the end of all his dreaming. My father needs dreams like some people need meat and water."

Sebastian nodded. It was a condition he understood well, had seen a dozen times over. It was not one, however, that he intended to succumb to. Dreams were a whetstone to sharpen your goals, not an end in themselves. "Are you still worried I'll steal your father's dream away from him?"

Nell frowned and looked down at her hands, as if contemplating the smooth, short lengths of her fingernails. "I'm not a suspicious person normally, it's just—"

"In other words, yes, you are," Sebastian said dryly. He leaned back against his satchel, legs stretched out in front of him, hiding the twinge he felt. Why should she trust him? Even now he was keeping secrets from her, failing to tell her the truth about what he'd discovered. But her wariness bothered him, far more than reason and common sense said it should.

Nell was quiet for a long moment, looking thoughtfully into the fire. The warm light caught the rings of her curls, making them glow like pink gold. "It was easier when I thought you were a ghost. Then I could have whisked you away like that"—she snapped her fingers and grinned at him—"if you got out of line."

"You don't really believe in all that, do you?" Sebastian said, propping himself on one elbow. "Ghosts and bonfires and black magic? You can't tell me you do. You're a scientist's daughter, you understand about evidence and the importance of facts. Those other things are just fairy stories."

Nell frowned. "There are a lot of things people think are just ignorant fancies. My father caught a horrible disease in the jungle once. His arms and legs swelled up like balloons, and he couldn't eat or drink or speak. The local medicine man made him medicine from grubs and ground-up parrot feathers, and chanted for three days to save him. Science would have pronounced my father incurable, and he would have died. But fairy tales saved his life."

Sebastian frowned and threw his crab shells into the fire, which hissed and spat sparks in protest. "Doubtless he would have survived anyway. Some men's constitutions are terrifically strong."

"But why? Why should one man, strong as an ox, die of a disease while his spindle-shanked neighbor survives it? What makes one man's *constitution*, as you call it, stronger than another's?"

"That's just the way things are," Sebastian said.

"Exactly. That's what I'm interested in. The way things are. Not the way science thinks they should be, all neat and tied up with a red ribbon to be presented at the Royal Society, but just the plain way things are."

Sebastian shut his eyes and settled back against the soft roll of his satchel. He was surprised by how good this felt—to be here, with her, sitting by a campfire and talking. To have eaten a fine meal, and hear the soft rush of the waves on the shore, and feel the mild tropical night air on his sunburnt skin. Even the mosquitoes didn't bother him. "You have an interesting mind, Miss Jolley."

She snorted. "You're not an irredeemable dullard yourself, Dr. Kane."

It was Sebastian's turn to laugh. "Thank you so much." He pushed himself up to face her. "Listen, we'd better get to sleep. We have a long day ahead of us tomorrow."

"We do? Why?" Nell sat forward, creamy jade eyes sparkling with curiosity.

He leaned forward to scoop sand in the fire, dousing it and hiding the expression on his face. "Ah, the bowsprint. I need to make my . . . repairs. In the morning. As soon as possible."

"Oh, that." Nell yawned and leaned back. Lit only by faint moonlight, he could just see her roll one of his shirts into a makeshift pillow. "Don't hurry yourself on my account. If I never get back on that beastly thing in my life, it'll be too soon."

"Would you rather stay here, then?" Sebastian's voice was soft enough that for a moment he wasn't sure she had heard him.

After a long moment she answered. "It wouldn't be so bad, would it? Crab dinner every night, and nothing to do but swim and pick flowers and watch the water change color?"

Sebastian's mind flooded with images of Nell's pale body, all lean, sweet curves, stretched languidly against the smooth flat stone. Her only covering had been a necklace of flowers, but they'd enhanced rather than hidden her small, high breasts. She'd made no attempt to shield herself from him. Instead, she had flicked the sand delicately from her arms and looked straight into his eyes, as if she showed her naked form to men every day.

Free love, she'd said to him that night in her father's house. Her father's house, for God's sake! *The only true way for men and women to live together in harmony is through the frank, open sharing of free love.*

Sebastian's throat felt too thick to talk, and at any rate he didn't have the first idea what to say. The girl might be a shameless wanton—though Sebastian had to admit, in many years of experience, he had never known a wanton quite like *this* before. But that didn't mean he had to take advantage of the situation. Nell was Professor Jolley's only daughter, and that placed her well out of limits. From now on, he'd just have to be sure she realized her outrageous ideas were unwelcome and inappropriate. Sebastian turned over, hoping he could get some sleep. He would find the Maenad as soon as possible and get the hell out of here. The sooner they got off this damnable rock, with its seductive, fragrant breezes and total absence of civilized mores, the better.

CHAPTER ☾ SIX

*W*hen Nell woke up, Sebastian was gone. The sun was still low in the sky, and the world was painted in cool lavenders and pale blues rather than the hot jewel colors of late morning. Nell wrinkled her nose and reached for Sebastian's discarded shirt, and rolled it up to shield her eyes.

The shirt carried his scent, faint but unmistakable. It carried her back to the dream she'd been having, a dream of a suntanned young man with a ready scowl but laughing brown eyes, and of the way his arms would feel around her. The dream and the teasing scent of his skin on his shirt made her feel peculiar all over—not happy and not sad but just . . . anxious. Anxious for something to happen, she didn't know what.

"Wake up, sleepyhead," came his gruff voice above her, and a few drops of something cold landed on her bare ankles.

"Oh!" she said, sitting bolt upright, his shirt falling into her lap. "Watch where you hold those things!"

Sebastian was holding two silvery mullet above her legs, letting them drip seawater onto her. "You seemed like such an energetic little thing, I never would have taken you for one to sleep the day away."

Nell pulled her bare legs beneath her and scowled up at him. "I do not sleep the day away, I just don't see any need to jump out of bed at the crack of dawn. And I firmly believe that the best way to marshal one's energies is to get enough sleep at night."

Sebastian laughed. "I don't think I've ever seen you this way. Like a cross little girl."

"I am not cross and I am not a little girl and I would very much appreciate it if you would watch where you're holding those damned fish!" Now that her legs were out of the way, the cold, wet mullet were dripping onto her arms, their morose faces seeming to stare at her as they swayed.

"Here, you hold them while I build a fire. I don't want to get sand all over them by putting them down."

She stood up as he handed them to her, and she scrambled up to sit on one of the large rocks, holding the fish out to drip. "Are you always like this in the mornings?"

He looked up at her, surprised. "Like what?"

"This cheerful and efficient," she said, speaking the words as if they were *obnoxious* and *vile*.

"Afraid so," he said, and actually began to whistle as he built the fire.

Within a half hour, they had roast fish for breakfast, and Nell was beginning to feel a little more human. "So you're going to work on your boat today?"

He looked at her, his brown eyes suddenly keen. "Yes. Would you like to join me?"

Nell shook her head violently. "No thanks. I'll amuse myself here."

She thought she could just see the suggestion of a smile creasing the tanned corners of his eyes.

"Right," he said. "I'll leave you my pistol."

"What for?" she asked, shocked. "If I run across an alligator, I'm certainly not going to shoot it. There are easier ways to chase them off, you know."

"I'm worried about more dangerous game."

"You have smugglers on the brain," she said, cleaning her hands by rubbing them on the rocks. "Anyway, you'd never hear a pistol shot all the way out on your boat."

"Then you'll just have to shoot to kill," he said blandly, reaching into his satchel and pulling out the pistol. "I don't want to be worrying about your safety while I'm . . . repairing the boat. Do you know how to work one of those things?"

"More or less." She looked uncomfortably at it. Nell knew how to load and shoot, but she didn't like guns. They made a wretchedly loud noise and frightened off all the animals.

"Try hard not to shoot yourself," he said, standing and throwing her his old felt hat. "Wear this, it'll keep you from getting too red. I'll see you later."

"I'll try to be properly dressed when you come back," she said, folding her hands demurely over the pistol in her lap. Now why on earth had she said that? He'd been utterly horrified yesterday, when he'd stumbled across her basking in the sun, so why should she throw that in his face? She found her face warming.

"That sounds like a good idea," he said dryly. He tucked his machete and his notes into his satchel.

"Why do you need that?" she said, pointing to the machete.

He looked sharply down at it for a moment, then at her. "To get back to the dinghy. It's still tied up on the beach where I landed. I'll row it around when I come back."

Nell nodded, watching his back as he walked away from her, the way the lean muscles moved beneath the soft white cloth of his shirt.

She missed him when he was gone. She didn't know why she should. He was bad-tempered most of the time, and even when he wasn't, he made her feel funny. Not funny like laughing and being happy, the way her father did. Funny like the first time she'd eaten pickled eels and couldn't decide if she liked them or not. She'd kept eating bite after bite, still not sure, but unable to stop herself.

She stood abruptly and began to pick her way along the rocky beach, looking for shells. As she found them, she arranged them in a wide circle on a flat slab of limestone, the tiniest ones at the center, then a daisylike ring of fragile ram's horns, then a band of alternating jewel boxes and broken angel wings.

Sebastian was a little like Auntie Mab, she decided. He had what Auntie Mab called "queer ways," something the old woman was decidedly proud of. He hadn't demonstrated any further attempts to treat her like chattel, but then again, there wasn't much for a chattel to do in the keys. With a little work you found some food, and with a little more you cooked it, and beyond that the idea of menial labor didn't make much sense.

He hadn't answered her question last night, about whether he'd like a life on these islands, with nothing to do but swim and lie in the sun. Probably that meant he didn't. He was driven, the way her father could be driven, though Nell herself saw precious little use in it.

When her flowerlike arrangement of shells was complete, she leaned against the rough bark of a gumbo-limbo tree to admire it. The water in front of her was calm today, a glaze of turquoise striped with bands of cobalt and pale amber, and murky violet where the turtle grass grew.

She might as well face it: She was a grasshopper and Sebastian was an ant, and once he had found the Golden Mermaid for her father, they'd part company and never see each other again. She could hardly imagine a less suitable companion—the man was overbearing and rude and hopelessly old-fashioned. He didn't have the faintest interest in the political and social ideas that were buzzing through the great minds of the world like some giant, invisible swarm of bees. And he thought she was a spoiled hoyden.

Nell frowned, though the sun was beginning to warm on her face. Maybe she truly *was* a spoiled hoyden. Her uncle Bartholomew certainly thought so. She'd lived with only her father for so long, and Theophilus Jolley was nothing if not an indulgent parent. Sebastian's reaction when he'd caught her sunbathing told her that there was a vast collection of social rules and obligations that she truly knew nothing about. But how was she to know what was proper behavior for a young lady in the larger world, and what could be attributed simply to Sebastian's pigheadedness?

She sighed loudly, turning her back on the shells and the rich colors of the water as if they, and not a young man with laughing brown eyes, were troubling her. She wasn't going to think about Sebastian Kane any longer, and she wasn't going to drive herself into a state over what the rules and regulations of polite society might be. She was who she was, and from where she stood now it didn't seem like such a bad life.

Something about the view of the other keys from where she stood rang a bell in her mind. The six nearest islands formed a shape a bit like the Ursa Major, the beach she stood on nestled within its bowl. A string of tiny keys, little more than rocks with bits of scrub attached, formed a handle that curved slightly west.

As soon as she saw the pattern she knew where she had seen it before: in her father's papers, the maps to the Golden Mermaid. She had remarked on the way the scattered islands resembled constellations. And if her memory served her correctly, that meant that this very island was the best place to look for the Bathing Maenad.

Nell's grin was so broad she felt like her face would crack. Wouldn't Sebastian feel sheepish! She could have danced at the thought of how she'd tell him. *Oh, I thought you might like to know, we happen to be directly on Jacques D'Epiques's island.* No, too casual. *Guess what I've discovered?* Too childish, and it sounded like she gave a dead mackerel for what he thought.

Well, she had time to think of how she would break the news to him. She entertained, for one guilty moment, the thought of not telling him at all—of simply finding the Golden Mermaid on her own, letting him thrash around looking for it, and calmly presenting it to her father when they returned home. But that would be too nasty of her—Sebastian wasn't a bad sort, just a bit of a grump.

She gathered up her few things, twisting her old dress around like a rope and tying it belt-fashion around her waist. She considered for a moment leaving the pistol—it would become tiresomely heavy to carry—but it would probably get sand blown into its works, and would almost certainly get rained on, neither of which was probably very good for a pistol. Nell wanted nothing to get in the way of the delicious moment when she crowed to Mr.

Scientific Mind that she, not he, had found out they were on Despicable Jack's island.

She jammed the pistol into her makeshift belt, thrust the old hat Sebastian had left her on her head, and headed down the coast toward their rowboat. She'd swim out to the boat to tell him the good news. She could hardly wait.

The walk back was not a difficult one. The overgrowth was still clear from yesterday's walk, and Nell wondered again why Sebastian had bothered to bring the machete. The thing was wretchedly heavy, worse even than the pistol, and the lush mat of ferns and strangler fig would hardly have sprung back overnight. Perhaps Sebastian had taken the advice of the old salts a little too literally, thinking that trees really did spring from the ground in an hour or two in the keys. He was a frightfully literal-minded man, after all.

She walked quickly, thinking she would catch up with him, but he must have run the whole way. After a short time, she found the rowboat, left high on the beach where they'd tied it. The sand around it was pristine; there was no sign that it had been moved, and no trace whatsoever of Sebastian Kane.

Nell felt, for the first time, the total desolation of this place. Even compared with Forgotten Key, where she at least had her father and the goats for company, this island was a wild, empty scattering of stones in the water, almost unearthly. The changeable sea had gone deep green, like a shimmering plain of grass, lapping calmly at her feet as if to apologize for yesterday's outburst. And Nell Jolley was perfectly alone.

It took Nell a long moment to understand what the still-abandoned boat could mean. Something must have happened to Sebastian. And she had told him so many times there was nothing to worry about on the keys! For the first time she entertained the possibility that there truly might be smugglers here—the legends about Despicable Jack were known throughout the keys and beyond, and surely scholars were not the only men interested in ancient treasures.

Sebastian's pistol dug into her hip, and she realized

she had left him all but defenseless. A machete was all very good and well, but it would be little use against a dirty band of pirates with blunderbusses and cannons and God knew what else.

Nell took a careful look around. There was not a footprint, not a broken leaf, not a trace of anyone or anything who had been here since last night's tides had washed their tracks away. She turned around and headed directly where she'd come from. The bandits must have waylaid him before he'd gotten to the boat, then. Nell eased the pistol from her belt and cocked the trigger. Whoever these brutes were, she'd take care of them.

Nell took pains to keep her steps quiet as she pushed through the undergrowth. The keys could play tricks on you; one moment the ocean's roar drowned out all sound, and then the wind would change and you could hear the rustle of a pigeon's wings from across the island. She eased slowly through the mass of leaves, keeping the pistol raised in her right hand, ready to lower and fire if she were caught by surprise.

Finally, about halfway between their camp and the rowboat, she found a break in the undergrowth leading to the interior of the island. If she hadn't been looking for it, she'd have assumed it was nibbled away by the tiny Key Deer that swam from island to island. But this damage was rougher, carved out by man, not beast. This is where those vicious thieves had taken Sebastian.

Nell stepped into the shade of the path through the trees, and the sudden chill raised the hairs on the back of her neck. She had begun to sweat, walking in the morning's building heat, but here the air was cool and fresh. Butterflies flitted around her like flying flowers.

She swallowed hard, realizing that she might actually have to *shoot* at least one of the smugglers. An image rose unbidden before her, of a man crying out in pain as she pulled the trigger. But she had no choice. If she were going to rescue Sebastian, she would have to put aside her squeamishness.

The huge web of an orb spider grazed her face, and she brushed it impatiently away, pushing slowly through the lush wall of green. She attuned herself to the slightest sound that might reveal the smugglers' whereabouts, but the low-growing forest was nearly silent, all sound muffled by the thick, damp leaves.

Finally she heard it, the rhythmic staccato hacking of a machete. Then there was silence again. Nell tightened her grip on the pistol, trying not to think about her aching arm, and pushed on. Ruthless, she must be ruthless, acting without hesitation when she caught up with the smugglers. Sebastian's life might depend on her ability to keep her cool.

Finally she caught a glimpse of white, a shirt back seeming to blaze against the green darkness, then disappearing around a curved path.

Nell wiped her palms on her trousers and adjusted her grip on the pistol. She took a deep breath and pushed through the overgrowth. "Hold it right there!" she called, surprised that she was able to keep her voice from cracking. "Don't move!"

A figure in a white shirt and dun-colored trousers stopped dead ahead, his back to her, a shapeless black hat covering his head. He clutched a worn scrap of paper in his left hand, and a wickedly curving machete in his right.

"Hands up where I can see them!" she barked.

The figure stiffened, then growled, "What the hell—" He turned as if to face her.

Nell had no time to think, no time to ask herself whose voice attached itself to the form ahead of her. All she could see was the silvery arc of the machete as it curved toward her, and the powerful arm beneath the white sleeve—an arm that could fling the machete into her face.

In no more time than it took to blink, Nell found herself holding her arm straight out in front of her, pointing the pistol roughly in the man's direction, and pulling the trigger.

CHAPTER ☾ SEVEN

The black hat flew from the man's head like a startled bird, as he wheeled around to face her. His clear brown eyes were dark with outrage. "What in the name of hell do you think you're doing?"

Nell could only stare, stunned, at Sebastian. "Where'd you get the hat?" she finally asked, horrified, not knowing what else to say.

He was on her in an instant, taking the pistol from her hand with a ruthless twist. "You nearly killed me! What in blazes were you thinking?"

"The smugglers—" she began, shaking her head a little to try and clear her mind.

"What smugglers?" Sebastian asked, suddenly wary.

"The ones who kidnapped you. You never made it to the rowboat. I just came from there." The words sounded stupid, worse than stupid, as they lay there in the air.

"You haven't seen anyone?" Sebastian insisted.

Nell shook her head no. "Why weren't you wearing that hat before? I would have recognized you if I'd known the hat."

"Will you leave off about the damned hat? I found it washed up with the rest of the debris on the beach, and thought it would do me a damn sight better than letting my head broil in this sun." He checked the bullets remaining in the pistol in a swift, unthinking motion.

"Then there *are* other men here!" Nell said, still

stunned that she'd nearly "rescued" Sebastian by blowing his head off.

Sebastian tucked the pistol into his own belt. "Could be, but I wouldn't count on it. I've seen storms wash up all kinds of flotsam—anything that can fall off a ship and is too tough to eat might end up here."

She'd shot at him. She'd nearly killed him. Nell felt dizzy and a little sick, and she grasped the low branch of a poisonwood tree to balance herself.

"Nell, are you paying attention?" Sebastian's voice cut through her mental fog.

Her face grew hot, as much with anger as embarrassment. "No, I wasn't."

"I asked what you're doing here. I thought I told you to stay put."

"You told me you were going to repair the *Minerva*," she said evenly, regaining her calm.

He blinked once, then took his eyes from her, looking over her left shoulder. "I needed to cut some wood, to make the repairs."

"You can't repair a boat with green wood. Just how long were you planning on staying on this island?" Her mind was clearing now, and she was beginning to wish she had that pistol back, so she could wave it around under Sebastian Kane's treacherous nose.

Sebastian sighed impatiently. "Well, it wasn't wood exactly that I was seeking, it was vines. To make ropes with."

"And what's that for?" She pointed to the paper, now rumpled and damp, still clutched in his left hand.

Sebastian looked at the paper as if it were a deadly scorpion, and for a moment Nell thought he might actually fling it to the ground. "I had an idea. About the island. So I thought I'd check it against Professor Jolley's notes."

"Seeing as you had them conveniently in your satchel," she pointed out.

"That's right. Here now, this is nasty, rough work, no place for a young girl. Why don't you wait for me back by the rowboat? I think I'll keep hold of the pistol for now."

Sebastian spoke rather too quickly, and touched her elbow as if to shepherd her off.

"If you'd just wanted to stop and check his notes, why did you keep them in your hand while you were blazing your trail?" Nell asked, looking him steadily in the eye.

Sebastian looked at her for a long moment, the light brown of his eyes looking insidiously warm and trustworthy. He ran his hand roughly through his hair. "I guess you've caught me, haven't you?"

Nell couldn't figure out why she wanted to cry, why she wanted to kick and scream and shout her head off. She took a step backward, away from him. "I wish I *had* shot you."

He moved toward her, shrugging apologetically as his eyes asked for her forgiveness. "I realized that this might be D'Epiques's hiding place, and I wanted to check a few things out, that's all."

"You lied to me," she said, turning away from him so he wouldn't see the tears welling in her eyes. She'd been an idiot. How could she ever have begun to trust him? He was out to cheat her father, nothing more, and he had just *pretended* to enjoy her company last night, when they'd talked above the lazy crackle of the fire.

"A sin of omission," he said, taking her lightly by the arm. Slowly and gently, he turned her to face him, his eyes kind. "Nell, you must admit, you're something of a handful when you get an idea into your head."

She bit the inside of her cheek hard, to keep herself from bawling her eyes out. "I'm sorry you find me so horrible."

Sebastian laughed at that, not unkindly. "I don't find you horrible." He was quiet then a moment, looking at her as if she were something rare and precious. "I don't find you horrible at all. I just find you more than a little troublesome at times. I wanted to investigate a bit further before telling you, to keep you from going off and doing something rash."

Her eyes stung, and she was losing her battle with tears. She wanted to trust him, with a want that pressed at her throat in a painful lump. "Rash? Me?" She couldn't keep from laughing then, at the expression on his face when she'd shot at him, and with her laughter the tears spilled over. "All I did was nearly shoot your head off."

"Hush, hush," he said gently, taking her into his arms. "Have I made you so sad as all that?"

Nell gave herself up to the release of tears, shutting her eyes against the wonderful feeling of being next to him, of feeling her cheek against the warm, solid weight of his chest. "It's just that I thought we were f-f-friends," she sobbed, "And then you t-t-tried to trick me."

Sebastian cursed softly beneath his breath and gathered her closer, wrapping her in the sweetness of his arms. She could feel his lips brushing the top of her head, and she felt a warm shiver all through her belly. "I guess that was a pretty rotten thing to do, wasn't it? I'm sorry, Nell. I underestimated you, and I shouldn't have."

His hands stroked her back, and suddenly she did not want to cry at all. The warm shiver spread outward, like a swallow of hot brandy. She hiccuped, and looked up into his eyes.

He touched her cheek with his fingertips, brushing at the traces of tears. "Do you think you can forgive me?"

She was getting lost in him, in the warmth that stole over her and the lean, brown planes of his face and the laughing eyes that had gone quietly serious. She was getting lost, and she found she didn't mind it a bit. "I think I can," she whispered.

Something dawned over his face, a hunger, and she wondered for a wild moment if the warm shiver hadn't enveloped him, too, if he didn't feel these feelings that were making her stomach jump like a slivery mullet leaping from the water. "Nell," he said, his voice soft as he touched her cheek, her chin.

And then he lowered his mouth onto hers, and she lost herself entirely. The warm shiver in her belly became a flood, and she knew nothing but that she wanted him to keep doing this, to keep the touch of his mouth on hers.

His tongue teased at her lips, and she opened to him like the soft unfurling of a moonflower. She met his tongue with her own, shyly at first, then more boldly as she heard his harsh groan and felt him pull her to him more tightly. She could feel the pistol at his belt grind into her belly, but she did not mind it. She did not mind anything. Sebastian Kane was kissing her as she had no idea she could be kissed, and there was nothing, nothing else in the world.

He broke away from her, his eyes shiny as black pools. "Nell, this can't—"

Nell was horrified as she let out a loud hiccup. "Can't what, Sebastian?" she asked, hoping he'd ignore the hiccup. "Kiss me again."

He put his hands on her shoulders and stepped firmly away from her, his expression unreadable. "I don't think that would be a good idea."

Nell's heart gave a painful squeeze. "Didn't you like it?" she blurted, hiccuping again. Damn it all, here a man had kissed her so that she felt it straight down to her toes, and she had to go and ruin it by getting a case of the hiccups like some five-year-old child.

Sebastian let her go then. "I liked it very much. It's just that—"

Nell hiccuped. "It's just that you think I'm an infant," she said crossly.

He looked extremely uncomfortable, and adjusted the pistol in his belt. "I think you're very young, yes. A lot has happened in the past few days, and we've become friends. And it's only natural that friends, every once in a while—" He broke off, as if confused, and tried again. "You see, between men and women, there are certain consequences . . . that is to say . . ."

He was blathering on in precisely the same way her father had when she'd asked him, at seven years old, how babies got made. She remembered it very clearly, just as she remembered her father's scientific, if rather dull, answers. "There needn't be a child, you know," she said, trying to be helpful. "If you simply remove the interested article just before the end, there isn't the least danger."

It was the wrong thing to say, she saw that immediately. His tanned face blanched, and he looked horrified. "What did you say?"

"The interested article," she repeated in a small voice. "You remove it. Just before the finish."

He took three quick steps back from her, as if she'd grown fangs and long horns. "What the hell could you know about it?"

"As a matter of fact—" she began.

"No! Don't tell me. Good God, you're no more than seventeen."

"I'm eighteen, actually, and it isn't so complicated as all that, you know," she pointed out.

His face was hard, almost angry. "You will not mention the subject in my presence again."

"But I thought that perhaps you wanted to—" She broke off. She wasn't exactly sure *what* she'd thought, but she'd been quite certain that the smoldering kiss had something to do with what men and women did to make a child. And she'd read Sappho and Ovid—it seemed clear that such things were intensely pleasurable. If they could, indeed, prevent the begetting of a child, which Sebastian naturally might find a trifle burdensome, why shouldn't he be willing to share this pleasure with her?

"I do not," Sebastian said, nearly shaking. He wiped his forehead, which had broken out in a sweat, with his shirtsleeve, and turned away from her to look for his hat. "For God's sake, woman, the matter is closed."

"Fine! I wouldn't have cared to—" Nell lacked the vocabulary to describe what she would or would not have cared to do. "Well, I wouldn't have, with such a dreadful coward!"

His warm brown eyes blazed. "What did you call me?"

"You heard me. All that nonsense about the lure of adventure—ha! You think you're some kind of modern Jason, but you're more like some silly old-fashioned . . . *bookkeeper!*"

"It's clearer to me now than ever that Jason would have been a lot better off if he'd just steered his way clear of women!" Sebastian shouted, sinking his machete into a coconut palm.

Nell let out an outraged yelp. "I knew it! You disdain half of the species—the smarter half, I might add—just because we're female! Of all the irrational, pigheaded, antiquated—" Nell was searching her mind for suitable adjectives when the look on Sebastian's face changed in an instant, from anger to wary watchfulness.

"Nell, hush for a moment—did you hear that?"

Annoyed, Nell nonetheless quieted herself and listened. "I don't hear anything other than—" But then she caught it, the distinct murmur of male voices. "Sebastian!" she whispered. "There's someone else on this island!"

Sebastian nodded grimly as he tugged his machete free of the palm trunk. "And they're not far away. We'd better find someplace to lie low."

The voices raised to a shout, and a break of raucous laughter.

Nell took him by the hand. "I know someplace we can hide."

She began to lead him back down the path he'd cleared. The rumble of the men's voices grew louder. One of them let out a raw howl, punctuated by the blast of gunfire.

Nell's eyes met Sebastian's in an instant of perfect understanding. She had turned and was trampling her way through the tangle of ferns even as he softly cried out, "Run!"

CHAPTER ☾ EIGHT

*N*ell and Sebastian ran for all they were worth, Nell leading them down the path and out to the beach. The men—and it did not sound like there were many of them, perhaps no more than two—were fast on their heels, cursing and laughing and letting out the occasional burst of gunfire.

"They must have heard us," Sebastian said, swallowing a curse as a thorn apple lashed his cheek. "And they'll be on the lookout for our boat."

They broke out onto the beach, and Nell grasped his hand firmly. "Come this way. I know a place where we'll be safe." It took her only a few minutes, running at full tilt, to reach a clump of limestone rocks, laced through with holes and patched again with limpets and barnacles. They formed a shape something like a well, a ring of stones around a hole over the water. "Come on!" she cried, as she scrambled up the lip of the well.

Gunshots rang out again, ricocheting off the trees. "What the hell are you doing? You'll be a sitting duck up there."

"Trust me!" Nell hissed, and then disappeared into the limestone well's mouth with a splash.

Sebastian cursed long and bitterly as he followed, taking the rocks with only slightly less agility than Nell, who, he decided, was surely part monkey. He paused a moment at the rocks' edge, listening for their pursuers. He could hear individual voices now—two, he thought, one deep and one high. Both of them sounded drunk. Sebastian held his breath, shut his eyes, and dropped himself down the dark, rocky hole.

The water was warmer than he'd expected. He pushed his wet hair out of his eyes as he bobbed to the surface, and let out a satisfying curse.

"Over here!" cried Nell. "Ahead of you, to your right!"

He made out the outlines of her form in the darkness. They were in a limestone cave with high walls, and Nell was perched on a rock ledge some feet above him. He swam over to her, fighting the water's tendency to slam him into the limestone walls, ducked beneath the water to release himself from his satchel, and handed it up to her.

She took it wordlessly, then shook herself like a water dog as he hoisted himself up onto the ledge.

"How'd you know about this?" he asked.

"I saw it yesterday, when I first swam to the island. I used to love to tramp around sea caves."

"Why didn't you tell me? You knew I was looking for a secure place to camp."

Nell shrugged. "Who wants to spend the night in a cave? I thought we'd be more comfortable on the beach."

"We'll be more comfortable if we don't get ourselves shot to pieces," Sebastian muttered.

The men's voices grew nearer outside, until Sebastian was certain the men were standing directly above their heads. The men's wild laughter told him his instincts had been right. "They're drunk."

"Ugh," Nell said, as if she'd uncovered a spider. "No wonder they're behaving like baboons."

"How do you know what baboons act like?" Sebastian said, smiling despite himself.

"My father used to tell me stories about them, and about the other exotic animals, when I was small," Nell said.

Sebastian laughed softly. "I'm beginning to see that you might have had a somewhat untraditional upbringing."

"Don't most parents tell their children bedtime stories?"

"I think the average American child hears more about the Three Little Pigs and Red Riding Hood than about baboons and orangutans."

"Those men are certainly *not* behaving like orangutans," Nell said crossly. "Orangutans have excellent manners."

Despite the water's warmth, the air in the cave was cool, and Sebastian found himself shivering in his wet sleeves. "This is all very interesting, but I think we'd better make a plan. I doubt the gun will do us much good after the dunking I just gave it. We'll have to wait until they either get bored and move on or pass out. Either way, we need to move quickly as soon as the coast is clear. I'd rather not have to confront them openly."

Nell sneezed. "Is it just me, or is it cold in here?"

Sebastian swallowed the curse that rose to his lips. "Being around you, I've noticed, does distinctly unsavory things to my vocabulary. Yes, as a matter of fact, it is getting cold in here."

The cave walls were smooth and damp, and in the distance Sebastian could hear a faint drip. "Come on," he said, pushing himself to his feet. "There's more to this cave than this ledge—let's see how far back we can go."

Nell agreed surprisingly easily, for Nell, and the pair of them felt half-blindly along the rock ledge. The light was dim, but the cave's mouth was wide enough that they could make out all but the darkest shadows. They felt their way along the cool walls, the shadows growing steadily darker.

Nell moved ahead of him, her small form sliding easily between the narrow split in the limestone, as if moving through a near-black cave was of no greater moment to her than crossing a meadow. The air grew stale, redolent of brackish water and the stifling dark of caves. And the walls around them grew darker still, the white limestone glowing faintly like the moon hidden by clouds.

Sebastian looked down at the water below, where a strip of phosphorescence in the water glowed like an unearthly lantern.

Finally Nell cried out in soft pleasure, as they came upon a beam of yellow sunshine. In this moon-pale darkness, the sun was like a stream of warm honey.

"Another entrance," Nell said confidently. "Now all we need to do is figure out how to get to it."

Sebastian moved to stand behind her, looking up at the new entrance. It was high above their heads, forty feet or more, a radiant patch of light against the cave's cloak of darkness. When he looked down around him again, sun-blind, he could hardly make out the cool white shapes around him. "I think the answer to that is, we don't. We're stuck here until our friends upstairs get bored."

As if in response, the men began shouting, in what sounded like a rip-roaring fight. The voices were close, but not too close.

"Right this moment it sounds like they're more interested in killing one another than in chasing us any longer." Nell placed a warning hand on his wrist. "Mind your step—this is the part that gets dangerous. If you can't see the ground beneath you, look into the shadows until you can."

Sebastian followed her advice and moved slowly around this new cave. It was spacious enough, warmer than the one they'd left. He peered into the gloom, trying to make out the sculpted limestone forms.

Suddenly Nell gave a sharp cry, and Sebastian felt his heart beat like the luff of a sail in a changing wind. "What is it, what's wrong?"

"Over there." She pointed to a loose jumble of stones and shells. As Sebastian's eyes accustomed to the darkness, he realized they were not stones at all, but a pile of polished white skulls, grinning at him with macabre glee.

And unless he was very much mistaken, they were human.

Chapter ❨ Nine

$\mathcal{N}$ell was the first to speak. "Is it Despicable Jack's horde, do you think?"

Sebastian swallowed. "Hard to tell. It could be smugglers, pirates, there's no shortage of bloody stories on these remote keys." He moved closer. The skulls were not thrown together in a heap, but piled quite precisely. Ringing them was a thicket of long thigh bones, like a crown of thorns.

"I think I'm going to be sick," Nell said quietly.

"Would you rather we left?" Sebastian asked, suddenly feeling that this was very much the wrong place for Nell to be.

"No," she said, her voice stronger now. "I want to see what's under those bones."

Together they moved the pile, bone by bone. Sebastian was surprised by how heavy they were. He'd half expected them to be light, insubstantial as the hulls of dead insects. But they were thick and heavy, as if with the weight of their bloody histories.

Beneath the skulls was a tangle of hands, some clasped as if in ghoulish friendship. And beneath the skeletal hands was a carved teak box, painted with D'Epiques's characteristic mark—a mermaid drinking a bottle of rum.

Nell shivered. "This is it, isn't it?"

He nodded. "I think so."

She turned to him. "Are you sure you want to do this?

This is the end of your dream. What will you have left when the search is over?"

Sebastian found himself grinning. "I have a couple of ideas. Help me get it open."

They worked at the lid, but it held fast. "Do you think wc'll have to use . . . those?" Nell asked, shuddering as she pointed to the bones.

"These bones have been desecrated enough," Sebastian said. "If this blasted thing isn't haunted already, it'll be a miracle."

"I hope you aren't succumbing to irrational fancies," Nell teased. "I thought you were going to leave the ghost stories to me."

From what seemed like very far away, Sebastian could hear the shouts of the two men above. The fight seemed to have disintegrated into a maudlin, drunken stupor. At least they'd give up firing their guns for the moment.

"With any luck, the locals won't be telling ghost stories about *us.*" He set the blunt edge of his machete on the seam bctwcen trunk and lid, and leaned. The lid gave a groan, then an outright creak, and finally gave way, sending up a cloud of moldering dust.

"Ugh!" Nell shielded her face with her hand. "I suppose no one's touched this in a hundred years."

"And we stumbled across it by accident," Sebastian said, realizing it for the first time himself. "If you didn't have such a knack for getting us into trouble, we would never have come here."

"I have not gotten you into trouble," Nell said airily, frowning at the burst of laughter from the men above their heads. "All I've done is introduce a little adventure into your life."

"I've been sailing the *Minerva* all over the globe looking for a pirate's treasure. I thought that *was* an adventure," Sebastian said wryly.

Nell shook her head. "An adventure needs a jolt of the unexpected once in a while. Maps and notes are all very well, but a real adventure begins when you haven't got a clue how things will turn out."

"The life with you, crazy Nell, would definitely be an adventure," Sebastian said with a grin. The words made him feel strangely warm. *Life with Nell.* The idea should have made him run as far and fast as he could, but instead he found it rather . . . appealing.

"Well?" Nell cried, exasperated. "You've been looking for the Mermaid for six years now. Aren't you the least bit curious now that it's practically in your hands?"

"I want to savor this," Sebastian said. But it was not only the discovery of the Maenad he wanted to savor. It was being here, in this damp cave lit only by a bit of phosphorescence in the water and a single slim sunbeam, with this impatient slip of a girl beside him.

Nell sat back on her haunches and let out a tragic sigh, as a child might. "Very well. I'll just wait here until you decide you've *savored* long enough."

Sebastian laughed aloud. "All right, all right. She's been asleep for a hundred years—let's wake her up."

He took a cloth bundle from the top of the trunk. It had an evil, musty smell, like something cursed. Nell was right—he *was* beginning to succumb to irrational fancies. He unwrapped the cloth slowly. Whatever was inside was too small and insubstantial to be the Bathing Maenad. He peered at the opened packet in his hand, and let out a long, low whistle. "Well, if the Mermaid's not here, this will help take the sting out of it." He plucked out one of the objects and handed it to Nell—a heavy gold ring set with a stone the size of a finch's egg.

"What is it?" Nell asked.

"Amethyst, I'd guess."

Nell slipped it onto her finger and admired it. "I suppose it's very gaudy, but I like it." She brought it up to her face to examine it more closely. "Oh, look, it's little people!"

Sebastian leaned over to see, and felt his face grow hot. The gold setting was a tiny carving of a man and a woman, locked in a very intimate—not to mention athletic—embrace.

"Maybe you'd better give it back to me," Sebastian croaked.

"Don't be wretched, Sebastian. You'll get your precious ring back, don't worry." Nell sounded offended, as if he'd accused her of stealing it. "Just let me wear it a few minutes."

"It's not my ring," Sebastian said gruffly. "You're as entitled to it as I am. It's only . . ."

"It's only what?" Nell brought the ring up to her nose to examine it again.

Sebastian clasped his hand quickly over hers, and her gaze rose to meet his, startled.

He felt an electric tingling as their hands touched, as her eyes met his in the half darkness. He should not be touching her, she should not be so near. They were silent a moment, watching, wary as two cats. "Let's see what else is in here," he finally said, breaking the silence.

He turned away from her, grateful for the distraction. But the chest provided more than he'd bargained for. He pulled up fistful after fistful of treasures: rings, necklaces, golden mirrors, and several small statues. All were as erotic as the amethyst ring. Apparently Jacques D'Epiques was something of a specialty collector.

Nell held up a large round pendant depicting a nymph struggling in the arms of a satyr. "Look, they're dancing!" she cried, squinting in the dim light.

"Ahh—" Sebastian said, his throat suddenly cottondry.

"Oh, they're . . . oh!" Nell cried. "But they're—"

"Yes," he agreed. "Quite."

She fell silent, and Sebastian with her. Suddenly the wide limestone cave seemed too small, and impossibly warm. Sebastian tried hard not to think of the amorous poses depicted in the treasures, but the harder he tried, the more aware he was of Nell's warm body beside him, and his tortured memories of the glimpse he'd caught of her on the beach.

Nell's breathing was quick and shallow. Was she as aware of him as he was of her? Sebastian remembered her outrageous comments about free love and interested articles, and suddenly his principles about Theophilus Jolley's wild daughter seemed irrelevant as fairy dust.

He shook off the thought. The air in the cave was thick, and he wasn't thinking clearly. He couldn't be.

"Do you think that's the Maenad?" Nell asked, pointing to a bundle near the bottom of the trunk, larger than the others.

"I think it might be."

Nell swallowed audibly. "Let's open it."

The bundle was heavy in Sebastian's hands. Suddenly the realization sharpened in his mind. This was it—the dream he'd chased halfway around the world. Perhaps Nell was right. Maybe now that he'd found it, he would feel empty.

He glanced over at Nell, who was watching him quietly, those sultry-innocent green eyes looking more unearthly than ever in the sea cave's darkness. There were dreams left for him, if only he had the courage to pursue them. And courage was a commodity Sebastian Kane was known for.

He unwrapped the bundle and carried the statue over to the weak beam of sun to see it as clearly as possible. Nell followed close behind.

The Maenad was not so large as he'd imagined her, but she was infinitely more lovely. A laughing girl with curls to her waist, carved in marble with exquisite subtlety, leaned back lazily against a golden sea rock. Her eyes were half-shut, and she seemed to revel in the feel of the sun on her face. Gold waves, the gilt still largely intact, washed her ankles.

The statue was less frankly erotic than the rest of Despicable Jack's trove, but the pleasure that washed over the Maenad's face was as real as if she'd been a flesh-and-blood woman, lying on one of the key's rocky beaches, her wet hair drying in the sun.

"She looks just like you," Sebastian whispered, realizing too late he'd spoken aloud. It was true. The mix of innocence and sensuality, the way the girl's whole body seemed to yield to lazy, uncomplicated pleasure, reminded him of her. He was assaulted anew by the memory of Nell stretched out along the rocks, her pale flesh creamy against the rough white and gray of the limestone.

"Oh my," Nell said in a small voice.

"I'm sorry, forgive me, I should never have said that," Sebastian said quickly. He was all but gulping for air now. She was too close to him, he was saying foolish things, and she wouldn't slap his face the way any properly brought up young lady would. Nell wasn't properly brought up, she was a heathen whirlwind. And right at this moment, Sebastian was glad.

"Sebastian?"

"Yes?"

She leaned closer to him, damp and warm, her curls smelling of seawater. Her mouth was close to his, and he could feel the soft heat of her breath. "Would you please . . . kiss me again? The way you did before?"

The fight was lost, he knew it now, and he found he didn't care. "Nell, you know that I want you, don't you? You know what that means?"

"I know what it means. I want you, too, Sebastian."

He felt the cool goose bumps on her arms and the warmth of her sunburned shoulders as she wrapped herself around him and gave herself up to his kiss. His sex leapt to life as he held her, pressing itself insolently between them.

She broke away from him for an instant, startled, then dropped one hand down, her ginger touch soft against the fabric of his pants. "Oh! It's very . . . it's quite large, isn't it?"

He growled, a growl that began deep in his belly and rumbled up in his throat, but there was no anger in it. Only possession, and wanting, and hunger. "Be quiet, sweetheart," he said softly, as he covered her face in feathering kisses.

She trailed her hand lightly down the length of him, her touch gentle but insistent as her mouth found his. She kissed him, then, hard and urgent, her tongue sliding into him, possessing him with all the hard hunger he felt for her. Her hands moved slowly around and down his back.

"What are you up to, wench?" he growled, shutting his eyes against the pleasure of her hands on him.

"Taking off your wet things," she said roughly, peeling his shirt off in a single motion.

Sebastian heard a moan slide from his throat.

Nell slid off her own shirt and set it aside. She sat

there looking at him, her green eyes suddenly serious. "Sebastian, I'm . . . I'm a little bit scared," she confessed, her voice small in the darkness.

"Good God, Nell, so am I." He leaned forward to kiss her again, kissed her with a smoldering fire that lit the last corners of his chilled frame. Her hands roamed boldly over him, belying the fragility of her voice, and he dared to touch her, to brush his hands across the line of her collarbone and over her shoulders and across her breasts. She drew her breath in sharply at that, then let it out again in a long, slow sigh of pleasure.

Her hands roamed down the hair on his chest to rest at the waist of his trousers, and he realized he was holding his breath. "I want to . . . see you," she said, tugging gently.

Sebastian swallowed. She was moving fast, too fast, he felt caught in the whirlwind of her. Everything in him screamed that it was wrong to do this, that she was the daughter of a man he respected, that she was so young. But she wanted him, with the same burning intensity that was roaring in his ears, deafening him even as he slid his trousers down, even as he tugged at the drawstring holding up her own sodden sailor's pants.

She was tense at first, frightened perhaps of being there beneath him. A sensuous creature, his flawless little mermaid, but not so experienced as he had guessed. His sex lay between them, hard and long across her belly, and he thought he might die of wanting her. But still he held himself in check, tasting her mouth, letting her taste him.

He slid his hands from cupping her face down to caress her breasts, his thumbs toying with the nipples. Pink, they were sugar pink. And now they were hard, and she was beginning to wriggle beneath him. He felt a sharp stab to the belly, as if he were being murdered by pleasure. He broke away from her mouth to kiss and lick her breasts, sucking each nipple long and slow. Her breath was ragged now, and when he nipped at her gently—so gently, more a caress than a bit—she broke out into an inarticulate moan.

He moved up to kiss her mouth again, his thumbs

resuming their stroking of her hard nipples. "Can you feel how much I want you?" He thrust his hips an inch forward, so that his sex slid slightly along her belly. He shut his eyes at that, afraid to say more for fear his voice would give way.

"Y-yes, I feel it, Sebastian. I . . . I want you so much. Please . . . I don't know what I want . . . please me, Sebastian."

He smiled and reached his right hand down to stroke the curls between her legs. They were slick, and he parted her easily, but he did not penetrate her. He merely kept his fingers sliding back and forth across the entrance to her, moving only the tiniest fraction into her with each stroke.

Her breath was quiet now, but fast. He let his thumb stray to seek out the hard bud of her pleasure, and flicked it gently. She responded with a sharp intake of breath. He flicked it again, then again, stroking it as he pushed his finger slowly inside her. Long, slow strokes, joining her, filling her, the way he would fill her when she was ready for him.

But she was ready for him now, he knew. Tight, yes, but hot and slick and panting with the anticipation of it. If he wished, he could drive into her and finish the torment with a few quick strokes.

Sebastian had never been one to take shortcuts.

He slid his hand free of her, and she made a small, plaintive whimper. "Please don't stop!"

He moved down, skin sliding against skin as he knelt between her legs, the stone floor hard and cold beneath his knees. "I promise you, I won't," he said, and then he bent down to kiss her in the deepest, most intimate kiss of all.

Nell thought she must certainly die, as she felt the soft pressure of his lips and tongue on her, on the place that demanded to be stroked. She had not known—how could she have known? He kissed her with small, light sips, lighting on her like a hummingbird, then moving away again. She could feel the span of his hands on her hips, as she arched up. He pressed her down again, and bore down on her with his mouth, devouring her in small, rhythmic bites, consuming her.

Her fists were clenched at her sides, but she reached up to press him down on her, to demand that they finish this. She did not know what lay at the end of this path, but she knew she would have killed to get there. She wrapped her fingers in his hair and pulled his mouth to her.

The light sipping motion became a slow, persistent stroke of his tongue, and he insinuated his finger into her. She felt invaded at first, wanting almost to move away from that probing, insistent finger, but as he stroked she felt her world begin to dissolve around her. She could feel the pull calling out to her, calling her to join in an ancient and terrifying dance. Almost, almost, she had the strength to resist it, but it called to her, called in the rhythmic motion of his mouth and the sliding of his fingers—two now, and then three, stretching her, testing her, pushing her. And still she hungered for more, felt her deepest muscles clinging to his fingers as the dance called out to her in a wild whirling, a frenzy and a song she could not deny. And then she stopped denying it, and she leapt into the magnificent annihilation of the whirlwind, and she was lost.

CHAPTER ☾ TEN

$\mathcal{N}$ell could not believe she did not lose consciousness, but somehow she found herself still in this dimly lit cave with this dark, magic man and his dangerous tongue. "I . . . what was . . ." she began, feeling a little foolish and utterly drained.

"Hasn't any man ever done that for you before?" Sebastian asked, his voice indulgent and more than a little proud of himself.

Nell shook her head. "No."

He laughed then, a soft, rich sound that echoed from the walls. "I see." He stroked her lightly, touching her hips, her thighs, the plane of her belly. She shivered a little. "The next time, I want you to be with me."

She had no idea what he could possibly mean, and for the first time in her life she felt shy. He had opened up some dark place in her, a place she'd never known existed. She was a little afraid of it, and of him. "With you?"

He cursed softly in the darkness. "I forgot. The interested article. Ah, well, it can't be helped."

He stretched up to kiss her again, pausing briefly to nibble at her breasts. His mouth smelled of her, of earth and ocean, and she felt the sweet darkness curl again in her belly. Surely he couldn't bring her to that place again. And yet she found herself responding to him, felt the wetness flowing in her as he slipped his tongue in and out of her mouth, in the same sultry rhythm he had used when he had knelt between her legs.

She felt a hardness brushing her, and felt him poised there where his mouth had been, as if he were seeking out her wetness. She wanted that hardness within her, a full joining with him. She arched her hips up to meet him, so that her belly pressed against his and he pushed against the entrance to her.

"Christ, you are so goddamned beautiful," he whispered, reaching down to stroke the bud of her pleasure again. "Everything about you, your look, your smell, your taste." He made a choked sound as he pushed inside her.

Nell's eyes flew open. This was very different. He was huge, he would split her in half. "Sebastian, I—" she began in a choked whisper.

He drove into her then, pushing inside her with one long, merciless stroke, and for a moment she knew that this searing pain meant she would die.

Then he was still. "Oh, Christ. Nell. Why didn't you tell me?"

He began to pull away, to leave her, and in that instant Nell knew that this was right, that this was meant to be. She took his buttocks in her hands, and pulled him hard against her. "Don't leave me, Sebastian."

He slid into her again, a deep, slow stroke, and Nell felt a wince of pain, but also a hot shock of pleasure.

"You're a virgin," he whispered, astonished, almost pained. "Nell, beautiful Nell, why didn't you tell me you were a virgin?" He bent down to kiss her, his mouth gentle and warm, yet his hardness was still strong and insistent, beginning a slow, sweet rhythm inside her.

She curled her hips up against him and let out a soft moan. "Not anymore," she managed, and then she reached up to kiss him, and she could say nothing.

They danced together, legs entwined, as he moved inside her with a slowness and a sweetness she thought would surely drive her mad. His body was hard against hers—not just the sexual part of him, but his arms that pinned her gently beneath him, and the planes of his back as she ran her hands over him, down the roundness of his buttocks. He shifted position, propping himself upright on his hands, and she felt a jolt of pleasure as he moved inside her.

"Sebastian, yes, there."

He laughed softly, his hips quickening slightly. "Like that?"

What she said next was not quite intelligible, but it did not need to be. As he quickened, she followed him, dancing the ancient dance, satyr and maenad, Adam and Eve. She thought of one of the statues Sebastian had pulled from the chest—a nymph astride a golden Bacchus, her head tossed back in pleasure. The thought sent a hot thrill to her loins, and she felt the heat begin to build again, a fire that threatened to burn her to fine ash.

"I want you with me, beautiful Nell," Sebastian whispered, and he reached a hand down to toy with her, his thumb flicking across the bud of her pleasure as he moved inside her, faster, stronger.

"Sebastian . . . I'm going to—" Nell broke off, not knowing the words, knowing only that she was crying out with the pleasure of him, that the pleasure was washing over her in wave after endless wave, and then he left her body, abruptly, and he was crying out in a long guttural cry like a joyous sob, and then he was still.

They slept there, curled together, for what felt like a long time. The sliver of light from the crack in the rocks above lengthened, spilling over their skin and across their faces like a yellow-gold watercolor wash.

It woke Nell first, and she gave Sebastian a nudge. "Hey, sleepyhead. I think it's getting late."

Sebastian's eyes opened, and Nell felt her heart break with sweetness. He smiled. "Hello, lover."

Her face grew gently warm, and she smiled shyly at him. "It's getting late," she repeated. "Maybe those men have gone."

Sebastian yawned and stretched, and Nell privately noted that the sight of his hard, muscular body was quite aethestically appealing. So much so, in fact, that she regretted the notion of leaving the sea cave. It would be much nicer to stay here, to take pleasure with him again and then sleep again.

So that was love between men and women. It was not what she had expected. What they had done did not remind her of Ovid's sly sniggering, and it did not seem a casual trading of pleasure. She found herself caring what he thought of her and hoping he was pleased by her.

Her stomach rumbled angrily, chasing any notion of staying in this cave from her mind. They would have to leave, to find their way off this island and back to the world, and with it all the rules and logical order Sebastian lived by.

Perhaps Nell could find a way to live in such a world, as well. The thought made her feel like a songbird choosing to go live in a cage. But how else would she be with Sebastian? She was quite sure that she wanted very, very much to be with Sebastian.

Sebastian was sitting cross-legged on the ground, looking distracted as he ran his hands appraisingly over the Golden Mermaid. "It's all her fault, you know," he said, looking up at Nell with a smile that flashed dazzling white in the slant of the afternoon light. "So wanton, and so beautiful. *She'll give ye your heart's desire, or drive ye mad with longing's fire.* That's it, isn't it? I think she's done both."

Nell felt a shiver of pleasure that crept down to her toes. "Was what we did madness, then?"

"Absolutely," Sebastian said, sounding pleased. "You've made me as crazy as you are, Mad Nell."

"I wouldn't have thought you'd want to be mad," Nell said. She didn't know what was wrong with her. She should be happy, but she felt unsure and nervous, afraid for the first time in her life that her happiness was about to slip from her fingers before she had truly known it.

"I didn't, at first, but it's what I needed," Sebastian said, leaning forward to kiss her on the nose. "Come on, wench. I'm going to make you very unhappy."

She felt a little stab in her throat. "Unhappy?"

"I'm taking you back to the boat, if we can slip past our friends up above. We'll be safer there. I can repair the bowsprit tonight, and we'll be sailing back to Forgotten Key by morning. You should see your father again tomorrow afternoon. I can't wait to see his face when he sees we've found the Maenad."

Nell bit her lip. She wanted to cry out, to fall into Sebastian's arms and beg him to take her with him. Anywhere, she didn't care. But there was no sense in behaving like a hoyden. If she conducted herself with a bit of decorum, perhaps he would see that she would make him a very good partner after all. A very good . . . wife. That was what she wanted, wasn't it? To live by his side, and take care of him, and share his secrets late into the night?

She only knew she could not bear to lose him now that she had found him. "Yes, you are quite right," she said, forcing a reasonable tone.

"Are you all right, Nell? You don't regret what happened here, do you?" He touched her cheek, and his voice was soft, a caress.

She shook her head, squeezing her eyes shut to force back the tears. "No, of course not. It was . . . it was wonderful."

He smiled at that and planted a gentle kiss on her temple. "That's what I was hoping you'd say. Look sharp, then. We're heading home."

They were dressed and moderately respectable-looking within twenty minutes. Sebastian wrapped the Mermaid back in her cloth, and stuffed the statue into his satchel. The rest of Despicable Jack's treasure he wrapped in a single bundle and gave to Nell, to carry slung over one shoulder. "Right then. Off we go."

They traced their way back to the cave's mouth. The tide was higher now, and they had to swim the last part of the way, but the water's surface was only a few feet from the round, well-like opening. They lifted themselves out without trouble, despite their wet clothes.

Nell's heart felt as heavy as her cold, clammy shirt as she walked along the beach. Why hadn't he said something about making her his wife? The conventional thing to do would have been to insist they marry immediately, and for once Nell found herself longing for the conventional thing. Perhaps he didn't want to marry after all?

She had given herself to him with such simplicity, without any notion of how heavy a thing love truly was. Love. She was in love with Sebastian Kane. The thought made her miserable.

They walked quietly, aware of every insect's buzz and frog's peep. But they saw no sign of the men who had chased them.

Finally they came to the shallow inlet where Sebastian had tied the rowboat. Nell eyed the thing with suspicion. The rowboat might bring her to Sebastian's world, with its rules and laws and proprieties, or it might take her back to Forgotten Key and to a loneliness she'd never noticed before now. Either way her mouth felt dry and faintly bitter.

She supposed this was what it meant to grow up. If so, growing up was overrated.

Sebastian tossed his satchel into the boat with a heavy thud, and Nell threw her bundle of erotic treasures in after it. They were silent as they rowed back to the *Minerva,* Sebastian concentrating on pulling the oars, and Nell wondering just how she would ever fit in a world where ladies wore shoes and proper hats and expressed only the mildest of opinions.

When they got to the *Minerva,* Sebastian was the first aboard, climbing the ladder with practiced ease. Nell took his helping hand, though she hardly needed it. Immediately he saw some rope out of place, frowned, and set himself to fiddling with it.

Nell turned her back to him a moment, and toward the jewel green of the island, with its ropy mangrove tangle opening onto a stand of coconut palms. A zebra butterfly drifted past her on the freshening breeze. Maybe it wasn't a very sensible or logical world, these warm, sweet islands, but it was her childhood, and she would miss it.

She turned to face Sebastian again and took a deep breath. She even pasted on a brave smile, ready to face the future, whatever it held. She had said a million times that she wasn't a child any longer, but for the first time, she felt it might be true.

But before she could take her first step toward her

new life, Sebastian's head shot up, and he cried, "Nell, look out!"

The hatch creaked with a harsh shriek beneath her, the deck clattered with heavy steps, and before she could turn around, her arms were clutched by a pair of hairy male hands.

CHAPTER ☾ ELEVEN

$\mathcal{N}$ell thrashed against the hands clutching at her, and managed to free one arm. She was pleased until she felt the sharp jab of a knife at her waist.

"That's it, girly, just calm down," came a voice from behind her. It was an odd voice for a man, almost shrill.

Nell twisted her head to get a better look at her captor, but he responded with a poke of the knife. "Eyes front, girly," he growled.

"Let her go," Sebastian said, with such quiet authority that Nell could not quite believe the man didn't obey.

"Think it's going to be that easy, eh?" The man laughed a nasty little laugh. "You came here for the Golden Mermaid. Well, we want it."

"Never heard of it," Nell said quickly. "We just had a little trouble with our boat, we went to the island to find something to eat."

"You shouldn't try to lie to him, lady," another man said, pulling himself up from the hold. Nell blinked. The newcomer was the skinniest, most forlorn-looking soul she had ever seen, looking more like Ichabod Crane than like a dangerous smuggler. "Ralph Black's a terrible 'un, Despicable Jack's twin, you know. He has what they call an obsession about Jack, can't get him out of his mind. And all the old salts say Jack's treasure is on this key." The man spoke softly, as if he were apologizing.

"Dang it, Bland, don't mention our names! Now we'll have to kill 'em. Drat it, why can't you remember the simplest thing?" The man named Black punctuated his reproach by jabbing at Nell's midsection with his knife.

"Well, if you're going to kill us, I'd appreciate it if you did it all at once, instead of poking me to death," Nell said crossly.

"You don't take me serious, is that it, lady? You don't think I'll really do it, do you? Do you?" Black's voice grew shriller as he shouted the words in her ear. "Me and Jack, we're twins separated by the centuries. You got any idea what that means, lady? It's fate, that's what it is. And I want that damned treasure. I know you two got it, it's wrote all over your faces. Anyways, we heard you fighting on that island, and don't nobody fight like that 'less it's over money. Give it over."

"Why should we bother, since you've already decided to kill us?" Nell asked, archly sweet.

"Nell," Sebastian said in a warning tone.

"You ought to tell her to mind her manners, mister," the one called Bland said, dusting off his trousers with fastidious movements. "Black's the devil when he's angry. These keys haven't seen nothing so fierce since Despicable Jack."

"Yes, you've mentioned that," Sebastian said dryly. "Why don't you tell us what it is you want?"

"The Mermaid," Black said quickly, and Nell swore she could hear him licking his lips. Could hear it, in fact, from a region well below her shoulder. Mr. Black might consider himself Jacques D'Epiques's twin, but Nell was beginning to suspect her captor was positively Lilliputian. She twisted her head to catch a glimpse of him, but he tightened his grip on her arm and jabbed her again. "I said eyes front!"

Sebastian's face took on a contemptuous air. "We know where Jack's treasure is, all right, every doubloon of it, but why should I tell you? The girl's right, if you're going to kill us, you have nothing to bargain with."

The forlorn one, Bland, nodded. "He's right, Black. You gotta admit, he's got a real point there."

"Shut up!" Black snapped. Nell was sure of it; the man was minuscule. She thought she could feel his breath on her shoulder blades. "Where is it? Tell me, or I'll carve her up!"

"Since I'm going to die anyway, go ahead and carve," Nell said irritably. "This is getting very tiresome."

Black cursed. "All right, then, I won't kill her if you tell me."

Sebastian's mouth curled in contempt. "Why should I trust you? Despicable Jack would have been lying, and I'll bet you are, too."

The man gave a frustrated little yelp. "You'll be sorry you didn't take me seriously. You will!"

"You could torture her," Bland pointed out helpfully. "That would make him tell us. He's not going to want to see her tortured."

Sebastian looked genuinely upset at this, and Nell frowned. Honestly, if Sebastian were going to take these two ridiculous men seriously, they'd never get out of her. "Go ahead and torture me, I don't care. You can torture me all afternoon if you like. Sebastian won't care. He doesn't even *like* me."

"Nell, be quiet," Sebastian said irritably.

"Yeah, girly, be quiet," Black said, pinching her arm with his meaty little hand. "We men have important negotiating to do."

"Now if it's the Mermaid you're interested in . . ." Sebastian said, as if musing to himself.

"Yeah?" Black said, curious despite himself.

Sebastian narrowed his eyes and leaned back against the helm as if lost in thought. "The way the *real* old-timers tell it, the Mermaid was only the first clue to Jack's bloody horde. Find her and you find the secret to a treasure so valuable Jack's ghost is still guarding it. We found a hiding place on the island, all right, but he didn't keep his real treasure here. Only a few doubloons and pieces of eight, ordinary stuff. We didn't even bother picking it up."

"There's pieces of eight all over these keys," Bland agreed. "Nothing special there."

"Shut up, Bland. Go on, mister. I'm listening."

"Well, a few months back I bought a map from an old sea dog who told me that Jack buried his real treasure in

Tierra—oops!" Sebastian shut his mouth suddenly. "Well, never mind where, exactly. But I could sell you that map."

"Black, he must mean Tierra del—"

"Shut up, Bland!" Black shouted furiously. "What do you want for the map?"

"Leave the girl. We don't care what your name is, we're fortune hunters just like you are. We're all professionals here, surely. You win this round, perhaps some day we'll win another. Surely we can behave like gentlemen?"

"Jack was a gentleman," Black said, boasting. "A proper one, from France. With a castle, and serving girls, and a velvet hat with a feather in it. I read all about it in a book."

"The feather was red," Bland put in helpfully. "I saw the picture."

"And you know, Jack was a great man for the ladies," Sebastian said with a sly wink. "He would never have harmed a woman—unless it was strictly necessary, of course. How about it, Black? The girl for the map? Seems like a fair trade to me."

"I'd have to say it was fair," Bland said. "That one I couldn't argue with."

"Shut up, Bland," Black said mechanically. "How do I know you two won't kill us as soon as we've got the map? I need some kinda guarantee."

"Oh, I like that," Nell said. "Here you are holding a knife to me, and you accuse us of being untrustworthy! It's too much, it really is—ow!"

Black had poked her again. "I thought I told you we men had negotiating to do."

"I might try to get the drop on you," Sebastian said coolly, "but you know I'd never make it. You boys are too fast for me. Let go of the girl, I'll give you the map, and we go our separate ways."

Bland's forlorn brow wrinkled as he pondered this. "They might have a point, Black. On the other hand, maybe they don't."

"Shut up, Bland," Nell and Black said in unison.

"All right. We take the map, and . . . and the rowboat. Between us we got enough guns to blast Fort Jefferson to the promised land, understand? So don't get any ideas about gunning us down for the map. We're too fast for you, boy, you said it yourself."

"I certainly did," Sebastian said, ducking his head to hide what Nell suspected was a grin. "I just need to go down to my cabin to get the map. Then you can be on your way, with no hard feelings."

Black eased the knife free of Nell's midsection, and she took a deep breath in relief. It really was *very* uncomfortable, having a knife point poking at one that way. She was about to yank herself free of the nasty little creature and toss him over the side when she felt another, colder sensation at her temple.

"I'll just mind the girl while the gentleman finds the map," Bland said pleasantly. He held a very long, very ugly black pistol to Nell's temple. No one on the boat made a sound as he cocked it.

"I thought we had an agreement," Sebastian said quickly. "What are you trying to pull?"

"I'm not trying to pull anything," Bland said. "I just want to make certain you keep up your end of the deal."

Black danced around from behind her, and as Nell had suspected, she towered over the man by nearly a foot. "This ain't the way it was supposed to work, Bland."

Bland blinked as he held the gun to Nell's head. His hands were remarkably steady. "I think you should go get that map now, mister."

Black rubbed his hands together nervously. "Um, maybe you'd better do what he says. Bland gets a little funny sometimes."

Sebastian backed slowly toward his cabin, holding his hands high where Bland could see them. "I don't want you getting nervous on me, friend. You've got nothing to worry about. You get your map, I get the girl, everyone's happy."

Nell was suddenly disinclined to make sarcastic remarks. Black was a nasty little thing, but she hadn't thought for a moment that he would really stab her.

Bland, with his peculiar calm and his steady hands, was another story altogether.

Sebastian backed down the stairs to his cabin, was gone from sight no more than an instant, and came back holding a piece of paper high above his head. He kept both hands visible, and moved as smoothly and quietly as a panther stalking prey.

Black busied himself with the dinghy as Bland took the map from Sebastian with his free hand.

"Come on!" said Black. "We got what we wanted, Bland. Let's go."

Bland gave Nell a pleasant, friendly smile, and Nell found herself genuinely terrified. "I'm sorry if I frightened you," he said evenly.

"Don't worry, you didn't," she said, her voice a dry croak.

"Come on!" Black said urgently. "Leave her!"

Nell swallowed, her mouth dry as a pailful of dust. "You don't suppose you could leave us our bags, do you? They're just some crabs we caught for dinner. I'd be obliged to you."

"Nell, to hell with the damned bags!" Sebastian barked, his voice genuinely angry. "They aren't important."

Nell dared a glance at him, moving her eyes rather than her head. The jewels were wrapped in her old dress, lying half-forgotten on the deck, but the Bathing Maenad was in Sebastian's bag. "I don't want you to . . . to go hungry because of me."

"The bag isn't important," Sebastian said again, looking steadily into her eyes. "They can have it."

Bland backed slowly away from her, and the sensation she felt when the gun was no longer pressed to her temple made her distinctly light-headed.

"Come on!" Black said, his face turning red. "Let's just get out of here!"

Bland tipped his head in an oddly polite farewell, stepped neatly into the dinghy, and Black began to row for all he was worth as Bland leaned back and laid the gun gently on the seat beside him.

Nell's knees felt like seaweed, and she all but crumpled into Sebastian's arms as he rushed up to embrace her. "Why did you do that?" she asked, sucking in air in deep breaths, as if she'd been underwater.

"Do what?" Sebastian murmured, burying his face in her hair, wrapping her in his body as if he were a warm, protective cloak.

"Give them the Mermaid? They would have given us the bag, they didn't know what was inside. Surely it was worth a try."

"It wasn't worth a try," Sebastian said flatly, still wrapped around her. "I've seen the look that was in Bland's eye before. Black was nothing but a little thug, but Bland was genuinely out of his mind."

"But the Mermaid's gone!" Nell said, shaking now. She leaned into Sebastian's warmth, taking from him the strength she needed.

Sebastian's chest was shaking, and Nell looked up at him. He was laughing. He was actually laughing. "I know where she's going."

"You do?"

"She's going to Tierra del Fuego. Weren't you listening?"

"Oh, come on, do you think they're going to believe that cock-and-bull story? 'A treasure so valuable Jack's ghost is still guarding it?' You couldn't fool a five-year-old with that."

"Maybe not, but Black believes me. And Bland will probably follow Black, at least until he gets it into his head to cut the poor bugger's throat." Sebastian wrapped himself more tightly around Nell, and she pressed her cheek gratefully against his chest. "Anyway, you were probably right. I wouldn't know what to do with myself, having found the Maenad after all this time. I need a few months to get used to the idea."

"So now you'll go after them?" Nell said in a small voice.

"What do you mean *I'll* go after them? Having a gun held to your head didn't scare you off treasure hunting, did it?"

"No, of course not!" Nell said, indignant as she pulled

back a fraction. "It's just that—I didn't—just what are you trying to say, Sebastian?"

Sebastian took her chin in his hand and lifted it, looking down into her eyes in a way that made her sweetly dizzy. "It won't be much of a life with me, you know. I spend an awful lot of time on boats."

Nell's throat felt tight, and she couldn't keep from laughing, though tears were spilling from the corners of her eyes. "I can't tell you how much I hate boats."

"I know you do, sweetheart. But if you think I'm leaving you behind on land, to get into God knows what kind of trouble, you'd better think again."

Nell swiped at her eyes with her sleeve and took a deep, shuddering breath. "If you honestly believe you can keep me out of trouble, you're crazier than I am."

Sebastian threw his head back and laughed aloud, and folded her up in him, and kissed the top of her head. "You may be right about that, Mad Nell. I'll take you around the world, to places you've only dreamed about, and after we get the Maenad back we'll find another treasure to hunt. And in a hundred years of life together, I'd probably never teach you to stay out of trouble. But I'm damned well going to give it a try."

PROLOGUE

DECEMBER 1848

*B*lizzard-whitened winds blasted across the desolate
high moor country, enshrouding gorse and heather in a
sheet of shimmering ice. Gales surged down the open
hillsides and into the churchyard, moaning across the
ice-encrusted gravestones that shouldered against one
another in the December darkness. Then the winter
wraiths combined their attack, encircling the old stone
Parsonage at the edge of the village, shaking it and
shrieking,

Let me in!

Like relentless, malevolent ghosts, they battered the
brittle windowpanes, wailing their demand for the
warmth and life inside.

Within, three unmarried sisters huddled by the fire in
the dining room, trying to ignore the death call that grew
louder with each tick of the clock. Charlotte drew her
chair closer to the fire and tucked her heavy skirts
around her ankles. She adjusted the queer little spectacles on the bridge of her nose, then resumed reading
aloud from the book she had purchased at the stationer's
shop the day before. It was the work of an American
writer, Emerson, which she found intriguing. Perhaps it
would please her sister Emily, who sat next to her large
yellow dog on the rug, pale and still, holding onto her
rosewood writing box with a kind of quiet desperation. If
only Emily would have let them call a doctor, Charlotte
agonized, glancing at her stricken sister in the flickering
firelight. Then she looked up, and her eyes met those of
her other sister, Anne, the youngest of the three at
twenty-seven. There she saw a reflection of her own
grief. They both knew that now it was too late. There was

little they could do for their brilliant but determined sister except stay with her until the end.

Suddenly, Emily's shoulders hunched, and she was wracked by a deep and terrible cough that echoed into every chamber of the house. Across the hall in his study, her father tried in vain to concentrate on reading his Bible, peering at the printed page through a large magnifying glass. His heart was heavy as the snow-laden clouds outside, knowing he would soon bury another of his children in the cold vault beneath the stone church floors.

The spasm subsided, and with trembling fingers Emily opened the writing box that had been her closest friend and confidante through the years. She knew and was grateful that she hadn't much time left. Only one thing remained to be finished in her waning lifetime.

Inside the box lay a slim, red-covered volume that, until this moment, only Emily knew existed. For the past three years she had written in it furtively almost every night. She had kept it hidden beneath the mattress of her small bed, risking exposure of a dark and dangerous secret should one of her sisters discover it. But it was a risk she had been willing to take, because writing was the only way she had been able to sort out her terrifying thoughts. Writing had led the way through the treacherous anger, fear, and despair that had at times engulfed her like the mists on the moors, leaving her lost and helpless. Writing was the rock of sanity to which she clung desperately after a chance encounter on the moors had sent her hurtling into a frightening chaos of emotions that she neither understood nor had the experience to control. With no one to confide in, she turned, as always, to the patient page.

A sob escaped her throat, and the effort sent her into another coughing fit. Surely it couldn't take much longer, she thought. She hadn't known her dying would be so attenuated.

> *I know there is a blessed shore*
> *Opening its ports for me, and mine;*
> *And, gazing Time's wide waters o'er,*
> *I weary for that land divine . . .*

Emily had planned to burn the diary earlier, when the others were not looking, but she'd waited too long. Her sisters had become anxious nursemaids as her illness worsened, hovering 'round her, not leaving her a moment alone in weeks. The clock on the stairwell chimed the quarter hour. Emily paused. She had no choice but to carry out this final task before their eyes. Slowly, with great effort but steadfastly, Emily ripped away the first few pages, crumpled them, and threw them into the fire. The flame leapt momentarily, consumed the tidbit, then returned to its normal glow.

Startled, Charlotte closed the book she was reading and leaned forward. "Emily, what is that?"

Her sister's only reply was to turn her back squarely to Charlotte, tear more sheets from the book, wad them, and feed them to the flames.

"Emily, stop!" Charlotte cried out in alarm. She knew her sister prized her privacy, but she could not sit by and allow Emily to destroy her work, for there would be no more of her strong and energetic poetry, no more strange and moving novels like *Wuthering Heights*. If Emily Brontë had created more work than what Charlotte had already found, Charlotte felt it her duty to rescue it from the sure death Emily obviously intended for it. The poet might go to her grave, but her poetry must live on. Charlotte sprang from her chair and knelt by Emily's side, eager to see what the volume contained.

Emily slammed the book shut and crossed her arms over it. Charlotte was such an impossible meddler. I should have burned this long ago, she thought, disgusted. She looked up at Anne.

"Help me," she whispered, her words ending in a rattling cough.

Anne looked from Emily to Charlotte, uncertain what to do. She knew Emily was loath to give the outer world so much as a glimpse of her private thoughts, even in her poetry. But did she not recognize her worth as a writer? Of them all, Emily was the true genius. But Anne had long since given up trying to understand her difficult and enigmatic sister. Right now, all she wished to do was ease Emily's pain. Whatever she had written, it was clear her sister did not want it to survive her. "Yes," Anne said quietly at last, and looked at Charlotte. "Let her be."

"No!" Charlotte insisted. "You know how she is. She'll destroy all the beauty she has created. I won't let her do it!"

"It is hers to destroy if she wishes," Anne said patiently.

"It is *not* hers," Charlotte cried, vexed at being crossed by her normally compliant younger sister. "Those poems belong to everyone who loves her work."

Emily tore more pages from the diary and crumpled them hastily. She handed them to Anne, who dutifully threw them into the fire. "Not poems," Emily managed.

"A novel?" Charlotte could not bear the thought. "Is it a new novel you were working on?" She reached out and attempted to wrest what was left of the volume from Emily's grasp but stopped short when her sister's deep gray-blue eyes froze on hers, daring her to intrude further. Charlotte sighed and backed away, and Emily resumed the chore at hand. When the last of the diary was gone, her secret would be safe. Hopefully, the savage wind and rain on the moors would have destroyed the letter she'd foolishly left under the message rock.

Since she didn't believe in heaven or hell, she had no fear that she would burn for what she was doing. Dying now would put a natural end to the horror almost before it began. She was safe. Her family was protected. Her secret was secure. Emily felt light-headed with relief as the last paper blazed and the cover turned to ash.

The flames crackled contentedly, like the purr of a cat with a belly full of cream. Emily tried to breathe deeply the fullness of her release, but consumption stole her breath and allowed only another coughing fit. The clock on the stair struck ten. Emily nodded to Anne in gratitude for her help. Then, without speaking, her two sisters helped her off the floor. She refused further aid and made her way slowly, painfully, up the stairs. She eased down onto the narrow bed in the tiny, unheated room that had been her private quarters since she'd returned

home for good six years ago. In the dark, she listened to
the wind wailing outside her window.

Let me in!

Throughout the night, the tempest continued its assault
on the darkened Parsonage, and the following day,
shortly after two o'clock, a windowpane finally burst under the force. The icy wind found Emily on the sofa in
front of the fireplace, and without hesitation, completed
its mission of death.

CHAPTER ONE

$\mathcal{T}$hunder shook the sodden skies over London as Alexander Hightower topped the stairs of the Underground, exhausted to his bones. Across the traffic-choked avenue the chimes from Big Ben somehow managed to overpower the street noise below, where red buses roared and taxicabs honked, competing with private cars and commercial trucks in the muddy, endless race of commerce.

One o'clock.

Alex drew the black mackintosh closer around him and moved under the protection of a nearby archway. Above him pigeons clucked and cooed in the shelter of windowsills and alcoves, the rain sending their residue like so much whitewash to the pavement below.

He spotted a display of umbrellas in the window of a nearby souvenir shop and decided immediately on his first purchase on British soil.

"I'll take that one." Alex indicated the largest black one in the lot. He paid the vendor with soggy pound notes, opened the umbrella with a snap, then ventured into the heavy traffic, making his way across the circle and past the park.

One o'clock.

He had exactly two hours. Two brief hours until he had to face Maggie Flynn. And into those two hours he had to cram what under more leisurely circumstances could easily take him several days.

Damn!

He walked briskly, dodging puddles, wishing he hadn't agreed to this afternoon's meeting. He was in no shape to spar with Maggie Flynn. His clothes were rumpled, travel-worn from the long night spent cramped in the coach class seat on the flight from New York. He was in need of a shower, a shave, and a nap. But as it was, he'd barely had time to check into his hotel and sling his bags into the room before starting off again.

Maggie Flynn, it would seem, had bested him again.

Alex reached the ancient shrine of Westminster Abbey, where a service was in progress inside the magnificent Gothic structure. Organ music swelled to the tops of the intricate arches and reverberated off the smooth stone walls, loud enough to shake the crumbling bones that lay beneath the floors and in the toms and vaults. Lightning flashed fiercely through the majestic stained-glass windows, and moments later thunder echoed throughout the cavernous cathedral.

Alex felt the hair on his arms stand on end, and he shivered. He was not a religious man, but if there was a God, he thought it likely He might call this place Home.

But it wasn't God he had come here to see. He waited until the music died, the aisles emptied, and a tall man in a red coat indicated that the Royal Chapels would be reopened. Then Alex made his way through the gate among the throngs of other sightseers, paid his three pounds, and entered a time warp.

Tread softly past the long, long sleep of kings . . .

They were all there, virtually every monarch who had held power over Britain since there was a Britain. Edward the Confessor, who established the Abbey, followed by a parade of Henries, Richards, and Jameses along with their wives and consorts and various and sundry relatives. He paid his respects to Queen Elizabeth I, whose carefully carved marble effigy slept peacefully atop her tomb. In the room opposite, given almost equal space, the bones of that throne-usurper, Mary Queen of Scots, reposed restlessly for eternity. Lightning flashed, eerily illuminating the sepulcher.

Alex moved on, filing past the ancient coronation chair and the legendary Stone of Scone. Most of Brit-

ain's monarchs had been crowned on this chair, and he
was duly awed by the sheer weight of the history that
surrounded him.

But it was another kind of hero he'd come to honor
today. Royalty of a different sort from whom he sought a
silent blessing for his improbable quest.

He stepped into the South Trancept, better known as
the Poet's Corner, and allowed the moment to envelop
him. Here his true heroes were either buried or memori-
alized. The giants of English literature. Those whose
works he had studied and taught and loved most of his
life. Dryden. Dickens. Johnson. Kipling. Hardy. They
were all buried right here, beneath his feet. The walls,
columns, and floors were filled with memorials, tributes
to the likes of Milton, Shakespeare, Wordsworth, Byron,
Shelley, Tennyson, Coleridge, and many more.

And then, there to the right, Alex spied an inconspicu-
ous, inornate square framing three names, engraved in
plain letters:

Charlotte Brontë
1816-1855
Emily Jane Brontë
1818-1848
Anne Brontë
1820-1849
With courage to endure

Another streak of lightning pierced the afternoon
gloom.

Alex stood for a long moment, gazing at the memorial,
wondering what these three strange and provincial
women would think about having been enshrined here.
Charlotte, who sought fame and fortune, would be ec-
static, he felt certain. Anne, in her own quiet way, would
be pleased. And Emily, at the very least, would approve
of the plainness of the memorial.

Alex allowed himself a small smile. As a scholar of
early Victorian literature, he had studied the lives and
works of these three writers so long and so intensely he
felt as if he knew them intimately. He knew what clothes

they wore and what food they ate. He knew much of their suffering, as well as their victories. At times he felt almost a part of the family.

His eye was drawn to the middle name on the memorial—Emily Jane Brontë. Of them all, she was his favorite. Perhaps because she was the most elusive. Little work remained from which to try to piece together the personal and literary puzzle she presented. Less than two hundred of her poems existed, many only fragments, along with one strange and darkly fascinating novel, *Wuthering Heights.* She had lived only thirty years and died after a short illness. It was her death Alex found most inexplicable about Emily Brontë. A young woman. A strong will. A premature death. She died, he theorized, if not by her own hand, then certainly by her own design.

> *O for the day when I shall rest,*
> *And never suffer more!*

His theory, that Emily's death was, in essence, a suicide, was not popular among Brontë devotees.

Although many concurred that in those final months she seemed to have lost the will to live, most attributed it to her grief over her brother Branwell's death, while others offered more complex psychological explanations, including *anorexia nervosa.*

Alex alone among his contemporaries in the world of academe had dared mention suicide. Emily Brontë was, after all, something of a sainted literary figure. A scholar's monarch. One was not welcome to loosely question tradition.

But Alex sensed there was something that had driven this intensely private woman to take her own life, not with a gunshot or a dram of poison, but rather in a way that would not raise the suspicion of others, based on her past behavior.

Through willful neglect.

What else but a deep and unyielding desire for death would cause her to refuse, totally and absolutely, all medical help when she became so gravely ill? Something devastating must have happened to her in those last few months, something so frightful and traumatic that death had seemed the only escape.

Something she had successfully hidden from snooping biographers like himself.

Alex had been vocal about his opinion, both to his students and among his colleagues, and the latter had called his hand. The academic world, like science, scorns conjecture. His peers, Maggie Flynn foremost among them, demanded proof.

Put up or shut up.

The showdown was to be a formal debate that loomed like a menacing storm at the end of the summer.

Having a gut-level feeling was one thing. Finding solid evidence to back it up was quite another. Alex had studied every available Brontë resource in the United States, but still had nothing stronger than a hunch to present, based on his interpretation of some of Emily's work. The only element of her life he had so far been unable to examine was her environment—the wild and haunting moors of northern England which she had loved deeply and which had influenced virtually everything she wrote.

So tomorrow he would travel to Haworth, the small West Yorkshire village that had been her home. He planned to review the material available at the Brontë Parsonage Museum Library there. But more than that, he wanted to walk the rugged countryside she trod, breathe the air she breathed. It wasn't in a library, he felt, that he would find an answer. If he found one at all, it would come from insight gained by personally experiencing the forces that had touched her and molded her life.

It wasn't much to build his seditious suicide theory on, but it was the only strategy remaining. He must uncover Emily's secret, for unless he found arguable proof, in late August, in front of many of the world's preeminent scholars of English literature, he would be torn to shreds over the issue by another expert in the field, Dr. Maggie Flynn.

Maggie.

His colleague.

His former lover.

Alex stared at the letters carved in the cold marble memorial. "Why?" he murmured. "Why did you choose to die?" He ran his fingers across the engraved name.

"Emily," he entreated softly. "Answer me."

Rain, driven by a sharp easterly wind, pelted against Selena's cheeks as she dashed from the old farmhouse. The gale whipped a long strand of dark hair from beneath the knitted cap she wore, lashing it with a sting into one eye. Unsure of her footing on the slippery, sandy mud, she made a careful run for the old Land Rover parked in the drive.

Overhead, gray clouds scudded across the tops of the moors like large sheep in need of shearing. On the verdant squares of pasture below, real sheep huddled for shelter behind drystone walls that formed uneven geometric quilts over the landscape for miles in every direction. The world was cold and wet from four straight days of rain.

Selena got into the dilapidated vehicle and turned the ignition, concerned whether the square-backed wagon would make it all the way to London and return. The ancient engine bucked and snorted. She ground the starter again. Nothing. She beat her palm against the steering wheel and pumped the accelerator furiously. "Come on!"

At last the car rumbled to life, and after letting it warm up, Selena slipped it into gear and backed carefully up the steep drive into the lane. She allowed herself one last glance toward the house, where a bedraggled black and white border collie sat on the stoop, staring at her with sad, accusing eyes.

"Damn it, Domino. Why don't you have the good sense to stay out of the rain? And don't look at me like that. I'll be back tomorrow. By noon. I promise."

She was apprehensive about the long drive to London and hoped the rain would let up once she was out of storm-riddled Yorkshire. Glancing at her watch, she regretted having committed to visiting Matka en route. Selena had to be at the gallery in London by five.

But she'd promised, and she knew her grandmother would be watching the clock.

The nursing home where Matka lived was new and modern. The receptionist greeted her with friendly efficiency. Matka had reported the food was good and the place clean.

But it hurt to see the woman who, through sheer tenacity of spirit had somehow managed to hold the fragile pieces of Selena's childhood together, confined to a wheelchair, her body rendered mostly immobile by rheumatoid arthritis. Matka's manner was always gruffly cheerful whenever Selena visited, but her granddaughter suspected the brightness was a front, a show put on for her benefit, like the old Gypsy used to do for her customers in the fortune-telling booth.

Selena found her grandmother in her favorite spot beside the fireplace in the Community Room, a small package of a woman sitting in a wheelchair, hidden behind the wall of the daily newspaper she was reading. "Hey, Gran!" She poked her face over the papers and kissed the wrinkled forehead.

"Stars in heaven, child! You like t' a taken my breath. Where't y' come from, appearin' like tha' out o' nowhere?"

"You knew I was coming," she reminded the wizened woman. "I'm on my way to London."

Matka squinted, her clouded dark eyes focusing on the young woman. "London, eh? What'd y'be doin' in London?"

Selena picked up the paper and folded it noisily, impatient at the game her grandmother seemed to play with increasing frequency, the one called I Don't Remember. "You know that, too, Gran. Those paintings of mine I told you about. They've been on exhibit in a gallery there. The show's over, and I'm on my way to fetch them. It's been on a month. Got a lot of good reviews, too. I even sold a few."

Matka snorted and chewed her toothless gums. "Paintin's! An artist, y' want t' be? Wha' kind o' life would tha' be for a girl like you?" Like a locomotive, she was building steam, getting set to roll into her favorite subject.

"You ought t' find a nice man and settle down, have children. You'll soon be meetin' thirty, you know . . ."

Her voice trailed off, and Selena said nothing. She found it difficult to defend her choice of lifestyle to her Romany (and sometimes surprisingly traditional) grandmother. She pulled an ottoman close to the old woman's chair and took the gnarled, aged hands in her own.

"We've gone over this before, Gran," she said, summoning patience. "Think about it. Do you *really* believe that getting married and having a family would be the best thing for me?"

The old woman looked at her with eyes that saw more than what was in front of her. Neither said a word for a long while, each remembering Selena's violent childhood, the stormy parents who had deserted her at different times, in different ways. They both knew it was only after Matka had come to live with them that Selena had known any security or happiness.

Selena didn't like to think about those days. In fact, there was much she had carefully buried deeply inside her so she would no longer remember the horror. But she remembered when the old woman's brightly-colored Gypsy wagon was parked for good in the shed behind her parents' small home. She recalled how sad Matka had been to leave her wandering life on the road, but how glad she herself had been to find one loving soul in her life. The young girl and the old woman had clung to each other as the terror and turmoil of her parents' lives raged around them.

"It's the curse," Matka would swear, wringing her hands.

"No, Gran," Selena would reply under her breath. "It's the whiskey."

Witnessing her parents' unhappiness, Selena doubted she would ever marry, but her grandmother never gave up hope that she would change her mind. Because, in spite of the old woman's superstitious belief that an ancient curse hung over the family, Matka prayed that one day, by some miracle, the hex would be dispelled and one of her line would at last be free to love without pain.

That one had to be Selena. Because her raven-haired, olive-skinned granddaughter was the only one left, the last descendant of this branch of the ancient line of fabled Abram Wd, King of the Welsh Gypsies.

Selena did not believe in any such curse. Her parents' problems had been caused by nothing more mysterious than financial stress and alcoholism. Matka's story about the curse, Selena felt, was just a Gypsy superstition.

And Selena refused to let her Gypsy ancestry control her life.

Sure, she loved the romantic stories Matka had woven for her as a child as they sat together by the fire on cold nights, tales of the old woman's vagabond life. But Selena knew it was their Gypsy heritage that drove her father's anger, her mother's despair. Her father had left his own caravan behind when he was only a boy, seeking his fortune in wartime England. He had been too young to fight, so he'd gone to work in a munitions factory.

But life for a young Gypsy wasn't easy in the *Gorgio* world. When anything went wrong, he was blamed. When anything was stolen, the Gypsy did it. In his first job, and in every other job, it happened again and again, until he simply gave up. That's when the drinking began, and the fights. And his misery didn't end until he pulled the trigger one dark, rainy night, sending his body to the bottom of a cliff outside of town. In spite of no longer being brutalized by her husband, her mother never recovered from his suicide, and Selena found her one morning, dead of alcohol poisoning.

Matka patted Selena's hands and shook her head sadly. "The curse has a strong hold on our family. No one's escaped it in a hundred and fifty years. Perhaps it has touched y' already, makin' y' lonely, afraid of love." She sighed heavily.

Selena wanted to shake her grandmother and cry out, "There is no curse!" For intellectually, she didn't believe in such nonsense. That stuff belonged in fairy tales.

She would have pressed the point, if it hadn't been for the paintings.

Selena hadn't shown Matka any of her recent work,

even though it was the old woman's money that had paid for her education at the École des Beaux Arts in Paris, because Matka would have spotted the letter in an instant.

The letter.

That impossible letter that Matka still kept, brittle with age, in the drawer of her bedside table at the nursing home. Selena wished she had it now. She would burn it and be done with it. The damned thing had caused nothing but torment and tears to countless of her superstitious ancestors.

And now, it seemed, it was insidiously invading her own creativity, somehow manifesting on every canvas she painted. No, she didn't dare show her art to Matka, for the old Gypsy would insist that the curse was attacking the only thing she loved—her work.

Ironically, it was the continuity of the images in her work, especially the scraps of the letter, that had led Selena to some measure of recognition in London. Actually, the reviews *had* been good. One writer had even compared her favorably to Léonor Fini. The bizarre nature of her surrealistic compositions had captured the equally bizarre taste of trendy London, and she had sold several pieces. Tom Perkins had already asked her to show again in the fall.

But she couldn't keep painting like this—the same picture, in essence, over and over again. It was as if she were possessed when she went to her studio. She'd pick up her brushes, determined to stay away from the mauves and grays, the campfires, the dancing bears, the wild ponies, the monkey's head, and above all, that ubiquitous scrap of letter that made its way onto the canvas regardless. Sometimes it was pounded beneath the horse's hoof. Sometimes it was burning in the fire. Sometimes the monkey reached out with it teasingly, as if handing it to the viewer. Selena wished Matka had never shown her the letter or told her about the curse.

She wished she wasn't a Gypsy.

She wished she could paint a bowl of fruit.

June 2, 1845

How beautiful the Earth is still
To thee—how full of Happiness;
How little fraught with real ill
Or shadowy phantoms of distress;

How Spring can bring thee glory yet
And Summer win thee to forget
December's sullen time!
Why dost thou hold the treasure fast
Of youth's delight, when youth is past
And thou art near thy prime?

June 4, 1845

    I should not write this lest Charlotte come snooping, for he made me promise not to tell anyone of his whereabouts. And yet it is all so strange I am loath not to record it. I will mark it now, and maybe tomorrow awaken to find it only a mad dream anyhow, like all the rest.

    When I was upon the moors today, late in the afternoon, I climbed the ravine along the back hill. I do not know what made me go there today, because it is not common for me to walk that way. I was busy playing at Gondal in my mind and watching the water splashing down the beck, and I did not see what lay in front of me. Neither did I hear anything unusual, until my foot struck a low mound that stretched across the path. Then I heard an awful moan, and I saw that an injured man lay half hidden in the grass. Keeper heard it, too, and came running, ready to attack, but I held him off. I was not frightened, but I picked up a rock and approached him cautiously. He was the most ragged creature I have ever seen, and I guess from his dress he is one of those they call gipsie. He wore a silk kerchief knotted about his neck, and a large earring in one ear. His shirt was dirty and torn and stained with blood from his cuts. He opened his eyes while I stood there staring, wondering what to do about him. He looked up at me, his face filled with pain, and asked if I was an angel! (He thought he was dead.) I told him no, I'm Emily Jane Brontë. I brought him *some water from the beck. He told me he had fallen from his horse, but I saw no horse nearby. Perhaps it ran away.*

He is badly hurt. I know his leg is broken, and he may have other injuries. He was in great pain, so much that it beaded in sweat on his brow though the day was chill. He would not have me summon help, though I fear for his life. I understand, for the gipsies are not welcome in the village and I, too, do not trust doctors on any account.

I helped him to take shelter beneath a large outcropping of rock and tried to make him comfortable, but when I left, he was pale and not awake. Tonight, I will save some broth and bread, and Keeper and I will steal away after everyone is asleep. I pray he is still alive. This must be a most secret adventure.

EMILY'S SECRET BY JILL JONES—LOOK FOR IT IN SEPTEMBER, FROM ST. MARTIN'S PAPERBACKS!

ANITA MILLS
ARNETTE LAMB
ROSANNE BITTNER

*Join three of your favorite storytellers
on a tender journey of the heart...*

Cherished Moments is an extraordinary collection of
breathtaking novellas woven around the theme of mother-
hood. Before you turn the last page you will have been swept
from the storm-tossed coast of a Scottish isle to the fury of
the American frontier, and you will have lived the lives and
loves of three indomitable women, as they experience their
most passionate moments.

THE NATIONAL BESTSELLER

CHERISHED MOMENTS

Anita Mills, Arnette Lamb, Rosanne Bittner
_____ 95473-5 $4.99 U.S./$5.99 Can.